# Sugar Plum Dead

***Also by Carolyn Hart in Large Print:***

Mint Julep Murder
Dead Man's Island
Scandal in Fair Haven
Crimes of the Heart

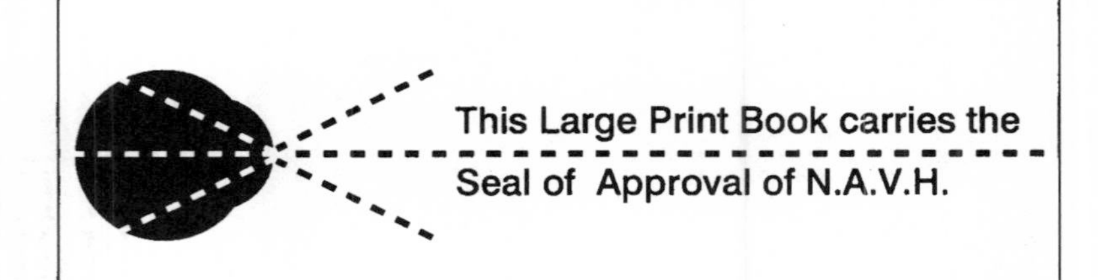

# Sugar Plum Dead

A Death On Demand Mystery

Carolyn Hart

**G.K. Hall & Co. • Thorndike, Maine**

This book is a work of fiction. Names, characters, places, and incidents either are products of the author's imagination or are used fictitiously. Any resemblance to actual events, locales, organizations, or persons, living or dead, is entirely coincidental and beyond the intent of either the author or the publisher.

Published in 2001 by arrangement with William Morrow, an imprint of HarperCollins Publishers, Inc.

G.K. Hall Large Print Core Series.

The text of this Large Print edition is unabridged.
Other aspects of the book may vary from the original edition.

Set in 16 pt. Plantin by Elena Picard.

Printed in the United States on permanent paper.

---

**Library of Congress Cataloging-in-Publication Data**

Hart, Carolyn G.
Sugar plum dead : a death on demand mystery / Carolyn Hart.
p. cm.
ISBN 0-7838-9377-9 (lg. print : hc : alk. paper)
1. Darling, Annie Laurance (Fictitious character) — Fiction. 2. Darling, Max (Fictitious character) — Fiction. 3. Women detectives — South Carolina — Fiction. 4. Booksellers and bookselling — Fiction. 5. South Carolina — Fiction. 6. Large type books. I. Title.
PS3558.A676 S84 2001
813′.54—dc21 00-054024

*To Sarah in gratitude for*
*all the laughter we've shared.*

# Prologue

"What am I going to do?" Happy heard her own voice, high, breathless, uneven. And shrill. Her mouth curved down, forlorn as a sad-faced clown. She stared in the mirror and spoke again. "Now, Happy, no more of this!" There, she sounded better, sounded like herself. A soft voice, sweet as summer berries. Appealing.

But the change in pitch didn't solve anything, didn't show her any way out of the cloud of discord that was going to surround all of them as surely as the December fog curled and eddied around the house, swirled over the marsh. Throughout her life, she'd made it a point to avoid unpleasantness. But this time . . .

Marguerite, of course, left trouble trailing behind her. She always had and always would. Daddy had called Marguerite Scarlett because every place that Scarlett O'Hara went, trouble followed. But he had nicknamed her, his other daughter, the child of his late middle age, Miss Happy-Go-Lucky, saying that when she breezed into a room, she made everybody happy. And she had, hadn't she? Even though the laughter in later years seemed too often to turn to tears. But that was when she moved on, happy-go-lucky, determined to be carefree. Because that's who she was.

Tears filmed Happy's blue eyes, eyes that so long ago had mastered the art of beguilement, eyes that had made a lifelong practice of never seeing anything they didn't want to see. For an instant, her protective mental mantle parted, just long enough to wonder how it might have been different. What if Daddy had called Marguerite Lionheart? Would Marguerite have envisioned herself as courageous and undaunted, devoted to her followers, rather than beleaguered and alone? What if, instead of Happy-Go-Lucky, her own nickname had been Maid Marian? Would she have been stalwart and steady?

Happy. She'd always tried to be happy. But how could she be happy when it seemed obvious that everyone in the family was destined to quarrel? As soon as the others learned of Marguerite's mad plan, tempers would erupt. The atmosphere was already tense. Scholarly Wayne, who usually kept his nose in a book and his study door shut, had taken to walking about the grounds, staring up at the house, a house he had always refused to leave. Self-effacing Alice, who'd put up with Marguerite through a lifetime of tempests, was increasingly somber. The others would arrive today: platinum-haired Donna, who loved objects more than people; bluff and hearty Terry, who swaggered and always needed money; and hapless Joan, who'd never really gotten over her divorce from Wayne. Even her own spunky Rachel was being difficult, flipping her dark hair, glaring at Happy with rebellious eyes. As for Marguerite, she was flaunting her the-world-be-damned look.

Marguerite: famous, still beautiful in a gaunt, haggard way, vain, spoiled, vulnerable. And, of course, rich. Very, very rich. Generous certainly in her own fashion, making a place for Happy and Rachel, for Wayne, and always welcoming Donna and Joan and Terry. But that generosity might end. Unless . . .

Happy fingered the gold chain at her throat. She felt a flutter of fear. Where could she and Rachel go? Nowhere, nowhere.

Deep in the recesses of her mind, a solution stirred. She shivered. Confrontation, a word and act alien to her. But she had to do something. And do it soon.

At least she could count on Pudge. She'd felt much better since Pudge had arrived. She'd traced him down in Puerto Vallarta. Trust Pudge to be in a warm place. Visiting friends, of course. There was never a fixed address for Pudge. His arrival yesterday had seemed an omen that all might come right.

For an instant, a sweet, happy smile softened her face, brought a glow to her eyes. Dear Pudge. They'd made quite a good pair, she and Pudge. Her smile dimmed. But it hadn't worked. Pudge had charm, but he was here for a while, then there. Sweet as could be, but always saying goodbye. In fact, she'd been pleased and surprised that he'd responded to her call. She'd invited him for the holidays. Time enough to ask his advice. Of course, she'd told him her worries about Rachel. Pudge adored Rachel.

Happy's eyes were suddenly shrewd. Pudge was probably broke. But that was all right. There was enough money. Or had always been until now. Oh, what was she going to do?

Wayne Ladson finished the sentence:

*. . . apparent that the appraisals of Abernethy and Turner slighted the importance of the Eastern urban laboring classes on Andrew Jackson's presidency. The question then arises . . .*

Wayne paused and stared unseeingly out the casement window at the terraced garden sloping down to the lagoon, a part of his mind still engaged in his essay, picturing Jackson's elegant face, high forehead, long slender nose, piercing blue eyes, rounded heavy chin. Interesting to wonder just how desperate Jackson had felt when promissory notes he'd signed in a land deal came back to haunt him.

Money.

Wayne's vague gaze sharpened. He felt a wave of distaste. Why did everything always come down to money? Then and now. Behind the dash and glamour of history were always columns of figures, pots of gold, hunger for land, for minerals, for power. He put down his pen. He was drawn to the past because it was at a remove, the passions and clashes reduced but still stirring, like the sound of distant trumpets. Abruptly, he pushed away the legal pad, stood and walked to the window.

Normally he would have worked throughout the day, taking time to eat lunch on a tray, absorbed and happy in his work. But he couldn't continue to ignore Marguerite's idiocy. Not that he cared what causes she embraced. However, that latest vague comment worried him. Marguerite had murmured, "The market is so high now. Why, the house could sell for as much as two million. Two million — why, that could make such a difference in psychic research." Surely she didn't mean to get rid of this house. She couldn't do that to him.

But, he realized, his gaze grim, she very well could. Dad had left the house to Marguerite, the house and all his estate. Of course, this was Wayne's home. Marguerite knew that. She'd never suggested that Wayne leave.

Psychic research. Dad would have hooted at that. How could Marguerite be such a fool?

Wayne stood at the window. Slowly, he began to smile. There might be a solution. There was the research he'd once done on the wave of spiritualism that swept the country after the Great War. He'd written a piece or two. He swung about, walked to an old wooden filing cabinet, pulled out the middle drawer.

Alice Schiller held the orchid silk dress carefully. She was always careful with Rita's clothes. That had been one of her duties for so long. She was accustomed to the feel of finery, had known loveliness secondhand for almost a lifetime. She stared into the ormolu-framed mirror into dark mocking eyes so like her own. Even after all these years together, she always felt a shock of amazement when she saw Rita's face, the so-famous face of Marguerite Dumaney. She remembered the first time they'd met on a set in Santa Monica and Rita, young then, had gestured to her. "Come closer. Let me see you." Rita had reached out, tousled Alice's dark red hair until it drooped like her own. "Some makeup and she'll be perfect. At least at a distance," and her low throaty laugh welled. It could have been insulting. Instead, Alice had looked into those compelling eyes and been enchanted as all the world was then. Almost forty years ago, the exciting years as Rita's stand-in punctuated by Rita's marriage, travel, successes and, finally, escape. When they left Hollywood, Rita tossed that richly auburn hair, still with its memorable wave, and said huskily, "Always leave while the band's still playing."

So many years. "Rita . . ." Alice carefully laid the dress on the bed, but then she stood straight and tall. She didn't really sound like Rita now, though she could still re-create that throaty drawl. She heard her own voice, thin and bloodless in comparison with Rita's, but challenging, nonetheless.

Before Alice could get the words out, Rita pushed back the gilt chair and turned, one thin, elegant hand outstretched. She was, as always, a dramatic actress, blazing eyes, hollowed cheeks, blood-red lips.

"Alice," the husky voice commanded, "you will do as I say."

Donna Ladson Farrell always flew first class. But not today. Her face was sullen as she boarded, angry at sitting in the tourist section, wishing she could shove Marguerite into the seat next to that squalling baby. How dare Marguerite send a cheap ticket! After all, she was Donna Ladson! She slammed into the seat and thrust her Louis Vuitton bag beneath the seat in front. She didn't have the miles to upgrade because there'd not been enough money to travel this last year. She'd just managed to keep the gallery open and make the first night parties in new gowns. But she couldn't get any more dresses, not until she paid the outstanding bills. Thirty-five thousand dollars. Outrageous how much it cost to dress properly. But if she didn't wear a new dress, the whispers would start, that she was old hat, and worse, that she was poor. No one in Hollywood would have anything to do with her if word got out that she was short on money. It was bad to be old; it was death to be poor.

Donna smoothed back a ringlet of white-gold hair. She might be sitting among hoi polloi, but she looked first class. She'd almost refused to make this hellish flight across country. But she had no choice. Marguerite was generous at Christmas. This time Donna needed a big infusion of cash.

Generous. Donna's mouth twisted. With Dad's money. The bitch.

---

Terry Ladson checked the fuel gauge. God, it was hell to be broke. He'd have to take on fuel before he could leave. The cruiser moved smoothly through the water. A dark green smudge loomed suddenly out of the low-hanging cloud bank. Terry's sunburned face split in a grin. Oh well, what the hell. It was always good to be on the water. If those last two charter parties hadn't canceled, he'd have been in the chips. Well, maybe not in the chips. There'd been the cost of rebuilding the motor down in San Juan and that old pirate had taken him for a cleaning. But when you don't have a choice, you pay the freight. Anyway, the food was good at Marguerite's and she'd always liked him. He was willing to bet she'd ante up at least ten grand. Then he could go to Bermuda. And someday — the old hag couldn't live forever — there would be money to burn. He envisioned a forty-five-foot yacht with mahogany paneling, the latest in sonar, big enough for a crew and he would be captain. . . .

He was still smiling as he turned the wheel and the cruiser headed for a familiar channel. He was never down for long and he always had a grand picture of himself, a hell of a swaggering guy in his white captain's hat and blue jacket. If he'd looked at his own photograph, he would never have noticed that he was middle-aged and running to a paunch with a too-red, bloated face topped by thinning hair.

---

Joan Ladson struggled to push her suitcase into the overhead rack of the bus. No one offered to help. She stood on tiptoe and shoved, then sank into a hard seat and stared out the window. She didn't see the graceful fronds of palmetto or the fences draped with bougainvillea. She clutched her purse. She mustn't lose her purse. It contained her return ticket. When she'd received the letter from Marguerite with the invitation to spend Christmas on the island, she'd wanted to fling it into the trash. Why should she go there and be humiliated, as she'd felt humiliated ever since Wayne and that girl got involved? At least Wayne hadn't married the little tramp. Joan had waited, expecting that final blow, but it never came. And now Marguerite asked her to come, demanded that she come, really. So she was on her way. She hadn't had a choice, really, even though the timing was awkward. She'd had to take off before the official Christmas vacation began. It was vintage Marguerite, asking everyone to come for her birthday celebration on the fifteenth, then stay for Christmas though that was ten days away. Could she be in the same house with Wayne for ten days? Well, she was leaving the day after Christmas. If the girls didn't need money, she wouldn't have come. But they did need money, more money than she as a librarian or Wayne as a teacher could manage — though, to give Wayne his due, he helped out as much as he could. But Eileen was in Europe for her junior year and it would be stupid to be there and never go and see anything. And Rosalie was expecting the baby next month and Chris had just lost his job and they needed everything.

Marguerite had everything. Joan stared at the window. How much would Marguerite give her?

Rachel Van Meer stopped beside the lagoon. She stared at her reflection, wavering, uncertain, making her look thinner than ever. She was just a jangle of bones. Thin and stupid and terminally ugly.

Mike didn't think she was ugly.

Mike . . .

She looked over her shoulder. The dumb house was so big it had more windows than a Disney castle. She hated the house. But if they hadn't come to live with Aunt Marguerite, she would never have met Mike. At least the place didn't seem so much like a mausoleum since Pudge and the others had come. And there were fun Christmas decorations everywhere. Best of all, nobody was paying any attention to her, not with so much company, and she could slip away and spend more time with Mike. Her dark mood was swept away by a flash of happiness, a feeling so unaccustomed and so delicious that she waited a minute longer, savoring the golden sensation even though she heard the steady snip, snip, snip of clippers, calling to her as clearly as throbbing drums.

Mike was there within the maze, clipping. And

waiting for her. Rachel glanced once more toward the house, the immense many-windowed house, then darted into the opening in the dark, tall, heavy-scented shrubbery.

The evergreen branches slowly ceased to move, the cessation as gentle and unremarkable as the curtain that slowly drooped into place at a window on the second floor.

Pudge Laurance ambled on the walk that curved around the harbor. He wasn't much for fog. Or early morning walks, for that matter. But he needed to get out of that house. No wonder Happy was spooked. Although she was vintage Happy when he tried to find out what was bothering her, fluttering her eyelashes and murmuring vaguely, "Everything will be all right. I feel so much better since you've come, and we do want to have a happy Christmas. We won't worry about a thing until after Christmas," and she stared at him with those huge blue eyes that begged for reassurance. Oh well, she wasn't the real reason he'd come to Broward's Rock. When Happy's call came — "Oh Pudge, it would be so nice to see you again at Christmas. And Rachel will be thrilled" — he'd had a swift picture of a long-ago Christmas and a little girl with golden ringlets, reaching up to him with chubby hands.

Christmas. Not a good time to be alone, wishing you could change things that could never be changed. He looked out at the foggy harbor. Damn pretty, the boats strung with Christmas lights, soft pools of color in the mist. He shivered. It wasn't really cold, but cold enough to a fellow who'd been on the Mexican Riviera. And damn refreshing after his encounter with Happy. Lord knows it was no wonder they'd split. He should have remembered, when she'd called, how maddening she could be. Didn't the woman ever come to the point? All this jumble about Marguerite and the awful man who was taking advantage of her. From what Pudge remembered of Marguerite, he'd like to meet the man who could take advantage of her. What harm did it do if the old girl wanted to dabble in ESP and talk to — he frowned, trying to remember what Happy had said — not controls, not gurus. Whatever, somebody on the Other Side. He grinned. You'd think ghosts — spirits? — would have better things to do than rock tables or talk with odd accents through heavy-breathing yogas. Yogas? No, no. Oh well, it didn't matter a tinker's damn to him. He would have turned Happy down flat except for the island. Broward's Rock. He'd not sent a letter to Dallas in a long time. They always came back: Addressee Unknown. But Judy's brother Ambrose lived on Broward's Rock. Pudge had called him a couple of times, but Ambrose wouldn't tell him a thing. Said Judy was through, it was over, leave it at that. Quite a speech for a man who measured out words like hundred-dollar bills. Ambrose had a little bookstore somewhere near the harbor. Maybe after all these years . . .

Pudge had pretty well given up his quest. But

maybe, just maybe . . . His shoes clicked on the boardwalk. He walked faster. There, down at the end.

He reached the window and looked up at gilt letters:

DEATH ON DEMAND

He checked the display. Lights twinkled on a small Christmas tree. Red letters hung from a green strand: SANTA'S PICKS FOR A MYSTERIOUS CHRISTMAS. The books were arranged in a semicircle: *The Last Noel* by Jean Hager, *A Holly, Jolly Murder* by Joan Hess, *Midnight Clear* by Kathy Hogan Trocheck, *Mistletoe from Purple Sage* by Barbara Burnett Smith, *Ransome for a Holiday* by Fred Hunter and *We Wish You a Merry Murder* by Valerie Wolzien.

Times must have changed. As he remembered, Ambrose was a private eye fan, loved John D. MacDonald, James M. Cain and Erle Stanley Gardner.

He pulled at the doorknob and a CLOSED sign jiggled. Oh. Hours: ten A.M. to six P.M. Monday through Friday, ten A.M. to 4 P.M. Saturday. The store would open in about fifteen minutes. He was turning away when he saw the small gold letters at the bottom of the window:

ANNIE LAURANCE DARLING, PROP.

# One

Annie Laurance Darling crouched on the floor by the coffee bar. She peered into a deep crack. Maybe if she got a skewer she could reach the silver bell. A skewer? This was a bookstore, not a culinary shop. Whatever made her think of skewers? Probably the box of Diane Mott Davidson books waiting to be unpacked. Readers loved books with sleuthing cooks at Christmas. Maybe she'd better order some more of the Katherine Hall Page and Janet Laurence titles.

Annie popped to her feet, tried to push back a loop of yarn into her sweater and glared at Agatha. "Agatha, this is my favorite Christmas sweater."

The elegant black cat lifted a languid paw, the same paw that an instant before had swiped swiftly through the air and ripped the silver bell from atop the green yarn Christmas tree on Annie's red sweater.

Agatha tilted her head and looked for all the world as if she were smiling.

Annie finally grinned. "Okay. I don't blame you. It's what anybody deserves who goes around with a bell dangling from their front. Happy holidays, sweetie." Annie reached out, carefully, and stroked the velvet-soft fur, then moved behind the wooden bar and poured Kona coffee into a mug. Each mug at the Death on Demand Mystery Bookstore carried the name of a famous mystery. This one emblazoned: MURDER FOR CHRISTMAS by Agatha Christie. She also had a mug with the English title: HERCULE POIROT'S CHRISTMAS.

Annie held the warm mug and smelled that wonderful Kona aroma. How cheerful to think of lacy waterfalls and champagne music when it was cold and foggy outside. Annie loved the South Carolina Low Country and especially the barrier island of Broward's Rock, but even she had to admit that December, with its sharp winds and drab brown marshes, was a good time to stay inside, read wonderful mysteries (perhaps *Renowned Be Thy Grave; Or, the Murderous Miss Mooney* by P. M. Carlson, *Death at Dearly Manor* by Betty Rowlands or *False Light* by Caroline Llewellyn) and drink Hawaii's best coffee. December was also a good time for shelling, especially an hour or two after dead low tide. Yesterday she and Max had found channeled whelks and two lettered olive shells. The olive, South Carolina's state shell, was glossy with a pointed spire. Max had picked up the first olive and smiled. "Hey, this one's perfect. A Low Country Christmas present just for us."

Annie grinned. She adored Christmas, but sometimes she thought Max loved the holiday even more. Last night they'd made red and green taffy and one evening soon they would whip up a batch of divinity. As far as Annie was concerned, there was never time enough in December to do all she wanted to do. There were boxes of books to unpack and a big stack of luscious bound galleys to read. Publishers sent out early paperback versions of forthcoming books to alert booksellers, and many of her favorite authors would have new books out in the coming year: Anne George, Harlan Coben, Peter Robinson, Deborah Crombie and Caroline Graham. Hmm, what riches. Her Christmas present to herself would be the time to savor these books.

Annie picked up the fragrant coffee, happily drank. Christmas was her favorite season. She loved everything about it: the tangy scent of pine, decorating the tree, the lighting of an Advent candle at church each Sunday, buying presents and wrapping them, making divinity and pumpkin bread. After all, Max wasn't the only chef in the family. . . .

She put down the cup. Family. Christmas was a time for families. She'd always envied friends with big, sprawling, though sometimes noisy and cantankerous families. Her own memories were, perforce, of small gatherings. But happy ones. There were the years with her mother before she died. Later Annie had come to the island to spend the holidays with her Uncle Ambrose, a taciturn man who seldom spoke but whose every gesture to Annie spoke of love. These recent years, Christmases with Max. Dear Max, who always looked toward her when he entered the room and whose dark blue eyes held a special warmth that was for her alone. Dear Max, who was definitely not the Prince Charming she had imagined. Oh, of course he was charming and handsome and sexy, but he was light-years different from any spouse she'd ever envisioned when she was growing up. To be honest, she'd thought of someone like herself: serious, intense, hardworking.

"Agatha, have you ever heard of the Odd Couple?"

Agatha lifted her head to sniff the coffee mug, wrinkled her black nose.

Quickly, Annie said, "Well, we aren't *that* odd."

From the front of the store, Ingrid Webb, her longtime clerk and friend, called, "Annie, are you talking to that cat again?"

Annie called back, "Ingrid, she didn't mean to bite you."

"Humph." There was a slap of books being shelved.

Annie understood Ingrid's coolness. Of course Agatha had damn well meant to bite. Agatha was bright, quick, gloriously beautiful and exceedingly temperamental.

Annie bent down, whispered, "Agatha, you shouldn't have."

Agatha eyed the green-yarn Christmas tree on Annie's sweater.

Annie took a step back. Not, of course, that she was afraid of her own cat. But prudence prompted retreat.

Prudence. Yes, Annie knew she was prudent.

Max was not prudent, although he was too mellow ever to be reckless. Max didn't believe in schedules. When they traveled, he was always ready to turn down an enticing road even if it wasn't going in the right direction. He liked the unexpected. Max was handsome and fun and adventurous — and lazy? She brushed away the word. To be fair, Max was quite capable of intense and excellent work. It was only that he so rarely found any reason to work. Max was debonair and clever and kind. So, all right, he wasn't an overachiever. Okay, okay, he wasn't even an achiever.

Did it matter?

So far, so good.

She felt a sudden breathlessness. Why had that phrase come to mind? She could over the years hear her mother's light, dry voice: "So far, so good." Implicit in the words was the suggestion that the future was yet to be proved. Her mother had said it about the course of friendships, the quality of clothing, the promises of politicians.

Annie stepped behind the counter, turned on the water to wash the mug. What a silly phrase to come to mind now. After all, her mother had reason to be wary, to distrust current good fortune. Nonetheless, despite the fact that it was only the two of them, she'd made every Christmas glow and Annie held those distant days in her memory, shining like the long line of luminarias they'd put down their walk to light the way for Santa Claus.

Annie turned off the water, dried the mug and replaced it on the shelves behind the coffee bar. Speaking of Christmas, she needed to get busy, Christmas lists to make, parties to plan, special groceries to buy, mincemeat and pumpkin, pine nuts and candy canes. But for now, it was time to concentrate on the store. Although mornings were never terribly busy, the store would open in a quarter hour and there were sure to be a few shoppers, especially since the weather was foggy. Ingrid had readied the front counter, and Annie needed to call and check on a shipment of Dick Francis books that hadn't arrived and print out the invitations to the store's annual Christmas party. First there was regular work to be done. She lugged the stepladder from the showroom, then unwrapped the paintings stacked against the back wall. Every month, she hung five watercolors by a local artist. Each painting represented a scene from one of Annie's favorite mysteries. The first customer who identified each painting by title and author received a free book.

Not, of course, a collectible. Annie glanced toward her New Treasures table where she arranged recently acquired firsts. She was especially thrilled to have found *The Sea King's Daughter* by Barbara Michaels, *The So Blue Marble* by Dorothy B. Hughes and *Dark Nantucket Noon* by Jane Langton.

It took only a moment to hang the paintings. Annie climbed down from the ladder and admired the watercolors.

In the first painting, a lean, dark-haired man knelt on the carpet in front of a safe. He concentrated, eyes intent. There was an aura of underlying sadness about him, of difficult times and dark days, even though his face was young. A tube led from a box on the floor to one ear. Another tube led from the box to the safe, fastened next to a small window with five dials by a rubber suction cup. Nearby, an older man with sandy hair lounged in a comfortable chair, smoking and watching.

In the second, the hospital operating room was large and green-tiled. Glass cabinets held supplies and metal sterilizing drums awaited scalpels and clamps. A huge circular metal lamp beamed down on the operating table. Their faces stricken with shock, two surgeons, an anesthetist, a chief nurse and two assistants stared at the leaden gray face of the dead patient.

In the third, the group of people on the terrace, high above a river, looked constrained and ill at ease. At a glass door leading out to the terrace, an older woman placed a restraining hand on the arm of a dark young man who stood close to a beautiful young woman. The older woman's face was grave. She was a compelling figure, despite the fringe of mousey brown hair, dangling pince-nez and old-fashioned brown dress with a bog-oak brooch as a demure decoration.

In the fourth, a single-masted white ketch rode quietly on the steel-gray water of the estuary. The name was painted on the hull, *Peacock*. A young woman rowed a dinghy, a basket and milk jug carefully balanced midships. She handled the sculls with competence. Her face was eager, intelligent, quite lovely and utterly determined.

In the fifth, the group in the shabby drawing room appeared stiff and uncomfortable. An old woman, her white hair mussed from sleep, stared toward the doorway with bright pale cold seagull's eyes. She sat on an Empire sofa, her hands folded in her lap. There were three men, two of whom had an official air, one of them a youngish spare man in a well-tailored suit. A pleasant-faced man in his forties stood by a lean dark woman with hazel-gray eyes, a gypsy swarthiness and a sardonic expression. All eyes were focused on the doorway. A young girl of fifteen or sixteen in a school coat and childish low-heeled clumpish black school shoes stood next to a police matron. The girl's darkish blue eyes were set wide apart in a heart-shaped face. Mouse-colored hair and hollowed cheeks gave the face charm and pathos. The lower lip was full, but the mouth too small. So were her ears. They were too small and set too close to her head.

Annie knew her smile resembled Agatha's when licking whipped cream from an unwary coffee bar customer's cappuccino. But a shopkeeper did what a shopkeeper had to do. No way was she going to put up paintings of Christmas mysteries. Those would be duck soup to her customers. As for the books represented here, no one could say they weren't among the best of the British mysteries — even if they were all written fifty years ago. Her best customer, Henny Brawley, prided herself on her knowledge of British mysteries. Maybe, maybe not.

Okay. So far, so good.

She felt an instant of stillness, then shrugged. The recurrent phrase only meant she realized there was much yet to do. The front windows were done, but there were all the interior Christmas decorations yet to put up. She'd hang the garlands of holly next, the glossy green leaves and vivid red berries superb harbingers of the season. It would look awfully nice for the party, when longtime customers were invited for egg nog and sherry and offered a ten percent discount on all book purchases if they donated a book to The Haven, the island's public recreational center for teenagers.

She found the holly garlands in a long, heavy box on the storeroom worktable. She pulled the box into the coffee area. Climbing up on the step-ladder, she looped the garland around exposed beams, humming "Rudolph, the Red-Nosed Reindeer," with pauses for an occasional "Ouch!" as the sharp leaves pricked her.

One end of the swag drooped across the coffee bar.

Eyes glittering, Agatha whipped her paw, knocking the holly on the floor.

The phone rang. Annie glanced over the book stacks. "Will you get it, Ingrid?" And smiled. Ingrid's tribute to the season was a huge red bow that wobbled atop her iron-gray perm.

Ingrid picked up the phone. "Death on Demand, the finest mystery bookstore east of Atlanta. How may I — Oh hi, Pamela." Ingrid pointed at the phone, then at Annie.

Annie shook her head so vigorously, the stepladder wobbled.

"She's hanging holly right now. No, not really hanging it," Ingrid explained patiently, "she's wrapping it around the exposed beams in the coffee bar. . . . Yes, it's very pretty."

Annie reeled in the strand and flipped the end over a beam. Pamela Potts without a doubt. Pamela was an indefatigable volunteer for island charities and a very literal person. And lonely. Annie was already feeling a pang of guilt that she was evading the call.

"Would you like to leave a message? Oh? Something personal? Well . . ."

"I'll take it, Ingrid." Annie perched on the stepladder and took the portable phone from Ingrid, nodding her thanks.

"Annie." Pamela's serious voice quavered with uncertainty.

"Hi, Pamela, what's up? Ouch!" Blood welled from Annie's right index fingers.

"Annie!" Alarm lifted Pamela's voice.

"It's nothing. The darn holly . . ." Knowing this could entail a laborious description of the offending sharp leaf and her resultant wound, Annie said firmly, "What can I do for you, Pamela?"

A casserole for a church dinner? A donation to

the Salvation Army? But Max had already taken care of that. Annie was a firm believer in the Salvation Army, which offered hope to those without hope. A raffle ticket for an island charity?

"Annie" — Pamela's voice faltered — "you know that I don't gossip."

Actually, Pamela didn't. She was much too serious and, further, she was as good-hearted as she was dense.

"Of course not." Annie tossed the holly over the back of a chair. As she walked behind the coffee bar and picked out another mug — REST YOU MERRY by Charlotte MacLeod — she said soothingly, "Don't pay any attention to what people say."

There was a startled pause. "Annie, what are people saying?"

Annie poured more coffee. It wouldn't do any good to bleat at Pamela. And an explanation . . . Annie sighed. "Sorry, Pamela. I was talking to Ingrid. What did you say?"

"Oh. Well. The thing about it is, I absolutely empathize with the right of every individual to grieve as he or she wishes. I mean" — her voice deepened with earnestness — "there are God-given rights."

Annie carried her mug around the bar and slid onto a stool. She glanced at the clock. Opening in five minutes. Surely by then . . . "I couldn't agree more," she said heartily. She sipped the coffee.

"So you understand that I find this very, very difficult."

"I'm here for you, Pamela." Annie waved away Ingrid, who was looking anxiously toward her.

"You always have been." A ragged breath. "That's why I feel I must tell you about Max's mother, even though I obviously came upon her in a most private, delicate moment. Oh, and Annie, I was with Gertrude Parker."

Annie sat bolt upright. Her brain absorbed three messages at once:

Pamela Potts didn't have a problem. The problem, whatever it was, belonged to Annie and Max.

Max's mother, with the best will in the world and flashing an absolutely enchanting smile, was capable of creating problems which would confound even Judge Judy.

And whatever Laurel had done, word would reach even the least curious and most unsociable on the island because Gertrude Parker's mouth never shut.

"Laurel." Annie pictured her mother-in-law, her fjord-blue eyes, her smooth cap of golden hair, her patrician features. You'd never think just to look at her — Well, maybe you would. There was Laurel's otherworldly gaze. To put it nicely. Actually, loopy was an equally appropriate description. Oh Lord. What in the world could Laurel have done? A most private, delicate moment? Did Annie even want to hear what Pamela had observed? Probably not. Almost certainly not. Did she need to hear? Oh yes.

"Annie, are you there?" Pamela spoke gently.

"Yes. I'm sure everything's all right." Annie was proud of her self-command. Then she ruined it by demanding worriedly, "What's wrong?"

Pamela oozed reassurance. "Annie, don't be upset. I assure you that Gertrude and I didn't intrude."

"That was good of you." Annie took a deep breath. "Now, if you could just explain. . . ." Annie was reminded of the old vaudeville joke when an actor, greeted after a humorous skit by neither laughter nor applause, leaned over the lights and said, "And now my partner and I are going to come into the audience and beat the bejesus out of you."

"We were at Sea Side Cemetery —"

Annie felt the tension in her shoulders ease. The cemetery — that didn't sound too threatening.

"— taking Christmas wreaths to the soldiers' graves. And you know that gravestone with the steering wheel?"

Indeed Annie did. It was a favorite spot to take island visitors, and chauvinist islanders considered it right on a level with the nose-up Cadillacs buried along the highway outside Amarillo. However, even the headstone's biggest boosters admitted the island couldn't compete with Savannah since the publication of *In the Garden of Good and Evil.* Still, the steering wheel headstone remained a point of pride. It was the resting place of a locally famed stock car racer. The inscription read:

JOHNNY GO-DOG DAVIS
JUNE 5, 1944–MAY 22, 1968
FROM CHAMPION RACER
TO GOD'S FASTEST CHARIOTEER
GO-DOG, GO!

"And Laurel was there!"

Annie gulped coffee in relief. She hadn't known her mother-in-law was keen on stock car racing, but what the hey! Live and let drive.

"Pamela, I appreciate your —"

"She was talking to Go-Dog." Pamela's tone was sepulchral, but even so, Annie heard the Southern intonation, "Go-o-o Dawg."

Annie slid off the stool, paced back and forth. "She couldn't talk to him," Annie said gently. "He's dead, Pamela."

"Annie, I swear, it was the spookiest thing — I mean, I don't want to insult anyone's beliefs and I firmly support everyone's right to approach the hereafter in whatever manner they find most comforting —"

Annie braked the philosophical discussion. "I'm sure you do. What did Laurel say?"

"She didn't say anything to us."

Annie spoke through clenched teeth, the better to refrain from verbal assault. "What did Laurel say to Go-Dog?"

"Oh, she wasn't actually talking to Go-Dog. I mean, he wasn't there, Annie."

Annie was proud of her measured tone. "What did Laurel say while standing by Go-Dog's grave?"

"She was asking him for help. She wanted him to look up someone named . . . I think it was Roderico or Rodolfo or something like that . . . and tell him to get in touch with her, that she had received the one message and now she was waiting for more, that she didn't know what she should do about some family matters and she just knew that he and Go-Dog must have met and if Go-Dog would pass along her request she would be awfully grateful. That's when I yanked Gertrude back into that path that runs behind the big pines and marched her out of there. But Annie, I thought you ought to know."

"Yes. I appreciate your telling me. Yes, we should know." Was it possible that Laurel had finally skidded beyond the normal barriers? She had always been spacey, but there had been an earthy, solid base beneath her enthusiasms. And, frankly, a fey sense of humor that enjoyed tweaking the pompous and especially the proud.

But this . . . "Thanks, Pamela." Annie clicked off the phone. Should she talk to Laurel? Or should she tell Max? After all, Laurel was his mother.

Max's mother. Max's ocean-blue eyes were so much like Laurel's, brimming with good cheer, refusing to take the world too seriously, intent upon good times. Heredity. Surely Laurel hadn't gone bonkers. Annie refused to entertain the possibility that Laurel had been bonkers forever. No. That wasn't true. But this graveyard soliloquy must be investigated. Did Laurel need help? If she was talking to a steering-wheel headstone, yes, she did.

The front doorbell jingled. Annie looked up at the clock. Ten o'clock. Agatha stretched, flowed through the air to land on the heart-pine floor and then she was gone, slithering into a favorite nesting spot beneath the Whitmani fern. The fern's raffia basket had a lopsided bulge in front, courtesy of Agatha. Agatha always disappeared when a stranger entered the store.

Well, Ingrid would take care of everything.

Annie didn't bother to retrieve her red jacket from the storeroom. Max's office was only a few steps along the boardwalk that curved around the harbor. She would likely find him immersed in *Golf Digest* or the *Atlantic Monthly* or the *New York Times.* The fact that he was able to keep abreast of all current affairs simply underscored, in Annie's view, the paucity of demands on his time. Max always retorted that anyone in the service industry had to remain informed. He considered himself a member of the service industry in view of his rather unusual business — Confidential Commissions — which offered help to anyone with a problem. Confidential Commissions wasn't, of course, a private detective agency. "Confidential Commissions," Max would say earnestly, "strives to assist individuals who are perplexed, bewildered, bedeviled."

Okay, bub, Annie thought, have I got a candidate for you. She was so absorbed in her thoughts that she was halfway up the central corridor before Ingrid's call stopped her; stopped her, in part, because of the peculiar, choked sound of Ingrid's voice.

Annie looked toward the cash desk, at Ingrid, with her eyes wide, her jaw slack, one thin hand outstretched protectively toward Annie.

Forever after, Annie would retain an indelible imprint of her surroundings, the True Crime books to her right, the Christie collection to her left. Edgar, the sleek black stuffed raven, looked down with glassy eyes. A cardboard display case in front of the children's mystery section held an assortment of George Edward Stanley paperbacks.

And she would always remember her first glimpse of the stocky middle-aged man and his familiar, oh so familiar rounded face with hopeful gray eyes, mist-dampened sandy hair, broad mouth, sandy mustache flecked with gray, and spatter of freckles. He wore a yellow crew neck sweater over a tattersall shirt, chino slacks, tasseled loafers.

The bookstore receded, the brightly jacketed books and Ingrid's shocked face and the heart-pine floors blurring. She saw only the man standing a few feet from her. She stared into eyes that mirrored her own, at features that were a masculine version of her own. She saw the flutter of sandy lashes.

That was the way she blinked when shocked or upset.

He tried to speak, struggled for breath as she struggled.

"Annie?" A clear tenor voice.

She simply stood there. And waited.

He stepped forward, reached out.

She held up her hands, palms forward.

"Annie" — there was wonder and hope and delight in his voice — "I'm your dad."

# Two

She took a step backward.

"God, Annie." A smile crinkled the too-familiar, too-strange face, a smile that found a ready home. This was a face accustomed to smiling. "You're so beautiful. You were a beautiful little girl. And now . . ." Those damnably familiar, yet strange gray eyes filled with admiration.

Her sandy hair, her gray eyes. And yes, her smile. She felt utter confusion.

He held out both hands, strong hands. "I've looked for you for a long time, Annie." His smile was eager, sweet, engaging.

Sudden anger flamed through Annie's icy calm. "Have you?" Her voice was thin and tight and uneven.

Ingrid came around the cash desk. Annie felt Ingrid's hand on her arm, but the touch seemed far away.

He took a step forward. "Annie, I wrote and wrote. But the letters came back Addressee Unknown. I —"

"I don't care." She spaced the words like barriers at a closed road. She remembered in a jumble all the Christmases when she used to pray for a daddy like all of her friends and the tears that stained her pillow and the questions she never asked her mother. She thought of scraping by and making do and going without. She remembered the years when she'd spun fantasies about her father, and she remembered even more clearly the years she'd no longer spun fantasies, when the idea of a father was remote and unreal. He had never been there for her. Never.

She stared at him, saw his smile slip away, his eyes widen, his hands drop.

"You walked out a long time ago." She spoke crisply, as if to a late deliveryman, polite but firm, dismissive. "As far as I'm concerned, you can keep right on walking."

Eyes straight ahead, Annie moved past him, brushing against his suddenly raised arm. For an instant, her heart quivered, but she yanked open the door and plunged out into the fog. She broke into a run, her steps echoing on the boardwalk though the fog dulled the sound. Behind her, she heard a call, muffled by the fog.

"Annie, Annie, please —"

Annie banged into Confidential Commissions.

Max's buxom blond secretary looked up, a tiny Christmas wreath blinking from her bouffant hairdo. Her welcoming smile froze, then fled. She pushed back her chair. "Annie, what's —"

Annie was already across the narrow anteroom and flinging open Max's door.

Max lounged in his oversize red leather chair, holding a copy of *Golf Digest*, feet propped on an Italian Renaissance desk that would have looked at home in a Vatican office. A putter leaned against the desk. The in box held a dozen varicolored golf balls. The desk lamp was twisted to illuminate the artificial putting green.

"Max!"

She scarcely had time to see his shocked face, he moved so fast, and she was clinging to him, clinging with all her strength.

"Annie, what's wrong?" Instead of Max's usual easy, amused tone, his voice was hard, the tone of a man prepared to attack whoever had hurt her. It was like watching a shaggy, well-loved Irish setter transformed to a German shepherd. Her Max, her affable, civilized, laughing Max with a glint in his eye and a grim set to his mouth.

Annie looked up, seeing a face she knew well, handsome features and Nordic blue eyes and golden hair with the glisten of wheat in the sunlight, and a face she'd never seen, eyes steely, jaw taut.

"It's my father." Her voice was still clipped and harsh.

Max slipped his arm around her shoulders, drew her to the red leather sofa. "Father?"

No wonder his voice was puzzled. He knew Annie's family history as she knew his — in bits and pieces. She'd never said much about either of her parents. Why talk about things that hurt when there were always so many happy things to discuss? And, of course, Annie's mother had died of breast cancer years before Annie had met Max. All Max knew of Judy Laurance were snapshots in albums and one studio photograph, a delicate face with sparkling blue eyes, a high-bridged nose, hollow cheeks and a pointed chin. Straight dark hair parted in the middle. The high-necked blue polka-dot granny dress had a lace collar.

The picture didn't reflect Judy's grave smile or the way her eyes lit when Annie came into a room. Annie had always wished she'd looked like her mother, but she knew she didn't with her short blond hair and serious gray eyes and round chin.

She looked past Max, not seeing the bright modern paintings on his walls, seeing instead the figure of a stocky man with sandy hair and mustache and a round face with laugh lines.

Now she knew where her face came from.

She didn't care.

"I don't care," she said explosively.

Max grabbed her hands. "Annie, what about your father?"

"He walked in the store. Just now. I don't know where he came from. Or why. Oh, he said he's been looking for me. For years." Finally there was a prick of tears. "Max, that's not true."

Max squeezed her hands. "It could be true, Annie."

"No. You remember how you found me?" She looked into dark blue eyes that softened as he smiled.

It was a favorite memory. She and Max had met in New York when he was involved in off-Broadway plays and Annie was an aspiring young actress fresh from Southern Methodist University in Dallas, Texas. They'd looked at each other across a crowded room and when their eyes met nothing was ever the same for either of them.

Except Max was rich. Annie was poor.

Max had lived in big houses all over the world. Annie had grown up in a shabby bungalow in Amarillo.

Max dabbled. Annie flung herself wholly into any enterprise.

Max delighted in ambiguities and prized the unexpected. Annie insisted upon order and effort.

Max took almost nothing seriously. Annie took everything very seriously.

Max proposed the second time he saw her. Annie left town.

She did have a reason: her Uncle Ambrose Bailey's unexpected death. But she left no forwarding address.

"It didn't take you any time at all." Annie pulled her hands free, gestured energetically. "You called SMU, got the name of one of my roommates, phoned her and, presto, you came to the island."

"I knew you'd gone to SMU," he said mildly.

"He could have figured it out. Anybody can find anybody with the Internet. The point is" — now her gray eyes were deep pools of resistance — "he didn't try. He didn't really try."

Max sprawled back against the soft cushion, folded his arms behind his head. "He came to the store today." Her husband looked at her gravely.

She sat up stiffly. "So I should jump up and down and shout with joy?"

Max gazed up at the ceiling. "You lost your mom." He was silent for a moment and the office was so quiet she could hear the dull boom of the foghorn out in the harbor, a sad, forlorn, lost sound. His blue eyes swung down to meet her gaze. "You've been all alone. Maybe you ought to give him a chance." Then he said quietly, "My dad was too busy working to have any time for me, too busy making more money when he had so much he could have used stacks of it for firewood. Then he died."

Max's father would never walk into this office.

Annie folded her arms. "He could have found me if he'd tried." She was past the shock now, but resentment lodged deep inside, hard as granite. She pushed up from the couch. "I'm okay. But he's twenty-five years too late, Max."

Max rose, too. When he started to speak, she reached up, touched his lips. "And we have plenty to do. With Christmas and everything."

Christmas, a time for families. She pushed away the thought. She wasn't a sucker for sentimentality. Families . . . She clapped a hand to her head. "Max, listen, I had a phone call. Your mom . . ."

Laurel walked across the dance floor toward them. Annie couldn't help observing her mother-in-law more carefully than usual. Annie turned toward her husband, looking from Laurel to her son. What an incredible resemblance: the same golden hair, the same handsome features (or lovely, as sex decreed), the same eyes — No, dammit, Max's eyes might, on occasion, gleam with eagerness, soften with tenderness, dance with glee, tease with amusement, but they were never spacey.

As for Laurel, no one, not even Max, could deny that tonight Laurel was at her spaciest. Spacey and lovely, her golden hair curled softly around her patrician face. Laurel lifted a beautifully manicured hand, the coral polish an exact match for lips now curved in a sweet (otherworldly?) smile.

Annie shot another look at Max, then wished she hadn't. Now was not the time to be reminded of how much Max looked like his mother. Annie didn't want to ponder family resemblance and the fact that on this island, right now, was a man with her face, an unreliable Johnny-come-lately she never wanted to acknowledge. But acknowledged or not, her father's reality couldn't be denied. Just as no matter what she or Max did, nothing could change the reality of Laurel. Or the unreality. . . .

The band belted out "Chattanooga Choo-Choo." The Island Hills Country Club had always been an enclave for music of the forties and fifties, responding to the tastes of its members, but the recent revival of swing on college campuses had resulted in a weekly Friday night dance attended by members of all ages, not simply jiving geriatrics. Their table was near the front, so they had a good view of the dancers.

Laurel beamed at Annie and Max. "My dears" — the husky voice was kind, tolerant — "the minute I saw you, I came straight to you."

Max rose. "Hi, Ma." He grinned in his usual easygoing fashion.

Just as if, Annie thought resentfully, nothing remarkable had occurred.

Annie cleared her throat. "Laurel." She spoke loudly.

Laurel's gaze moved to her. "Dear Annie." As if Annie's presence absolutely, positively topped off a day packed with glorious moments.

Annie wasn't deflected. "I came by your house. I called. I left messages. I need to talk to you."

Max was waggling a hand. She didn't need a primer in body language to understand. Max had not taken seriously Annie's report of Laurel's session with Go-Dog. He had, in fact, hooted with laughter, rolled those dark blue eyes and murmured, "Good old Go-Dog. I'll bet it made his day." Max dismissed Annie's efforts to contact Laurel as unnecessary. "But if it makes you feel better . . ."

Annie ignored Max.

Laurel's eyes widened. "What a wonderful idea. To talk, dear Annie." She cupped her hands as if cradling a rainbow. "However, this evening there are so many wonderful friends I must greet." She glanced happily around the ballroom.

Laurel was undeniably one of the loveliest women in the room. But there was more to Laurel than sheer beauty. She exerted an attraction to the opposite sex that Annie compared to a tidal pull. As Laurel paused at their table, elegant in a cocktail-length ice-blue dress, men headed their way. Men of all ages and all stations. A retired admiral. The mayor. The captain of the high school men's tennis team. A waiter. A visiting golf pro. Howard Cahill, an old friend and sometime beau. Fred Jeffries, intrepid sailor and current beau.

Laurel knew, of course, and she showered hellos and lifted a graceful hand and the men eddied around her, each eyeing the other and awaiting an opportunity to break through. "So many friends to greet," she murmured. "You and Max are such a dear couple. Do have a lovely —"

"Laurel, please. Laurel, what were you doing at the cemetery?" As Annie leaned forward, the music stopped and the last word seemed to reverberate.

Did faces turn toward them? Or was Annie simply imagining the feeling that hundreds of eyes covertly observed their table? Certainly the long list of messages taken by Barb at Confidential Commissions and by Ingrid at Death on Demand and the frenzied blinking of the red light on Annie and Max's home answering machine were not figments of her imagination. Laurel may have been seen only by Pamela and Gertrude, but the eyes of two had done the work of hundreds. Call after call reported hearing about Laurel's cemetery visit. The facts were garbled by some:

"Max, I really hate to tell you, but Junie Merritt

said Agnes Phillips told her sister that your mother put a model of a demolition derby car by the double-trunked live oak at the cemetery . . ."

"Max, fun is fun, but pantomimes at the cemetery . . ."

"Max, apparently Laurel is going to take vows! Now, I haven't heard what kind of vows, but will the church let a woman who's been married five times . . ."

"Annie, I left word on Laurel's machine, but she hasn't called. Please tell her we'd like to have her speak at our luncheon next week and tell us about the Other Side. Everyone is so excited . . ."

"Annie, I hope you can arrange things quietly for Max's sake. Perhaps a nice rest home might be . . ."

"Annie, Go-Dog is my very favorite driver. I haven't been able to get in touch with your mother-in-law, but I'll do anything . . ."

In the pause after Annie's plea, Laurel placed a hand over her heart. "The cemetery." She could not have projected her husky voice more professionally from the apron of a New York theater. She waited a beat, her limpid eyes circling the room. "I've had no success yet, but in my heart I know Go-Dog will come through, just as he always did on Memorial Day." Murmurs across the ballroom sounded like muted cheers. Laurel smiled with utter confidence. "I've asked Go-Dog to find Arturo. I know he will."

"Go-Dog, go!" a deep male voice shouted.

Smiles flashed. Heads bent in eager conversation.

Annie glimpsed a flash of utter satisfaction in Laurel's eyes, a sharp, totally cognitive flash.

Laurel lightly patted Annie's arm. "Your aura is rather worrisome, dear. A rather mustardy color. However, Max" — she blew a kiss at her son — "is . . . oh, it's coming to me . . . aquamarine, undoubtedly." A throaty laugh. She turned toward her admiring coterie, "Oh, Howard, Fred, how utterly divine to see you both," and swept away.

Annie looked after her with amazement. A beau on either arm. Hot damn. But beneath Annie's admiration, worry pulsed. That satisfied look of Laurel's — what did it mean?

Max bent down, kissed the top of Annie's head. "Come on, sweetie, it's vintage Laurel. She's having a blast. Everybody in the room heard that exchange. She's obviously decided to be the village eccentric." He was half amused, half exasperated. "If there's anyone in town who hasn't heard about her performance in the cemetery, they will know after tonight."

Annie stared across the floor at Laurel, still circled by admirers. All male, of course. "Why does she want to talk to him?"

Max blinked. "Annie, don't ask questions that can't be answered. Who knows? It can't be anything too serious. They were only married for two years."

Annie had never sorted out the order of Laurel's spouses. Max's father, of course. And a sculptor. Arturo, the race car driver. A general.

And a professor. Maybe Arturo was the most fun.

Max grinned. "Actually, I liked Arturo. Laurel called him Buddy. Man, did he drive fast!"

The band swung into "Tuxedo Junction." Max grabbed her hand. "Come on, Annie, let's dance."

Annie felt the old familiar thrill course through her. She loved to dance, but she wasn't sure you could always dance your troubles away. As she and Max swung onto the floor, she couldn't quite dismiss her memory of Laurel's savvy, satisfied look.

Or the face of the man who'd left her and her mother behind so long ago.

A pale streak of silver speared into the dusky room, the crescent moon free for a moment from scudding clouds. Annie lay wide awake, Max's body curved next to hers, his arm warm over her waist, his breath soft against her neck. The silvery beam briefly illuminated a white wicker divan and a table with photographs and a small china Christmas tree decorated with sugarplums. When she was little and awoke in the December night, she imagined sugarplums dancing along the moonbeam. The ever-present Great Plains wind rustling the sycamore trees became Santa's husky laughter as he directed his sleigh over head. The pale moonlight wavered, was gone, prisoner again of the capricious clouds. How many years had it been since she'd pictured plump and luscious sugarplums on an avenue of silver?

How many years . . . ? She moved restlessly.

Max's arm tightened, pulling her nearer. "Penny for your thoughts?"

Christmas memories fluttered like brightly patterned cards slapping into a pile . . . a heavy snow and the rush of icy air as her sled careened down a hill . . . her mother's face flushed from the heat of the oven as she lifted out loaves of pumpkin bread meant for gifts, but there was always one for Annie . . . the procession at the Midnight Service, joyous and triumphant . . . opening presents on Christmas morning . . .

"He was never there." Her voice ached with unshed tears. "I used to think . . . oh, when I was really little . . . that someday he would come. I even wrote letters to Santa Claus. Oh well." Now her voice was dry, removed, cool. "I grew up."

Max gently turned her to face him and their faces were inches apart on the pillow. "Annie, maybe —"

"It's too late, Max." But she knew as she spoke that her father's unexpected appearance, this confrontation with a past that she had never even known, had cast her adrift on a sea of memories, expectations, losses — and fears. Was her father's instability a part of her? She'd always made plans, followed them. How much of that tenacity sprang from her early loss? Would she ever walk away from those who cared for her?

"But he's alive." Max's hand gripped hers. "My dad . . . well, I guess I always knew he wasn't really there for any of us. I kept thinking some Christmas he would really see us, my sisters and me. But he could scarcely wait for the presents to be unwrapped to leave. He went to the office on Christmas Day."

At her involuntary movement, he rolled over on his elbow, stared down in the darkness. "I mean it. Christmas Day. There was always something he had to see to. Oh, he came home for dinner, but I don't think he was ever aware of us. It's like we were invisible and he lived in a world bounded by work. If he had lived . . . But I don't think he would have changed. I swore that I would never be like him. Never."

Annie felt a rush of tenderness for the little boy whose father never saw him. Maybe that was worse than a father who was never there. At least she hadn't had to deal with a quartet of stepfathers. She reached up, gently touched Max's face.

He turned his mouth, kissed the palm of her hand.

She felt his lips spread in a smile. She looked up and the moonlight flared again and she saw his familiar grin and the gleam in his blue eyes.

"But you can't say the girls and I didn't have fun with Ma." His voice was light and lively. "And I guess she made us feel good about Dad because she's always had good taste in men — so he must have been fun sometimes."

Fun. Annie felt a pang. Max had devoted his life to fun. No one pursued pleasure and good times with more élan.

Fun — wasn't that why her father had left her mother? She and her mother had never talked about her father, about who he was or why he left or what he had done with his life, but she remembered standing outside the living room one afternoon when she was fourteen and listening to her mother and Uncle Ambrose and hearing her mother's quiet, bitter comment, "All he wanted was to have a good time." Annie had known they were talking about her father. That was all she heard, whirling around and hurrying down the hall to her own room, flinging her schoolbooks on the bed and thinking: So that's why he left, so that's why!

"Hey, Annie, let it go." Max's arms slipped around her; his lips brushed her cheek, slipped softly toward her mouth. "It's okay. We're okay."

Were they? Her absent father, his distant father, his ditzy (surely it was no more than that!) mother, how much did they matter for Annie and Max? Just for an instant she lay still, and then her lips opened and fear was lost in passion.

# Three

Annie glanced in her rearview mirror. That blue Ford had been behind her red Volvo on Saturday when she went to the store. She'd spotted it on Sunday afternoon when she and Max went to the club for brunch. Now it was behind her this morning, obviously having waited for her to pass one of the side roads that opened onto Sand Dollar Road. It didn't take the perspicacity of G. K. Chesterton's Father Brown to guess the identity of the driver.

Annie picked up speed. It didn't matter. Her too-late father could trail her around the island from now until next summer and she wouldn't change her mind. She had too much to do, including shopping for Max and thinking about the future — a future that did not include the driver of the blue Ford. She slammed out of her car, ignoring the Ford as it parked in the lane behind her. Whistling "Jingle Bells," she hurried toward the boardwalk.

Red and green Christmas garlands were wrapped around the light poles and strung along the seawall. The sun sparkled on jade-green water and boats ranging from sailfish to yachts. Annie took a deep breath and looked beyond the harbor to a pod of porpoises playfully diving. It was already in the fifties and would reach the low sixties, a December day that made winter seem far away. A happy day, and a day she was determined to keep that way, despite the blue Ford. And Laurel.

Annie heard footsteps behind her.

She walked faster, reached Death on Demand, unlocked the door and hurried inside. She moved purposefully down the center aisle, accompanied by Agatha, who nipped at her ankle in between emitting sharp yowls.

"I am not late," Annie protested. "And you have dry food; delicious, nutritious dry food." Annie picked up speed and was glad for evasion skills perfected in long-ago soccer games. She reached the coffee bar unscathed, shook down fresh food, opened a can of dietary soft food.

Agatha glared, then crouched over her bowl.

Gradually, Annie relaxed. The front door hadn't opened. Okay, should she string the Christmas lights around the mugs shelved behind the coffee bar? Or unpack some of the boxes of books that had arrived Saturday? She moved briskly to the storeroom and picked up the box marked COFFEE BAR CHRISTMAS LIGHTS.

As Annie deposited the box on the coffee bar, the phone rang. She reached out.

"Death on Demand, the finest mystery bookstore east of Atlanta." She loved the phrase, which rolled over her tongue as easily as a Godiva chocolate.

"And south of Pittsburgh," came a cheerful voice.

"Henny!" Henrietta Brawley was Death on Demand's best customer, a club woman of enormous skill and dedication, a gifted actress, a former schoolteacher, a onetime Peace Corps volunteer and she was, most of all, one of Annie's best friends. Annie felt only a small pang as she realized that Henny, vacationing in Pittsburgh, had probably done a lot of her book shopping at Mystery Lovers Bookshop in the Pittsburgh suburb of Oakmont. But this wasn't the season to be piggy. "Say hello to Mary Alice for me." Annie had met Mary Alice Gorman, the ebullient owner, at a mystery conference.

"Will do. Annie, I've actually seen the hospital where Mary Roberts Rinehart went to nursing school!" Sheer delight lifted her voice. "I tried to figure out the wing where she and the others were quarantined with that smallpox outbreak over Christmas of 1895."

Annie lifted the lid of the box, pulled out a strand and began to untangle it. Why had she put the lights away snarled like a ball of yarn attacked by Agatha?

A black nose poked over the edge of the box.

Oh. Right. Agatha had no doubt helped with the dismantling last Christmas, which might have encouraged a dump-it-in-fast mentality. A black paw patted the end of the strand. Annie reached for another strand. Maybe she could work with this one while Agatha investigated the first.

"Gosh, Henny, the actual building?" Mary Roberts Rinehart, once the grande dame of American mystery writers, had entered nursing school in late August of 1893 at the tender age of sixteen. It was there that she met a handsome young surgeon, Dr. Stanley Marshall Rinehart, who tutored her in German (an excuse to meet) and later would become her husband.

"Yes. I even walked down the halls. But I don't know where the smallpox ward was. In Christmas 1895 when she was quarantined with a rowdy group of patients, she and Stanley sang Christmas carols to quiet them down. You know, they both had excellent singing voices. Oh, Annie" — a sigh of pure happiness — "I am having so much fun. Except —"

Annie pushed the stepstool behind the coffee bar, climbed, and carefully clipped the strand to the edge of the mug shelves.

"— I'm snowed in. Eight inches and it's still falling. So I decided to make a few calls."

Annie reached the end of one strand, leaned perilously sideways to snag another from the box. Agatha crouched to jump for the dangling end. Annie slipped loose a bracelet of bells and tossed it over Agatha's head. The cat turned in midjump. Annie was applauding her own quick-wittedness and missed most of Henny's sentence. ". . . wondered if you'd spoken with her."

"Henny, you're the first person I've talked to this morning. Except for Max." The second strand clipped into place nicely. Annie reached for the third strand.

"I hope Max isn't too worried," Henny said quietly. "I'm afraid Laurel truly needs psychiatric help."

The strand slithered from Annie's hands, caromed off the counter, clattered to the floor, one end landing in Agatha's water bowl.

"You talked to Laurel?" Annie sat down on the ladder.

"Well, you know how it is to talk to Laurel." Henny sighed. "Annie, she is trying to communicate with that race car driver. You know, her third husband. Or maybe he was her second. And he's dead. When I asked why, she would only say, 'I must. I must,' and then she skittered off, oh, you know how she does, and she chattered about crystals and gamma rays and auras —"

"Henny, you remember that woman — I don't recall her name, Ophelia something or other, and she lived at Nightingale Courts —"

"Of course I remember," Henny interrupted crisply. "That's when Ingrid disappeared. Right after your wedding."

That frightening disappearance had been solved with the help of Henny and Laurel. "You remember how Laurel wandered around murmuring about the boundaries of the mind and how we should open ourselves up to cosmic fields —"

"This time it's different." Henny spoke with finality, and Henny was not an alarmist. She was smart, empathetic, clever, a world-class mystery reader, and Laurel's good friend. "I'm sorry, Annie. I'll bet Max won't admit there's a problem" — Henny knew both of them very well indeed — "and I know it's Christmas and you're busy as you can be, but Laurel needs help." There was a pause, then she added, her tone puzzled, "I tried Miss Dora first. She stays in touch with Laurel. But, Annie, it was the oddest thing. Miss Dora was evasive."

Annie stared at the phone. This pronouncement was almost more shocking than Henny's concern for Laurel. Miss Dora Brevard, the doyenne of Chastain, South Carolina, was direct, to the point and never minced words.

"Anyway, I could probably get to Nome before I could get home. The airports are closed, but I have a huge stack — Oh well, Annie, have a great Christmas — but see about Laurel."

Annie didn't even try to retrieve the felled light strand from Agatha, who was pulling it toward the front of the store. Instead, she walked slowly up the central aisle. By the time she reached the cash desk, she had the beginnings of a plan. It took six calls to find Pamela Potts.

"Oh hi, Annie." Pamela took opportunities as they came. "You are so good to call. I'm sure we can count on you for two casseroles, can't we? I'm at the church now and we need to restock the freezer."

Annie would have promised anything short of Max on a platter. "Listen Pamela, what time of day did you see Laurel at the cemetery?" Annie glanced toward the clock. A quarter to eleven.

"The church bell was striking, Annie. It was straight-up noon."

"Thanks, Pamela."

Max kept his expression pleasant but noncommittal as he shook hands with his visitor. But he felt stunned. Annie's dad. Max glanced at the picture on his desk, dear Annie with her steady gray eyes and sandy hair and grave smile, then looked at an older, masculine version of that treasured face.

Pudge Laurance stared at Annie's picture for a measurable moment, too, before he spoke. "You're Annie's husband?"

Max stood a little straighter, felt the intensity of another pair of gray eyes. He was absurdly pleased when Pudge Laurance smiled, a smile uncannily like Annie's, and said softly, "You love her?"

"I do." Max said it as firmly as he had spoken on the memorable day of his and Annie's wedding.

Pudge grabbed Max's hand, pumped it again. "I'm Pudge Laurance and I need your help."

Max found his visitor was instantly likable, his face genial, his tone affable. There was charm here and an appealing plaintiveness. But Max stepped back, folded his arms. "Annie doesn't want to see you. She said" — Max cleared his throat — "that you were twenty-five years too late."

Pudge's eyes were deep pools of sadness. Lines

etched a suddenly anguished face. His mouth drooped beneath his mustache. "Please." He pointed at the chair in front of Max's desk. "Will you hear me out?"

Sandy hair, gray eyes, a face with lines that told of laughter and good humor. Max looked again at Annie's picture. She was so determined. And so hurt. Maybe there weren't any words that could undo the silence of twenty-five years.

What harm could it do to listen?

Max waved toward the chair.

Pudge's grin was both insouciant and sad, ingratiating and abashed. It caught at Max's heart.

Dust curled from beneath the Volvo's wheels. In the thin light of the December sun, the long avenue beneath the live oaks had the murky quality of a grainy black and white photograph. Swaths of Spanish moss hung straight and still. The springlike warmth of the day didn't pierce the glossy green leaves. Annie shivered and rolled up her windows. It didn't take much imagination to hear the clip-clop of black hearses pulling a funeral hearse. A local legend held that on nights of the full moon, a tall woman in a long black cloak walked restlessly up and down the lane, seeking her husband who had been lost at sea in 1793.

Annie abruptly braked as a raccoon darted across the road. There were always explanations for sightings of that sort — a raccoon, for example, partially glimpsed, or an odd play of shadow in the lights of a car (but not in the

1800s), or simply a projection from the viewer's mind.

Whatever, Annie picked up speed. The sooner she got out of this dim tunnel, the happier she would be. Probably Laurel wouldn't come to the cemetery today. But the only way for Annie to judge Laurel's mental state would be to see for herself. She was more worried by Henny's call than she wanted to admit. Max, of course, continued to refuse to entertain any thought that Laurel's actions might be a cause for concern.

The road curved to the right and came out of the live oak tunnel on a bluff above the Sound. The water glistened like polished jade. Stone walls marked the boundary of the cemetery. An iron gate marked the entrance. The gate was open.

Laurel's latest car, a bright blue restored Morris Minor, was parked near a line of pittosporum shrubs to one side of the small whitewashed chapel which every year came closer to extinction. When first raised, the little chapel must have been far distant from the bluffs facing the Sound. Erosion at the pace of three feet a year from the force of tidal currents and storm surf had brought the crumbling shoreline within a stone's throw. Henny Brawley was chair of a committee raising funds to move the chapel. The cemetery, laid out to the south, was as yet in no danger.

Annie parked behind the shiny Morris. The slam of the Volvo door startled a deer in a nearby shrub. The deer bolted, its fluffy white tail readily visible in contrast to its dusky gray winter coat.

The onshore breeze rustled the shrubs as Annie stepped through the gate. Graves with tumbling, weathered headstones seemed to be tucked at random among the graceful slash pines, glossy-leaved magnolias and, of course, the ever-present live oaks. Annie was not a graveyard habitué. She looked around and felt as out of place as a redneck in a tearoom. She had no business here in this serene enclave of peace and farewell.

She would have turned back, but she heard a faraway murmur, the sound of a voice she knew well. Annie took a deep breath and walked swiftly, following the dusty gray path as it wound past family lots and occasional lone graves. Some of these bore fresh Christmas wreaths. She stopped to look down at one grave:

WALTER WALLACE
APRIL 12, 1840–JUNE 16, 1863

It didn't take a history book to know that war had claimed a short life. The wreath was so fresh that when Annie leaned down to straighten the bow, she could smell the fresh pine. Pamela Potts had come this way.

The husky voice murmured on the other side of a clump of pines.

Annie ducked through the pines, slipping a little on slick golden needles. She pushed aside a limb.

Laurel had obviously given some thought to her appearance. Annie wondered what it revealed of her mother-in-law's psyche that she had selected (quite a nice foil for her blond beauty) a navy wool gabardine jacket with gold-cord-trimmed sleeves, peaked lapels, six gold-tone crest buttons and flap pockets with a gold-and-white-striped blouse and white wool slacks. The gold cord on the jacket matched the gold-trim chain on her navy kidskin flats. Laurel looked equally ready to man a flotilla or tap-dance in *The Pirates of Penzance.*

A half dozen graves ranged on ground sloping down from a ridge. Laurel stood with one hand on the marble steering wheel that jutted from the largest gravestone.

". . . know that you are most likely very busy. Why, if the crowds cheered for you here, I can imagine the shouts that must ring among the clouds." A faint frown marred that beautiful face. "Can shouts ring among clouds? One might think there would be a damping effect. Well" — a small laugh — "no matter. I'm sure there are sound engineers who have studied this problem in depth. If, indeed, it is a problem. But I am sure" — there was a burst of confidence in her husky voice — "that race you must. Why, what would heaven be if we could not pursue the activities which afforded us the most joy in our earthly realm?" Laurel smoothed a tendril of golden hair stirred by the wind.

Annie thought of five husbands and earthly joy.

"Each heart must follow its proclivities. So" — Laurel patted the steering wheel — "I know you are racing. And therefore" — a sunny smile —

"I'm sure that you know Buddy. Oh, how Buddy loves to race!" She clasped her hands together. "Dear Go-Dog — I hope you won't mind my addressing you so familiarly, but I feel as if we are confreres, I have ventured so often to this quiet glen — please" — and now her tone was brisk — "tell Buddy that I truly must speak with him." There was the slightest hint of impatience. "I know he's busy, too." Her eyes widened. "Oh dear, I hope you aren't competitors. But no, no, I would not have been led here were that the case and truly I have to thank Providence for this opportunity." She beamed at the marble steering wheel. "I awoke one night with the clearest picture in my mind — stock cars, a great smash-up — oh, that was such a shame, Go-Dog, and you were in the lead — and a white marble steering wheel. It led me right to you. And I must depend upon your good offices because dear Buddy is buried in Milan and I truly haven't time to go there. I need his advice. I have decided to liquidate a great amount of stock — oh, those particulars are neither here nor there — and use it for the good of mankind. Now, there are those who might have difficulty seeing Buddy as a financial adviser. But" — she leaned closer to the stone — "once I was getting ready to sell my Microsoft stock and do you know what happened? Buddy's little red Porsche simply zoomed into my room late one night and he jumped out. He looked dashing in his racing goggles and soft leather hat and white silk muffler — fringed silk — and he said firmly, *'Ne vends pas ces stocks, ma chérie.'* " She raised an eyebrow. "Oh yes, Buddy was Italian, but he also spoke French when — well, at some of our more special moments. Of course, I held on to that stock and you know how well it's done. So I won't listen to anyone but Buddy. Now, it may be that I shan't have to bother you again." A soft laugh. "Although I hope I've not been a bother. Do you know, I think you and I should have got on famously had we met at an earlier time." A pause. "When you were alive. Because I feel so drawn to this lovely spot." One coral-tipped hand was flung wide. "However, it may be that I am being led. I received the loveliest call from a Friend. That's a Friend of the Library, Go-Dog. In any event, she's told me about the most marvelous place to reach out to the Other Side — the Evermore Foundation. She said its president — Dr. Swanson — is simply wonderful! The kindest man, and he is able to put you in touch with everyone! Well, not exactly everyone. No frivolous or mean-spirited contacts are permitted. Don't you think that's lovely? To keep the plane of connection at a very high level? But I wanted you to be the first to know because you may be responsible for that call." She wagged a pink-tipped finger playfully. "Of course, if I don't speak with Buddy, I will hurry right back to you. Good-bye for now, Go-Dog." Laurel gave the steering wheel a final soft pat.

Annie plunged down the slope, skidding a little on the pine needles.

Laurel reached out to keep her from falling. "Annie, my dear. What a pleasant surprise."

Annie looked deep into bright blue eyes. Crazed blue eyes? "Laurel . . ." Despite Annie's firm intention to sound casual and unconcerned, she sounded like a Budweiser lizard spotting a frog. "You can't talk to dead people."

Laurel's laugh was as light and sweet as distant wind chimes. The gaze she bent on Annie expressed chagrin, disappointment and just a soupçon of embarrassment. "My dear, I would have expected better of you." Clearly the embarrassment was on Annie's behalf. A delicate sigh. "But we all do what we can do. I'm sure you mean well."

"Laurel." Annie looked deep into those eyes, searching for even a hint of humor. Laurel had evidenced other odd enthusiasms through the years, wedding customs and saints and ghosts and Shakespeare, but she had not sought counsel from the dead. Especially not financial counsel.

Laurel's eyes met Annie's, her gaze kindly, interested and utterly serious. She clasped her hands to her heart. "Annie, you will excuse me, I know, but I feel compelled to continue my quest. I know that if I can talk to Buddy, everything will be all right." Her lower lip trembled. "You see, I have felt quite frightened and it came to me — things do, you know — that everything would be all right if only I could talk to Buddy."

Laurel frightened! Annie couldn't have been more shocked had Go-Dog suddenly materialized beside them. She stared at her mother-in-law and saw uncertainty and despair in her eyes and bowed shoulders in the elegant jacket and an aura of frailness and confusion.

Laurel pressed one hand to her lips, then she looked past Annie.

It was painful to Annie to see the effort it took for Laurel to lift her face and manage a smile.

But Laurel was almost her old insouciant self when she called out, "Gertrude, what a pleasure to see you." Laurel clapped her hands together. "Why, Annie, look who's here! It's Gertrude."

Annie looked over her shoulder.

Gertrude Parker's long, horsey face sported a strained smile and she had the decency to avert her eyes from Annie.

Annie stared at her frostily. Clearly Gertrude had crept up to hear Laurel's soliloquy, intending to bring an eyewitness report to as many islanders as she could reach by phone and E-mail before the ten o'clock news.

"Hello, Laurel, Annie." Gertrude's voice was a high whinny. Her eyes glistened with interest. She came even with Annie, stepped past to look avidly at Go-Dog's grave.

Laurel gazed around the clearing. "Isn't this cheerful! So many of us converging right here!" Laurel looked beyond Gertrude and Annie toward the pines. "Are you with Gertrude?" Then she blinked. "Oh my. Oh, Annie."

Annie didn't look around again. She knew who stood behind her. Worry about Laurel was swept away by a furious spurt of anger. How dare he follow her! And wouldn't this be a choice item for Gertrude's gossip mill? What would she emphasize, Laurel's tête-à-têtes with Johnny Go-Dog Davis or the intriguing appearance of Annie Laurance Darling's father? Annie could imagine Gertrude's unctuous tone: *Well, my dear, I am not one to gossip, but I was out tending to some graves, oh you know, I just feel it is my duty at Christmastime, and I happened to overhear Laurel Roethke, you know, she's Max Darling's mother, and she was talking, that's the only way I can put it, she was simply having a conversation with Go-Dog Davis. And to cap it off, here came Annie Darling and she looked like she was worried to death.* (A little giggle.) *And then, you won't believe this, but this man came up behind us . . .*

Annie was damned if she was going to give Gertrude anything to crow about. She said briskly, "Laurel, my" — it took enormous effort — "father's visiting and, of course, he's eager to meet you."

Annie had to hand it to Laurel. No one would imagine there was anything peculiar either in the circumstances of this meeting or in the locale. Laurel bestowed a charming smile on Pudge Laurance. "Such a pleasure. We have so much in common, don't we? Our dear children have truly made a love match and isn't that simply the greatest achievement of all?" As Laurel burbled, she somehow maneuvered Gertrude — surely she didn't actually push her — toward the path and they were walking out of the cemetery.

Annie knew that Laurel, with her uncanny ability to pick up on nuances, perceived Annie's turmoil and she was deflecting Gertrude just as surely as a magician whips a red scarf to conceal the hidden ace. Gertrude kept attempting to turn and look back at Annie and her father, but Laurel firmly grasped her arm and moved them ahead at a rapid rate. And, of course, Annie thought sourly, she was also avoiding a grilling by Annie.

Annie allowed herself to lag back. She didn't intend to talk to her unwelcome companion, but she was not eager to end up by the gate to face Gertrude's scrutiny. She walked slowly and stared down at the dusty gray path.

"There's something rotten going on." Pudge Laurance reached out and gripped Annie's arm.

She swung to face him, yanking her arm free. She realized abruptly that he wasn't looking at her. He had stopped, too, but his eyes followed the women on the path as they curved around a clump of pines and out of sight. His pleasant face was somber, his gaze worried. He tugged at his mustache.

"What do you mean?" Why should he care about gossip? Besides, no man would likely pick up on Laurel's artful handling of Gertrude and the reason why. As for Laurel — and no doubt he, too, had overheard that disturbing soliloquy — why should he care what Laurel did?

He bent his head, deep in thought, fingers still tugging at his mustache.

In the silence, Annie studied the man who

meant both too much and too little to her. He might have been any island visitor, a blue polo shirt and white crew-neck sweater, khaki slacks, running shoes, but his intelligent features were too bleak for a man on a holiday. He looked up, and his eyes demanded her attention.

"This Dr. Swanson she talked about —"

So he had overheard Laurel.

"— he's the guy Happy says is taking advantage of her sister. He . . ."

Annie folded her arms, held them tightly against her. She shut out his voice. What was it he had said that first day — "Annie, I've looked for you for a long, long time"? Had she ever, even for an instant, believed that he had come to the island seeking her?

"Happy?" Annie's voice was harsh. "Who's Happy?"

Pudge Laurance shoved a hand through his hair. A lock dangled forward and he looked boyish — boyish and uncertain. He swallowed. "Happy's my ex-wife and her sister is —"

Annie didn't wait to hear. She broke into a run, the dust scuffing beneath her feet. She never wanted to hear about this wife or any wife. Ex-wife. That would be expected, wouldn't it, of a man who wasn't there for anyone, not for Annie's mother or Annie or this Happy, whoever she was. Annie felt the hot rush of tears. He hadn't come to the island to look for her. She should have known that right from the first. She happened to be living where he came to see an ex-wife. That was right in character, wasn't it? His arrival had nothing to do with Annie.

As she burst through the gate, veered toward her car, she saw Laurel's outstretched hand, heard her soft, "Oh," and she saw, too, the avid delight in Gertrude's face. Ignoring them both as well as the shout from behind her, Annie slammed into the Volvo, twisted the ignition, pumped the gas and jolted the Volvo back far enough from the blue Morris to swing around and gun toward the dim tunnel beneath the live oaks.

# Four

A light flashed on his phone. Max pushed back his Christmas list — wouldn't Annie be pleased with the elegant parchment map of St. Mary Mead? — and punched on the speaker phone.

"Max Darling." He scanned the rest of his list:

A treasure box tied with a red ribbon with contents that should amaze her.

A yellow cashmere sweater.

A box of Godiva raspberry truffles.

A little book with quotes from Jane Austen's novels.

A handwritten promise . . .

"Max, Pudge Laurance." The speaker phone magnified the despair in Pudge's voice. "I've blown it. I should have waited and let you talk to her. Now, God, I don't think she'll ever listen to me. But I was just trying to tell her about that guy your mom's involved with."

Max pushed back the list, sat up straight. "My mother?"

"Yeah. Listen . . ."

Max listened. When Pudge finished, Max chuckled. "Sounds like Laurel, all right. Listen, Pudge, I guess every family has some" — Max paused, drew a huge question mark, festooned it with headstones — "unusual members." Max knew that was not very explicit, but if Pudge hung around long enough, he would surely get used to Laurel. Although it was odd that Annie, who had coped with enthusiasms ranging from wedding customs to old-fashioned hand fans adorned with quotes from Shakespeare, should be so concerned about Laurel's efforts to communicate with Buddy. "I'll talk to Annie about it," Max said reassuringly. "Maybe she's overreacting because she's upset about seeing you." Sure, that could be the case. Max drew a cat with its fur standing on end. Annie reacted to her father like a cat sighting a Doberman. And good old Pudge was a cocker spaniel if he'd ever met one. "You know, Pudge, you shouldn't have sprung it on Annie that you'd married again. At least not at this point."

"But she asked me . . ." Pudge's voice trailed away. "I was trying to explain because I thought Annie should know about this Swanson guy. But she didn't give me a chance to finish. And Max, I'm afraid it's more serious than you think. Everybody's furious over here." There was a thoughtful pause. "Except Happy. Of course, she can't ever act mad, it's not in her job description." His tone was dry.

"Job description?" Max added a bow to the cat's collar. Not that anyone would ever collar Annie.

"Oh, Happy's such a — well, I shouldn't be critical. She means well. God, does she mean well!

But being around her is like existing in an alternative universe. Happy absolutely refuses to admit that it isn't the best of all possible worlds even when something's really bugging her. And something is driving her nuts or she wouldn't have asked me to come here. But that isn't the reason I came. I came because I thought old Ambrose might finally tell me where Judy and Annie were living. I didn't know about Judy. Dammit" — now he was indignant — "if Judy hadn't written me off, I could have kept in touch with Annie. And I would have. Max, do you think Annie will ever believe me?"

Max didn't have an answer. Annie was hurt and she'd been hurt for a long, long time. "Let's take it one step at a time, Pudge."

"I'm almost ready to get the hell out. This mess over here is enough to push everybody over the edge. Then they'll all be nuts like Marguerite. She's convinced this Swanson dude has a pipeline to Eternity and she's been shoveling money at him. Happy moans about it, but something more is worrying her. I can't put my finger on it, but she acts damn odd when we start talking about her sister and the rest of the family. As for Marguerite, everybody glares at her and the old hag is having the time of her life. She's planning a dinner in Swanson's honor. Even Happy looks glum. If it weren't for Annie, I wouldn't spend another night here. Well, Annie and Rachel. Rachel's a good kid."

"Who's Rachel?" But Max's tone was absent. An idea began to form.

"Rachel Van Meer, Happy's daughter by her second marriage." Pudge's voice softened. "She was a little kid when Happy and I got married." He drew his breath in irritably. "That's another thing. Happy and I have been going 'round and 'round — Well, anyway that doesn't matter to you. But I think you better check out this Swanson. Your mom was talking about money . . ."

Max wasn't worried about money. Laurel's assets were pretty well tied up in trusts. His dad may have been a workaholic, but he obviously had a good line on his wife. Max drew a stack of greenbacks wrapped in chains.

"Wait, wait a minute." Max pressed his fingers against his temple. "Hey Pudge, I've got an idea! What do you think about this?"

A pier extended into the harbor. Annie had it to herself. The wind off the water was cold despite the thin sunlight. She stood with her parka zipped, gloved hands on the railing, staring out at a distant buoy bobbing in the swells. A flock of herring gulls, their summer white now dusky and streaked, sailed overhead, angling out toward a fishing trawler. Annie shivered. But it wasn't the wind chill that made her feel sheathed in ice like a polar explorer trudging across a harsh and terrible whiteness.

Why, after all these years, should it hurt so much that her father had not sought her, that he had come to the island to see his ex-wife? So Annie was an afterthought. So what else was new?

Annie blinked against tears. Okay, all right, she was a big girl now. She had Max. The sudden thought broke through the sheath of ice. Warmth pulsed through her. Max. Okay, she wasn't going to let her father's appearance ruin the holidays for her or for Max. They were going to have a bang-up Christmas, full of good cheer, good humor —

Laurel. There could be no pursuit of Christmas pleasure if somebody was taking advantage of Laurel.

Annie swung around, walked hurriedly, her shoes echoing on the wooden planking. When she reached the boardwalk fronting the shops, her footsteps slowed. She stopped outside the plate-glass window of Max's office. Max and Barb could easily round up information on Dr. Swanson. It was either appalling or wonderful, depending upon your attitude, what could be learned on the Internet within the space of a few minutes merely by clicking a mouse. Orwell's Big Brother would have loved cyberspace. With the day coming when a life history will be embedded in a disk on a plastic card, anonymity will be no more. But a computer search could wait. She picked up speed. First she needed to find out whether there was indeed something sinister about the man or whether the problem was the state of Laurel's mind. Annie still believed that the old-fashioned art called conversation offered nuances and shades of meaning a computer screen could never deliver.

Annie passed the windows to Death on Demand. She felt a pang of guilt, leaving Ingrid to deal with the Christmas crowd, but Ingrid could call on her husband for help if hordes of shoppers arrived. However, though business picked up nicely during the Christmas season, throngs were unlikely.

As Annie drove the Volvo out of the harbor parking lot, she punched a familiar number on her cell phone, knowing success would probably commit her to another couple of casseroles.

Pamela Potts answered on the first ring. "Hello, Annie."

Annie felt an instant of surprise. Obviously, Pamela even recognized Annie's wireless number on her caller ID. Caller ID and the myriad of modern technological gadgetry continued to diminish some of the standbys in older mysteries, such as the anonymous phone call, the unidentified bloodstains, the mysterious stranger. As for the winsome heroine trapped at midnight in the old cemetery, all she had to do now was whip out her cell phone.

Annie turned left from Sand Dollar Road onto the dusty, gray winding road that led to the Lucy Bannister Kinkaid Memorial Library and reference librarian Edith Cummings, who, in a very different fashion from Pamela Potts, knew everything worth knowing on the island of Broward's Rock.

Clutching her cell phone, Annie bluntly asked, "Pamela, do you know Dr. Swanson?" It was not necessary to be indirect with Pamela. It would never occur to Pamela to wonder why a question had been asked.

"Oh, Annie." Pamela's voice might have quavered with the same unease had Annie presented her with a box of tarantulas.

Annie braked for a half dozen deer trotting across the road. "You don't like him?" There was a pulsing pause. Annie curved around the front of the three-story Greek Revival mansion that housed the library and pulled into a parking spot next to a line of palmetto palms. "Pamela?" Annie switched off the motor.

"Some things are wrong." The words came slowly. "God warns us not to deal with black magic or the occult —"

Annie could picture Pamela, her blue eyes wide and serious, her hand tightly gripping the receiver.

"— things which are not of this world. Annie, that's what Dr. Swanson does. That's why, even though I am a member of the Library Board, I got up and left in the middle of the lecture he gave there."

Annie knew there could have been no more brave or telling act on Pamela's part.

"Annie, don't have anything to do with him. Please." A gasp. "Is Laurel involved with Dr. Swanson? Oh, Annie, you must save her!" A ragged breath. "Forgive me if I have said too much." She hung up.

Annie clicked off her cell phone. As she walked to the back steps of the library, unease swirled within her. Annie knew a sophisticated listener might smile with quiet amusement, but Annie knew, too, that Pamela, earnest, kind, literal and serious, represented basic goodness. And basic goodness was not a laughing matter.

"Mmm, sexy." Edith Cummings, a reference librarian with enthusiastic appetites, winked at Annie. "Laurel may be interested in more than his crystals."

"Crystals?" Annie pictured chandeliers glittering at a winter ball.

Edith placed her hands on the Information Desk counter and leaned forward, dark eyes gleaming. "Emory Swanson." She emphasized each syllable. "His name's a mouthful, but I'd pick him for Bachelor of the Year anytime. He spoke to the Friends a couple of months ago and I'll have to hand it to the man — he gave a spiel any medicine man would envy while managing to look like a banker. You know, inspire confidence." She smoothed back a strand of wiry black hair. "And lust. But not for money."

Annie had a confused image of a sloe-eyed Harrison Ford in pinstripes. "What does he look like?"

Edith glanced around the Lucy Kinkaid Memorial Library. "Everybody's Christmas shopping," she observed. "Except me and thee, and I'm only here because I'm a working stiff." Edith reached beneath the counter and lifted up the SECTION CLOSED sign. Plopping it next to the computer terminal, she pointed a thumb toward the stairs. "C'mon. You're a library patron. I can help you find the materials you're seeking even if it requires deserting my post and relinquishing the pleasure of addressing the serious inquiries that I receive this time of year. Such as, 'Do you have "Jingle Bells" available in Icelandic?' or 'What kind of buttons does Santa Claus have on his jacket?' " She bustled out from behind the counter.

Annie followed her up the stairs, Edith bounding eagerly ahead. Annie hadn't been upstairs since last summer and some momentous meetings involved in planning a Fourth of July celebration that culminated in fireworks and murder.

Edith was already tapping on the third door to the right of the stairs. Gold lettering on the panel read: FRIENDS OF THE LIBRARY. But she was opening it as she knocked. "Like I said, everybody's Christmas shopping. Until the holidays are over, it'll be quieter up here than Tombstone with Wyatt Earp in town. Come on back here."

Annie joined her at the second of two gray filing cabinets against the back wall.

Edith rummaged in the top drawer. "Here we are." She thrust a folder at Annie. "Every meeting in the history of the Friends is documented since its inception in 1936."

Annie forbore to reply, *Huzzah.* She flipped open the green folder and found the minutes of the meeting called to order at 10 A.M. October 12, a transcript of the guest lecture, presented by

Emory Swanson, Ph.D., entitled "Manifestations of Psychic Phenomena in the Modern Era," and a brochure.

Edith leaned over Annie's shoulder, tapped the brochure. "He handed them out. You know, Laurel's on the Library Board. I'll bet she was at the meeting." Edith slid the minutes out of the folder and rustled through the stapled sheets. "Yeah. Here's her name on the attendance sheet."

But Annie was studying the substantial brochure, printed on exceedingly heavy, pale mauve stock. The outer panel featured a pen and ink drawing of a brick plantation house. Beneath it, gold letters in light gothic script trumpeted:

*Chandler House*
*Evermore Foundation*
*Broward's Rock Island, S.C.*

"I've heard the esteemed doctor has quite a fancy layout. He must have asked the real estate agent to lead him to the spookiest house on the island. Or maybe" — Edith's tone was skeptical — "he spotted it in a crystal. Hey, that may be the coming answer for information junkies. Who needs the Net? No more interminable delays while one phone line squabbles with another or five thousand teenage boys absorb every circuit to check out — Well, we've been having some discussions here about where the boys go on the Net. But here's a glitch-free way to connect to our future. Simply grab a crystal, peer deep within and You Will Be

Led. Or something like that. Anyway, that's the old Chandler place. You know it, don't you?"

Annie did. The Chandler house, built in 1832, was one of the more remarkable extant plantation homes in all of South Carolina. Two stories and an encircling piazza were supported by seven brick arches on each side. The house overlooked the marsh and was surrounded by pines and live oaks, buffering it from the nearest homes. Annie and Max had attended a New Year's Eve dance there several years ago on a stormy night with wind howling around the house. Despite blazing logs in four huge fireplaces, cold drafts eddied through the ballroom. They had danced out of the ballroom into a broad hallway and ended up beneath a sprig of mistletoe and not a breath of cold touched them.

Edith folded her arms, leaned against the filing cabinet. "Open the brochure."

Obediently, Annie unfolded the heavy paper. Faint ivory streaks in the mauve background gave the brochure a marbled appearance. The first inside panel announced:

*The Crystal Path*

> Amidst the clamor of earthly life, sensitive natures can easily become alienated, overcome —

Edith said impatiently, "Don't read that guff. Look at his picture!"

Annie's gaze slid over the second panel, where the text alternated with artistic photographs of three crystals, a yellow one in the shape of a lotus, a green one in the shape of an elephant tusk and a brilliant white one in the shape of a globe. In order, they were named Serenity, Perception and One World.

Annie moved on to the third panel and looked into the forthright gaze of Emory Swanson, Ph.D. Dark brown eyes crinkled in good humor. A slight smile softened ruggedly handsome features, a bold forehead, jutting nose, blunt chin. His silver hair was a thick tangle of close-cropped curls. He sat behind a desk, one strong hand gently cupped around an oblong white crystal. Books filled the shelves behind him. Every color in the photograph exuded warmth, from the beautifully tailored brown tweed sport coat with the merest hint of a red stripe to the ruddy mahogany of the desk to the bright book jackets.

"Wow," Edith murmured. "Isn't he the best-looking thing you've seen since Ezio Pinza?"

Annie wrinkled her nose. "If you like that type."

Edith clapped her hands to her head, stared at the ceiling. "Jeez Louise!" she exclaimed. Edith was a mystery reader on a par with Henny Brawley and this exclamation was a favorite of Gar Anthony Haywood's ex-cop sleuth Joe Loudermilk. Edith flounced her hands. "How about Jeff Chandler?"

Annie grinned. "Better. He played lots of private eye roles."

"You have," Edith intoned, "no taste. You'd take Jeff Chandler over Ezio Pinza? That's like preferring Victor Mature to Cary Grant."

Annie ignored that gibe. Her eyes studied the compelling face in the photograph. The longer she looked, the more worried she felt. Swanson's straightforward gaze came from heavy-lidded eyes that had a secretive air, and the lips, despite their gentle smile, were sensuous and utterly confident.

She had a swift memory of Laurel, with her troubled eyes and slumping shoulders.

"So what's this about crystals?" Annie pointed at the pictures of the shining glass shapes.

Edith's eyes were sardonic. "Oh well, of course, Swanson doesn't do anything so passé as a crystal ball. I mean, shades of Madame Who-sis in a turban. No, ma'am. He's New Century. And that is crystal on a cost level with Lalique or Tiffany. He brought that yellow one, the flower" — she pointed at the lotus — "and placed it where the sun was slanting in from a window and it blazed like diamonds. And he has this deep voice that makes you feel like you're in a tent with Ronald Colman." A sigh. "Okay, with a guy you'd like to be in a tent with." She peered at Annie. "Pierce Brosnan? Brad Pitt? Leonardo di Caprio? Oh, he's probably too young."

Annie glared.

Edith grinned in utter satisfaction. "Anyway, when Swanson spoke" — Edith tilted her head and her face scrunched in thought — "you felt like you were being wrapped in layers of cashmere warmed in the sun. He stared deep into the crystal and his voice got lower and lower and he described time stretching backward and forward, a golden highway, and the ineffable joy of slipping from earthly ties to walk in light and peace and listen to those who have gone before and will come after."

"And?" Annie prompted.

Edith's dark eyes crackled with a vivid, skeptical intelligence. "Sweetie, I enjoyed wrapping up in his cashmere voice, but I last took a ride on a turnip truck when I was about six and was invited on a snipe hunt and left holding the bag. Nevermore, saith both I and the raven."

Annie frowned at the handsome photograph. "I've never heard of him. The Chandler house belonged to the Rossiters the last I heard." Hugh Rossiter was a computer consultant and his wife was a golfer.

"They got a divorce a couple of years ago. She moved to Arizona and he's in California." Edith plopped in a swivel chair and grabbed the computer mouse and began to click. "Let me see . . ." She peered at the screen, typed, clicked, typed, clicked. "Okay, sweet baby," she crooned to the screen. Images flashed. "Voilà, Annie." A dark brow quirked. "My, a travelin' man, all right."

Annie pointed at the screen. "Will you print it out for me, Edith?"

At the stop sign on Sand Dollar Road, Annie hesitated for an instant. Should she turn right and get back to the store? Or . . . She flicked on her signal, turned left, drove a hundred yards and turned left again on Red-Tailed Hawk. She drove slowly, seeking the winding private road to the Chandler house. It was right along here. Yes. She turned left again on a rutted, bumpy, dusty road. Annie wasn't impressed. If the Evermore Foundation was so damn well connected, you'd think they could pave the road.

The road curved around a bamboo thicket. Annie braked and stopped in front of a huge metal gate attached to stone pillars. On either side of the pillars stretched a tall spiked iron fence. A small intercom was attached to the left pillar.

Annie stared. The last time she'd been to the Chandler house, there was no gate, no fence, definitely no intercom. Dr. Swanson might like to talk about travel on a golden road, but apparently he had strong feelings about anybody using *his* road. In the thin sunlight, the house looked brooding and withdrawn, the front piazza in deep shadow.

What would happen if she went up and poked a button on the intercom? What if she said she was interested in learning about Evermore? Could it do any harm?

Ignoring little bumps of presentiment that were probably a product of Max's oft-stated advice to THINK before she acted, Annie was out of the car and within reach of the intercom when a deep-throated growl erupted to her left.

Startled, she swung toward the fence, then,

flailing, stumbled back, hands automatically lifted in defense.

Two Dobermans lunged toward the gold-tipped spikes, saliva drooling from dark lips agape in throat-deep snarls. Over the frenzied growls, a cold voice demanded from the intercom: "State your business."

The dogs barked and jumped, jumped and barked.

Annie backed toward her car, tried to still her trembling hands. She ignored the repeated request and flung herself behind the wheel. As she drove away, fast, she wondered a great deal about the peace and harmony espoused by Dr. Emory Swanson.

# Five

Max paused outside the heavy wooden door of Parotti's Bar and Grill. Parotti's was an island institution, an all-day café and tavern and fish bait store just opposite the ferry landing, all owned and operated by Ben Parotti. Ben ran the ferry when he damn well pleased and his bar and grill provided the best fried catfish and hush puppies on the island, as well as bait, charter fishing trips and beer on tap. Annie loved Parotti's, especially the fried oyster sandwiches. Thankfully, Ben still offered succulent down-home food even after his recent marriage and a wife who had added quiche and lemonade to the menu and fresh flowers in vases to the old scarred round wooden tables.

Marriage did change some things. Scrawny, pint-size Ben no longer scuffed around in long underwear tops and stained corduroys held up by a knotted cord from an old flannel bathrobe. In fact, the last time they'd been over for lunch, Annie had murmured to Max that Ben looked like a Broadway dancer in his spiffy double-breasted blue blazer and white ducks, an opinion which would probably have sent Ben posthaste to the nearest secondhand store for an old outfit.

But Ben was a prime example of the miracle of marriage, the willingness to take into account a partner's hopes and desires and fears.

Max took a deep breath and shoved open the door. Ever since the call from Pudge Laurance, he'd expected to hear from Annie. He'd called Death on Demand, home and her cell phone. She'd fled the cemetery, angry and upset. But when she finally called a few minutes ago, she'd not even mentioned seeing her father. She'd just said, "Max, I know it's late. But I haven't had lunch yet. Can you meet me at Parotti's?"

Of course he could.

He waited a moment for his eyes to adjust to the dimness, then walked swiftly across the wooden floor.

Annie waved from a booth not far from the line of coolers filled with squid, chicken necks and chunks of fish which added a pungency to air laden with the odors of old grease and beer. She stood and waited for him, eyes huge in a pale face, hands clenched.

He pulled her close, held her tight, smelled for an instant the freshness of her hair, the delicate scent of her favorite Estée Lauder powder, and wished for wisdom.

Annie stepped back and looked up at him, then slipped into the booth. She didn't say anything, but her eyes were wary.

Max took his place opposite her and felt that an abyss stretched between them instead of an old plank table carved with lovers' initials.

"You've seen him." She spoke calmly, but her voice was cool and remote.

Max looked at a face both familiar and unfamiliar. Yes, this was his Annie, sun-streaked hair, gray eyes, eminently kissable mouth, but he didn't recognize this carefully composed, grave mask which hid her thoughts. Was she angry? Grieving? Despairing?

Max hesitated, uncertain what he should say. Annie would never forget his words. And what right did he have to push her toward the father who had abandoned her? All right, so he liked Pudge. Obviously, he didn't really know the man, but Pudge had warmth and charm and, dammit, he was Annie's father.

Sudden anger glinted in Annie's eyes. "So he raced from the cemetery to you. If he calls you again, tell him what I said, Max. Tell him I said it's twenty-five damn years too late."

Max would have jumped from an airplane, scaled a mountam, swum a wave-crested river to erase the tears from her eyes. He spoke slowly. "He called me. I told him exactly that, Annie."

Those shiny eyes watched him.

"He said you were the only reason he came to the island, the only reason he's staying on the island."

She listened intently.

Ben Parotti stood a few feet past their booth, out of Annie's vision, and his worried eyes darted back and forth between them.

Max dropped one hand where Annie couldn't see and wiggled his fingers and Ben slipped away.

"But he said he had to call me. Because of Laurel. Pudge said —"

"Pudge?" Annie's voice was strange. "Is that what he's called? His name is Patrick."

Once again Max knew this was dangerous territory and how galling it must be for Annie to realize that Max knew her father's nickname while she did not. "Annie, listen. You trust me, don't you?" He reached across the table, gripped her hands. "I know you're upset. I know you can't be expected to simply dismiss the past, but I hope you will give him a chance. Just give him a chance."

She squeezed his hands, pulled hers free and brushed back a tangle of blond hair. "Max, don't push me." She pressed her fingers against her cheeks. When they dropped, her gaze was determined and somehow fiercely impersonal. "He doesn't matter right now." Speaking fast, she described Laurel in the cemetery, concluding, ". . . she's frightened and she truly believes everything will be all right if she can talk to Buddy. Maybe that wouldn't hurt anything, but she's vulnerable, Max, and she's going to go to this foundation —"

"I know. Evermore Foundation, run by a Dr. Swanson. Pudge told me a great deal about Swanson." His voice was grave.

Annie's eyes flashed. "Oh yes. Pudge's ex-wife. The reason he's here."

Max decided the less said about Pudge's ex-wife, the better.

Ben Parotti was lurking near a potted palm, another of the new improvements. Max waved at him. "Here's Ben, Annie. Let's order."

Annie managed a smile. "Hi, Ben."

Today Parotti wore a Jack Nicklaus green sport coat and pale yellow trousers. "We have two specials, fish chowder with corn fritters and oyster pie with a spinach salad and a raspberry vinaigrette. And apricot tea."

"Oh, I don't know," Annie said blankly. She waved her hand. "Anything."

Parotti shot her a shocked look. He put his hand to his mouth, muttered to Max, "Missus under the weather? I'll do her a double special fried oyster sandwich."

Max nodded. "Fried oyster sandwich for Annie. I'll take the chowder. Two apricot teas."

Parotti looked at her anxiously. "I'll bring a double order of fritters," and he hurried away.

Annie stared at the table. "It was decent of him to come and tell you about Swanson." She took a deep breath. "Okay. He said he had to tell you about Dr. Swanson. Look what I've got here." She opened her purse, pulled out a sheaf of papers. She pushed them across the table. "There's something wrong about Swanson. The longest he's ever stayed in one place was five years. That was in Nashville. He moves to a town and sets up a foundation and puts out fancy brochures with all this guff about the Golden Road and Emanations of Light and Seeing Our Way and then the first thing you know, wham, the foundation shuts down, he moves to a new town, starts over again."

Max scanned the thick sheaf of papers. "You're right. And a different name every time. In Nashville, the New Vision. In New Orleans, Points of Light. In Laguna, Shimmering Spirit. In Seattle, the Golden Road. But there's nothing here to indicate any trouble with the law or with his credit. No bankruptcies. In fact, it looks like his credit's pretty choice." He raised an eyebrow. "How did you get all this financial stuff?"

Just for an instant, the old Annie looked at him, laughter in her eyes. "My lips are sealed." Then the laughter fled. "Laurel shouldn't be involved with this."

"I agree." That was true enough, Max thought. But his real concern wasn't Laurel. His real concern was Annie. And whether it was wise or foolish, he wanted her to see Pudge, to be around him long enough to sense what kind of man he was. Once again, Max chose his words with care. "Pudge's ex-sister-in-law is Marguerite Dumaney —"

Annie's eyes widened at the mention of the legendary actress.

"— and apparently she's deeply involved with this crystal stuff. Dumaney's convinced she's connected with her dead husband. This has upset everybody in the family. So Pudge has hired me to find out what I can about Swanson." Max stared into cool gray eyes.

"I see." She spoke evenly, but she no longer looked at him.

"Annie —" He reached across the table.

Parotti clomped across the wooden floor. "Here you go, Annie, the double deluxe fried oyster sandwich. I made the tartar sauce fresh this morning myself."

Annie smiled. "Thank you, Ben. Nobody in the world makes a better sandwich."

Chowder sloshed over the brim of Max's bowl as Parotti kept his eyes on Annie.

Waiting until Parotti turned away, Max unobtrusively sopped up the spillage.

Annie munched on her sandwich, closed her eyes. "Hmm. The best!"

Max waited until he was halfway through the chowder. Annie's color was better and she no longer looked like a soldier staring up a gun barrel.

"So" — and he kept his voice casual — "Pudge thinks it would help if we met Swanson on a social basis."

Annie was suddenly still. She put the remnant of sandwich on the plate.

"Marguerite Dumaney's celebrating her birthday tomorrow night. Pudge will wangle us an invitation. He said Swanson will be there and we can meet him. Swanson won't have any idea Laurel's my mother."

Annie sipped the tea, then said precisely, "That sounds like an excellent plan. You can talk to Swanson and that should help you decide how to approach Laurel. Here, you'd better keep the stuff

I got on him." She swept together the printout sheets and held them out to him, a woman obviously pleased to discharge any and all responsibility. And further effort.

Max was afraid he understood only too well. He stared into suddenly dark and remote gray eyes. "You and I —"

"No, Max. I'm not going."

Annie unpacked books like mad. Only ten days until Christmas. This was her best holiday season yet. As always, there were customers with odd but fun requests, including the homesick Left Coaster who wanted books set in northern California. Annie obliged with titles by Elizabeth Atwood Taylor, Susan Dunlap, Janet LaPierre, Janet Dawson, Chelsea Quinn Yarbro, Shelley Singer, Marcia Muller and Linda Grant.

If Annie had odd and uncomfortable moments — and she did — she assured herself that married couples didn't always go in tandem. Tonight Max could manage on his own. After all, it was his mother.

And her father.

The unexpected thought shocked her. She folded her lips in a tight line and bent to shelve a raft of Lillian Jackson Braun paperbacks.

Agatha materialized from beneath the Whitmani fern. The elegant black cat slithered between Annie and the shelf.

Annie looked at Agatha. "No. Huh-uh. You're smart, sure. But no way."

Agatha stared at her with opaque golden eyes, rubbed her whiskers against *The Cat Who Saw Stars*, flicked her tail and moved down the aisle toward the coffee bar.

The bell at the front door of Death on Demand gave its familiar, cheerful peal, followed by Ingrid's soft murmur of inquiry. Annie picked up six more books, trying to remember the order of publication, then paused as an angry young voice rasped, "No, you can't help me. I want to see *her*." The emphasis on the pronoun was startlingly hostile. "Annie."

Annie was on her feet and starting up the aisle when a teenage girl came flying toward her, skidding to a stop only steps away.

They stared at each other.

The girl — she couldn't be more than fifteen — planted her feet apart, slapped thin hands on hips hidden beneath a floppy oversize shirt and a huge unzipped canvas duck jacket that sagged down her shoulders and dangled near her knees. Ragged bell-bottom jeans splayed over black sports sneakers that added at least two inches to her height. Despite the voluminous clothes, she looked like a Dickens waif, her wrists smaller than the span of a thumb, her eyes huge in a bony face still seeking its adult shape. She poked her narrow head forward, a tangle of dark curls framing blazing brown eyes, angular cheekbones and trembling lips.

Annie had a sudden memory of Agatha as a kitten, a frightened stray, eyes glittering, stiff-legged, tiny mouth agape in a furious hiss. Annie lifted her hand.

"So here you are." The girl's high voice quavered. "All stuck up and happy. Wearing a Christmas sweater. Just like you hadn't ruined Christmas for me and Pudge." Those big dark eyes glared. "You don't care, do you? Did you know I used to dream about you and write letters to you? My big sister, that's what I thought you would be. Pudge told me all about you when I was little. He said he'd looked for you everywhere, and he knew we would be crazy about each other, that you'd be a great big sister to me. And now —"

"Wait a minute." Annie's face felt hot. "Who are you?"

The girl jammed her hands in the big slanted pockets of the grimy red coat. "Nobody to you, I guess. I'm just Rachel. But I hate you. You've made Pudge cry," and she whirled and ran toward the front door.

Max slammed the front door. "Hi, gorgeous."

Annie, stretched out on a white wicker couch with flowered cushions, listened from the terrace room and knew he was scooping up Dorothy L., their rollicking white cat who adored him.

"Max?" Annie sat up, looked toward the front hall.

His face surprised and pleased, Max appeared in the doorway, Dorothy L. riding on his shoulder. "I didn't expect you to be here. I thought you were working tonight."

"Ingrid and Duane are handling the store." Annie looked at the mantel, at the clock now chiming the hour. "What time's your dinner?"

"Seven."

There was a moment of silence.

Max's gaze was hopeful, then slowly the light in his dark blue eyes faded. "Well, I need to shave. See you later."

Annie listened as his steps crossed the entrance hall and the swift thud as he hurried upstairs.

Pushing up from the couch, she stood uncertainly for a moment, then whirled toward the terrace. Grabbing a jacket from the row of hooks, she yanked open the door. Once outside, she shivered and pulled on the nylon jacket. Head down, hands in her pockets, she plunged down the path toward the lagoon. But not even the cool misty air could sweep away the turmoil in her mind, dampen the memory of those big, dark, angry eyes, such forlorn, young, aching eyes.

Annie clattered onto the pier, stopped at the end, hands tight on the railing, It was too dark to see and no moon tonight. Fog wreathed the trees, rose in miasmic swaths from the cold dark water of the lagoon.

"I don't owe her anything." Annie wanted to sound tough. But she heard the sadness beneath the veneer. "Oh damn, damn, damn." Why did Rachel remind her so much of herself at that age? Why did it hurt so much? Okay, all right. So it was no fun to see a kid in pain. Didn't everybody have to grow up, learn that dreams are just dreams?

Annie wasn't anybody's big sister. Just like she hadn't been her father's daughter. That kid — Rachel — she'd had Pudge for a father. That was more than Annie had ever had.

There was a hot flick of jealousy at the thought. But it wasn't Rachel's fault. Rachel was just a kid, a kid wearing clothes too big for her because she hated being skinny, a kid who still had dreams.

Annie remembered another kid, who dreamed of sugarplums and waited for the father who never came.

The breeze rustled the winter-browned cattails, but Annie heard a light young voice: ". . . I hate you. . . . You've made Pudge cry."

Annie felt the tears on her cheeks. She yanked free a hand, swiped at her face, then turned and ran up the pier.

As the Ferarri zoomed down the drive, Max said gently, "Relax, Annie, relax."

"Who's going to be there? Besides my erstwhile father." She half turned to watch Max. In the light from the dash, his profile was endearingly familiar yet strange, as everything had seemed strange since a man she didn't remember had walked into Death on Demand and disrupted the world as she knew it. She had always ascribed Max's insouciance and refusal to be serious to a streak of laziness. How wrong she had been. What else didn't she know about her husband?

He flipped up one finger at a time. "Our hostess, Marguerite Dumaney, onetime leading lady, now reclusive grande dame. Reputed still to be hauntingly beautiful. A well-to-do woman, courtesy of her late husband, movie mogul Claude Ladson. She also inherited money from her father and made buckets in Hollywood, but she has a great talent for extravagance. She's still flying high on the Ladson bucks. Marguerite's stepsons, Wayne and Terry, stepdaughter Donna, and Wayne's ex-wife, Joan. Wayne teaches history over at Chastain College. Terry has his own charter boat. Donna runs an antique store in West Hollywood. Joan's a librarian at a little college outside of Chicago."

"Lots of ex-wives around," Annie muttered. "How come all these people are here?"

"It's a holiday gathering, plus they're here specifically for Marguerite's birthday party tonight. Pudge said the household consists of Marguerite, her companion Alice Schiller, her sister Happy, Happy's daughter Rachel Van Meer, and Wayne Ladson. Visiting are Pudge, Donna Ladson Farrell, Terry Ladson, and Joan Ladson. That, according to Pudge, wraps up the Ladson family except for Wayne and Joan's daughters. One is in Europe, the other is very pregnant on the West Coast. Donna and Terry have both been married and divorced but no kids."

Annie raised an eyebrow. "I'd say the Ladson family has a little trouble with interpersonal relationships. So it's probably going to be one big happy family. Not. Oh well, birthday parties are usually fun." She ran her fingers through her hair, knew she was stressed. "So they're all here for a birthday bash. Do they like their stepmom that much?"

"Hmm." Max's tone was cautious. "I didn't get that impression. More that Marguerite is the Big Daddy Warbucks and everybody pretty well taps when she says dance."

But Annie had lost interest in Marguerite Dumaney and her entourage. She squinted at Max. "How come her sister lives with her?" If Happy had been married to Annie's father and had a daughter Rachel's age, she was not young.

"Pudge didn't say, but I got the idea it might be money. Or the lack of it. Happy's been married three times, each one poorer than the last, and like the rest of the Ladson kids, she grew up rich but Marguerite got the money when their father died." Max slowed and peered into the dark night. A raccoon loped across the road. "Apparently, Happy's always had a talent for deadbeats. I mean —" he began hastily.

Annie said sharply, "Including my father?"

"I didn't put that well. Pudge pays his bills. But he's never made a lot of money and neither did her other two husbands, so Happy ended up broke not long after she and Pudge split. Anyway, Happy will be at the party, as will Rachel, her daughter from her second marriage. Plus the Ladson siblings, Wayne, Terry and Donna. And Pudge. And Wayne's ex-wife, Joan. And us. Oh, and Marguerite's companion, Alice Schiller. They've been together since their Hollywood days when Alice was Marguerite's stand-in. She's always in attendance. And the crystal man, of course. Pudge says it will be easy to keep everybody straight. Marguerite's a star. Her companion is a pale imitation of the original. Happy is always happy. Or trying damn hard to look happy. Rachel's the kid. Wayne has a short, neat beard. Terry's face has seen too much sun and been in too many bars. Donna might be pretty if her lips didn't have a permanent pout. Wayne's ex-wife looks sad or mad most of the time. Apparently, the crystal man is the only happy camper in the bunch."

Max turned onto Sand Dollar Road, picked up speed.

Annie clasped her hands together, staring out the window into the winter dark and the huge pines briefly illuminated by the car lights. "The only reason I'm going is the girl. I don't want to talk to my father. Tell him that."

"Pretend it's just another party." Max sounded jovial, but his glance toward her was searching. "That will make it easier."

"Just another party," she said bitterly. "Oh, sure. Given by a crazy, rich ex-actress for a man who thinks crystals are a path to another world. And what a swell guest list, a bunch of down-and-outers fawning over the rich relation. And featuring — oh, this is just a minor note — an emotional girl who wants me to be her big sister, a man who happens to be my father and a stepmother I've never met. Some party."

Max reached out, squeezed her hand.

She looked straight ahead. "You and" — she hesitated, then said, "Pudge . . . that's a damn silly name."

Max slowed, peered ahead. "Why aren't there any streetlights?" He turned into a bricked drive. A signpost announced: MARGUERITE DUMANEY.

It was an oft-voiced complaint since his arrival on the island. "A more natural environment," Annie replied absently. She continued briskly, "Okay. You and Pudge have talked this over."

"He said Happy's upset about tonight, but he can't get her to tell him why. I told him we'd try to talk to Swanson, see if we can find out what he's up to. I'll lead him on, then announce at some point that Laurel's my mother and see how he reacts."

"Happy." Annie shook her head. "That's even sillier than Pudge."

Max shot her a glance as he squeezed the Ferrari between a silver Bentley and Pudge's blue Ford. "We're here."

"Just another party . . ." Annie murmured.

# Six

Annie had always enjoyed the flair for originality on Broward's Rock, unlike Hilton Head, where zoning laws determined everything from house color to yard decorations (one plantation prohibited children's treehouses). As she and Max walked up the wide shallow steps that rose in gradual tiers, she realized zoning laws might have a reasonable basis. This house — or should she call it a mansion or a castle or perhaps an architect's nightmare? — certainly qualified as individual. It rose at different points to four stories and the building materials included chrome, bronze, quartz, cedar, stucco, New England clapboard, tile and copper. Rooms jutted at odd angles and the whole was topped by a thirty-foot aluminum tower. A red banner wrapped around the tower was no doubt intended to look like a candy cane. It looked more like a spaceship in an alternate universe.

"I'd guess six," Annie whispered.

"Huh?" Max took her elbow and steered her around a fifteen-foot, barnacle-encrusted, upside down anchor leaning against a pile of rocks. Holly garlands dangled from the flukes.

"Six architects at least." She stopped, pointed

to her right. "Max, look at that!"

A glistening glass whale spewed varicolored streams of water in the center of an enormous bricked fountain. Just past the fountain, huge boulders arched, creating a cave. Tongues of fire flickered within the cave mouth. Suddenly the fiery plumes billowed and a dragon's head emerged. A Christmas wreath bright with holly encircled the dragon's neck.

"Cool!" Max marveled. "Do you suppose Hot Breath's guarding a treasure chest?"

"With golden doubloons? Maybe." She moved swiftly ahead. "I guess you can take the girl out of the movie set, but you can't take the movie set out of the girl. Let's see what other wonders await us."

They walked on a cobbled bridge across a moat to a massive wooden door studded with glass bubbles pulsing with changing colors: orange, purple, rose, aqua, gold. Each bubble was encircled by a miniature Christmas wreath. Max pulled a silver chain and a bell pealed.

When the door opened —

Max smiled. "Mr. and Mrs. Darling."

— Annie was relieved to be welcomed by a slender older woman with a perfectly ordinary appearance. Dark red hair drawn sleekly back emphasized a bony face and intelligent eyes. A Christmas tree brooch was the only spot of color against a high-necked navy silk dress.

"I'm Alice Schiller. Please come this way." She led them down a two-story flagstone hall. Along the wall marched a row of miniature spruce trees decorated with shiny green bows.

Annie was a little disappointed at the dusky medieval tapestries. Surely an old set of armor or a moose head or flickering candles would have been more appropriate. Their shoes clicked on the stones and far ahead light spilled through an arch and voices murmured.

Their guide stepped aside for them to enter a long drawing room where Marie Antoinette might have enjoyed cakes and conversation, the plush furniture decorated with carved acanthus leaves, scrolls, ribbons, flowers and scallop shells. Heavy maroon velvet hangings draped twelve-foot-tall windows. But the eye was drawn immediately to the far end of the room and the older woman in crimson silk who lounged in a Louis XV armchair on a low dais. The entire wall behind her was covered by an eighteenth century Flemish tapestry. A spotlight in the ceiling, not harsh but soft and silvery, played down over her, emphasizing the rich auburn of her hair, the blazing dark eyes, hollowed cheeks and bloodred lips, the fiery dress and an out-flung hand, the long tapering fingers brilliant with glittering diamonds and rubies. Flocked Christmas trees strung with blue lights sat at either end of the dais, but they were small and didn't detract from that lounging figure. The bejeweled hand made an imperious gesture.

A thin voice beside Annie said quietly, "She wants to meet you."

Annie glanced into Alice Schiller's dark eyes, noting that her auburn hair was flecked with silver. But those deep-set eyes, hollow cheeks and full lips . . . Annie glanced at the dais, then looked in surprise at the woman beside her.

Pale lips, bare of color, stretched in an ironic smile. "Yes, we still look alike. When we were young, I could fool everyone. Even her husband." A shrug. "But that was a long time ago. And looks matter more to Marguerite. She says I'm a dowdy old fool without an ounce of style. But that's all right. Style belongs to her. Come, it's best not to keep Marguerite waiting."

The long room looked curiously empty despite the assorted chairs and sofas. Like courtiers subservient to a queen, the other guests stood near the dais, watching as Annie and Max and their guide neared. There was easily enough space in the room for a party of fifty. Perhaps the grandeur and immensity of the room contributed to the sense of sparse occupancy, gave the handful of people standing near the dais the forlorn appearance of shipwrecked survivors on an uninhabited atoll, uneasy at their present state, wary of their future.

As they grew nearer, Annie was even more aware of their hostess's gift for drama. Marguerite Dumaney's presence made those near her bloodless and negligible. Her attendants were within range to be summoned, yet not quite close enough for conversation.

Annie managed a meaningless social smile. She knew Pudge and Rachel, of course, and she'd seen the brochure with the photograph of Emory

Swanson. The others she tried to identify from Max's description. The lanky man with longish gray hair and quizzical eyes and a sleek goatee must be Wayne Ladson, the stepson who lived here. The chunky red-faced man who rocked back on his heels like he was standing on a boat had to be Wayne's brother Terry. Annie took one swift look at an elegantly dressed woman with a sour face; a dowdy, plump woman who stood very stiff and still; and an effervescent blonde with a sweet smile, and tabbed them as Donna, Joan, and Happy.

As she and Max stopped in front of the dais, Annie was acutely aware of Marguerite's entourage. Her father appeared blonder than she remembered, in a bright green silk blazer. There he was, so familiar and so alien, her face, her honey-streaked hair, her gray eyes. But she didn't know him and she never would. Not if she could help it. Pudge stared at her anxiously. Behind him loomed a ten-foot stone jaguar. The oversize sculpture made him look small.

Wayne Ladson's tweed jacket hung from thin, stooped shoulders. He nodded toward them, his sensitive face formal but not unfriendly.

Terry Ladson's eyes lit with appreciation as Annie neared. Sensual lips curved in a slow smile. Annie knew his type, always on the prowl, with a preference for married women.

Donna Ladson Farrell's gaze passed over Annie and Max without interest. She cupped her cheek in her hand, quite consciously posed to afford the best view of her exquisitely made-up face.

Joan Ladson's wispy gray hair needed a permanent. Her dress was nice quality but a decade old. Her hands were clasped tightly together, and she determinedly avoided looking toward her ex-husband.

Happy Laurance — and how unsettling it was to share the name — half turned to watch Annie and Max walk near. Curly blond hair cupped a round, kindly face that managed, oddly, to combine distress and welcome. She blinked and the anxious lines around her eyes smoothed out. Drooping pink lips pressed together, then curved determinedly in a sweet smile. "Hello, Annie." The words wafted in a conspiratorial whisper promising a warm welcome, after, of course, Annie and Max were presented to the queen.

Emory Swanson's hand rested lightly on the back of Marguerite's chair with just a faint hint of possession. He was even handsomer live than in a photograph, his wiry silver hair tousled, his brown eyes bright with enthusiasm, his smile infectious. Annie suspected the smile was the product of careful practice. Without it, his face would have looked aggressive and challenging.

But these were the bit players. They faded into the background as Annie looked into Marguerite Dumaney's unforgettable face, black eyebrows arching over eyes that glowed with intensity, a high-bridged nose, hollowed cheeks beneath gaunt cheekbones, skin smoothed by tinted powder, lips as scarlet as her dress. She slowly rose, her movements as graceful as a ballerina's, and as studied.

Alice Schiller stepped to one side. "Marguerite, here are Pudge's daughter and son-in-law, Annie and Max Darling."

Marguerite stepped forward, long, slender hand outstretched, fingers heavy with rings. Rubies blazed, emeralds flashed, diamonds glittered. Vivid, talon-sharp nails echoed the color of her lips and dress. "My dears."

The throaty drawl evoked a fleeting memory, a darkened movie house, Annie all of seven or eight and a woman's face huge on the screen. Annie was grateful for Max's tight grip on her arm. He was an anchor in a world with undefined boundaries.

"Life" — Marguerite paused just long enough for every face to turn toward her — "is family." Her deep voice throbbed with emotion. Her dark eyes were pools of yearning.

Annie could almost smell popcorn. But she couldn't pull her eyes away from that haggard yet lovely face.

Marguerite swept off the dais, cupped Annie's face in smooth, cold hands.

Annie fought away a shudder at the touch of those icy, dry hands.

Marguerite leaned so near that a silky strand of hair brushed Annie's cheek. "You. Your father. My sister. A rapprochement after years of separation. What higher calling can we have than to come together?" Marguerite dropped her hands, whirled toward Pudge and Happy. "Come." She clapped a bony hand on Annie's shoulder.

Max's grip on tightened on her arm. He murmured softly, "Annie."

Annie's face flamed. She almost exploded, and then she saw her father's stricken face, eyes wide with dismay, mouth parted in anguish. Annie's anger shriveled like a popped balloon. She stared into his eyes and knew her father hadn't invited this trumped-up scene. He was as distraught as she. Why should they let this bizarre old woman yank at their emotions like a puppeteer with helpless marionettes?

Annie ignored Marguerite's tug. "It's a great pleasure to meet you, Mrs. Dumaney. I've always been interested" — this was true — "in the history of old films. I believe you were one of my mother's favorite actresses. Of course, that was a long time ago."

Marguerite froze, her head poked forward, her eyes drawn in a scowl, her bloodred lips pursed together.

Pudge stroked his mustache, hiding a smile. Happy gave a tiny gasp. Rachel giggled. Wayne Ladson's eyes gleamed. Terry Ladson mouthed, *Naughty girl,* but kept his face turned away from Marguerite. Donna Ladson Farrell arched pencil-thin brows. Joan Ladson moved uneasily.

Emory Swanson bounded off the dais. "Marguerite, you always exhibit the most exquisite sensitivity." He slipped an arm familiarly around her shoulders. "Your empathy has been prompted by your own sense of family, your devotion to your husband. You promised to show me his portrait . . ." and his hand was firmly on her arm, moving her away from the little pool of silence created by Annie.

Wayne Ladson strolled toward Annie and Max. He held out his hand. "Wayne Ladson. You'll have to forgive Marguerite. She can't resist grandstanding. So you're Pudge's daughter. Glad to meet you. Pudge was always my favorite uncle-in-law."

Wayne led them around the room. Happy was effusive and gave Annie a hug. Donna's eyes cataloged their clothes, and she warmed up a bit. Joan was nervous and Terry too friendly. Annie and Max spoke with everyone except Rachel, who peered at them from the shadow of an indoor honeysuckle trellis festooned with twinkling miniature Christmas lights. Rachel hung back, her eyes pinned on Annie, forlorn eyes almost lost in the shadow.

A trim young woman whom Annie recognized from the country club brought drinks. Annie opted for ginger ale. She wanted all of her wits quite clear and unbefuddled. She whispered to Max as Happy headed for them, "I was mean."

"No." His eyes were admiring. "You refused to roll over and play dead. The old devil could use a few more wake-up calls. But play it cool for the rest of the night. Remember, Swanson's our objective."

"I'll be good." She gave his arm a squeeze as he

moved off after Swanson and Marguerite, who stood at the far end of the room looking up at a portrait.

Happy's plump hands clutched Annie's. "Annie, oh, Annie." She might have just sighted a diamond necklace. "You are so lovely, so dear. I can't tell you how much it means to Pudge to have found you after all these years."

Annie stared into eyes brimming with well-meaning, but already flitting past Annie to watch Marguerite Dumaney and Emory Swanson as they gazed at the portrait that hung over a fire-place fit for a baronial hall. "Oh dear, that man. Oh, I wish I knew what to do. I am so afraid of what may happen. Marguerite is so vulnerable."

Annie's automatic defensiveness about her father and his late arrival in her life slipped away as she felt the tension in Happy's tight grip and heard the quaver in Happy's sweet, light voice.

"Your sister seems remarkably capable of taking care of herself." Annie's tone was dry as she dis-entangled her hands from Happy's moist grip.

"Oh, Annie" — Happy leaned near as if they had been confidantes for a lifetime — "you simply don't understand. Marguerite, of course, is bril-liant, simply brilliant. And she is so beautiful. But don't you think beauty can be a curse?" She looked earnestly at Annie. "It has always set her apart —"

Annie felt confident egotism and selfishness were likely more responsible than beauty, but she found herself nodding in agreement.

"— and made her so lonely. Of course, she was passionately in love with Claude. That explains so much about Marguerite. Nothing mattered but that she should have him. Nothing and nobody was going to stand in her way. And of course she got him. Marguerite always gets what she wants. But Claude never loved her as much as he loved the boys' mother. That was Ellen, you know —"

Unfamiliar names and old emotions swirled around Annie like no-see-ums on a summer day, impossible to escape, uncomfortable to experience.

"— and I always thought Ellen died of a broken heart. Of course, everyone had warned her not to marry Claude. She was just a girl. Seventeen, I think. And she met him at a dinner party at her own house. Her father was an actor and Claude was going to produce his next film. Claude and Ellen ran way and got married not even a month later. Oh, her parents were so upset. Claude was that kind of man, you know, so attractive to women and always ruthless." Happy shivered. "That's where families have a responsibility. To make sure impressionable young girls don't get carried away by their — well, children know so much about sex these days. It's just dreadful what they see on television, and some of them having babies when they are just thirteen or fourteen . . ."

Annie blinked. A swarm of no-see-ums would seem controlled and directed in contrast to Happy.

Happy's round face looked suddenly mulish

and determined. ". . . I simply won't let Rachel ruin her life. I won't do it."

"Rachel?" Annie looked toward the Christmas-bright arbor.

Rachel glared out of the shadow, her frown a sad contrast to the holiday's lights.

"Even Marguerite is right sometimes." Happy followed this obscure pronouncement with a decided head shake. "It's not that working-class people aren't perfectly wonderful. Of course they are. But Mike's too old for Rachel. Why, he's nineteen! And if he were truly nice, he wouldn't take advantage of a girl who is really still just a baby, now, would he?" She pressed her hands to her cheeks. "I am so upset. And to have Rachel be so ugly — I don't know what's gotten into her. And Pudge. Well, he isn't actually her father, though you'd think he was to hear him talk. Now, I'm sorry, Annie, but you might as well know that Pudge has quite a temper. However, I told him and I told Rachel, I will not permit this to continue . . ."

*Not actually her father . . .*

Nor Annie's.

Annie didn't want to think about Rachel and Pudge and Rachel's apparently unwise romance with a boy named Mike. She looked toward Max, seeking rescue, but he was deep in conversation with Wayne Ladson, who stood with his hands in his pockets, talking to Max while watching his stepmother and Dr. Swanson.

From the sanctuary of the indoor arbor, Rachel's dour gaze focused unwaveringly on her mother. Pudge talked earnestly with Joan, who had a slight flush on her pale face and looked more relaxed. Alice checked the time on her wristwatch. Terry continued to eye Annie with interest. Donna stood with her arms folded, her hard face petulant, her eyes intent on Marguerite and Emory Swanson. The aging actress and her attentive companion continued to look up at the portrait. Marguerite's hands reached out as if in appeal.

Annie sipped her ginger ale and peered down the long room. "Is she talking to the portrait?"

Happy's face drooped. "I'm afraid so, yes, I'm afraid so. That is, Marguerite claims she's talking to Claude and she's very insistent. Absolutely insists they are speaking to reach other. Just as if he were . . . here." Happy smoothed back a tendril of hair. "Oh, it's such a worry. At first I was glad she'd met Dr. Swanson. She seemed so excited. And then" — Happy's voice skittered higher — "I found out that he encourages her in the wildest, the most extraordinary ideas. Marguerite believes that she and Claude — that Claude comes — Oh, I don't know whether she claims actually to see him, but she talks about the crystal path and how easy it is to travel and all it needs is effort and, of course, guidance. That's where he" — the pronoun was sharp and Happy's face tightened in a scowl as she pointed toward Swanson — "comes in. He's the guide. That's what he says, that he is simply the guide, that each person experiences the reality of an expanded universe in an individual manner. I think that's just so much nonsense . . .

Annie agreed, but Marguerite Dumaney was definitely animated, her haggard face uplifted. She was engaged in a passionate conversation, but not with the man who stood so protectively at her side. A conversation, by definition, requires at least two persons. A conversation is an exchange of speech. Yet Emory Swanson, his silvered head bent, was silent, his lips closed while Marguerite talked and listened, talked and listened, head tilting coquettishly, lips stretching in an adoring smile. Annie's spine crinkled the way it did when she read a Douglas Clegg horror novel.

". . . and I told him so." Happy tugged at the neck of her pearl-encrusted pink sweater as if the collar choked her.

Annie realized she'd missed a spate of invective. It wasn't hard to catch up. "I'm sorry. What did you tell Swanson?" Perhaps it was as chilling to watch Emory Swanson as Marguerite. His pleasant expression and relaxed stance were so at variance with a normal response to a conversation that simply could not be occurring. Did he hear Claude speaking? Surely not. But if he didn't, his acceptance of Marguerite's behavior was unconscionable. Annie decided she would ask him at her first opportunity.

"I told Dr. Swanson he'd better be careful. If he keeps up this nonsense, there's no telling what Marguerite may do. Why, she was talking at one point about selling everything and using the money to go to the desert and build a huge monument of Claude's face. Now, Claude loved himself better than anybody else, except maybe Ellen, but even he would think that was a waste. Claude was . . ." A tiny flush mounted in her plump cheeks. "Well, I don't want to be vulgar, but Claude was definitely a natural man and he just immersed himself in food and drink and sex. Why, Claude would think a stone face in the desert was silly. And Marguerite" — Happy's voice was suddenly firm — "has family responsibilities. And that reminds me" — she fluttered her hands — "I'd better see to dinner. Marguerite likes for everyone to be seated by eight." She squeezed Annie's elbow. "Perhaps we can talk some more after dinner. About you and Pudge. Dear Pudge. He is simply the sweetest man and I want you to know that, even though I am simply furious with him right this minute," and she turned and pattered away.

As Happy scurried around the arbor, heading for an archway flanked by palms, Rachel glowered.

Obviously, Rachel and Pudge were in Happy's doghouse. Annie glanced toward her father. Pudge slumped alone on a cobalt sofa, his face weary, gently stroking a calico cat curled in his lap. Annie tried to control the glad little quiver in her heart that Pudge liked cats, too. But liking cats wasn't enough. She forced herself to look away. The conversational groups had shifted. Max was moving toward Emory Swanson. Wayne Ladson intercepted Marguerite as she drifted dreamily toward him. Alice stood beside a huge gong next to the palm-framed archway. Mistletoe dangled from the center of the arch. A few feet away, Terry's face no longer looked genial. He looked, in fact, like a man who'd like to fashion a particularly unpleasant end for the charming Dr. Swanson. Donna flashed her brother a warning glance. Joan looked everywhere in the room except toward her ex-husband.

Annie's nose wrinkled in distaste. It appeared their hostess intended to spend the evening chatting with her dead husband. Annie would have walked out the door except this was why Max had come, to see the crystal man in action. Annie didn't want to have a damn thing to do with Marguerite Dumaney and her peculiar beliefs.

Annie looked again toward her father. Her gaze slipped across the shadowy indoor arbor. Rachel huddled beneath the arch of greenery, withdrawn, sullen, miserable. Annie hesitated. Obviously, Pudge and Rachel had made Happy mad. Was it any business of Annie's if Rachel and her mom had a fight? None, of course.

Annie looked toward Rachel. Rachel's lips quivered. Annie stared into sad, angry eyes and walked toward the twinkling Christmas lights of the arbor.

# Seven

Max paused in his casual progress toward the evening's lion, Emory Swanson, to watch Annie. Annie, the rescuer. He'd seen her reach out to others so many times, to people who were hurting, to animals that were abandoned. Now she was responding to the pain in a troubled teen-ager's face. He glanced toward Pudge. Their eyes met. Pudge looked proud.

All right. Rachel was in good hands. Now it was time to get to work. Max intercepted Swanson near the wet bar. "It's a pleasure to meet you, Dr. Swanson. I've heard so much about you. Ms. Dumaney believes you are definitely a wizard."

Was there the tiniest flicker in Swanson's attentive brown eyes? He had never, of course, heard Marguerite mention Max's name. "Call me Emory, please." His deep voice oozed bonhomie. "Marguerite has remarkable psychic gifts. I suppose you are an old friend of hers?"

"Marguerite's family has a long connection with mine," Max said smoothly. After all, Pudge was his family in a real sense and Pudge went back a long way with Happy. And if Max's claim gave him some legitimacy with Swanson, well, so much the better. Max gestured vaguely toward

Wayne. "Wayne and I couldn't help noticing Marguerite's conversation with Claude. Now" — Max tried to appear both earnest and slightly credulous — "how in the world did she manage that? Or is it all in her head? After all, we didn't hear Claude's voice."

Swanson teetered back on his heels and gave Max a condescending smile. "No, of course not. Only Marguerite hears Claude."

"So you don't?" Max fought down a burning desire to jam his thumbs in his mouth and give a Bronx cheer.

Swanson's limpid gaze never wavered. "That's not to be expected." His tone was patient. "The connection is between Marguerite and Claude. I have simply been able to help Marguerite focus so that she achieves her goal of communication."

"But this connection" — Max raised an eyebrow — "could all be in her mind."

"Not at all." Swanson folded his arms and smiled pleasantly, with only a hint of smugness. "Marguerite can be sure that this connection is now, at this moment, and for the future because Claude has informed her of his wishes."

"Wishes?" Max stared into amused eyes.

"Oh yes. Claude apparently has strong feelings about the path Marguerite should follow. I think" — and now Swanson's amusement was scarcely masked — "that the family will be most interested."

Annie ducked inside the arbor. "Hiding out?"

She sniffed. Honeysuckle. She reached up, touched a strand. Yes, it was real and it was blooming. But nothing could be too surprising in a huge mishmash of a house guarded by a fire-breathing dragon in a mock cave and a spouting whale beached in a fountain.

"Yeah. What's it to you?" Rachel's voice was sullen, but her dark eyes were pools of misery. As Annie stepped nearer, a thin hand yanked loose a strand of honeysuckle, crushed it. The sweet scent hung in the air.

They stood so close, Annie could hear Rachel's shallow breathing. The small space pulsed with emotion. Rachel seethed with anger, resentment, bewilderment, hostility.

Annie hesitated. Was Rachel simply a teenage mess? It would be easy to dismiss her volatility as the turmoil engendered by raging hormones and unfinished personality. But Annie thought it was more than that. This girl was consumed by anger, anger made even more painful to observe because of her obvious vulnerability. Whatever was wrong, Rachel was near an explosion.

"Trouble with your mom?" The very words carried Annie back a decade, to whispered confidences among friends as girls bewailed their mothers, their obtuseness, their jealousy, their small-mindedness. Even then Annie had known she was an exception. She and her mother rarely disagreed. Annie never knew whether it was because there were only the two of them or whether they enjoyed a special gift.

Rachel gripped a spoke of the huge wagon wheel that formed one side of the arbor. Her curly dark hair hung down in her face. "I hate her. I *hate* her. She's awful. She treats me like I'm a stupid kid. That's how they all treat me." Her voice rose. Tears welled in her eyes. "I hate this house. I hate —"

The deep tone of a gong reverberated.

Annie opened her purse, pulled out some tissue. "Here. Come on, Rachel. It's time for dinner."

"I don't want any dinner." Rachel swiped at her face, jammed the tissue in the pocket of navy silk slacks that flapped around pencil-thin legs. The sleeves of the bright red wool cardigan hung almost to her skinny knuckles. This was the Dickens waif in dress clothes and her appearance was perhaps even more forlorn than in the oversize grunge of the afternoon. Rachel's eyes gleamed. "If I don't show up, it will piss off Aunt Marguerite and that will put Mother into a spin. She's like a cat on hot rocks about Aunt Marguerite. Who cares what the old hag does with her money? Of course, they all care a lot. They're greedy pigs. Mother tries to act like she doesn't care about the money, that she's just worried —"

"Annie." Max's warm hand touched her shoulder.

Annie looked around with a smile. "I know. Time for dinner. Rachel and I are just coming. Rachel, this is Max," and she took that bony arm and gently tugged, turning Rachel toward the palm-framed archway.

As they walked, the girl between them, Annie managed not to grin. Yes, Rachel was a bundle of burgeoning hormones; witness her immediate fascination with Max. Annie applauded Rachel's good taste. After all, Max definitely was the handsomest man in the room — oh, all right, Swanson was a close second — but tall and well-built Max was by far the sexiest with his rumpled blond hair, vivid blue eyes and expressive mouth. And Max, bless his kind heart, had immediately noticed Rachel's red-rimmed eyes and drooping face and was ladling out the Darling charm by the bucket.

Annie and Max stepped inside the archway. They both came to a full stop, eyes wide.

Rachel stood with her hands on her hips and watched them. "Honestly, you look like you just spotted an extraterrestrial with a boom box. My friends can't believe it, either." Her small mouth twisted in a sardonic grin. "Mike said we could make a fortune if we had tours at twenty bucks a head and charged an extra five to see the dining room."

So it was a dining room. Annie slipped her arm through Max's, pulled him along. After all, they could look when they were seated.

Rachel chattered and led them toward the table. ". . . half the length of a football field. See, the far end is a jungle. It has sprinklers and heat machines and everything and it's really a rain forest. Can't you smell it?" Rachel wrinkled up her nose.

Annie could. The dark, rich scent of dirt and vegetation and moisture cloyed the air.

"We had a couple of monkeys, but they got into a fight and Harry pushed Sally off the bridge. Do you see the bridge?" Rachel pointed up at a rope bridge that stretched from a clump of trees in the rain forest the length of the room to a landing that jutted from a spiral staircase that rose to the ceiling. Faux Christmas stockings, decorated with elves and deer and snowmen, hung every few feet from the bridge.

"The staircase opens into the tower." Rachel's tone was matter-of-fact. "Watch your step."

Rachel spoke in time to prevent Annie from plunging into an indoor pond. Actually, it was more than a pond. Perhaps canal was a better description. The four-foot span of water circled an island that held a jade-green glass table. Arched bridges spanned the water at twelve, three, six and nine o'clock.

Alice Schiller waited on the island. "This way, please."

In a moment, they were all seated at the circular table, Emory Swanson to Marguerite's right, Terry Ladson to her left, Wayne Ladson opposite Marguerite. Donna Ladson Farrell, Max and Joan Ladson sat between Swanson and Wayne. Happy, Rachel, Annie and Pudge sat between Terry and Wayne. An immense green candle served as the centerpiece, with Christmas balls heaped around the base. The sweet scent of pine mingled with the heavier odor of water.

A stocky manservant moved deftly around the table.

Annie declined wine. She turned determinedly toward Rachel. "Is the rest of the house this unusual?"

But Rachel was leaning toward her mother. She hissed in a voice Annie could barely hear, "I don't care what you say. If you won't let me see him, I'll run away. You can't be so mean."

Happy's plump hand gripped her daughter's thin arm. "Rachel, hush." Her tone was soft, too, but implacable. "This isn't the time or place —"

Rachel pulled her arm free, knocking over a silver goblet of ice water. She pushed back her chair, came awkwardly to her feet, like a stumbling colt. Her angular face flamed. "Don't look at me. Leave me alone." She turned and ran, clambering across the bridge, her steps clattering on the stone floor of the huge room.

Annie quickly set the goblet upright and unobtrusively patted her soggily cold skirt and ached for Rachel, diminished and furious, running from humiliation, certain that everyone was laughing at her.

Pudge quickly handed Annie his napkin. "Here," he said softly. "Poor kid."

Happy's plump face tightened into a stiff mask. "I'm sorry. Rachel's not been feeling well. I hope you will excuse —"

Marguerite Dumaney's drawl overbore her sister's hurried words. "Of course she feels well, Happy. The child is simply having a marvelous"

— the word stretched and stretched — "time. Actually, a fine performance. One I might almost envy. I can't wait to behold the scene when she discovers that her Romeo prefers money to her. It cost very little to put paid to that budding romance. Perhaps we can all convene here tomorrow night for an encore. Now let us —"

Annie knew she was coming into the drama during Act II, but it wasn't hard to understand. There was a boy and Rachel cared about him and — for what reason? — Marguerite offered him money to stay away from the girl. And he took the money. Annie hated the thought. What would this betrayal do to a girl just beginning to look for love?

Just for an instant, Annie's eyes locked with Marguerite's. The actress arched a brow in amusement and her voice never faltered.

"— enjoy our dinner, for I will have a much more exciting announcement when we conclude. I have found truth." Her eyes burned with a zealot's conviction. "I asked each of you here to help me celebrate my birthday. But the true celebration will be in the liberation of our spirits from the terrible weight of possessions. Everything I have, everything here" — one hand swept in a slow arc — "shall be dedicated to finding truth. We shall take the Golden Path."

Her words fell into strained silence. Happy's plump face sagged. She pleated her dinner napkin and stared at her sister in dismay. Terry Ladson's red face was suddenly hard and wary. Pudge muttered, "Not to be upstaged . . ." Wayne fingered his beard, his face carefully expressionless, his eyes cold. Donna's sharp features were suddenly pinched and frightened. Alice's face echoed Marguerite's dramatic beauty, but instead of Marguerite's complacent self-absorption, Alice looked bleak, her features sunken and drawn. Joan took a deep, trembling breath.

Emory Swanson, however, looked pleased. Exceedingly pleased. He sat at ease in his chair, his eyes gleaming with triumph.

"But" — and Marguerite's gaiety was in stark contrast to the dark resistance surrounding her — "we must all be patient until after dinner. Now, Emory" — and she turned to her right — "tell me again about the golden crystal. That's the one I . . ."

Conversation creaked into being, jerky and disjointed. As Annie picked at her salad, desperately aware of Pudge to her left and Rachel's empty space to her right, she heard snatches:

Emory Swanson's reassuring balm, ". . . know that you yourself hold the keys to many kingdoms and . . ."

Max's dear voice, a solid spar in a sea of unpleasantness, ". . . specialize in helping people with problems. No, I don't . . ."

Joan Ladson's slightly querulous tone, ". . . can't believe how much everything costs today. And I just have to get a new car . . ."

Alice Schiller's dry comment, ". . . has never been able to control herself so . . ."

Donna Farrell's harsh whisper, ". . . has she lost her mind?"

Wayne Ladson's exasperated mutter, ". . . had no idea she'd gotten in so deep until . . ."

Terry Ladson's puzzled query, ". . . what's all this about crystals?"

Happy Laurance's anxious flutter, ". . . Marguerite doesn't realize how upset . . ."

The words swirled and buzzed, disconnected and unimportant. Annie's being was concentrated on the physical presence of the man who sat next to her, on the well-formed hand that nervously turned his wineglass, on the sheen of his bright green jacket, on the face turned toward her with its sandy mustache. She knew he looked at her even though she stared straight ahead.

"You were nice to Rachel." His voice was a musical tenor.

The manservant whisked away salad plates.

Annie picked up her roll, tore off a portion, buttered it. "It's hard to be her age."

"She told me she came to see you."

The dinner plates were served, sea bass with a bleu cheese sauce, stuffed artichokes and sautéed winter vegetables.

Annie slowly met his gaze. Before she could discipline her mind and her heart, the thought came tumbling through her sweet and clear as a fine white wine that he was nice with honest eyes and a kind mouth. Her face tightened. He hadn't been there for her. He had never been there for her. She didn't owe him a thing.

Pudge leaned closer. "Annie, did your mother ever tell you about the night we met?"

She stared into his eyes, feeling a jumble of conflicting emotions. Yes, she wanted to know. He could re-create a moment in time that she had never known. He could bring her mother to the table, young and eager and full of hope and the beginnings of love. But every word he spoke forged a link between them and Annie wanted no link. Not now. Not ever. He had proved he couldn't be trusted.

"She never talked about you." Annie's voice was harsh.

Pudge sighed. "I don't suppose I blame her." He sounded very tired.

Annie poked at the fish, though she knew she couldn't eat anything. One painful word at a time, she said jerkily, "The night you met —"

Afterward, she couldn't recall anything of that dinner, the taste of the food or the sounds of other conversation or the odd surroundings of that water-encircled table. She ate, yes, but most of all she listened and learned.

"— my sister Amy asked me to help her that night. She taught fourth grade. I was in town on leave. I was a second lieutenant in the infantry . . . in the hall carrying a Humpty Dumpty made out of egg cartons and I bumped into this pretty girl . . . Judy was in her first year as a kindergarten teacher . . . you don't look like her, you know —"

Annie knew.

"— her hair was as black as midnight and her

eyes shone like sapphires. Delicate features, but a firm chin. Very firm. Deep-set eyes and hollowed cheeks and a rosebud mouth. I never gave another thought to helping Amy. She found me after the open house and asked if I intended to take up residence in the kindergarten room." Pudge's mouth curved in a rollicking grin. " 'Hell yes,' I told her. I knew then that I wanted to marry Judy. I told her . . ."

The dessert plates were removed.

Marguerite rose. She waited until every eye was on her and the only sound in the huge room was the susurrant wash of surrounding water.

Annie marveled at Marguerite's impact. Yes, it was all a piece of stagecraft, from the silver beam of light trained upon her to the carefully timed pause. Stagecraft, yes, but magic, too. Rich auburn hair swayed around the haggard, still-elegant face. Black strokes of makeup made the smoldering eyes darker, larger, mesmerizing. Her bloodred lips parted.

"Life" — Marguerite leaned forward, looked at each in turn — "and death. Forces greater than any of us." It was a declamation, her deep, husky voice imbuing the words with grandeur. One hand, the scarlet-tipped nails bright as flame, slowly encompassed them.

The audience — and they were indeed an audience — probably wasn't reacting as Marguerite wished. The watching faces exhibited caution, wariness and uneasiness, but no one appeared captivated or impressed. Except, of course, the attentive, oh-so-pleased Dr. Swanson.

"It has been my great good fortune to realize that I possess an extraordinary capacity for reaching beyond this world." Her crimson lips spread in an exalted smile. "I have a responsibility to myself, to society, to the world. Therefore I shall divest myself of the encumbrances of this world and dedicate myself and my fortune to the great efforts being made by Emory Swanson."

Swanson looked up at his benefactress, his expression one of humble self-deprecation.

She smiled down at him. "Oh, I know you've counseled me to give this great consideration, to be sure that I can follow the Golden Path. I know I can." She clasped a hand to her heart. "I am led. I shall endow the Evermore Foundation —"

Terry Ladson stood so quickly his chair clattered to the stone floor. "Marguerite, you can't be such a fool." His red face was mottled.

Happy struggled to her feet, too, twisting the napkin in her hands. "Marguerite, you mustn't. This isn't what Claude would want."

Wayne Ladson waved a languid hand, but his eyes were angry. "Calm down, everyone. Let's hear what Dr. Swanson has to say. What is this Golden —"

The lights went off.

Though the lighting had been dim, except for the silver spot trained on Marguerite, the transition from light to utter darkness left Annie straining to see and feeling as though black velvet pressed against her eyes. Sounds pulsed around her, Marguerite's imperious voice demanding, "The lights. Someone see about the lights," Happy's frantic bleat, "I don't like this," the scrape of a chair, Alice Schiller's sharp cry, "Marguerite, be careful."

Alice Schiller's warning frightened Annie. Schiller's husky voice throbbed with fear — fear for Marguerite, fear for a woman hell-bent on destruction. What was happening in the darkness? What could happen?

The lights came on.

Annie's heart thudded. She stared toward the head of the table.

Marguerite Dumaney stood rigid, her features sharp-edged, her lips twisting in a furious scowl. Her gaze, dark eyes hooded and implacable, swept the table, then paused, eyes locked on the single gardenia that lay on the table in front of her. The transformation was slow, her face softening, lips parting in wonder and awe. Slowly, hand trembling, she reached down, lifted up the gardenia. A flush suffused her cheeks. Her lips scarcely moved, and the sound was a whisper. "Claude." Then, loud, strong, triumphant, her voice filled the huge room. "Claude." She held the gardenia to her cheek, then thrust the flower toward Emory Swanson. "Claude always gave me gardenias. Always. He wants us to know he's pleased. He is reaching out to me across the great chasm."

Wayne Ladson smoothed his beard. "Pretty dramatic, Swanson. How did you bring it off?" Admiration mixed with sarcasm.

"That's what I'd like to know." Terry hunched forward in his chair and glowered.

"Claude always gave her gardenias." Happy's eyes were wide and shocked. "He did."

Donna's mouth curved in a derisive smile. "Don't be an idiot, Happy."

Joan lifted her glass with a shaking hand. "Where did the flower come from?"

Pudge looked up at the lights.

Alice Schiller stared at Marguerite, her face tight with foreboding.

Max's gaze was focused on Emory Swanson. Annie understood why. When the lights came on, faces around the table reflected surprise, uncertainty and shock. And that included Emory Swanson.

Whoever — or whatever — spun a sweet-scented gardenia through the air to fall in front of Marguerite was unknown to Swanson. And that, Annie thought, might be the most peculiar and unsettling fact of all.

Marguerite cupped the gardenia in her hands, smiled at it tenderly. "Oh, Claude. Claude." She moved away from her chair, stepping out of the light.

Everyone watched her go.

At the bridge, she turned. She lifted the gardenia, touched it to her lips. "Claude. Forevermore."

# Eight

Annie waited until Max slammed his door and turned on the motor. "So who rigged it?"

"The single gardenia?" Max's tone was dry. He drove cautiously down the drive. "Damned if I know. But that's why the lights went out. In addition to setting a spooky stage, the lights had to go out."

Annie understood. It would be a little awkward simply to pull the posy out of a pocket. That lacked any otherworldly connotation. No, the gardenia had to arrive unseen and thereby appear to be proof of an active spirit attempting to communicate with those still earthbound. In the early twentieth century, attendees at séances marveled at flowers presumably created from ectoplasm by the medium's control. Annie didn't believe in materialized ectoplasm, nor in poltergeists, unruly spirits usually linked to destruction. She agreed with skeptics who wondered wryly why any spirit would waste its time in eternity cavorting about tooting horns, flinging flowers or communing under control names ranging from Chief Sitting Bull to Sister Corinna. Annie shivered, but not from a waft of icy otherworld air. The car was cold and she didn't like the picture in her mind, someone at the table waiting until the perfect moment, somehow cutting the lights, then tossing that sweet-smelling flower toward a deeply vulnerable woman.

"Marguerite's a mess, isn't she?" Annie leaned back in her seat, glad to be free of the house and its seething, volatile, distraught occupants. "But I'd say somebody made a big mistake. Swanson definitely came out the winner."

"I guess so." Max's tone was thoughtful. And puzzled.

Annie peered at him. "*Guess* so? Oh hey, Max. The flower simply reinforced Marguerite's conviction that she was communicating with Claude. Or I suppose she'd say that Claude was communicating with her. A gardenia! You'd think she'd have better sense. Anyway, I looked at Swanson just as the lights came on and I swear he was absolutely astonished. Now, I know the man's an actor, too, but just for an instant there was complete surprise."

"Then what?" Max asked slowly.

She was sure Max had watched Swanson, too. "Oh well, he played along. Who wouldn't?"

Max braked, then turned into the street, the thin headlight beams illuminating the live oaks. Silvery swaths of Spanish moss were briefly glimpsed, then gone. He drove slowly, alert for wandering deer. "So you think one of the others rigged the lights and threw the flower, with the net result that Marguerite's even more convinced that Swanson is her link to Claude?"

"No doubt about it. I'll bet whoever did it is simply sick." Annie doubted the flower thrower could appreciate the irony.

"That would be pretty stupid." Max strained to see, prepared to stop for either raccoons or deer. "Funny thing is, I don't think anybody there is stupid." He shot her a glance, husbandly ESP, and said swiftly, "Happy's not stupid. Sweet and even a little silly and credulous, but not stupid. Besides, if anyone there besides Marguerite was tempted to credit Claude with the flower, it was Happy."

Annie recalled Happy's wide, amazed look, her tremulous voice, and grudgingly agreed. "Okay." She ticked them off on her fingers. "Swanson was shocked, then bland. Happy wasn't sure it was Claude, but she was damned scared it might be. Wayne immediately accused Swanson of fakery. Terry and Donna also thought Swanson threw the flower, and Alice Schiller . . ." Annie frowned. "Max, Alice looked worried."

Max picked up speed. The road was fenced on both sides for a stretch. "I'm with Alice. Because the appearance of the gardenia didn't make any sense. Oh sure, if Swanson set up the flower, it made lots of sense. But if he didn't, someone is playing a very strange game. Why reinforce Marguerite's belief in the supernatural? That's what someone did."

"It's ugly," Annie said bluntly.

"Ugly and dangerous." Max frowned.

Annie said crisply, "I'll bet Alice knows who threw the flower."

Max glanced at Annie.

She moved impatiently in her seat. "Alice is about as savvy as Marguerite's nuts. The way Alice looked at Marguerite — I think she's frightened for her."

Max slowed again as the fences ended. "Marguerite was too busy playing to the house to get a feel for the audience. I came away with a singularly nasty feel. She's infuriating a bunch of people. You'd think Swanson, just for his own good, would have tried to keep her quiet about plans to turn her money over to him."

"To the Evermore Foundation," Annie corrected.

Max shrugged. "Same thing. And they all know it. But you have to hand it to the old dame, she can put on a good show." He turned the Ferrari into their road.

Annie felt warmer. The heater was working and they were almost home. She leaned forward, glimpsing the twin lights on their porch. "Oh well, it isn't our problem. God, what a house and what a zoo. I don't like any of them. Marguerite Dumaney's a self-centered, crazed old harridan. I wouldn't trust Emory Swanson with a wooden nickel, much less a fortune. Happy lets her sister push her around and, worse than that, she didn't stick up for Rachel. Wayne cultivates that tweedy professor image, but he has the eyes of a lion tamer. Donna has all the charm of the alligator in our pond. Terry looks like a blackjack dealer in a casino. And Joan should have stayed home if all she can do is glower at her ex." Annie's eyes narrowed. "I'd be interested to know what Alice thinks about her boss. But" — and the relief was evident — "I don't have to give a damn about any of them."

Max said softly, "Annie, you talked to Pudge."

She wanted to cling to their discussion of unexplained gardenias and unattractive people. Yes, she had talked to Pudge and she liked everything about him: She liked his kind face, she liked the sound of his light tenor voice, she liked the feeling it gave her to sit next to him.

There was still a core of coldness around her heart. Pudge Laurance couldn't be trusted. That's what she had to remember. Now and always. He could not be trusted. Ever.

The Ferrari lights swept over their front lawn. Annie grabbed Max's arm. "Max, look, on the porch. . . ." A small figure huddled on the wooden bench.

Max jammed on the brakes. Annie was out of the car and running. Max's door slammed. He left on the lights.

A thin, bloodless face turned toward them. Her brown eyes vacant and glazed, Rachel's stare didn't waver. A tracery of blue veins stood out against gauze-white skin.

Annie reached out, gently touched a cold cheek. "Rachel, let's go inside." Annie pulled the girl to her feet as Max held open the front door. Annie put her arm around the bulky oversize jacket hanging from thin, slumped shoulders. She led

Rachel into the living room to an overstuffed sofa. As they sank into its comfort, Annie murmured, "Max, some hot chocolate. And an afghan."

Max turned toward the hall.

"Rachel" — Annie gently held icy hands — "they'll be worried."

The girl's eyes flickered. Her mouth twisted. "Nobody cares about me." She swallowed. Her words came at intervals, as if it took all her strength to speak. "You were nice to me tonight."

Annie's throat ached. Words should never be that hard to say, not for anyone and certainly not for this bewildered, drained girl.

Max stepped softly near and handed Annie a beige and blue afghan.

Annie squeezed Rachel's unresponsive hands, then gently spread the warm afghan over her. "Rachel, what's wrong?"

Red-rimmed eyes stared stonily ahead. Rachel's lips quivered. "Mike wouldn't talk to me."

Annie had a cold sense of foreboding. Mike was the nineteen-year-old gardener. Happy thought he was too old for Rachel. At dinner, Marguerite said she had found it easy to discourage his interest in Rachel. "Tonight?"

Tears slowly trickled down Rachel's white cheeks. "I called and he hung up on me. I rode my bike to his house. I went up to the front door and his mom opened the door. She's always been nice to me before, but tonight she shook her head and said Mike was busy." One hand straggled out from beneath the afghan, swiped at her cheeks.

"She looked sad. Then she shut the door. I went around to the back. Mike's room is by the back steps. I knocked on his window. I've done that lots of times." Her high voice was open and guileless. "Sometimes it would be real late and he'd push the screen out and I'd climb in." She pulled the afghan up to her neck. "He opened the window and told me to go away, told me to go back to the big house. He said —" She swallowed jerkily. "He said he never wanted to see me again."

A spoon clinked as Max placed the tray on the coffee table.

Annie picked up a mug, held it out. "You're cold, Rachel. Max has fixed some hot chocolate for us. Here, he makes great cocoa, I promise." She talked and tried desperately to think. What should she say to Rachel? What could she say? What, actually, did Annie know? There was Marguerite's cruel statement that Rachel's "Romeo prefers money to her." The inference was clear. Marguerite offered Mike money to dump Rachel, and he accepted.

Rachel took the cocoa, sipped, but her eyes clung to Annie.

Annie took a deep breath, wished for wisdom and felt the beginnings of a slow, deep anger. Who the hell did Marguerite Dumaney think she was? Perhaps she acted on impulse. Perhaps Rachel, sullen and hateful, had made her angry. Perhaps, giving Marguerite every benefit of every doubt, she had felt it was quite all right to use any means to protect Rachel from an unwise alliance at an unwise age. And, Annie realized in a rush, Happy must have acquiesced. Was it in reference to this that she'd said so obscurely at the time, "Even Marguerite is right sometimes?" If confronted, the aunt and mother would with some justification retort that their fears had been well founded or Mike would never have traded "love" for money. They could feel pleased that they had protected Rachel. But why hadn't they weighed the cost? Were they so old, so benumbed with age and experience and cynicism that they had no inkling what this would do to Rachel? Rachel's heart and mind were reaching out beyond herself for the first time, foreshadowing what would someday be a full and frank search for love. But this was just the tentative beginning, the budding of a delicate, fragile trust. Marguerite's brutal, public destruction could sear Rachel's heart, make her incapable of ever trusting anyone. Annie knew, knew better than she wanted to admit, just how indelible are the effects of broken trust.

"People can mean well and do the wrong thing." Annie's eyes slid away from Rachel. Damn, how could she tell her?

"Annie . . ." Rachel's voice was as faint as the beat of faraway wings.

Reluctantly, Annie met her gaze.

Her eyes boring into Annie's, Rachel placed the half-filled mug on the coffee table. She pushed back the afghan, slowly came to her feet. "What do you know?"

Annie reached out, but Rachel took one step back, another. "Tell me what you know." Her thin young voice was harsh.

"At dinner . . ." Annie searched for words, but there weren't any good words, not for this moment. "Marguerite said" — no, Annie couldn't put it on money, she couldn't do that to Rachel — "that she'd persuaded Mike not to see you anymore."

Rachel wrapped her skinny arms around herself.

"They don't understand," Annie said quickly. "They don't mean —"

"They?" Rachel looked at her intently.

"Marguerite and your mother. They —" Annie stopped. What had she done? She shouldn't have linked the two. If Rachel ever discovered that Happy agreed with Marguerite, perhaps even approved of Marguerite offering Mike money, Rachel would be shattered. But, of course, she would find out. If nothing else, Marguerite would tell Rachel, would take enormous pleasure in telling her, would likely spell out the exact amount, describe whether the sum was handed to Mike in a check or cash. Oh damn, damn, damn. "Rachel, please, grown-ups do the wrong things sometimes." Like Pudge going away. The thought was deep inside. She pushed it away. "You're very special. Someday you'll find someone to love, someone who loves you —"

"They've taken Mike away. I hate them. I'll make them sorry." Rachel whirled and ran for the door.

Annie glimpsed her face, burning eyes, a rising flush of anger, lips pressed hard together. The door banged.

"Wait," Annie called. She ran after Rachel, Max close behind her. On the porch, they stared out into the darkness.

Max turned. "I'll get a flashlight —"

"It's too late, Max. She's on her bike." Annie clattered down the steps, started for the car, stopped. "We can't catch her. There are too many trails. Max, I'm frightened. Where do you suppose she's gone? We should have taken her home."

"I'll call Pudge." It took him only a moment and then he was back to the porch, Annie's cashmere shawl in one hand, a heavy-duty flashlight in the other. "I got him. He'll watch for her. But just in case, let's drive out, see if we can spot her. Pudge will call us on the cell phone if she comes in."

As the Ferrari moved slowly up the road, Annie hung out the open window, shining the flash toward the bike trail that sometimes hugged the road, sometimes plunged deep into the pines. They were a half mile from the Dumaney house when the cell phone rang.

Annie snatched it up. "Hello."

"Annie, she's home. I'll talk to her." Pudge's pleasant voice was tired but reassuring.

Annie felt like a storm-tossed castaway thrown a thick lifeline. Pudge would take care of Rachel. He would keep her from harm. "Thank God."

The awful sense of fear and responsibility receded, leaving her almost lightheaded with relief. Her voice bubbled. "Tell her that . . ." she paused, then plunged ahead. "Tell her that her big sister" — Annie felt an odd flood of surprise and warmth and uncertainty — "is counting on her. Tell her everything will be all right." Annie knew that her message couldn't bind a gaping wound, but words of love always help, no matter how deep the pain. She knew also that nothing would ever erase this night from Rachel's memory.

# Nine

Annie looped a garland of red and green tinsel over the glossy black feathers of the stuffed raven who overlooked the cash desk of Death on Demand. "Cheers, Edgar."

Ingrid said, "Hey, it takes years off his age. Hand-*some*." A Santa Claus hat perched on Ingrid's iron-gray curls.

As Annie started down the central aisle, she grinned at Ingrid. "Everything looks nice, doesn't it?" Now the store was fully decorated, tinsel garlands crisscrossing the coffee bar area, a Santa's List of Stocking Stuffers attached to the end of every row of shelves, and two trees decorated with candy canes and foil-wrapped chocolate Christmas bells, one by the entrance, the other in the cozy reading area. A customer donating a book to the children's library at The Haven picked a piece of candy. In its place, Annie hung a cane or bell made of paper and inscribed with the donor's name.

Annie sighed happily. "People are nice, Agatha." So far the count was up to thirty-six books for The Haven, including lots of Nancy Drew and Hardy Boys mysteries.

From the front of the store, Ingrid called out,

"Depends upon which books you choose. Have you read the latest Dennis Lehane?"

"Not in this lifetime," Annie responded. Annie's taste ran more to genteel crime and happy (as much as possible) endings.

Agatha batted at a foil-wrapped bell.

Annie reached down, avoided a whipping paw, stroked Agatha's sleek fur and listened for the phone. Or maybe Max would come down the boardwalk and tell her in person. She paced back toward the coffee bar, poured a mug. She glanced at the title of a book lying on the coffee bar, *Death at Wentwater Court.* If reading choices reflected psychological yearning, then, yes, truth to tell, she'd rather be in England in the roaring twenties with Carola Dunn's vibrant heroine Daisy Dalrymple than restlessly awaiting information she wasn't sure how to use or whether to use. And beneath that uncertainty ran a twin stream of worry. She'd called Laurel several times this morning and had no response from her. Of course, Laurel could simply be out. She could also be avoiding calls from Annie or Max. In between those calls, Annie had looked up the number to Marguerite Dumaney's house. Several times, she almost dialed, but her hand dropped, her face furrowed with indecision. Last night she had felt close to her father. This morning, she realized again that he might be a parent to Rachel, but he wasn't a parent to Annie.

As for Rachel, maybe Annie should keep her nose out. Why should she think there was even a chance that Mike wasn't a louse? Annie's jaw set. For a lot of reasons. Because Annie credited Rachel with good taste. (All right, Rachel was in Pudge's corner and maybe Annie should think about that, but not right now.) Because when it came to bad character, Annie was sure Marguerite Dumaney was in a class by herself. Because, as all mystery lovers know, things often are not what they seem; maybe in this instance, a poor young man hadn't preferred money to a casual dalliance with a young girl.

What if it turned out to be true as hell? What if Mike — and Annie had never met him, couldn't even guess at his intentions, honorable or dishonorable, or at his affections, sincere or fake — didn't care a rap about Rachel?

If so, that was truth, and truth had to be faced. But Annie liked to prove things for herself.

The phone rang. "For you," Ingrid called. "Max."

Annie snatched up the receiver. She listened and made notes. "Mike Hernandez. Parotti's Gas'N'Go? Okay. Thanks, Max." Before he could hang up, she added hurriedly, "I've called Laurel a couple of times and left messages. I haven't heard a word."

Max pushed aside the legal pad with its notes about Mike Hernandez. Everything he'd learned seemed to indicate Mike was a nice guy. No trouble in school. Hard worker. Ambitious. Maybe too hard a worker? But he used the money he earned to help his family and to go to school.

Max shoved back his chair, reached for his putter. He dropped a ball on the indoor putting green, Annie's thoughtful gift to him. Max bent his knees slightly, addressed the ball, stroked. The ball headed right for the hole, then veered past. He took three steps, tapped in. Sweet of Annie, especially since she worried about his tendency to prefer fun over industry.

Fun. Yes, he valued fun more than effort. Although he was willing to put effort into fun. The most fun of all was Annie, with her serious gray eyes and laughing lips. Sweet, serious Annie. Max bent, picked up the ball, walked slowly to the edge of the green, dropped it. But he simply stood with his putter, his eyes abstracted. Annie and Pudge. Laurel and the smarmy Emory Swanson. What could he do about Annie and Pudge? About Laurel and the crystal man?

For the first, he had an idea. Annie would never be rude to anyone in her own home. How about a dinner for three, cooked, of course, by Chef Max? Steak béarnaise. Rice pilaf. Spinach salad with hot bacon dressing. Crème brulée.

For the second, maybe it was time for him to have a chat with Laurel. Annie insisted Laurel was truly at risk with her efforts to contact her late husband. Certainly, after observing him last night, Max agreed that Emory Swanson was a formidable personality. But Max had always been certain that Laurel had plenty of sense. Yes, she loved to dabble in the odd and unusual, but most of it was simply for fun. His lips quirked. Yeah, he and Ma liked to have a good time. However, Annie insisted Laurel's preoccupation with the dead was dangerously different.

Max leaned the putter against his desk and reached for the phone.

Parotti's Gas'N'Go was catty-corner from Parotti's Bar and Grill, which was, of course, across the street from the ferry which also belonged to Ben Parotti. The Gas'N'Go was one of two gas stations on the island. Ben's was the largest and it also offered bait and assorted groceries. Ben hiked the prices, but you had to expect to pay for convenience.

Annie filled her tank at a self-serve island. The front door jangled as she pulled it open.

A young man knelt by the canned goods section, rapidly shelving soups and vegetables. He pushed to his feet and hurried behind the cash register. "Yes, ma'am." He glanced at the computer screen. "That will be twelve dollars, please." He was medium height and slender with dark curly hair, wide-spaced brown eyes and a dimpled chin. Yes, Annie could imagine that at fifteen she would have been enchanted, too. As she opened her billfold, she glanced swiftly at him. His downcast eyes didn't see her. His face was somber, his lips a thin line of unhappiness.

She placed the bills on the counter. "Mike . . ."

He glanced up, startled. He automatically sorted the money into the till, pushed the register shut and stared at her. "You're Rachel's sister. What do you want?"

Rachel's sister. That's what Rachel must have told him. Rachel must have described Annie, her words tying gossamer threads of belonging. If Annie had ever doubted Rachel's need, she never would again.

"Yes. I wanted to talk to you." Annie wanted him to be the person Rachel had believed him to be. Annie wanted it as badly as she'd ever wanted anything.

His black brows creased in a hostile frown. "How come? Did they send you to get the money back?" His eyes blazed.

Annie felt a sick acceptance. Oh, damn everything. Damn Marguerite and her silly sister and this handsome, cruel boy. "How could you do this to Rachel?" Annie burst out. "How could you treat her this way? She loves —"

"Money," he interrupted bitterly. "A fancy car. They promised her a fancy car and she agreed never to see me again. Then that old bitch tucked a hundred-dollar bill in my shirt pocket . . ."

Annie could well imagine the scene. Marguerite Dumaney staged it, as she staged everything in her life.

". . . and told me to use it for school, that I'd have plenty of time to study and 'better myself' without Rachel chasing after me." He slammed both hands down on the glass counter. "Don't laugh at me, damn you."

Annie reached out, grabbed his wrist. "Oh,

Mike, no, I'm not laughing, or yes, maybe I am laughing because they aren't going to get away with it. Rachel didn't trade you for a car. That's all a lie. She thinks you've dumped her for no reason. Probably they've told her by now that you took money and promised not to see her again, but we can fix it."

His eyes, dark and huge, clung to Annie's. "Rachel didn't?"

Annie grinned at him. "Rachel didn't. We'll take the money back —"

His eyes widened. His lips parted. "Back? I burned it."

Annie stared at him. What was it Max had told her? Mike had three jobs and went to night classes to pick up college credits. What did a hundred dollars mean to him? How many hours did he have to work to earn a hundred dollars? She squeezed his arm. "Good for you."

Max leaned against his desk. He smiled as he clicked off the phone. First goal met: Pudge would be their dinner guest tonight. Now for Laurel. Max punched the numbers, listened, frowned. "Ma, Max. Give me a ring when you get in." He clicked off the phone, dropped it on the desk and strode across the room. He wasn't a believer in ESP, but he had a picture of the phone ringing and his mother's head tilted to listen.

Annie moved her car away from the gas pump,

but didn't pull into the street. She picked up her cell phone.

"Dumaney house." The voice sounded familiar and yet not quite as Annie recalled Marguerite Dumaney's tone. She realized the speaker must be Alice Schiller. Of course, Marguerite would not answer the phone, probably hadn't answered a phone in years. After all, no star can be reached directly.

"May I speak to Mr. Laurance, please?" Mr. Laurance. Annie felt an odd sensation in her chest.

"One moment, please." That so-familiar voice was brisk, neither pleasant nor unpleasant.

It was a lengthy wait. Annie wondered where Pudge was staying in the huge, strange house.

"Hello." Her father's voice sounded grim.

"What's wrong?" She blurted the question instinctively, then felt her face flush. Whatever problems he had in that house, none of it was any of her business. Hurriedly, she added, "This is Annie. I want you to give a message to Rachel. Can you do that for me?" She had her voice under control now, firm and pleasant. She might have been talking to an acquaintance, politely requesting casual assistance.

His reply was equally formal. "Yes, I'll be glad to do that. Or I'll be glad to try." A tired sigh wavered over the phone. "I can't promise success. Things are a little difficult here at the moment. Rachel's locked in her room. She's furious with Happy and Marguerite."

"Well, she's going to be even madder." Annie felt an instant's hesitation. Yes, she was going to throw gasoline on a fiery blaze with who knew what kind of resulting explosion. But further straining Rachel's relations with her aunt was a reasonable price to pay for reaffirming Rachel's confidence in herself. As for Rachel and her mother, maybe Pudge could help Rachel see that Marguerite was a master at manipulating her sister and may well have also lied to Happy about Mike and the money. "Marguerite pulled a fast one." Annie quickly explained. "I promised Mike I'd tell Rachel."

"I should have known," Pudge said slowly. "I'm not surprised."

"Please ask Rachel to meet me out in front of the house." Annie remembered the fake cave with the dragon's head. "By that cave."

Max braked the Ferrari to a stop next to a black Mercedes sedan parked alongside Laurel's blue Morris Minor. He hesitated. Obviously, Laurel had company. Max checked his watch. Almost eleven. He opened the door and, contrary to his usual practice, eased it quietly shut. Who was she seeing, that she was ignoring all calls from him and from Annie?

Max walked slowly past the Mercedes. The windows were up and the interior looked as spotless as a showroom model. As far as he was concerned, there was something unnatural about a car that gave no hint to the driver's interests, pursuits or occupation.

In his Ferrari, a golf bag poked up from the well behind the seats, the new *Golf Digest* was stuck in a side pocket and a couple of paperbacks lay on the floor of the passenger side, the latest by Jay Brandon and Michael McGarrity.

Laurel's pink stucco house always looked summery, even in the thin December sun. Max was halfway up the shallow front steps when he heard a soft murmur of voices. Max paused and looked to his left, toward the oyster shell path that curved behind bamboo leading to a gazebo with a superb view of the marsh. Max bent his head, listening hard. Again that soft murmur. Laurel had to be in the gazebo with her guest. Although the day was warm, December certainly wasn't a peak month for marsh watching. The dying cordgrass was a dingy brown instead of the bright yellow-green of summer, and the breeze off the water was cool and dank, with the smell of rotting vegetation.

Max ran lightly down the steps. He ignored the crushed oyster shell path, opting instead for a slippery approach through a grove of pines, coming up behind the gazebo. He wormed through the pines, stopping when he could see the gazebo and hear the voices.

Laurel's denim jacket emphasized her silver-gold hair. She leaned forward, lifting a teapot, smiling tremulously at her guest. Her fine-boned face held a rapturous glow and her sapphire-blue eyes were as open and guileless as those of a child.

Emory Swanson held out his cup, his rugged

features softened by a gentle smile.

Max's hands twitched. He would have liked nothing better than to march up the gazebo steps, grab Swanson by the lapels of his expensive blue blazer and toss him into the cold, dark marsh water.

". . . I am astonished by your sensitivity, Emory." Laurel's husky voice wavered. "How right you were to suggest that we merge our souls into nature as we seek to follow the Golden Path. Here" — Laurel swept her arm to indicate the magnificence of the marsh and the surging waters of the Sound — "we can be at one with the ebb and flow of the tides. Why, it is simply primeval."

Max's eyes narrowed. He could envision a more concrete reason for Swanson's suggestion, a disinclination to have his conversations recorded. Removing a conversation to an unplanned, outdoor locale made any kind of recording very unlikely. Max might be overly suspicious, but he didn't think so.

"You respond to nature." Swanson's tone deepened. He spoke as if pronouncing a benediction.

Laurel refreshed her own cup, put down the teapot. "I respond," she said softly, "to you, to your leadership, to the grand vistas you can open for me. I have heard so many wonderful things about your evenings at the foundation. I would be so honored to be a part of them."

"The way is open to those who come with pure hearts. I believe" — he looked deep into Laurel's eyes — "that you are worthy."

"Oh, when may I come?" Laurel clasped her hands together. "I need so desperately to speak with Buddy."

He bent his head, as if in deep thought. "I must concentrate upon you, upon your needs. I will call when I feel the moment is right. And you must continue to make progress on the road." He slipped a hand into his jacket pocket. "I will leave this with you. I will know when you are ready."

Laurel gasped in delight and held up the pink prism, catching the rays of sun. "For me? Oh, Emory, what a great gift." Laurel held the prism to her lips.

He rose and bowed. "I will leave you now. Think. Meditate. Soon you will take your first steps on the Golden Path." His handclasp was firm, lingering, then, with a final smile, he hurried down the gazebo steps.

Laurel, the prism cradled to her cheek, slowly turned and moved gracefully across the gazebo to stare out across the marsh.

Max watched his mother, disturbed and uneasy. He almost started for the gazebo; then, frowning, he turned back, sliding on the brown needles. He reached the stand of bamboo in time to see Swanson come out of the gazebo path.

Max would have traded the pleasure of throwing Swanson into the murky marsh for a camera. If only he could have photographed Swanson's bold, predatory face, the satisfied gleam in his eyes, the arrogant smirk. The unguarded expression fled the moment Swanson sighted Max's car. Swanson slowed. He looked right and left, his gaze searching.

Max remained hidden in the pines. Let the bastard worry a little.

Swanson climbed into the Mercedes, his face smoothing out. Once again, a smug smile curved his mouth. His glance at Max's sports car was dismissive, as much as to say that it didn't matter, that Laurel was safely in his orbit.

Max stared at the dust swirling from the Mercedes' departure. "Pal" — Max's tone was conversational — "I am going to trash your ass. Count on it." Max's eyes glinted. If there was anything to ESP, Swanson should be feeling a prickle down his spine right this minute. If he wasn't getting a preview of trouble, Max had every intention of telling him to his face just as soon as he had a chance. But right now, Laurel came first. Max swung around and took the direct path to the gazebo, his feet crunching on the oyster shells.

Laurel still gazed toward the marsh. And she still held the crystal to her cheek.

"Mother." Max knew his tone was sharp, but, honestly, he was disappointed. He'd always been confident that Laurel's disregard for convention was simply a way of having fun, a pursuit he and his mother prized. He'd always insisted to Annie that Laurel was shrewd as hell beneath that dithery, amused exterior. For her to succumb to the unctuous suavity of a curly-haired, honey tongued, self-invented guru surprised and dismayed Max.

Laurel swept about. Her denim jacket sported red candy-cane buttons to match her long red skirt. She looked rather like an expensive Christmas figurine. Her blue eyes lit. Her shell-pink lips curved in delight. "Max. How lovely. I was just thinking about you. Oh, Max, look what I have," and she ran toward him, pattering down the gazebo steps, hand outstretched with the pink crystal.

She ran up to him and stood on tiptoe and murmured, her lips barely moving, the crystal held up to shield her face, "Quarrel with me. Loudly. Then stomp away. Midnight. Your terrace."

Max saw the urgency in her eyes before she whirled away, her skirt flaring. "Mother, what's that pink thing?" He remembered to frown.

She faced him, held the crystal up to catch the sunlight. "See how it sparkles? This is my gateway to the Golden Path. You just missed Dr. Swanson. Max, he feels that I am ready to become a part of the efforts of his foundation to reach out to the next world."

Max folded his arms. "Mother, for God's sake, the man's either a fool or a crook."

"Max" — her eyes widened in distress — "I can't permit you to say such dreadful things. Although" — and her smile was gentle — "Emory has warned me that the world hounds those who seek truth."

Max took two steps, stood close to his mother. "Mother, this is nonsense. Buddy would be the first to hoot at the idea of taking a Golden Path to talk to him. And I don't intend to let Swanson take advantage of you."

"Max, don't make me choose. Oh, please, don't make me choose," and she bolted past him on the path and ran toward her patio.

Max started after her, then paused as he saw a woman walk swiftly toward Laurel.

"My dear, I felt strongly drawn to you. I came at once." She was a slim, attractive brunette with hazel eyes and a squarish face.

"Kate, the crystal must have brought you here! Kate" — and now Laurel's smile was social and gracious — "have you met my son, Max? Max, this is Kate Rutledge. She's one of my new friends. I feel that I was led to her. Truly" — a bright smile — "good fortune."

Max looked from Laurel to Kate Rutledge. He was seized with an instinctive and violent dislike for the smiling woman who held out a long, graceful hand. Her voice was smooth and pleasant, her face well bred and intelligent, her gaze interested and vivid. Yet he sensed a mocking pleasure, a delight in his obvious discomfort.

"Led?" He had no trouble sounding explosive. He felt explosive. He stared at Kate Rutledge. "Are you one of Swanson's stooges?"

She drew back. "Laurel, perhaps another time. I didn't know you were engaged."

"Oh, Kate, I'm not. Definitely I'm not." Laurel slipped an arm through Kate's. "Come, we'll go inside."

Max caught up with them. "Laurel, we need to talk."

"Max" — she lifted her chin high — "I'm afraid there is nothing more to be said."

As the door closed behind Laurel and her guest, Max shouted, "I'll be back. There's plenty to be said."

# Ten

Parking out of sight of the big house, Annie hurried up the drive. This would not be a good time to encounter the reclusive actress. Annie could see no tactful way of explaining her call. Annie decided she would airily explain she had dropped in to see her stepsister, just a family call, and Marguerite Dumaney or any of the others could take that response any way they wished.

She was pleased that a row of willows screened the mock cave from the front of the house. The dragon head, sans fire, poked out peaceably from the rocky lair, reminding Annie of her favorite hole on the island's miniature golf course.

A thin figure burst from the shadows beside the fake cave. Rachel pelted down the drive, skidding to a stop in front of Annie. "Pudge told me. Did you really see Mike?" A thin hand grasped Annie's arm.

"I really did." Annie took Rachel's hand in hers, pulled them to a bench near the willows.

As they sat down, Rachel turned to face Annie. "Tell me what he said. Tell me every word." Rachel's eyes shone.

Annie talked fast, describing Mike's face and

the sound of his voice and the way he looked. Annie turned two thumbs up as she concluded, "and he burned the money."

Rachel clapped her hands together. "Yes, he would. That's what he would do." Her smile was pleased and proud. For a moment. Abruptly, the smile slid away, leaving her face composed but stern. She looked so young and so implacable. "They lied to us." Her eyes darkened. "If it hadn't been for you . . ." Her voice trailed away.

"I agree that" — Annie picked her words carefully, for this was dangerous ground — "it's important to remember that you have to believe in yourself. Trust yourself. But Rachel, you will have to talk to your mother, get things straight with her before you can see Mike. You have to understand that your mother wants to protect you."

"From Mike? That makes me so mad." Her voice cracked. "She doesn't have any right!"

Annie knew that Happy had every right. And it was possible that Marguerite had misled Happy, too. "Wait, Rachel. Don't quarrel with your mother. That's never the way to persuade anyone of anything. Let Pudge talk to your mother first."

"Oh, Annie." Rachel's face drooped. "She and Pudge aren't even speaking. He's going away. You'll talk to him, won't you? Please ask him to stay. I need him."

Annie tensed. Ask Pudge to stay? Oh no, that she couldn't do. That she could never do. She avoided Rachel's eyes, staring at the slick green plastic neck of the dragon. "They aren't speaking?"

Rachel pressed thin hands against her cheeks. "He slammed out of her room, and he rushed down the stairs. His face . . ." She shivered. "I've never seen Pudge look like that." She grabbed Annie's hand. "He'll stay if you talk to him. Or maybe he could come to your house." She jumped up from the bench. "Annie, thank you for everything. I'm going to —"

Running footsteps slapped against concrete.

Rachel's head jerked toward the sidewalk that curved around the willows. Annie pushed up from the bench.

Happy, her eyes brilliant with anger, her round face flushed, plunged into view, her gaze sweeping from Rachel to Annie. She stopped a few feet away, tried to catch her breath. "I saw you leave the house, slipping out." Her curls quivered as she glared at Annie. "You came from that boy, didn't you? You and Pudge, mixing in where you don't belong. Rachel's my daughter and I know what's best for her."

"Mother, Aunt Marguerite lied. She lied." Rachel's passionate cry hung in the quiet air.

Annie stepped toward Happy. "Let me explain —"

Happy clapped her hands over her ears. "I don't want to hear a word. Not a word. Everything's gone from bad to worse since Pudge came, and now you're causing trouble, too. Everything's so upsetting." Tears spilled down her plump face.

"I hate ugliness. Everything's dreadful now. Quarrels. And meanness. And I'm so frightened for Marguerite. She wants to give all the money to that dreadful man and she doesn't understand how they're all so angry. That kind of anger is dangerous. And now this trouble with Rachel on top of everything else. You just go home. Leave us alone. You don't belong here." Happy pointed toward the street.

Rachel grabbed Annie's arm. "I don't want her to leave. She's my sister. She's more of a sister to me than you are a mother. All you ever do is try to keep me from being happy. You don't care about me. You never have."

Happy took a step forward. Her plump hand whipped through the air. The sound of the slap mingled with Annie's shocked gasp and Happy's sob.

Rachel shuddered. She touched the cheek with its irregular reddening splotch. She backed away, one step, two. "I hate you. I hate you!" She whirled away and ran up the drive.

"Max" — it was a pathetic wail — "I don't know what to wear!" Annie stood in the middle of her walk-in closet and stared indecisively at the row of dresses, slacks and tops. She held a pair of white wool slacks and a red Christmas sweater in one hand and a short black dress in the other.

Max leaned against the doorjamb, eyes bright, lips curving in a merry smile. "I kind of like what you have on now."

Annie flicked a glance at the full-length mirror and her reflection, attired in shell-pink bra and matching bikini panties. She grinned. "You would." Their eyes met in the mirror and Annie loved what she saw. But — "Max, be serious. What should I wear?"

"I am serious," he murmured. He pushed away from the door and planted a kiss on her shoulder. "Mmm."

"Max." She wriggled free. "I have to decide."

He settled for a swift pat on her fanny and resumed his admiring stance in the doorway. "How about that pink outfit?" He walked to the far end of the rack and lifted up a hanger.

She studied the Battenberg lace jacket and the shell with a star lace inset and the silk slacks. "That's more for spring."

"Hey, it's eternal spring here. Usually." Even the Low Country could dive to the forties in winter. "You look wonderful in pink." He slipped the clothes free and handed her the blouse. "Not that it makes any difference. Pudge already thinks you hung the moon. You could wear a voodoo mask and a black cape and Pudge would be enchanted."

Annie clutched the blouse and stared at Max, her face doubtful. "Would he?" She whirled around abruptly, began to pull on the shell. Her words were muffled. "This is silly. It doesn't matter. Besides, he probably won't come." Her head emerged and she smoothed her honey-blond hair, determinedly not looking at Max. She slipped into the slacks. "Come on, let's go check dinner. Although we'll probably end up eating by ourselves." She was already in the jacket and stepping into silver flats and hurrying past Max. She waited for him at the foot of the steps, but her bright smile didn't hide the uncertainty in her eyes.

"He'll come." Max's tone was easy, confident. He turned to the stove and lifted a lid.

Annie leaned against the doorjamb, admiring Max's swift, economical movements, his concentration as he checked the meat, started work on the salad. She relaxed, pushing away her uneasiness over spending an evening with her newfound father, to savor this moment, the kitchen bright and cheerful with its white cabinets and copper-bottom pans hanging at the central workstation and blue-and-white-tiled floor that always made her think of a huge wave cresting and breaking. Her smile was soft as she watched Max, handsome face intent, thick blond hair tousled, a dish towel dangling over his shoulder, hot pad at the ready.

As he turned to pull down the oven door, he caught her glance and winked, a sexy, funny, happy wink. "What wine, do you think? Cabernet or . . . ?"

"Cabernet. I'll open it." She hummed as she opened the wine, made a last check in the dining room. She stood in the doorway. She had enjoyed setting the table. The china was the Holly Ribbons pattern from Royal Worcester, perfect for the holidays. She smiled as she lit the rose candles in cut-glass holders.

Holidays. All those Christmases without a father . . . Annie looked at the grandfather clock in the corner and felt cold and lost. It was a quarter after seven. Was Pudge fashionably late? Or was he not coming?

At seven-thirty, she opened the French door and stepped out on the terrace.

"Annie?"

She ignored Max's call, walked across the terrace and stared out into the darkness. She knew the lagoon was there, but there were no lights and no moon. Her hands clenched. Why had she set herself up for this? She knew her father wasn't reliable. God, how well she knew. Max had good intentions, of course he did, but he didn't understand about Pudge Laurance. Silly damn name. Silly man. But she wouldn't be caught like this again. Never again.

The terrace door squeaked.

She needed to have it oiled. It was nice to fasten on a specific, solvable problem. Tomorrow she'd find the 3-In-One and oil the hinges. Too bad she couldn't oil Pudge Laurance out of her life. She shivered, cold in her lace jacket. She wrapped her arms across her front and listened to Max's footsteps on the flag-stones, her mouth tight, her jaw set.

"Hey, it's cold out here. Annie, that was Pudge on the phone —"

She hadn't heard the phone ring. Well, at least

her absentee father had the grace to make an excuse. That was more than he had done for twenty-five silent years. Why should she have expected things to be different now? But she couldn't ignore the welling up of disappointment. Dammit, why did she care so much?

"— and he's on his way. He was awfully sorry, but there was a big dust-up with Rachel. He's coming as fast as he can."

Annie swung toward Max. "Trouble with Rachel? Did he say what happened?"

"No. But it must have been a bad scene. Pudge sounded pretty grim." Max grabbed her hand. "Come on. Hey, you're like ice. Let's go in."

Max insisted on building a fire.

Annie held out her hands, welcoming the waft of heat. "Poor Rachel. I still can't believe her mother slapped her! Poor kid. I wish I'd grabbed her and brought her home with me. But I couldn't. I mean, there was her mother glaring at me, telling me to go away. I swear, how much are they going to lay on Rachel? And I don't know whether she's ever had a chance to talk with Mike. I called twice this afternoon, but each time I was told she wasn't available. I don't know what that was supposed to mean. I'd swear she was there. It was Alice who answered. She always seems to answer. She has a funny voice. I mean, she sounds so much like Marguerite Dumaney, but with all the vim missing."

"Probably," Max said dryly, "it means that Happy told Alice not to put you through to Rachel." He moved to the wet bar. "A glass of wine?"

"I'll wait." She moved even closer to the fire. So okay, December weather on a barrier island was a far cry from winter as Northerners know it and the mercury had touched sixty-four in the afternoon, but tonight it was in the low fifties and cold to a Southerner. She wondered abruptly what kind of winters Rachel was accustomed to. And Pudge? Where had he spent his winters? How odd to know so little about people who were consuming her every thought. "I don't even know where Pudge has lived."

The doorbell rang.

They went together to the front hall. As Max pulled open the heavy door with its spectacular inset of stained glass, Annie found it hard to breathe. But when Pudge stepped inside, with a quick handshake for Max and a gentle kiss on her cheek, Annie found it easy to slide her arm through his, welcoming the nubby feel of his tweed jacket. It seemed very natural to look up as she led him through the living room into the den and to assess his face, to see how pronounced were the lines around his gray eyes, how drawn his cheeks. He sat beside Annie on a jaunty peppermint-striped sofa. As soon as they settled, Dorothy L. jumped up beside Pudge, then plumped herself in his lap.

He looked down at the fluffy white cat and smiled, a genuinely welcoming, pleased smile.

Max's face was a study. "Hey, she's my cat!"

Dorothy L. didn't spare a glance at Max. She turned her round face up and, blue eyes glowing, began to knead on Pudge's jacket.

Annie reached out her hand. "Don't let her snag —"

"Oh, that's all right. I haven't had a cat in a long time." He rubbed behind her ears. "Never in one place long enough."

Max brought them each a glass of wine. He grinned at Pudge. "I want you to know that Dorothy L. is very particular in her friendships."

"So damn particular," Annie said dryly, "that I am generally invisible to her."

Max attempted to look modest. "Obviously, she is partial to handsome and charming men. But who can blame her?"

It was a happy moment, but Annie knew it couldn't last, this little moment of peace with an elegant cat who had somehow known who most needed her love that night.

Pudge smiled down at Dorothy L. whose deep-throated purr was as cheering as the crackle of the fire and the lilt of a Schubert waltz. But despite the soft light from the Tiffany lamp, Pudge looked his age and more, his sandy hair and mustache liberally flecked with gray. He smoothed Dorothy L.'s gorgeous white fur, then looked at Annie, his face somber.

She spoke without thinking and it didn't seem odd to go directly to what mattered, to talk from her heart to his, even though this was only the fourth time they'd met since he arrived on the island. "What happened with Rachel?"

"I found her down at the dock, piling into a rowboat with her backpack and a sack of Chee•tos and a couple of power bars. She was trying to get the oars right and they were too heavy for her. If I hadn't seen her . . ." He sighed. "I was lugging my own suitcase. I couldn't wait to get out of there. It's a hell of a place. On the surface, everyone's polite. But you can feel poison. They're mad and scared and desperate. I don't know how Happy stands it. We never had any money, but we had a good time." He took a sip of wine. "For a while." He put down the glass, ran a hand through his sandy hair.

The gesture gave Annie an odd sensation, for that gesture was her own. How many times a day did she trail her fingers through her hair? She looked toward Max. He nodded and smiled.

"Anyway, there Rachel was, hell-bent to row to the mainland. She would never have made it. She promised not to run away if I would stay. So I carried my damn suitcase upstairs and unpacked it." His smile was lopsided. "Of course, Happy may have thrown my stuff out on the drive before I get back. But I can't walk out on Rachel."

He met Annie's searching gaze squarely, slowly nodded. "I'm a slow learner, Annie. I've been a damn fool more than once in my life. But I've learned something in the last twenty-five years."

Annie looked toward the crackling flames. She clasped her hands tightly together.

Pudge reached out, tentatively touched her

clasped hands. "I'm not asking you to forgive me. I'm not asking you to understand. I'm not going to make excuses. I'm just asking for a chance to prove that I can be your father."

The fire shifted, brilliant sparks whirling upward. Annie watched the fiery bits blossom and fade. His words were as bright as the sparks. Were they as transitory? She looked toward Max, at familiar eyes brimming with love and encouragement. Once, and it now seemed impossible it was true, she had left New York without telling him where she was going. She came to the island to escape his intentions, no matter how honorable. She'd been convinced they were too different ever to marry. Max was rich. She was poor. Max dabbled in fun endeavors, everything from diving for pearls to directing off-Broadway one-acts. She believed in work, the harder the better. Max was determined to enjoy life, avoiding pomposity, earnestness and any semblance of seriousness. She liked to have fun, but she never lost sight of her responsibilities. A feeling as cold as a blast of air from a polar ice cap swept over Annie. What if Max hadn't followed her to Broward's Rock? What if she didn't have Max? What if she hadn't taken a chance?

Across the years, she heard her mother's voice. Her mother had two short comments, depending upon Annie's situation of the moment: So far, so good; and nothing ventured, nothing gained. Odd to re-create her mother's dry tone at this moment in this company. Nothing ventured, nothing gained. That's what she'd said when Annie debated entering an essay contest (she won a trip to Six Flags), writing a letter to Jane Goodall (a handwritten reply), trying out for the lead in the junior play (she got it), applying for a scholarship to Southern Methodist University (all tuition paid). And she didn't regret the ventures that failed (she didn't make the basketball team, she lost the race for class president, she was rejected by Wellesley).

It was very quiet. The crackling of the fire was the only sound in the spacious, cheerful room. Annie gazed at the dear, familiar furnishings chosen by her and Max, green wicker furniture with striped fabric, a peeling-paint green washtub holding firewood, Low Country landscapes on three walls, her collection of miniature cats. All this and so much more, so *much* more, because she had taken a chance, had listened to her heart instead of her reason.

Now she must choose, heart or reason.

Her eyes rested finally on her father. She looked into weary gray eyes. What did he remember of her mother? He must have loved her once. Annie had adored her mother, a brisk, unsentimental, clever, interesting, prickly, kind woman. He would have stories of her, must have stories of her. They could talk together and her mother's spirit would be there, bright and funny and fiercely independent.

Nothing ventured, nothing gained. But that didn't mean Annie had any intention of succumbing to charm. She would listen. Listening committed her to nothing. She would also remember her mother's familiar judgment: So far, so good, and she would be wary. Her face was grave. She spoke softly. "Okay. I never say never." That wasn't her mother's aphorism. It was her own. But sure, attitudes run in families. Someday she would tell a daughter or a son: Never say never.

"Hey." Max bounded to his feet. "That's a toast. Never say never." They were all on their feet, their wineglasses pinging.

It was only red wine, but Annie felt like she was drinking champagne.

The giddy sense of exhilaration stayed with her when they reached the table. As they ate, Annie loved the way the glow from the fire highlighted Pudge's face. As Max served, Annie looked solemnly across the table. "I want to know everything," she said simply.

Pudge tugged at his mustache. "Fifty years in a flash." But he tried. "We were orphans and lived with my mother's sister in Gainesville. I worked odd jobs for spending money, sacking groceries, throwing papers. But I always snuck away to fish whenever I could. My sister still lives in Dallas. I called her to tell her I'd found you. She sends her love."

Annie could feel love: love from Max, love from this man who was speaking so quietly. Not even champagne can match the feeling of love.

". . . and I graduated from TCU —"

"A Frog!" she exclaimed.

They both laughed at Max's bewilderment.

"A graduate of Texas Christian University," Pudge explained. "I didn't know what I wanted to do. I liked selling and talking to people and traveling. Anyway, I ended up with a degree in business and a ROTC commission. That meant I went into the Army right after graduation. I told you how I met your mom. We didn't have time for a big wedding. I was being shipped out to Vietnam, so we had a small wedding. You were born while I was there. When I got back, we lived in Dallas." He pushed the food around on his plate, his face bleak in the ruddy glow from the fire. "I tried a bunch of things. But . . . I'd been a second lieutenant in the infantry. I came back from an ugly war to a world that hated the war. Nobody wanted to hear war stories from Vietnam vets. I tried a lot of things that first year back. I tried selling insurance. I was a property appraiser. I took our money and borrowed some and went halves on a restaurant. We were ahead of our times. It was a theme place, Jungle Louie's. My sister painted a safari mural. We had Chinese food and Vietnamese. One day my partner skipped town after emptying the bank account. I'd trusted him. Judy'd always said he was a flake. She was right. Then an old Army buddy called and he wanted me to come out to San Diego and we'd have a charter boat taking tourists out to look at the whales. God, it sounded like fun. I hadn't had any fun in a long time and I hated being in one place all the time. But . . ."

Judy wouldn't go with him. He went.

"Your mom stayed in Dallas. I went. I kept thinking she'd come and bring you. But she never did. One day I called and the phone was turned off. I wrote. The letters came back." He didn't look toward Annie. He stared into the fire. He lifted his shoulders. "And from there . . . I guess I've been everywhere, done a little of everything. But that's enough about me." He looked at her as if she were spangled with stardust. "I want to know about you."

What Annie didn't tell, Max did. When Max described his mother's efforts to help plan their wedding, he and Pudge laughed so hard they almost choked.

". . . harmonic convergence . . ." Pudge repeated.

". . . cosmic revelation . . . and a gold whale's tooth . . ." Max doubled over with laughter.

Annie smiled. Sort of. Though she had to admit that Laurel's influence had helped create a wedding that was still discussed in tones of awe on the island, recollections ranging from the Burmese love dance to the T-bones from Texas. Annie continued to insist that the rosy glow of the wedding dress resulted from sunlight through stained-glass windows. But finally, Pudge stopped laughing and said in a kind of wonder, "Your wedding. I wish I'd been here, Annie."

"I do, too," she said slowly. But his wishes and hers didn't matter. Yesterday never changes. Maybe she could change her feeling about the past. Maybe. But for this moment, she'd thought as much about the past as she could bear. When they moved to the den for their after-dinner coffee, Annie stirred in an extra teaspoon of sugar and directed the conversation to the present. "Do you think you can persuade Rachel to talk to her mother?"

Pudge trailed his hand through his sandy hair. "Oh, Lord, I hope. I don't know what's gotten into Happy. She's always been bubbly and fun. When she called and asked me to come, she wouldn't tell me what was upsetting her. She just kept saying that things were awful and wouldn't I please come. Frankly, I would have said no except she was here on the island. I thought I'd try Ambrose one more time."

How many times had he looked for Annie and her mother? But maybe that was a question better left unasked. What mattered was that he had come to the island and he had come in search of Annie.

Annie pushed away the thought that maybe the timing was convenient and the island a nice place to visit and it was one more destination for a man with restless feet. Instead, she said quickly, "What do you think now that you've looked everyone over? Do you think Happy is upset because her sister's involved with Dr. Swanson?"

Pudge rubbed his nose and frowned. "I can't figure out what's wrong. Oh sure, they're all upset about Swanson, and that includes Happy. But it's something more and I can't get her to ante, not a word. She just paces the room whenever we're alone and tells me she doesn't know what to do. Just before Happy got all upset about Rachel and the boy, she told me she was afraid of what Marguerite was going to do. Obviously, she knew about Marguerite's plans to fund that foundation."

Annie could pull from her bookstore shelves a dozen mysteries with variations on an old theme: Who gets the money? "Money can definitely cause problems, including murder. Christie knew that." Annie rattled off the first titles that came to mind. "*The A.B.C. Murders. Dumb Witness. Sad Cypress. After the Funeral.* And that's just Christie. There are lots more books about who inherits. Georgette Heyer. Patricia Wentworth. Mary Roberts Rinehart. Marguerite better be careful."

Pudge leaned back in his chair. "Oh, they're mad, but I can't see any of them bashing in her head. Happy's gotten herself so upset she can't think. I keep feeling there's something deeper behind it, not just this flap with Swanson. But they're all upset. Wayne isn't nearly as dreamy as usual. I noticed his eyes were pretty sharp when he stared at Swanson at that dinner. As for Terry, he looks like his favorite horse broke a leg. Donna badgers Wayne to do something. Joan bleats about how unfair it is to take away the children's inheritance. Alice is a cool customer. She doesn't give anything away. She kind of fades into the woodwork. She's trying to smooth things over, keeps telling everyone to be patient, that Marguerite has fancies but she always gets over them.

And, of course, Happy's a basket case. The trouble with Happy is that she's so damn determined to be happy! God, that's one of the things that drove me crazy and" — he shrugged — "helped me decide to move on."

Annie felt a faint chill. Yes, this was a man who always moved on. The sweet coffee lost its savor.

"Today I told Happy a few home truths. I told her she needed to get a grip and she had to get off Rachel's back. That's when Happy lost it. She started crying and moaning about her responsibilities, that no one else had to make the terrible kind of decisions she was making, but she had to do the right thing, no matter how hard it was, and I simply didn't understand and I'd never understood her or loved her and she just hated me and wished she'd never called me." Pudge's face reddened. "Hell, I know when I'm not wanted. I slammed upstairs and packed. I was ready to leave when I looked out the window and saw Rachel by the dock. There was something about the way she was moving, that I knew she was running away. I stopped that, but when I get back tonight, I may have to have it out with Happy. Dammit, she's got to understand about Rachel." He sighed, looked around the cheerful room with its bright prints and comfortable wicker furniture and bookcases and occasional mementos: wooden animals from a visit to Kenya, a framed letter written by Agatha Christie, Max's tennis and golf trophies, watercolors from past contests at Death on Demand, Annie's collection of Oaxacan woodcarvings.

"Nice," he said softly. "Nice. Being here is a great break from Marguerite's hellhole. You know, that woman's so damn poisonous, it's a miracle nobody's murdered her!"

# Eleven

Annie placed the silver in the dishwasher. "Thanks for having him come, Max."

Dorothy L. finished her bowl of finely chopped steak, settled back and began to clean her face.

Max scrubbed the broiler. Over the hiss of hot water, he said firmly, "He'll be back. And he had a good time. He needed it. I don't envy him, going back to that house."

Annie reached for the glistening grill and buffed it with the dish towel. On one level she admired Pudge for his determination to stick by Rachel. On another she resented his allegiance to a stepdaughter when he had never stuck by his own daughter. "It isn't fair." She spoke aloud.

"What?" Max looked up from spraying the sink.

Annie dropped the pan into the oven drawer. "I'm not being fair. I'm glad he wants to help Rachel."

Max draped the dishcloth over the sink divider. He reached out and pulled her close, warm and safe in the circle of his arms. "I have good feelings about Pudge, Annie. And about us. And about the future. Everything's going to be okay." He laughed. "And whenever we start to feel like we've got troubles, we can think about Pudge's ex-wife and her poisonous sister."

"Speaking of troubles . . ." Annie glanced toward the clock. Five minutes to midnight. She admired her mother-in-law's gift for the dramatic entrance. Laurel could likely have arrived at eleven, but no, there was a cachet about the stroke of midnight and Laurel was not one to miss her opportunities.

Max nodded. "I'll make some decaf."

Annie cut several squares of raspberry brownies. As she finished, there was a light knock on the French door to the terrace. The knob turned and Laurel stepped inside. Her dark cloak swirled. She flung back the hood. Her smooth golden hair hung in soft curls, framing her finely boned face. Her dark blue eyes darted a quick glance behind her. She pulled the door shut. "I do not believe I was followed." She handed her cloak to Max, stood on tiptoe to kiss his cheek. "My dear, you were magnificent." She sped to Annie and gave her a swift embrace. "I'm sure Maxwell told you how he and I staged a really most affecting quarrel this afternoon. It was simply superb the way he played up to my lead. Kate Rutledge heard it all. I'm sure word has traveled over the island." She beamed at Annie, dropped into a chair and reached for a brownie.

"Probably all the way to the cemetery. I suspect Go-Dog is quite concerned." Annie picked up a brownie, too. It wouldn't be fair to say she was mad at Laurel, but Annie didn't relish the fact that Laurel had made a spectacle of herself and worried Annie to pieces. Annie had intended to be cool, not to indicate by so much as the quiver of an eyelash that she personally had feared for her mother-in-law's sanity. Instead, she blurted, "Dammit, Laurel, what are you up to?"

Laurel daintily finished her brownie. "I believe they call it entrapment in some circles." She waved her hand. "Whatever."

Max brought a steaming mug to his mother, another to Annie. He sat beside Annie on the peppermint-striped sofa. Dorothy L. immediately trotted across the back of the couch and jumped to his lap. "Okay, Ma. You've got everyone on the island talking about your trips to the cemetery. Now, what's the deal about Swanson? And who's Kate Rutledge?"

Laurel nodded in satisfaction. "They are my link to the Golden Path. You see, my visits with Go-Dog were quite a success."

Annie almost choked on the hot coffee. She stared at her mother-in-law, who apparently thrived on midnight outings, her blue eyes dancing with pleasure, her pink lips curved in sheer satisfaction.

"Laurel, you did not talk to Go-Dog." Annie realized her tone was strident, but it had been a long day with too much raw emotion, especially the ugly scene at the Dumaney house when Happy slapped Rachel and ordered Annie to leave. It hadn't helped matters when Pudge was late to arrive and she thought that once again she'd hoped too much to see her father. And all through the day, she'd worried about Laurel.

"Annie, you are such a dear! So predictable. So earnest!" Laurel gazed at Annie in apparent admiration.

Max glanced at Annie, then said quickly, "Okay, Ma, okay. You've had fun. Everybody on the island thinks you're nuts. But we know you're not." He avoided Annie's skeptical gaze.

"Oh" — Laurel's tone was light — "of course, I am a little crazy. That's why Miss Dora thought of me. She called, you see. A friend of hers is in the toils . . ." Laurel frowned, cocked her head, murmured, "Coils . . . snare . . . web? Ah yes, the web of Emory Swanson." Just for an instant, her sparkling blue eyes were speculative and sharply intelligent. "A most unscrupulous man, I'm afraid. In any event, Miss Dora is quite concerned. Her friend is apparently signing over all of her property to Swanson because he has reunited her with her dead husband. Now" — Laurel's smile was gay and insouciant — "I have enough late husbands" — she looked fondly at Max — "to be quite aware that those who go before are always with us. That is not in question. But" — and her face was suddenly stern — "there is no need to clutch crystals and to sit in a darkened room with someone breathing heavily." Distaste flickered in her eyes. "No, indeed."

Annie looked at her blankly. Hadn't Laurel delved into ESP and the supernatural when

Ingrid Jones went missing right after Annie and Max's wedding? "But you and Ophelia Baxter —"

Laurel flicked her hand, dismissing Ophelia. "Fun's fun. Besides, Ophelia genuinely believes in ESP. She means well. I do not think" — and there was an unaccustomed severity to Laurel's husky voice — "that Emory Swanson means well in the least. He is, in fact, a grasping, clever, unscrupulous man who takes advantage of vulnerable women. So, of course, I told Miss Dora I would take care of it."

Max stroked Dorothy L. and studied his mother. "Just like that?" he inquired. "You told Miss Dora you'd take care of it? Of Swanson and the women who have fallen for his spiel?"

Laurel clapped her hands in delight. "Maxwell, you put it so succinctly. His spiel, yes, indeed, just like one of those medicine men who used to wander from town to town. People were so gullible. Not that they're any smarter today. There are all those stores with concoctions that promise to make you smarter, thinner, faster, pump you up or slow you down, drop your cholesterol, improve your sex life. . . ." She paused, gave a tiny head shake. "Why, they promise everything. When you think of the billions those companies make, it can be no surprise that Emory Swanson, who is quite charming and attractive, should be successful in taking advantage of lonely widows. But I shall fix his little red wagon."

Annie ate another brownie, simply for strength. "Okay, Laurel, let me get this straight. You've put on a charade that you're desperate to contact Buddy . . ."

Laurel nodded brightly.

". . . and you've convinced Swanson you're fair game."

"Is that why he gave you a crystal?" Max asked.

Laurel reached in her pocket, pulled out a triangular pink prism and held it where the light reflected in a shower of brightness. "My gateway to the Beyond. I shall devote myself to it publicly with great appreciation, and I shall cultivate Kate Rutledge, who seems always to be at the center of groups extolling the greatness of Emory Swanson. I am confident that soon I will be invited to a séance at Chandler house." She reached into her other pocket. "And here is Emory's ticket to trouble." She held in her palm a circular plastic object about the size of an eighteenth century snuffbox or a woman's small compact. The upper face of the pale gray plastic was grilled.

"A microphone?" Max guessed. He shook his head. "It's too little."

"A state-of-the-art tape recorder," Laurel announced impressively, "which can run for a week. It is programed to desist recording from midnight to ten A.M. to conserve energy." She bounced the small recorder on her palm. "What do you want to bet that within a week Emory Swanson in an unguarded moment will make a few statements that will shake the faith of even the truest believer?" Laurel relaxed back against the cushion. "All I have to do is get inside Chandler house. I am going to take a gift for Dr. Swanson, a photograph of myself" — was there just a bit of preening as she smoothed back a golden curl — "in a rather ornate frame with interlocking circles of plastic. This" — she held the small round recorder between thumb and forefinger — "fits very nicely within a circle. I shall insist that he keep my picture on his desk so that I may truly feel that we are in communion and that I am striving ever nearer the Golden Path." She dropped the recorder into her pocket. "Since I shall make it clear that I am willing to shower gold upon his efforts, I do believe that picture frame will sit on his desk as requested. And oh, what an interesting story I think we shall learn."

Max remembered Swanson's smug confidence as he walked to his car outside Laurel's garden. Slowly, he nodded. "Of course, you have to hope there's someone in his confidence who —"

"That kind of man," Laurel interrupted with finality, "always has an adoring woman at his beck and call. I did a little checking and I think it is quite significant that Kate Rutledge moved to the island about six months before Swanson arrived. By then she'd made herself quite familiar in island circles. She's active in all the best women's groups. She steers women toward him. Oh, quite tactfully and as if she scarcely knows him. The emphasis is always on the wonderful stories she's heard from others. I just have the tiniest little suspicion that he and Kate know each rather well. It will be such fun to hear what Emory has to say when he thinks no one else can overhear." Laurel popped to her feet. "Now I must fly." She pulled on her cloak, tucked her hair beneath the hood. "I didn't bring my car, of course. One can go everywhere on the bicycle paths." She paused at the French door. "Remember, now, dear ones, We Are Estranged. Night-night."

As the door clicked behind her, Annie grinned. "Having a hell of a good time, isn't she? A lady Bulldog Drummond?"

Max didn't grin in return. Frowning, he strode toward the French door. "Hey, I don't like this. I'll get the recorder from her. I'll get it in that house somehow. I'll find out if he has a burglar alarm" — most island homes didn't — "and I'll sneak into the house late one night and plant it in his office."

Annie was right behind him. "Not that house, you won't."

Max stopped with his hand on the door. "It ought to be easy. There are some big live oaks near the house. I'll bet I can get in on the second floor. Nobody's awake at two in the morning. I'll find out where his office is, scoot downstairs, plant the recorder and be out of there in five minutes."

"No way, Max. I went by there after I talked to Edith at the library. There's a big gate now and a huge fence. When I got out of the car, two snarling Dobermans tried to take the fence down to get at me." Annie doubted that even canine-savvy Holly Winters, Susan Conant's sleuth, would have an answer to those dogs.

Max opened the door, stepped onto the terrace. "She's gone." He turned back to Annie. "I don't like this. If Swanson finds that microphone, he'll know who brought it."

They stepped back into the den. As Max locked the door, Annie shrugged. "Even if he finds the recorder, what can he do? He might be furious, but you can bet he won't call the cops. He doesn't want any scandal to touch him."

Max checked the fire, made sure the screen was in place. In the glow of the embers, his face was somber. "It's not the police I'm worried about. Swanson's about to hit it big with Marguerite Dumaney. I don't think he'll stop at much to make sure the deal goes through. As for Kate Rutledge, I don't know if Ma's right about her being directly linked to Swanson, but the lady gives me bad vibes. Laurel may be up against more than she realizes."

# Twelve

Annie put down Rudolph the Red-Nosed Reindeer place mats, a jaunty Rudolph bounding over a chimney top. She began to hum.

Max opened the oven door and the kitchen smelled of cinnamon and fresh baking.

Annie smiled as he placed a Christmas-wreath plate in front of her. White icing oozed over the cinnamon roll. "Mmm, thank you," she said appreciatively. Annie picked up the morning paper and smiled at a photo from the North Pole. As she ate and read, she felt the familiar Christmas happiness, a compound of eagerness and panic, so much to look forward to, so little time to get everything done. Not only did she need to get her packages off to Max's sisters and their families, she was only halfway done with the rest of her list and now she needed to make some additions. What would suit for a newfound father and sister?

She looked over the top of the paper. "Max, maybe I could start with a stocking. The Spice Girls?" She looked at him doubtfully.

Max looked blank for a moment, then nodded. "Rachel? Oh, that's probably old hat by now. Why don't you ask Mike?"

"Max, you are brilliant!"

Max basked in her admiration.

Annie looked at him with a sudden surge of love. How wonderful to know that even a light compliment meant so much to him. But no more than his words always meant to her. She gave him a huge smile, knowing he would smile in return. He did.

"What could I get Pudge?" She put the paper down.

"How about a sweater?" Max looked suddenly eager. "Do you suppose he plays golf?"

Annie didn't know, but now the lack of knowledge didn't hurt. She and Max would be learning lots about her father. Somehow she was confident that Pudge did play golf and that he and Max would be golfing buddies. Of course Pudge played golf. What other answer could there be on a perfect morning with golden sunlight spilling into their kitchen?

Annie loved the glistening expanse of windows, windows everywhere, letting in the light. On a cloudless day the house shimmered with light, shining through windows and spilling down from skylights. But even on a cloudy day, the house made her happy because it reflected their love. That's what Pudge had felt last night. It was what she hoped he would always feel when he came to see them.

Annie felt afloat in happiness. Everything was going to be fine for all of them and this Christmas would be one they would never forget.

The phone rang.

Annie glanced at the clock. Eight-thirty on Friday morning ranked a little early for a social call. As Annie reached for the phone, she checked the caller ID: *The Island Gazette.* She frowned. "Hello?"

"Annie, Vince Ellis here." Vince was an old friend as well as owner and editor of *The Island Gazette.*

Annie knew him well, and the tone of his voice, concerned and carefully controlled, made her neck prickle. "Vince, what's wrong?"

"Maybe nothing," he said swiftly. "Thought I'd check. Is the Patrick Laurance staying at Dumaney house your father?"

Obviously Vince had heard that Annie's father was visiting the island. That Vince knew about her father's arrival came as no surprise. Vince always knew what was going on around the island. But he wouldn't call unless something was wrong. She stood quite still and stiff. "Yes."

"I picked up a call on the police scanner. There's been a murder there. A woman." Vince cleared his throat. "The police have rounded up everybody staying at the house. Apparently your father is missing. The police want to talk to him."

"An APB? Is that what you mean, Vince?" This was no time for Vince to try and soften his words. If the police had sent out an all-points-bulletin for Pudge, they must believe Pudge was somehow involved in the death. Or had something happened to him? "He's missing?" She was startled by a rush of panic.

"Hold on, Annie. He's probably out for a walk, something like that." Vince must have heard the fear in her voice. "There's no suggestion that anything's happened to him."

A murder at the Dumaney house and Pudge gone. Annie clutched the phone. The police couldn't be looking for Pudge. Not the tired-faced, genial man with her eyes and hair, not the man who had looked admiringly around her house and called it a happy place. But she felt sheathed in ice as she remembered his parting words about Marguerite, ". . . that woman's so damn poisonous, it's a miracle nobody's murdered her!"

"I'm sorry, Annie." Vince's voice was gentle. "Look, I'll see what I can find out. I don't know a damn thing more, who got killed or where or why the APB. I'll find out." Vince started his career covering murders in Miami. He knew how to dig. "I'll get back to you."

The minute Vince hung up, Annie called the Dumaney house. A busy signal rasped in her ear.

As the speedboat crested the swells in the sound, Annie shaded her eyes against the sun. She wanted to urge Max to go faster, but the boat was spanking against the water. Going by water was Max's idea and she'd approved at once. If Vince's information was accurate, if there had indeed been a murder at the Dumaney house, the drive would be barricaded, visitors barred. The chances of being let through were slim to none. Annie didn't think being the missing guest's daughter would get them past a police barricade. The missing guest! If the word hadn't come from Vince, a man she knew and trusted, she would have hooted at the idea. Even so, there must have been a huge mistake, a terrible misunderstanding, if the police truly were seeking Pudge. Pudge might not have liked Marguerite Dumaney, but he had no reason to kill her. He was just a guest. The police needed to look at Marguerite's family. They'd find plenty of suspects there. Annie wouldn't mind telling them so. Fine spray misted her face and hair, dampened her navy cardigan and gray slacks.

Annie pointed across the murky green water. "Look, there's the tower." The gay red bunting wrapped around the shiny aluminum tower made the Dumaney house easy to spot.

Max slowed the boat as they neared the estuary. Vegetation-choked hummocks poked up from the water. Max edged into a channel leading to the inlet. The small islands screened the shore. As the boat headed for the deeper channel, Annie craned to see. Through an open space, she spotted the Dumaney dock. Although too far away to be sure, she was afraid she recognized a tall, sturdy figure standing at the end of the dock. "We may have a welcoming committee. I think it's Billy." Billy Cameron was a good friend, but he was also a sergeant in the island's small police force. Annie tried different approaches in her mind: *Billy, I've got to see my sister,* or maybe, *Billy, what the heck does it mean that there's a pick up order out for my dad?*

Or would it be better to pretend they'd taken a spin (on a Friday morning when the store would be brimming with Christmas orders?) and dropped by to see Rachel, then insist upon staying — after all, they were family — when informed there had been a death? That's when families draw together. Nobody could dispute that Annie and Rachel were stepsisters.

Rachel. Annie felt a sudden breathlessness. What if Rachel or Mike had attacked Marguerite? They were certainly angry enough and so young that violent emotion could destroy judgment. "Max —"

"Shh."

Startled, she jerked her head toward him.

"Back there," Max murmured. He put the boat in reverse. They were in shallow water here, winding past the hummocks toward the estuary. Cattails and spartina quivered in the onshore breeze. Black ducks flapped into flight as the boat neared. A white ibis on a near hummock stood elegantly on a live oak limb. They passed so near, Annie could see the brilliant red of the ibis's bill and legs and the snowy white plumage.

Max watched over his shoulder, cautiously ran the boat in reverse. There was not enough room to turn in the narrow waterway. The boat slid quietly through the water, the sound of the motor a low murmur. They were in a world hemmed in by hummocks. A smell of rotting vegetation overlaid the scent of brackish water. The boat backed across a narrow channel between two hummocks. Max idled the engine and they looked into a dim corridor of dull water bounded by thick, tangled vegetation.

A rowboat was wedged at the narrowest point. Pudge Laurance, the muscles in his shoulders bunched, shoved hard against a hummock with an oar. At the sound of the motor, his head jerked toward them. He didn't speak for a moment. Finally, his voice oddly colorless, he said, "Guess I got myself in a mess. I'm stuck."

Annie looked in vain for the genial man she'd talked to last night. This sweaty, pale-faced stranger wasn't the man who had asked her to give him a chance to be her father.

"Pudge, what's happened? What are you doing here?" Did he know about the murder? Did he know the police sought him?

Pudge's eyes slid away from hers. "I forgot to check the depth. Pretty dumb. I thought I saw a marsh hawk and I poled in here. I poled too far."

Annie was her mother's daughter, direct and unequivocal. "The police are after you." She wished he would look at her, but he stared stubbornly at the green, rippling water.

"The police?" The muscles of his face tightened. Now he looked up, but he didn't see Annie. His eyes were wide, staring, speculative, shocked.

But not surprised.

Annie waited for the question that didn't come. He didn't ask why the police wanted him. Annie felt a swirling emptiness. He didn't ask.

"Pudge, hold on." Max's voice was calm. "We'll get you out. I'll back the boat in and you can climb aboard." Max eased forward, then back, and the boat inched nearer to Pudge. There was a rock and shudder as he climbed aboard.

Annie waited for him to speak. But Pudge slumped in the back of the motorboat, grimly silent.

Annie twisted in her seat. She felt the muscles in her face go slack. Her heart thudded.

Pudge's eyes followed her gaze, dropping to the front of his khaki slacks and the dark smear of blood on his left pants leg. As she watched, he shook his head back and forth, misery in his eyes. He stared at the stain, then fumbled in his back pocket and pulled out a handkerchief. Leaning over the side of the boat, he brought the wet cloth up and swabbed the stain.

Annie could have told him. Blood is hard to wash away.

Pudge scrubbed. Finally, kneeling by the rail, he spread the handkerchief, scooped up water, splashed it on his pants.

The boat headed for the dock. Over the roar of the motor and the rush of the wind, Annie cried, "What happened? That was blood, wasn't it?"

Pudge made no answer. Instead, he looked past Annie at the dock and the waiting policeman. Pudge took a deep breath and folded his arms across his chest, his face intent, absorbed, thoughtful, a man thinking as hard and fast as he could.

As Max nosed the boat against the pilings, next to a sleek red and white motorboat, the island police chief, Pete Garrett, strode briskly to meet them. The young police chief had taken the place of Annie and Max's longtime friend, Chief Saulter, when Saulter retired. Pete Garrett's round choirboy face, topped by slicked-down blond hair, was earnest, determined and pugnacious. They'd gotten to know him the past summer during the investigation into the murder of a Women's Club volunteer. Garrett dropped into the bookstore occasionally, but he was an acquaintance, not a friend. Right this minute, his eyes gave them an intent, measuring stare before they settled on Pudge.

Annie grabbed the ladder and climbed to the dock. The ladder creaked as Pudge followed. Whatever had happened, she didn't believe her father was a man who could hurt anyone. She felt that deep inside as surely as she'd ever felt anything in her life. She didn't know why he had run away — and it did look so much like flight — but Pudge wasn't stupid. Why would he row a boat into a shallow channel between hummocks? Certainly, if he was trying to get to the mainland, he would have rowed across the Sound. More importantly, he might have despised Marguerite Dumaney, but he had no motive to kill her. These thoughts swirled in her mind as she stepped in front of the police chief. "Pete, there's been some mistake." She tried to sound calm. "I understand there is a call out for my father."

Pudge came up beside her. "It's all right, Annie. I'll take care of this. Officer, I'm Patrick Laurance."

Max came up on the other side of Pudge. "Hello, Pete. What's going on here?"

Annie was acutely aware not only of her father and Max and Pete Garrett, but of the dock and the gardens, of the huge house and the quiet figures who became ever more distinct in her consciousness. Shock, fear and hostility emanated from watchful faces.

The weathered wooden dock stretched about twenty feet. It seemed uncommonly crowded, Annie and Max and Pudge, Chief Garrett and big, brawny, sweet-faced Billy Cameron. Her uneasiness deepened when Billy avoided looking at her. Billy and his wife, Mavis, had been their friends for a long time. Billy's sober look was proof enough that Vince Ellis's report was accurate. Yes, the police were looking for Pudge.

She glanced at her father, seeking some reassurance that this moment was wrong, that there had been a mistake. Pudge looked calm, but, standing so near him, she could feel his tension. Her eyes dropped to his tightly clenched hands. Perhaps he sensed her gaze. Slowly, his hands relaxed, hung at his side, but his face was taut, his eyes wary, his mouth a tight line.

Max appeared unruffled, totally at ease, his face grave but pleasant. Annie wished she had his capacity for exuding confidence, but not even the improved status of women in today's society had equipped her with a White-Male-Now-In-Charge-No-Matter-What persona.

In the bright sunlight, Chief Garrett's blond hair glistened. His khaki uniform was starched and fresh. His carefully blank face revealed nothing of his thoughts, but his eyes were sharp and suspicious. He studied Pudge intently, from his lined, tense face to his sweaty shirt to the slacks with the irregular wet splotch on the left leg. "Hello, Mr. Laurance. I'm Pete Garrett of the Broward's Rock police." A formal nod. "Annie, Max."

The wooden dock stretched through the marsh to the shore. Even in December, thanks to the subtropical climate, japonica, camellias, impatiens, lantana and roses bloomed in the garden. Dogwoods, azaleas and banana shrubs cascaded in tiers down to the marsh. A boxwood maze loomed dark and enigmatic between the house and a cattail-ringed lagoon. An oyster-shell path curved from each end of the colonnaded veranda, embracing a vine-covered arbor on one side of the lagoon, a gazebo on the other. The garden was as mellow as honey and as smooth as Southern whiskey.

The beauty of the garden emphasized the oddness of the house. Nothing could diminish the garish glitter of the aluminum tower or the mismatch of clashing materials, cedar and chrome and stucco and bronze and quartz and New England clapboard and glass and tile. Windows honeycombed the differing exteriors. Anything that happened in the garden or the maze or in the gazebo or on the dock could be observed from a dozen different spots within the house.

Perhaps the abundance of windows accounted for the convergence on the dock. Or perhaps, whatever had happened in the Dumaney house, Chief Garrett was the focus of all the inhabitants' attention. Everyone was there. Had they followed him to the dock like tails to a kite or robotic lemmings?

The circle of watchful faces at the end of the dock imbued the moment with menace. Annie felt menace, sharp and clear and hard as an ax head, menace directed at the man standing next to her. She slipped her arm through Pudge's. His glance at her was swift and sweet and remote.

She looked defiantly at those silent observers.

Wayne Ladson's pale blue eyes were cool and speculative, his sensitive, scholarly face hard and unfriendly. He smoothed his neat Vandyke beard.

Terry Ladson's ruddy complexion verged on purple. He held to the back of a garden bench as if the earth weren't steady beneath his feet.

Donna Farrell's pale blue blouse and simple gray wool slacks were a good foil for her icy blondness. One hand held tight to her pearl necklace as her eyes shifted uneasily from face to face.

Joan Ladson clutched a basket holding a half dozen roses. She looked like a suburban matron whose car had broken down on the wrong side of town.

Alice Schiller was almost invisible in the gloom

beneath low-hanging live oak branches. Wisps of Spanish moss dangled near her. Of them all, she looked most stricken, her hands twisting together. This morning her resemblance to Marguerite Dumaney was muted, her dark red hair straggly, her delicate complexion wan.

Chief Garrett stared at Pudge, but he spoke to Max. "We're investigating a murder. We received a call at nine minutes after eight o'clock reporting discovery of a body. We arrived at eight-twenty. We have met all the members of the household except Mr. Laurance. We would like to speak with Mr. Laurance." Garrett was well aware of the interested observers. "If you will accompany me, sir, we —"

Max took a single step forward. "Mr. Laurance will decline to answer questions until he has consulted with counsel."

Pudge almost spoke, then shrugged.

Chief Garrett looked from Pudge to Max. "Will you assure me that Mr. Laurance will be available this afternoon for an interview? If not, I will take him into custody now as a material witness."

"Definitely, Chief." Max was brisk. "How about two o'clock at your office?"

At Garrett's nod, Max took Pudge's elbow. "Come on. Let's go up to the house."

Pudge looked past Garrett at the watching faces. "Maybe they don't want me up there."

Max said loudly, "I know you intend to help as much as you can in the investigation with what limited knowledge you have of the situation. We all hope that Chief Garrett quickly uncovers the truth."

Annie would have liked to hug Max. He was telling the world — or at least everyone within earshot — that Pudge Laurance never killed anyone. Yet all Max knew was what she knew, that there had been murder and Pudge had blood on his slacks and he had taken a rowboat into the Sound.

No one spoke. The watching faces held suspicion and uneasiness as she and Max and Pudge started up the dock. They were almost to the shore when a piercing voice demanded, "Why is that man free?" This voice always reached the back row. This husky, throaty, deliberate voice had thrilled millions.

Marguerite Dumaney swept toward them in a jade-green silk robe.

# Thirteen

Her unforgettable face ravaged by grief, her eyes brilliant with pain and resolve, Marguerite demanded, "How can this be?" Her tone was low and anguished. "My sister lies dead, broken and disfigured, and this man walks free?" Her hand, the nails bloodred, pointed at Pudge. "Officer, I implore you, avenge my sister." A stark figure in a Greek tragedy could not have summoned more force.

Marguerite alive!

Annie stared, bewildered, at that dramatic figure; grief-laden, yes, but still a beautiful woman, her eyes deep pools of suffering yet burning with the fire of retribution for her dead sister. Her sister!

Pudge stumbled, stopped, shaken by her attack.

Annie whirled, seeking his face. In his sad and staring eyes, his sunken cheeks and drooping mouth, she read the truth: Happy was dead.

Happy, sweet-faced and kindly the night they met. Happy, angry and frustrated, striking out at Rachel. Happy, who tried so hard to live up to her name, avoiding conflict, ignoring trouble. Who would kill Happy?

In three long strides, Marguerite reached the dock. She flung out a hand toward dumpy, shaken Joan. "Tell him." Marguerite pointed at Chief Garrett. "Tell him what you saw."

Garrett lifted a broad hand. "That's fine, Mrs. Dumaney. Our investigation is far from complete. We intend to interview everyone. But for now —"

"I insist." Marguerite's voice throbbed. "The truth must be revealed. Here. Now. Joan" — her tone was imperious — "you shall speak." A pulse throbbed in the old actress's throat.

Garrett looked at Marguerite Dumaney uneasily, obviously displeased to have a possible witness publicly questioned, but unwilling to precipitate a stormy scene with an emotionally distraught woman who was also the sister of the victim. Annie recalled Garrett's address to the Broward's Rock Women's Club in which he pledged that the members of his force would always treat the community with concern and respect.

Joan Ladson drew in her shoulders. She glanced toward Wayne, carefully did not look at Pudge.

"Joan!" Marguerite commanded.

Wayne gave a short nod.

Joan cleared her throat. "I was down here in the garden. I love the flowers and I don't have anything like this at home." She looked around the luxuriant semitropical garden. Her lips twisted. "I live in an apartment." She pointed at a cluster of rosebushes. "I was cutting buds and I heard someone running." She shot a timid glance at Pudge. "He came down the path." She held tightly to the basket. "He was carrying something long, something wrapped in a blanket. He didn't see me."

Marguerite lifted her chin. Her eyes blazed. "What was his demeanor?"

"That's quite enough now." Garrett turned to Pudge. "Mr. Laurance, if you'll move along . . ."

Pudge looked toward the rosebushes where Joan Ladson had knelt, invisible to anyone hurrying down the path from the house. Pudge shook his head, not in negation but in dismay, as if this were just one more problem, one more fact to toss into a churning equation.

Every face was turned toward Pudge. Alice's intelligent eyes focused on the damp patch on his slacks. Wayne smoothed his beard and glared. Terry's color improved and he relaxed his tight grip on the back of the bench. Donna gave a little shake as if removing herself from sordidness.

Annie's sense of icy despair deepened. Why didn't Pudge explain? Surely there had been a reason, a good reason, for him to run down the path carrying God knew what. And why, oh why, didn't he say that he hadn't killed Happy?

But Pudge said nothing, his face abstracted, his eyes distant, a man dealing with a problem, collating, thinking, judging. Improvising?

Marguerite's instinct for drama led her to the heart of the moment. "Let the man speak, Officer. It's simple, isn't it? Let him say whether he is innocent." She stared at Pudge, her steely gaze unwavering. "Innocence" — the pause after the word was long, mesmerizing — "has no reason for silence."

Pudge matched her stare, his equally hard. "Playing to the box seats, Marguerite? Save it for the next matinee. Happy's dead and you don't give a damn." The hardness ebbed. Once again he looked bewildered and worried. He rubbed his eyes; then, head down, he brushed past the actress, strode up the path toward the house. Garrett hurriedly followed.

Max bent close to Annie, said softly, "I'll call Johnny Joe." Johnny Joe Jenkins was a lawyer on the mainland, young, bright, quick and savvy. If anybody could keep Pudge out of jail, it was Johnny Joe. Max added, "See what you can find out," as he started up the path after Pudge.

Annie knew it made sense for her to stay behind. Pudge would be all right as long as Max was at hand. All right? Would he ever be all right? What had happened? Who would kill cheerful, smiling Happy? How had she been killed? Where? When? Why did Pudge have blood on his slacks? Would Garrett notice the wetness? Of course he would. Annie wished she didn't feel so cold and lost. Pudge didn't kill Happy. Of course he didn't. Surely he didn't . . .

Marguerite's face flushed a dark plum. The queen had not dismissed her subjects. Her elegant features sharpened. Her mouth twisted. Eyes blazing, she took one step toward the house; then, almost without pause, so smoothly the moment of anger might never have been, her face sagged into lines of sorrow. One hand clutched at her throat. "My sister. My beloved sister." Tears welled, streaked down her face. She cried with the abandon of a lost child. "Oh, Happy, Happy." She reached out blindly.

Wayne stepped forward, slipped an arm around Marguerite's bent shoulders, gently guided her to the path.

Terry shot a skeptical look at his brother and stepmother. Instead of following their slow progress up the north path, he took a deep breath and headed for the south path, walking fast, and was soon halfway to the house. Donna flounced after him.

Annie couldn't hope to catch Terry or Donna without calling out. She didn't want to attract any attention. But Joan had stopped at the rosebushes to pick up the clippers.

Annie knew she wouldn't have a better chance. She took two steps, then felt a firm hand on her arm. "Mrs. Darling."

It was shocking to turn and look into that face so uncannily similar to the ravaged beauty of Marguerite Dumaney. Yet, after the first glance, the resemblance faded. Alice Schiller had no aura of power. Her makeup-bare face conveyed no passion, no presence. But the hand that clutched Annie's arm held tight.

"Will you help me?" There was an echo of Marguerite, but this voice was thin, unemphatic. In contrast to Marguerite's stylish green silk robe, Alice looked shabby in a worn purple velour blouse and faded black slacks. "I must hurry to Marguerite. She needs me."

Annie stared into intelligent eyes now filled with concern. This woman knew Marguerite Dumaney better than any of the others and she was frightened for the aging star. Annie felt confused. Had Marguerite's impassioned attack been a performance or was it real? Obviously, Alice Schiller saw pain instead of artifice.

As if in answer to Annie's unspoken judgment, Alice let go of Annie, took a step toward the house. "I don't know how Marguerite can bear this. She counted on Happy. Always." Alice took a deep breath. "I must go to Marguerite. But someone must help Rachel."

Rachel! Annie felt shaken, sick. How could she have forgotten Rachel? She'd looked around the garden and seen those watching faces and never once thought about Rachel. But it wasn't until Marguerite's arrival and attack on Pudge that Annie had realized that Happy was dead. That knowledge changed everything. Pudge had no real link to Marguerite, but his link to Happy was clear. Annie had been so bound up in Pudge and his obvious distress that she hadn't grasped what Happy's death meant. Oh, Rachel, poor baby, poor baby.

"She's locked in her room. She won't open the door. She yelled at me to go away, leave her alone." Alice looked hopefully at Annie. "You were nice to her that night at dinner and she's talked and talked about you, called you her sister, said she finally has a sister just like she'd always wanted. Will you see if she'll let you in?"

Annie stared up at the house, the house with so many windows. "Poor baby." When Annie's mother died, Annie had been only a few years older than Rachel. She would never forget her desolation, her feeling of being utterly alone, her sense of betrayal. Most of all, she had been incredulous. How could her mother be dead? How could her mother not *be?*

Someone should have seen to Rachel. How long had she been locked away? What did she know? Would she let Annie help? Though Annie knew better than most that nothing would ever help in one sense, but in another love always helped. She faced Alice. "I'll try. Yes, I will try. But first you have to tell me what's happened. I don't know anything, how Happy died or when or where, or who found her." Pray God it had not been Rachel. "I have to know before I talk to her." She needed to know for Rachel. She had to know for Pudge.

*Why hadn't Pudge denied killing Happy?* Annie pushed the thought away, stared at Alice Schiller.

Alice wrung her hands and looked anxiously up the path. "I must hurry." Her mobile face — and once again there was that echo of Marguerite's emotive brilliance — shifted, flattened, as if pummeled by shock. "This morning" — her thin voice dropped, mournful as a winter wind — "I was coming out of Marguerite's suite. The door to Happy's suite opened." Her eyes slid toward Annie, then away.

Annie remembered once diving into a wave and coming up enmeshed in slippery fronds of seaweed and the sweaty wash of panic as she thrashed to break free. Was this how Pudge felt? Were he and Max still in the house? There was no one down at the dock now, not even Billy Cameron.

Alice fingered the irregular chunks of turquoise in her necklace and continued to avoid Annie's eyes.

Annie knew, but she had to ask. "Who came out?"

"Mr. Laurance." The name dangled between them. Alice cleared her throat, then spoke quickly, the words tumbling out in that thin voice. "He poked his head out first, looked up and down the hall. He didn't see me. People often don't." She said the last calmly, without much interest. "He came out into the hall. He was carrying something. He turned away from me, toward the stairs. He looked back into the room and he shuddered. I thought perhaps he was ill. Then he reached out and pulled the door shut very slowly. There wasn't any noise at all."

Annie listened with growing despair.

Alice hunched her shoulders. "It was so strange. The minute the door closed, he ran. I was shocked. A moment before, I'd thought he was sick. Then he ran. He reached the stairs and went down them and he was gone. I walked up the hall. When I came to Happy's door, I stopped and knocked. I was on my way to see her. Marguerite wanted her to come for breakfast."

To push away the vision of Pudge bolting out of that room, easing shut the door, then running, Annie asked, though it scarcely mattered, "Was that usual?"

Alice nodded. "Oh yes. Marguerite needs attention, you know. Sometimes she'd ask Happy, sometimes Wayne, sometimes a guest. When she was bored with me for company." Once again she was matter-of-fact, not resentful, simply reporting. "This morning she wanted Happy. Happy never minded. She always liked visiting. She liked being with people. Happy . . ." She paused, swallowed, pressed a hand against her throat. "Everyone loved Happy."

Annie looked at her sharply, wondering if Alice heard the absurdity in her statement. Because someone sure as hell hadn't loved Happy.

Alice continued, almost as if to herself. "Happy was so bright and sweet. Serious, you know, and perhaps a little silly. Marguerite said she wasn't very bright. But that wasn't fair. Happy adored Marguerite. She wasn't the least bit jealous, either, even though Marguerite was already famous when Happy was just a little girl. We'd come to visit them and Marguerite was always in a whirl of parties and men following her about and she wasn't more than twenty then. Happy used to stay up late at night, slip out of her room, so that she could see Marguerite come in from a dance. Sometimes I think that's why Happy was never able to find the right man. She remembered those years and Marguerite the belle of the ball. This was several years before Marguerite met Claude and he simply swept her off her feet. He was much older, you know. I'm afraid he was married at the time" — Alice's tone was defensive — "but Marguerite had to have him. Hell wouldn't rest or heaven, either, until he was hers. I have to say, though it was a wrong way to start, theirs was a love match. Marguerite adored Claude until the day he died. I thought Marguerite was going to die, too. Oh, I had such a hard time with her. Happy came and helped. That was when Happy's first marriage failed. But Happy knew Marguerite needed her. And Happy was fickle, I'm afraid. Always looking for a great romance. But she was nice and sweet to everyone. That's why I knew something was wrong when she didn't answer my knock. Happy would never ignore anyone. Not like Marguerite. If Marguerite doesn't want to be bothered, she'll look right through you. That's why I opened the door. I shouldn't have. It isn't right to open someone's door without an invitation." Her tone was prim. "But I opened it." Her eyes closed. She gave a little moan. "Oh, Happy. I remember when I first met her." Tears edged from beneath those tightly closed lashes. "She was fourteen and she'd stay close to me when Marguerite was too busy for her. She was like a little sister to me." There was a lifetime of love in her voice.

Her eyes snapped open, wide and strained. "I opened the door. Oh God, so much blood."

Annie drew her breath in sharply, seeing in her mind the bright crimson splash of blood.

Alice pressed her hands against her cheeks. "I don't know how long I stood there. It seemed hours and hours. The sun was spilling in through the windows, pouring over Happy. She was slumped on the sofa, beaten down on the sofa, her poor head all broken and bloody. Blood everywhere, on her head and face and arms and dress, on the cushions, on the floor. Everywhere." Alice shuddered. "I closed the door and I went to find Wayne. I asked him to call the police." Just for an instant, her face thinned. "He had to look for himself, of course. Men are such fools. As if I didn't know what I had seen. But it didn't matter. I knew he would get the police when he saw. I went to Rachel's room. She has a funny little nook on the third floor." She lifted anguished eyes to Annie. "I tried to keep her there."

Annie understood and felt a curl of horror.

"I told her she mustn't go down there." Alice's voice rose. "She pushed past me and we struggled and she ran down the stairs and to Happy's door. Wayne caught her and held her. He picked her up and carried her up to her room. I locked Happy's door. When I went back to Rachel's room, she wouldn't let me in. Then the police came and they hunted for Mr. Laurance and no one could find him."

Annie couldn't see the cause and effect. "Why

did they hunt for him? Did you tell them you'd seen him at Happy's door?"

"I haven't been interviewed by the police yet. You see, there's not been time." She brushed back a strand of dark red hair. "Wayne called the police. They came and everyone gathered in the hall, everyone except Rachel. Oh, Joan wasn't there. I guess she was in the garden. It was all very confusing. She came in a little later and found us there and one of the policemen heard her say that Mr. Laurance went out in the rowboat. He wanted to know who Mr. Laurance was, and when he learned that he'd been married to Happy, he got all excited and he went to the stairs and yelled up. An ambulance came and more cars and they sent a policeman down to the dock. Terry was looking out the window, he kept a watch, and he saw your motorboat arrive."

They'd all streamed down to the dock, everyone except Marguerite and Rachel. Rachel was still locked in her room. As for Marguerite, it wasn't hard to imagine that she never permitted herself to be part of a crowd scene. She'd waited and, God knew, she'd timed her arrival perfectly if her intent was to increase police suspicion of Pudge.

As for Pudge, Annie couldn't imagine, short of a confession, what he could possibly have done to make his situation worse. But for the moment, as much as she wanted to help him, as much as she hoped she and Max could help him, he had to take second place now to Rachel.

Alice's report made it clear that the situation

was still fluid when she and Max and Pudge reached the dock. There had scarcely been time for Chief Garrett to look at the crime scene, get the names of those on the scene, and discover that the victim's ex-husband was missing. So Garrett hadn't interviewed anyone yet.

"The police will talk to everyone." Annie looked at Alice.

There was a moment of silence. Alice stared toward the house, her face uncertain and troubled. She touched her fingers to her mouth. Slowly, her expression hardened. She gave a resolute nod. "Yes, they will talk to me, won't they? I found her. I shall simply tell them the truth. Marguerite asked me to invite Happy to breakfast, so I went to her suite and knocked on the door. When she didn't answer . . ." Alice ignored Annie's startled face. "Come now, I must get to the house."

Alice turned and started up the path, walking with surprising speed.

Annie followed, questions bubbling in her mind. She didn't understand. Did this mean that Alice had no intention of telling the police that she had seen Pudge come out of Happy's room? Why should Alice protect Pudge? Alice had no reason to care about Pudge. Oh, she may well have liked him. Annie wouldn't be surprised to learn that her father made friends wherever he went. He was a man of charm and good humor. But all the charm in the world couldn't outweigh Alice's affection for Happy. Annie wanted to grab Alice's arm, stop her, be sure she'd understood.

But that was too great a gamble. Asking Alice, putting into words the unspoken promise of silence, could prompt a swift denial, cause Alice to divulge all she had seen.

Alice hurried up the curving steps at the south end of the veranda. She yanked open a French door, held it for Annie. They stepped into a narrow room that ended in a dark tangle of banana trees, thick vines, hibiscus and azaleas. The sweet scent of wisteria and the deep smell of rich earth cloyed the air. The room — it looked more like a ship's bar — might have been charming in a flamboyant fashion except for its occupants. Annie had seen more animation in an international flight lounge after a seven-hour delay.

Everyone was there except for Marguerite and Rachel. Red-faced Terry hunched on a barstool, his back to the room, but the mirror reflected his watchful eyes, moving slowly from face to face in the mirror. Wayne slouched in a wicker chair, bearded chin on his hand. Donna paced like a caged lioness. Joan, clippers in hand, bent over a low hedge, her back to the others. But her eyes slid toward Annie and Alice. A plump middle-aged woman with curly black hair stood still as a statue by a door at the far end of the bar, twisting a dish towel in her hand. She wore dark slacks and a bright pink blouse under a too-big white apron. She wasn't a family member, as far as Annie knew. The apron suggested she might be part of the domestic staff.

The only sound, other than the snip of Joan's

clippers, was Max on his cell phone. Max and Pudge stood by themselves near the archway. ". . . okay, Johnny Joe. We'll expect you. Thanks." Max clicked off the phone, nodded reassuringly at Annie. Pudge, his face bleak, simply stood there, not looking at anyone. The irregular splotch on his slacks was almost dry.

Patrolman Lou Pirelli blocked the archway leading to the front of the house. He noted Annie, whom he knew as he knew almost everyone on the island, but his noncommittal cop expression didn't alter. "Captain Garrett has asked everyone to wait here." He had a pleasant tenor voice, pleasant but firm.

Annie didn't hesitate. She walked up to him. "Lou, I've got to go upstairs. My little sister's locked in her room. It's her mother who was killed. Lou, she saw the body."

Pirelli's smooth round young face lost its veneer of blankness. His eyes darkened. So Lou had seen that room. "So much blood," Alice had said.

"We've got to make sure Rachel's all right. She's just a kid, Lou." Annie remembered that Lou Pirelli had a houseful of little sisters with great mops of black curls and laughing eyes.

Pirelli tugged a palm-size radio transmitter from his shirt pocket. "Captain, Pirelli here. Maintaining watch in terrace room as instructed. Request from Annie Darling to speak with younger sister. Sister is apparently the daughter" — Pirelli was puzzled, glancing at Annie — "of the victim. According to Annie Darling, her sister observed body and has since been locked in her room." He held the radio to his ear, nodded several times. "Yes, sir."

Annie moved to step past him.

Pirelli blocked her way. "Officer Cameron will escort you upstairs. He's on his way."

"I must go to Miss Dumaney." Alice Schiller was insistent. "She's upset. She won't understand why I haven't come to her."

Pirelli's round face didn't look quite so bland. "Miss Dumaney refused to remain here with the others. Captain Garrett let her go upstairs."

Annie imagined that had been a remarkable scene.

Pirelli pointed at a white wicker chair. "Everyone else has to stay here. Make yourself comfortable."

"Relax, Alice." Terry turned to face the room, his red face sardonic. "Marguerite's on a roll."

Alice whirled toward him, her face bleak. "It isn't funny, Terry."

His features hardened. "I'm not laughing. But this time you can't give madame a massage and a hot toddy and make everything right. You think I'm not sorry about Happy? Goddamn, she was the nicest person in this goddamn house. Marguerite's having a hell of a time. One bloody scene after another. But Happy's dead."

"We're all sorry, Terry." Wayne's cold blue eyes strayed toward Pudge. "Marguerite has to handle it her way. Leave Alice alone."

"I have to go to Marguerite." Alice turned back to Pirelli.

Pirelli shook his head, pointed again at the chair.

Footsteps sounded behind Pirelli. Big Billy Cameron loomed in the archway. He jerked his head at Annie.

Annie slipped past Pirelli, glad to leave the room behind, the room that smelled like moisture and dirt, the room that pulsed with uneasiness. As she followed Billy, their footsteps echoing on the flagstone floor, she steeled herself for what was to come.

# Fourteen

The archway from the terrace room led to the overfurnished formal reception area where she and Max had first met Marguerite Dumaney and her dinner guests on Wednesday night. Annie glanced to her left, where another archway opened into the dining room. Her mind juggled locations. The tropical garden at the north end of the terrace room also bounded the west end of the dining area.

Billy didn't spare a glance at the medieval tapestries or the plush furniture with its intricately carved scrolls and seashells and acanthus leaves or at the flocked Christmas trees at either end of the dais. He headed straight for the stairway. The double-wide curving staircase was dramatic, with black walnut balusters and railing and stone steps. Fresh pine garlands wound around the railing. The steps curved out of sight, hidden behind a stucco shell emblazoned with painted starfish and seashells and dolphins. Annie and Billy started up the stairs.

A stentorian rumble sounded above. The loud voice, a bulldog growl that had terrorized nurses for a half century, reverberated in the second-floor hallway. ". . . massive trauma. Autopsy won't show anything different. Somebody bashed the hell out of her, Pete. Struck, oh, I'd guess ten times, maybe fifteen, with something long and narrow."

Billy held out an arm to block Annie's climb. "Better wait a minute," he muttered.

Annie understood. She recognized that voice, too. Horace Burford wore a lot of medical hats on the island. He was chief of staff at the hospital as well as medical examiner. It was always smart to stay out of Burford's path when he bellowed. He hated to lose a patient, and he hated a death that shouldn't have happened.

Burford thudded around the curve, head thrust forward like a charging bull, his big-cheeked face distended in a scowl. His dark blue suit was a little too tight and shiny from wear. He'd loosened his tie, and his shirt was open at the neck.

Pete Garrett was right behind him. "Like what, sir?"

A choleric flush stained Burford's bulging cheeks. "I'm not a bloody mind reader. Bigger than a crowbar, smaller than a two-by-four." He jolted to a stop just above Annie. He twisted his head to peer up at Garrett. "You didn't find a weapon? It'd be damn bloody." He didn't give Garrett time to answer. "No weapon. Huh. Okay, look for something on the order of a broom handle. A bloody broom handle." He took two more steps, stopped again. "Blood. There'd be a hell of a lot. Spurts. Look for somebody pretty well drenched."

Annie didn't like the picture in her mind, but

she could have hugged Burford. Yes, Pudge had a smear of blood on his slacks but that was all, a single smear. It was the first positive fact she'd learned that might help him. *Look for somebody pretty well drenched.* But who would it be? No one had shown any evidence of blood. Had there been time for the murderer to bathe, discard stained clothes? Was she wrong in assuming that whoever killed Happy had been a member of the household? Had anyone checked to see whether an intruder could have reached her room? Surely Pete Garrett would consider all of these possibilities.

Burford continued to look up toward Garrett. "You better get a specialist from the state lab to analyze the stains. From what I saw, I'd say she was seated, murderer standing, blows delivered by the right hand. Anyway, if you find the weapon I can give you a better idea." He jerked around, noticed Annie and Billy, gave a short nod and thudded past them.

Garrett called after him. "Can you estimate —"

Burford shouted over his shoulder. "A guess. Rigor mortis well advanced. Maybe around midnight, maybe earlier. Hell, maybe later." Burford reached the base of the stairs and plunged toward the front door.

Midnight! Alice Schiller saw Pudge come out of Happy's room this morning. Happy had been dead for hours. It didn't mean a thing that Pudge ran through the garden. Except why didn't he rouse the house? What was he carrying? Why did he run away? But Annie moved up the steps, buoyed by relief. Happy had been dead for hours!

Garrett was waiting at the top of the stairs. He shot an impatient glance at Annie. "What's this about a sister? What sister?"

"Rachel Van Meer. She's Happy's daughter and my father's stepdaughter. My stepsister." Annie pointed up the stairs. "She's locked in her room. Up on the third floor. Pete, she saw her mother's body."

Garrett glared at Billy. "Nobody told me there was somebody else in the house besides the ones downstairs and Mrs. Dumaney."

Annie didn't try to explain that it should be Miss Dumaney or Mrs. Ladson. The fine points of Hollywood address wouldn't impress him.

"I'm sorry, sir." Billy pulled a notebook out of his pocket and flipped it open. "Everybody was milling around when we got here. Nobody mentioned a kid."

"A kid?" Garrett lost his curt, hurried look. "How old?"

"Fifteen. She's been by herself ever since they found Happy." Annie didn't like thinking about those two hours. Why hadn't any of the others thought about Rachel?

Garrett's round face creased in a frown. Obviously he was as unhappy as Annie that Rachel had been unnoticed for two hours. Garrett prided himself on taking charge and he must have felt that this morning's investigation was far from controlled. "Okay, Annie. You better check. Billy, hang close."

Annie understood Garrett's order. This was a murder investigation and he was in charge. Annie didn't mind Billy coming with her. Billy was a stepdad who loved his wife's son. Billy and Kevin fished and camped and kicked a soccer ball. Billy would help if he could, and there was no reason to care if Billy overheard what she and Rachel said.

Garrett watched as they walked across the landing to the third-floor stairs. They passed an open door. Annie darted a swift glance, then wished she hadn't. A miniature Christmas tree had tumbled from the end table next to a sofa that had once added charm to a sitting room. The sofa's fabric was a butter-yellow fabric accented by full-size red roosters. The red accents were picked up by the red, green and white rag rugs and a red and white quilt on one wall. Happy's body slumped stiffly at one end of the sofa. The maroon of drying blood splotched her battered head, her dressing gown, the sofa and the floor.

Annie carried the devastating picture with her as she and Billy silently climbed to the third floor.

Max walked the length of the terrace room and studied the tangle of ferns and shrubs and sweet-smelling trees. Joan Ladson stood on tiptoe to clip a dangling frond from a banana tree. She shot an uneasy look at Max.

Max gave her a reassuring smile, then turned to Wayne. Max pointed to a flagstone path that curved into the greenery. "Does that go through to the dining room?"

Wayne nodded. He walked toward Max, smiling. "Yes. It takes most people a half dozen visits to the house to get it straight. It's quite a house, isn't?" He spoke with evident pride. "It was Dad's pride and joy. You know who my dad was?" Wayne didn't bother to wait for an answer. "Dad made the greatest adventure flicks ever. He loved secret tunnels and caves and surprises. Like the jungle." He laughed aloud. "You ever been to Clifton's Cafeteria in L.A.? Rocks and a waterfall and lots of greenery. Dad loved to take us there when were kids. But he didn't do it on our account. No way. I'm surprised Dad didn't have a waterfall built in here. He about drove the architects crazy. They wanted the commission, but they fought his plans all the way. Four architects. When the second one walked out, they say he built a raft and set sail for the Caribbean, decided hammerheads were better company than clients. You know what" — Wayne's voice was pleased — "I think somewhere Dad's got the last laugh. It's a hell of a house. Have you ever seen it from the water when the sun's coming up? It's like a huge gaudy ring on a showgirl's finger. You know it's vulgar, but you damn sure can't take your eyes off of it. There's something to be said for vulgarity, you know. Crude exuberance has it all over staid respectability." He looked faintly wistful. "That was sure as hell true of my dad. He died the way he lived, flying a small plane into a storm. He shouldn't have, but he did. The story of Dad's life. The odd thing is, Marguerite understood that. I wouldn't have expected it of her. It's damn hard for Marguerite ever to separate any scene from herself long enough to see if there is anyone else present. But when he built this house, she supported him all the way. That's when I knew she really was nuts about Dad."

Max glanced toward the French doors. "How many entrances are there?"

Wayne's face sobered. "Yeah. That's a good question now, isn't it?" He looked sharply at Pudge Laurance.

Pudge still stood near the archway. He watched Max, a flicker of interest in his eyes.

Max said briskly, "The layout of the house may be important to others besides Pudge."

Wayne raised a skeptical eyebrow. "An unknown intruder? Bushy-haired, no doubt."

"Bushy-haired?" Joan repeated blankly.

Pirelli cleared his throat. "The captain said no discussion of the murder."

"Right," Max called out easily. As long as Max kept the conversation confined to the structure of the house, Pirelli wouldn't interfere. As for Wayne, Max didn't believe in bushy-haired intruders, either, but it wouldn't do any harm to let him and everyone else in the room believe that possibility accounted for Max's interest in the layout of the house.

Max glanced around the room. "Any scratch paper around here?"

Wayne nodded toward a bridge table. "There should be a score pad there."

Max strolled to the table, pulled out a side drawer. He picked up a tablet. "Do you mind if I use this?"

Wayne came up beside him. "What are you going to do?"

"I thought it might be useful to sketch the house, where the rooms are and the stairs and the doors. Although" — Max's smile was rueful — "I'm not too clear on the layout yet. Let's see, the front entrance leads to the reception area, and that's just through there." Max pointed toward the archway where Pirelli stood, still listening but clearly more relaxed.

Across the room, Alice Schiller moved restively in a wicker chair.

Wayne held out his hand. "I can do that." He pulled out a chair and dropped into it. He ripped loose a sheet, and began to draw in a quick, fluid motion, his face absorbed and interested.

Max slipped into the chair to Wayne's left. Joan sidled near enough to watch. Wayne finished the first drawing and peeled off another page.

Terry ambled over from the bar. "You've left out the tower."

Wayne shook his head. "The entrance is on the second floor."

Terry pointed at the first-floor plan. "Don't forget the rope bridge, buddy. I think the rope bridge was the reason *Architectural Digest* refused to do the house. Marguerite went into a decline for weeks."

Wayne laughed and added a rope bridge to the

first-floor plan. "You got it wrong, Terry. They didn't cotton to the fake cave on the front lawn. But they probably never liked Dad's movies, either."

Terry smothered a sneeze. "Remember his last movie? A jungle, an overgrown temple, a jade statue hidden in a well and a big son of a bitch of a dragon."

"A dragon in a cave. Dad had a hell of a good time. All he lacked was Harrison Ford as the lead. But that one grossed eighty million." Wayne grinned and finished the third floor, then got another sheet for the fourth. Last of all he drew the front of the house, including the glass whale and the cave with its resident dragon. He handed the sheaf of drawings to Max.

Max scanned the pages swiftly, appearing to give equal attention to each floor. But the second-floor sketch was the treasure. Yes, Pudge was across the hall from Happy, but Wayne, Donna, Marguerite and Alice were also on that floor. Joan was in a guest room on the third floor across from Rachel's room. Terry was staying on his cabin cruiser. Before Max tucked the pages in his pocket, he counted aloud, "One, two . . . Yes, I see. There are four entrances to the house." He looked at Wayne. "Is that right?"

"At least." Wayne pointed at the row of French doors. "They all open. Plus there's a door from the veranda into the terrace room, another veranda entrance to the jungle, and a back door to the kitchen."

"And the front door," Joan added.

Terry volunteered. "And more French doors into the informal living room." He looked at Wayne. "Who locks up at night?"

Alice Schiller pushed up from her chair. She paced toward them. "The doors were locked. I lock them every night. This morning, after Wayne called, I let the police in at the front door and it was still chained."

"I went down to the garden by that door. It was latched." Joan pointed at the door at the south end of the terrace room. "As far as I know, the French doors were locked."

"So, we few, we happy few," Terry said, his voice silky.

In a suddenly cold and ugly pause, footsteps sounded near the arch.

Annie hadn't had to guess at Rachel's room. She was glad because even genial Billy might have wondered if Annie hadn't known which room belonged to her stepsister. She knocked again while looking into the sensual face of Leonardo di Caprio in the full-length poster on the door. It seemed forever that she had stood there, knocking and calling. "Rachel, please, it's Annie." Had it been five minutes? Ten? Once Rachel answered, her voice thick. "Go away. Just go away."

Billy whispered, "Want me to see if I can get a key somewhere?"

Annie glanced at him, shook her head. She spoke again. "Rachel, my mother died when I was your age. Please, honey, let me in. Rachel, don't stay by yourself. I know how you feel." That couldn't be true in whole, but certainly it was true in part. "Please, Rachel. Rachel, it's not your fault." That was the terrible ache that others never understood, the awful sickening feeling that if you had only done something different at some time in some way, death would not have come. "Rachel, your mom loved you more than anybody in the world."

Abruptly, the door swung open. Rachel's skinny face was splotched and puffy. Red-rimmed brown eyes stared at Annie in piteous intensity. Her lips quivered. She gave a choked cry and plunged into Annie's arms.

Annie held her tight, pressed her face against Rachel's tousled curls, feeling the sting of her own tears as she grieved for Rachel and remembered long-ago grief that still scalded her heart.

Although Marguerite was accompanied only by Pete Garrett, their arrival transformed the terrace room, made it seem small and quivering with energy. Marguerite's royal blue silk slack suit rustled as she strode past Pirelli and Pudge, ignoring them. Her grief-stricken visage had given way to intense concentration, her bold features taut and severe.

Alice hurried toward her. "Marguerite, I tried to come to you."

Marguerite embraced her longtime companion. "Our loss," she murmured. A deep breath, then she stepped past Alice, moving into a pool of sunlight near the French doors. She stood for a moment, head bowed, auburn hair richly red in the sunlight, a strand falling across one cheek. Slowly, she lifted her face. Even though sunlight can be cruel, magnifying lines, emphasizing the ravages of age, Marguerite's haggard beauty was not diminished.

Max folded his arms and prepared to be entertained. He wondered if Marguerite was aware of the quiet resistance of her audience. Joan observed her former stepmother-in-law as she might note an aphid on a rose. A quiver of skepticism crossed Wayne's narrow face. Terry rocked back on his heels, his earlier, malicious amusement replaced by uneasiness. Donna's thin lips tightened. Pudge dismissed Marguerite with a glance. Alice looked wan and weary. The dark-haired domestic quietly chewed gum.

Pete Garrett's round face hardened. "Ladies and gentlemen, I appreciate your patience. I have spoken with Mrs. Dumaney —"

Marguerite's hand touched his arm. "I shall tell them." She looked at each in turn, a piercing gaze, and waited until all was quiet.

Marguerite clapped her hands. "Dear hearts, we must do our duty. Our duty is simple. We must" — her voice lifted into a clarion tone — "put aside our grief for the moment. I know you all will be reassured that I have had a conference with the authorities. We shall bend every effort of will to apprehend the person who so cruelly wrested life from our dear Happy."

Garrett moved restively. "Mrs. Dumaney —"

Marguerite took two steps forward. The simple movement relegated Garrett to the background. Once again the focus of all eyes, she lifted her hands, turned them out. "I have given Chief Garrett permission to search the house. Who knows what might be found that will help in this investigation. He has already searched my rooms. I know none of you will object to a search of your own."

# Fifteen

"You won't go away?" Rachel stood by the bathroom door, clutching her clothes.

"I'll be right here." Annie smiled. "I promise."

Rachel left the bathroom door ajar. Annie dropped onto a patchwork sofa, squares of turquoise and amber overlaid by circles of lime and marigold. She leaned back on the comfortable cushion, weary to the bone.

Rachel's beamed room, with a sloped ceiling to the south, glowed with colors reminiscent of New Mexico, the walls a dusty peach, Navajo throw rugs in scarlet, black, sand and gray, a rustic four-poster bed made of bleached wood bone white as a cattle skull. Donkeys laden with brightly colored pottery marched across the sandstone comforter.

The room was divided by the sofa into a sleeping area and a cozy nook with a TV, stereo, computer, printer, bookcases and — Annie counted — a stack of fourteen board games, everything from Pin the Tail on the Donkey to Monopoly to Scrabble. Chinese checkers were atop one bookcase. A snowman piñata hung from the central beam, a red porkpie hat, round black eyes, pink buttons, green boots.

A sweet and childlike room with only hints of a girl halfway to womanhood, the fashion magazines splayed open, the clutter of makeup bottles and brushes on the dressing table, a pair of high heels tossed in a corner.

Listening to the hiss of the shower, Annie forced herself to think. Persuading Rachel to shower and dress was the first step on a long road. Next was breakfast though Annie knew that Rachel would push most of the food away. Annie glanced at her watch. Just past eleven. Rachel was still grappling with the initial shock of her mother's death. She'd not asked any questions yet. Those questions were sure to come. Moreover, Pete Garrett would talk to Rachel. Annie was sure Pete would be gentle, but he would have his own questions, several that Annie imagined only too clearly:

*Was there any disagreement between your mother and your stepfather?*

*What was the nature of their quarrel?*

Annie pressed her hands against her temples. Rachel had no inkling that Pudge was a suspect. Annie looked at Billy, who was waiting patiently in the hall. There was no way to warn Rachel. Besides, what could be said? How could Annie explain what was as yet unexplainable? Why had Pudge run away from Happy's room carrying something and hurried through the garden and taken the rowboat? How did Happy's blood stain his pants leg? Why did he remain silent? Annie knew all the questions, but she had no answers.

She pushed up from the couch, her mouth and throat dry. How would Rachel react when she understood the import of those questions? Her mother dead, her adored stepfather under suspicion of the brutal crime . . . was there any way to shield Rachel?

Billy looked through the open doorway, his gentle face kind, but his eyes alert.

Annie knew he would call her back if she stepped into the bathroom, closed the door. "We'll go downstairs when Rachel's dressed. She needs some breakfast." And maybe there would be a moment alone, a chance to warn Rachel.

The shower cut off. The stall door banged. In a moment, the hair dryer buzzed. Rachel was brushing her hair, the ebony curls lustrous and fine, when she stepped into the bedroom. Her face was puffy and splotched and she looked very small in an oversize red-and-green-striped T-shirt and floppy denim pants, but there was an air of determination about her. Perhaps Billy, knowing Pirelli was on duty downstairs, would simply stand at the top of the steps, watch them descend. Maybe Annie could tell Rachel not to mention Pudge's quarrel with Happy, though no doubt others in the household had already reported that encounter to Garrett.

Before Annie could speak, Rachel burst out, "I need to talk to the police. I know who killed Mother." At Annie's shocked look, Rachel nodded her head vigorously. "I started thinking. I stood there in the water and it was like my mind opened up and everything came clear. I mean, why would anybody kill Mother? Then I knew." She bolted toward the door, looked up at Billy. "Are you the police?" Her voice quavered with eagerness.

Billy's face was serious and kind. "I'm Sergeant Cameron, miss. Chief Garrett will be glad to talk to you. If you'd like, we can go downstairs and find him. He'll be glad to hear what you have to tell us."

"I know what happened." She looked back. "Annie, come on." Rachel headed for the stairs.

Annie followed, Billy close behind.

A brisk voice rose up the stairwell. ". . . want to be clear, sir, that our search is with your permission and that you agree there has been no coercion of any kind."

Annie grabbed Rachel's arm. "That's Chief Garrett." When they reached the second floor, the hallway was crowded, the chief, Pudge, and Max standing in front of a door across the hall from Happy's quarters.

Happy's door was closed and sealed, a police tape strung in an X across the panel. Annie realized the initial investigation was complete, but Garrett had likely sealed the door with the intention of bringing in a bloodstain expert. The police tape also meant Happy's body had been removed.

Rachel stared at the closed door, her eyes huge, her lips quivering. Annie slipped her arm around Rachel's thin shoulders. Pudge was facing the door to his room and didn't see them.

Garrett nodded toward Pudge. "If you will open the door —"

Rachel pulled away from Annie, darted across the hall and flung herself at Pudge. "Oh, Pudge, Pudge," and she began to cry.

Pudge wrapped his arms around her. "Sweetheart, I'm so sorry." He looked down at her dark curls, his eyes wet, his face crumpled.

Annie's chest ached. She knew what Pudge meant. She was sure she knew what Pudge meant. He offered solace and comfort to a child faced with horror. But Annie didn't like the ferret-sharp look on Garrett's round face. Pudge didn't mean he was sorry because he had killed Happy. And what could be said? The usual bromides: *It's going to be all right. Everything works out for the best, I'll take care of it* — none of them applied here.

Rachel clung to him. "I wish it hadn't happened."

"I know." Pudge's voice was soft. "But we can't change what's happened."

The dark head burrowed against him. "Pudge, you won't go away, will you? Please don't go away."

"I'm here, Rachel." Pudge looked over her head at Annie. "And Annie's here." The warmth and thankfulness in his face brought tears to Annie's eyes. "Now listen, kid." He held Rachel away from him, looked soberly at her tear-spattered face. "We've got to get through some hard days, but we'll do it. Don't worry about the past. I'm here for you."

Annie felt cold. No blast of arctic air could have chilled her as completely as Pudge's words. *Don't worry about the past.* She couldn't pretend that she was an authority on her father. But those words didn't ring right to her. Why should he urge Rachel not to worry about the past? A sudden horrific vision surged through her mind. Rachel and her mother had quarreled. Rachel was hotheaded, passionate, undisciplined. She had been very angry with her mother.

Annie stared at her father and her stepsister. Everything shifted into place: Pudge running from Happy's room, Pudge rowing out into the Sound, Pudge with a smear of blood on his pants. Annie could feel the muscles in her face tighten. What would happen if she spoke out, if she asked Pudge what he had found in Happy's room?

It was almost as though she had spoken. Pudge's head jerked toward Annie. Warning blazed in his eyes, warning and a plea.

Annie stood frozen. She wanted to shout out that Pudge was innocent, that he would never have hurt Happy. The words ached in her throat. But if she spoke . . . Her eyes moved to Rachel.

Rachel nodded solemnly, her thin, tear-streaked face full of resolve. She swung around, stepped toward Garrett. "Mr. Policeman, I can tell you what happened." Her quavery young voice hung in the utter quiet of the hallway.

Pudge took two quick steps, grabbed her arm. He pulled her close to him. "Rachel, hush."

Garrett barked. "Step away, sir. Let the child

go." His hand dropped to the pistol in his holster.

Pudge loosed his hold, but he spoke fast and hard. "She doesn't know what she's talking about. She's just a kid and she's upset. Listen," Pudge looked desperately at Rachel, then at Annie, his face working. "Listen, I . . ." He stopped, swallowed hard. "I killed Happy. I didn't mean to. We got mad and — and she threw something at me and I didn't know what was happening —"

Annie knew what was happening. Despair washed over her like a smothering wave. Pudge must not do this. He must not. There was only one chance that she could save him. One chance. . . .

"Dad," she cried out.

It stopped him. He rubbed his face hard with his hand. "Annie" — his voice was broken — "please forgive me."

Rachel pressed the palms of her hands against her cheeks.

Garrett jerked his head toward Billy Cameron, who pulled out a notebook and a pen and began to write.

Max said sharply, "Pudge, shut up." His eyes were shocked and sad as he looked toward Annie.

"Dad, why don't you tell us about it," Annie's tone was gentle, as if she spoke to someone who had been very ill and was just coming back to consciousness. "You went in Happy's room this morning. About eight o'clock. Alice saw you. She saw you come out. Was that when you and Happy quarreled?"

She was aware that Garrett gave her a brief, hard stare, then fastened his probing gaze on Pudge.

"And" — it hurt to say it, but she had to continue — "when you hit her? Tell us what happened." She willed him to talk, wishing she could yank the terrible words out of his mouth, make him speak before he thought it through and realized that if there had been an angry shouting match, things thrown, Alice would have heard. And, more than that, that he had not been in Happy's room long enough for a quarrel and a violent death.

Pudge avoided Annie's eyes. He stared down at the floor and talked fast, "I don't exactly remember. It's kind of a blur. I went in and she started saying ugly things and she threw a cushion at me and I grabbed . . ." He stopped, his mind obviously racing. "I grabbed a poker from the fireplace. I didn't mean to do it. Then it was too late and I ran out of the room."

"Eight o'clock this morning?" Garrett walked up until he stood only inches from Pudge. "You killed Mrs. Laurance at eight o'clock this morning?"

Max took a step toward Garrett. Annie shook her head. Max stopped, his eyes puzzled.

"I guess that's right." Pudge looked at Annie. "Alice saw me? Yeah, that's right."

Garrett spit out two questions, his voice hard and angry. "Eight o'clock this morning? That's when you struck her with a poker?"

Pudge hunched his shoulders. "It was . . ." his face looked abruptly sick. "There was so much blood. I grabbed an afghan from the end of the bed and wrapped the poker in it. That's why I took the boat. I had to get rid of the poker."

Nothing sounds more true than lies mixed with truth. "So much blood . . ." Yes, Pudge went into that room and he found Happy dead and he ran with . . . what? Not a poker. But something he felt he had to get out of that room.

Rachel stared at Pudge in utter disbelief, too shaken for tears.

Annie watched Rachel. Whatever Pudge found, it must have belonged to the girl. But that didn't matter now. What mattered now was time.

Annie walked up to Garrett. She stood within inches of the police chief and her father. "Pete, tell him what time Happy died."

Garrett's eyes blazed. "How do you know?"

"Billy and I were on the stairs when Dr. Burford came down." She met Garrett's belligerent gaze without flinching. Annie didn't like the look in the young chiefs eyes. Garrett was mad and getting madder.

Garrett's cold stare moved to Pudge. "I want to inform you of your rights under the Miranda decision." He spoke slowly, clearly, his eyes never leaving Pudge's face. Then he asked, "Do you understand, Mr. Laurance?"

"Yes." Pudge's answer was harsh.

Max held up his hand. "Pudge, wait, you need to talk to —"

Pudge interrupted. “No. I want to get it over with.”

“Okay, Mr. Laurance.” The chief’s voice was calm and careful. “What time did you kill your wife?”

Pudge looked at Annie, at Max, at Happy’s closed door. He mumbled, “This morning, around eight. Hell, I don’t know exactly. What difference does it make? You can ask Alice. I’ve told you what happened. That’s all I’m going to say.”

Rachel stumbled toward Annie.

Annie opened her arms, held the girl tight and took a moment to whisper, “It’s all right. It’s all right. Pudge didn’t do it. He couldn’t have.” She raised her voice. “Pete, you know he’s innocent.” She heard Rachel’s soft sigh, felt the girl’s thin body relax against her.

Garrett folded his arms across his chest. His voice was clipped. “You do understand there is a severe penalty for lying to officers investigating a crime, Mr. Laurance?”

Pudge’s head jerked up. He had the look of a man rapidly reviewing what he had said and wondering where he made a mistake.

Garrett was as hungry for battle as a gored bull. It took great effort, but he held himself together, managed to speak in a level, even tone. “I’m going to charge you with obstructing justice, Laurance, and you are going to go to jail. But right now, I want some truth. You went in that room. You took the weapon. What was it?”

"A poker." Pudge's voice was stubborn. His eyes defied Garrett.

"What else did you take?" Garrett, too, knew there had to be a reason, a compelling, awful reason for Pudge's actions.

Pudge's lips set in a hard, tight line.

Garrett nodded toward Billy. "Get Tyndall." Joe Tyndall was the fourth member of the small police force. "We're taking him" — he jerked his head at Pudge — "into custody. Tell Pirelli to get the magistrate on the phone. I want a search warrant. I'm not going to let some slick lawyer throw my case out because we searched without a warrant."

Pudge gestured at his door. "Search away. You won't find anything." He spoke with utter confidence.

Billy spoke quietly into his handheld radio.

"We'll wait." Garrett's head jutted forward. "And we'll look, Mr. Laurance. Don't worry about that. And you're going to be in jail until you decide to tell the truth."

Rachel tugged at Annie's arm. "I don't understand. What's going on? Why did Pudge say he . . ." she couldn't say the words. "Why?" She stared at Pudge, her eyes wide and frightened.

Annie picked her words carefully. She spoke quite clearly and distinctly. "I think he saw something in your mother's room that worried him. I think he was afraid the police might —"

"Annie!" Pudge cried out. "No."

Annie whirled to face Pudge, still holding to Rachel. "Look at Rachel, Pudge, look at her. She loved her mother. She didn't do this."

Pudge lifted his hands in a plea to Annie, his face sagging in despair.

For a sickening twist of time, Annie wondered if she'd gambled and lost. She'd felt certain Rachel was innocent, that the shaken, miserable girl she'd consoled could not possibly be a murderer. But Pudge had been here in the house; he'd seen their quarrels; he knew Rachel far better than Annie did. And Pudge had run with a weapon, he'd run hours after Happy died, but, unless he killed her, he had no way of knowing how much earlier she had died. Should he have noted the darkening of the bloodstains, the rigidity of the body? He wasn't a man accustomed to violent death. He'd entered a room, found Happy brutally dead . . . and seen what?

Just for an instant, shock moved in Garrett's eyes, then he stared at Rachel.

Rachel understood, too. "You mean . . ." Her face creased into disbelief; then, slowly, it softened. "Pudge — you lied for me? Oh, Pudge, I didn't hurt Mom. I was so mad at her, but I wouldn't hurt her. Pudge" — Rachel's eyes glowed — "you lied for me."

Garrett took it all in and Annie knew he would root and dig until he knew everything that had happened, until he learned about Rachel and Mike and Marguerite and Happy and Pudge, every quarrel, every threat, every burst of anger. As for now, his eyes studied Rachel with steely objectivity. Kids kill. It happens, sadly, too often in a world where violence is celebrated in graphic detail as entertainment, and children grow up watching murder and cruelty on an everyday basis. Want to be a man? Make my day, blow somebody away. Pissed? Buy an AK-47, it isn't hard to do, and you've got a superb hunting weapon if your quarry is human.

Garrett's suspicious gaze swung to Pudge. Pudge was still high on Garrett's suspect list because Pudge could be dissembling, knowing that a confession to murder at a time long past the crime would be taken as a sign of innocence. "You heard the girl. So tell me about the weapon, Mr. Laurance."

Pudge still hesitated, remembered horror in his eyes. "I . . ." he swallowed, shook his head.

Rachel darted to him, clutched his arm. "It's all right, Pudge. Tell them."

Pudge looked into her pleading eyes. "Rachel, I'm sorry. I should have known better."

Rachel stood on tiptoe, kissed his cheek.

His arm around Rachel, Pudge looked shamefaced at Garrett. "I guess I was a damn fool. But if you'd seen . . ." He took a deep breath. "I went to Happy's room and opened the door." His eyes darkened with remembered horror. "I saw Happy. It was terrible. She was . . ." He glanced down at Rachel, stopped.

Rachel shuddered. "I know. Alice came up to my room and she tried to make me stay, but I ran down the stairs." Rachel pressed her hands against her face.

“Don’t,” Pudge urged. “Don’t remember that. Think about your mom the way she was. Remember her smiling.”

Garrett didn’t interfere. Instead, he waited and watched. Annie wished his face wasn’t quite so hard and disbelieving.

Rachel dropped her hands. “You found Mom.” She looked at Pudge. “Why did you run away?” Her voice was full of dread.

Pudge rubbed a hand hard against his eyes. “Just stupid. That’s all. I was afraid . . . Anyway” — he lifted his head — “I saw the poker there on the floor and one of your sweaters was lying not far from the sofa. I saw the sweater and I guess my mind snapped. I grabbed it and the poker and wrapped them up in an afghan and ran. I guess I’m just a damn fool.” Pudge sounded sick at heart.

“Was the sweater stained?” Garrett’s voice was sharp.

“No. Not at all.” Pudge shoved his hands through his hair. “It was dumb, but the minute I saw Rachel’s sweater, I panicked. If I’d had time to think, I’d have known better. I didn’t think Rachel hurt anyone. But —” he said miserably, “I thought the police might think so. Anyway, I grabbed the afghan, like I said, and wrapped it around the poker and the sweater and ran.”

“One of my sweaters. . . .” Rachel looked puzzled. “What color was it?”

Pudge was still for just an instant too long.

Pete Garrett gave him a hard, thoughtful stare.

Rachel blinked uncertainly.

"Blue," Pudge said finally.

"But I —"

"I'm not exactly sure." Pudge spoke fast. "It doesn't matter. "I —"

"It does matter, Mr. Laurance." Garrett swung toward Rachel. "I'll ask you to check your clothes. See if there's a sweater missing."

Rachel simply nodded.

Annie was sure there was no missing sweater. Whatever Pudge saw, it wasn't Rachel's sweater. She was sure of it, and so was Pete Garrett.

Pudge lifted his head, his face stubborn. "Whatever. I don't remember the color exactly. Anyway, I thought it was Rachel's. Maybe I was mistaken." He sounded relieved, as if facing the memory lessened its impact.

"Maybe you were." Garrett's tone was icy. He looked at Rachel. "We want to find out who killed your mother." The words were gentle, but Garrett's eyes were coolly observant.

Rachel's pale face was determined. "Well then, let me tell you who did it."

# Sixteen

"Wait a minute." Garrett's eyes scoured Rachel's face. He held up his hand. "Who's your closest relative? I want a responsible adult present when I talk to you."

Garrett didn't intend to be cruel, but Annie saw the spasm on Rachel's face as she grappled with the pain of her loss and with the terror of being alone, her mother gone and no one there to whom she belonged.

Pudge saw it, too. "It's all right, Rachel. I'm here. I won't leave you."

Garrett was impatient. "Isn't Mrs. Dumaney her aunt? I'll ask her —"

"No." Rachel's voice rose in a panicked squeak. "Not Aunt Marguerite. I hate her. I hate her!"

The police chief's eyes narrowed. He stared at that young tear-swollen face, distorted in anger.

Rachel spoke feverishly. "I can't tell you if Aunt Rita's there. She won't let me. Please, you've got to listen. Let Annie come with us. She's my sister. She's a grown-up."

Annie felt the bright burn of tears. *She's a grown-up.* As if Annie were one of those magical older beings with power. That's how children saw the world, themselves and grown-ups. If only

Annie had power, she'd use it for Rachel. But power comes to those who seek it.

Annie said briskly, "Max and I'll go with you. After all, Pete, Rachel is my sister and neither Max nor I were here this morning."

Garrett's mouth folded into a tight line. He had to feel hamstrung and beleaguered, his investigation impeded, imperiled and delayed. But he would want very much indeed to hear what Rachel had to say.

"That will work. Annie and Max will come with us." Rachel's tone was triumphant. "Come on. You need to see the theater."

"Wait a minute." Garrett looked at Billy. "Take Mr. Laurance downstairs with the others. Check with Pirelli about the search warrant. We'll be . . ." He looked at Rachel.

"In Uncle Claude's theater." She started up the stairs.

Pudge pointed up the stairs. "There's a small theater on the fourth floor. There's also a museum with Claude's movies and scripts and all kinds of memorabilia."

Annie and Max hurried up the stairs after Rachel and Garrett, one flight of steps, then another. At the top, Annie felt a little winded. So this was the fourth floor. Rachel hurried to an oak door, pulled it open. She flipped on the lights. The sixteen-seat theater was a miniature of the art deco film houses that flourished before World War II, ornate plaster-of-paris wreaths on the ceiling, a red velvet curtain, a small crystal chandelier, a glistening hardwood stage.

"Here's where Aunt Rita and that man come all the time." Rachel shivered. "She spends a lot of time up here watching those old movies. When that man comes, they turn down the lights and put candles on the stage and wait for Uncle Claude." Rachel's voice was high and quavery.

Annie looked around the small, musty room, so enclosed and far from light and life. Rachel's words evoked a scene of darkness and malignancy.

Rachel leaned forward, nodding earnestly. "He killed Mom because she knew something that was going to keep Aunt Rita from giving him all her money."

Garrett pulled a notebook from his pocket. "What man?"

"Dr. Swanson." Rachel looked toward Annie and Max, who were bunched in the doorway. "They know all about it. They were at Aunt Rita's birthday party Wednesday night. That's when she said she was going to give her money to him. Everybody's been furious." When no one spoke, Rachel added impatiently, "Don't you see? Aunt Rita wants to give her money to Dr. Swanson because she thinks he has some kind of magic that lets her talk to Uncle Claude."

"Black magic," Annie murmured. That was as good a name as any for trifling with the supernatural. Rachel went right past Swanson's New Age euphemism, the Golden Path.

"Anyway," Rachel said huskily, "Mom was really upset. Everybody was."

Except for Swanson, of course. Everyone else at that dinner had indeed been upset, including Happy Laurance. That was why, when Vince called, Annie had immediately assumed the victim was Marguerite Dumaney. Instead, Marguerite's charming, good-humored sister lay dead. Annie still felt astonished. Happy, a murder victim?

Garrett looked toward Annie and Max.

Annie said quickly, "Rachel's right. Marguerite made it clear. Apparently there's a lot of money. She inherited from her father plus she was married to Claude Ladson, a movie producer. He left his fortune to her, not to his children."

"His children?" Garrett looked puzzled.

"Marguerite's stepchildren," Max explained. "Wayne Ladson, Terry Ladson, Mrs. Farrell."

Annie nodded. "They were going to be out in the cold. Along with Happy Laurance."

"Will be out in the cold," Max amended. "I doubt that Marguerite has changed her mind."

"Mom wasn't going to let it happen." Rachel sounded utterly positive. "That's what I'm trying to tell you. Mom was real upset. I tried to talk to her about —" She broke off, her eyes sliding away from Garrett.

Annie understood. Rachel didn't want to tell Garrett about her quarrel with her mother and her fight to be free to see Mike.

"You tried to talk to her?" Garrett said quickly. "When?"

"Last night. After dinner. She was in the gazebo." Rachel clung to the back of a seat. "She told me to go away, that she'd deal with me later, that she had to think what to do. I asked her what she was talking about, she looked so worried and upset. She said, 'It's Aunt Rita. I've got to stop that man from taking all her money. I can do it. I'm not going to let him get away with it. It's robbery, that's all it is. He's a thief. Well, I know what to do. I'm going to talk to him and when I finish, he'll know it's no use. I can do that. I've got papers to prove it and I'm going to put them in a safe place. Or I could . . .' Then she shook her head and looked even more upset. 'Oh, I don't know which way to go. If I go to him, Marguerite will never forgive me. But I have to decide.' She nodded her head very hard. 'I will decide tonight.' She hugged me and said she was sorry about . . ." — Rachel's eyes slid toward Annie — "about the afternoon —"

Annie remembered the swift movement of Happy's arm and Rachel's red cheek.

"— and she told me to run on, that we'd talk tomorrow. She said she'd made up her mind, that it wasn't fair to Wayne and Terry and Donna for Marguerite to throw away all of Claude's money. She hugged me and said everything would be all right tomorrow." Rachel's thin face was drawn by misery and anger. "That man did it. He killed Mom."

Annie tried to picture a confrontation between Happy and Dr. Swanson, Happy threatening him. Would he attack her unless he knew where the papers were? Happy had told Rachel she was going to put them in a safe place. Would Happy have brought them out at such a meeting? Surely not. Happy's room, from Annie's brief glance, showed no traces of a search.

"You've got to find the papers." Rachel's eyes burned with intensity.

"There will be a careful search of your mother's belongings. Let me get this straight. . . ." As Garrett sorted out the relationships and the money and who Swanson was and where he could be found, Annie considered the possibilities. Did Happy call Swanson, threaten him? Was the call, if it was made, sufficient to alarm him into deciding to kill Happy? But how did he get into the house?

". . . lots and lots of money —"

Annie interrupted Rachel. "How would Swanson get inside the house?"

Rachel waved that away. "Maybe Aunt Rita gave him a key. Or maybe Mother let him in."

"At midnight?" Annie asked.

"Midnight?" Rachel's voice was thin. "Was that when —" She broke off, stared at the floor.

Garrett looked at her sharply. "Where were you at midnight?"

Rachel blinked. Her pale face was blank. "Midnight? I was in bed."

Garrett said nothing, simply waited. His manner remained courteous, but his bright blue eyes were skeptical.

The silence expanded. Annie tried to keep her

own face blank, but she was afraid that Rachel was lying.

Rachel's eyes moved uneasily around the room, but she wasn't looking at them. She was figuring and thinking — and scared.

"I see." Garrett's tone was neutral. His eyes dropped to his notes. "About the sweater Mr. Laurance saw . . . do you have a blue sweater?"

"No." She sounded puzzled. "Maybe it was someone else's sweater."

Garrett closed his notebook. "Thank you for your cooperation, Miss Laurance —"

"Van Meer," Rachel interrupted. "I'm Rachel Van Meer. Pudge is my stepfather."

Garrett opened his notebook, wrote swiftly. "We will take a formal statement later."

He was turning to go when brisk steps sounded in the hallway.

Billy Cameron poked his head inside. "Captain, we got the search warrant and started on the Laurance room. You'd better come."

As Garrett and Billy headed for the stairs, Rachel whispered, "What do they mean? Are they talking about Pudge's room?"

Annie felt her heart thud. She nodded and headed for the stairs. If Garrett saw them, he'd send them away. She looked over her shoulder, held a finger to her lips, moved softly down the steps, Rachel and Max behind her.

The second-floor hallway was empty. The door to Pudge's room was open. Easing across the hall, she peered inside.

There was nothing remarkable about the furnishings, a guest room for a man, twin beds with brown and black plaid spreads and matching drapes, a plain mahogany dresser, television, bookcase, adjoining bath. The open closet door revealed a half dozen hangers with shirts and slacks. Annie's gaze stopped at the open suitcase on the bed.

Garrett bent close to the suitcase.

Billy concluded, "I came for you as soon as I opened it."

"Get pictures, Billy. Tag the suitcase and the coat. Send it all to the lab." Garrett stepped back from the bed, his eyes still on the open suitcase. "That's what the murderer wore."

Bunched inside the suitcase was a yellow slicker, its surface mottled with dried blood, streaks and splotches of dark maroon.

Fingers clamped onto Annie's arm. "That's my raincoat. That's mine!"

Garrett jerked around at Rachel's piercing whisper. Irritation tightened the lines around his eyes and mouth until he looked at Rachel.

Rachel held on to Annie for support. She wavered on her feet, her face ashen.

"Get her out of here. Go back upstairs, all of you. Wait in that theater." Garrett was on his way to the door.

Annie grabbed Rachel, turned her away. She and Max supported Rachel between them as they slowly climbed the steps. On the third floor, Rachel stopped. "I don't want to go up there. I hate that place."

"We can wait in your room," Annie said quickly. She glanced at Max, but his head was turned as he looked down the stairs and listened.

Rachel leaned against the wall. She sucked in deep breaths and her color improved. "How did he get my raincoat?" She looked like a terrified colt, her eyes huge and staring. "My raincoat. It makes it look like I killed Mom." Her voice shook.

Annie reached out, grabbed her hand.

Max turned from the stairwell, though he still had a listening look. "Where do you keep your raincoat?"

Some of the panic eased out of Rachel's eyes. "Downstairs, in a closet off the main entrance. Everybody keeps their coats and stuff there. Sure. Anybody could have gotten it. He could have snuck in there and got my slicker."

Annie was having a hard time picturing Dr. Emory Swanson stealthily pilfering a raincoat, then slipping up the stairs to Happy's room. What did he say to Happy when he walked in on a chilly but dry December night carrying a bright yellow rain slicker? If he (or anyone else) brought the slicker, that argued premeditation. A poker grabbed up in haste suggested an argument ending in unplanned violence. But the bloody slicker had to be explained.

Was the sweater stained? Annie didn't like the question, but she couldn't ignore it. There had to be an urgent reason for Pudge to carry the sweater away. Was it really a sweater he was trying to hide? Was that a lie and had he grabbed up the raincoat? But if he ran with the poker and the afghan, why put the raincoat in his suitcase?

Clearly, Pudge had feared that Rachel was the murderer. Rachel could be guilty. There was no doubt that Rachel was distraught, but Rachel surely would be distraught if she'd argued with her mother and lost control and snatched up a poker and battered her to death. But if the killer wore the raincoat, the murder had to have been planned. Annie could understand a sudden fury, a loss of control, but she could not imagine Rachel as a careful, conniving, cold-blooded killer.

It seemed to Annie that everything hinged on the raincoat.

Or had Pudge told the truth and Rachel lied? Did she have a blue sweater? Could that be proved? Could she have worn the raincoat and this morning hidden it in Pudge's suitcase? But Rachel would never endanger Pudge. Would she?

Annie looked at Rachel, huddled against the wall, her face gray, her eyes pools of misery. Annie's heart ached. She reached out a hand, but before she could speak, Max moved swiftly toward Rachel.

"Is there another way downstairs?" He spoke softly. "Besides the main stairs? I want to see what Garrett's going to do."

Rachel pointed down the long hallway. "There are back stairs that go down to the kitchen. Come on, I'll show you."

As they passed closed doors, Rachel murmured, "That's Wayne's room. The first one on the right. The next one is a guest bedroom where Donna's staying. Those big double doors" — she pointed to her left — "are Aunt Rita's rooms. Alice is next to her."

At the end of the hall, she opened a door to uncarpeted stairs. They clattered down into a service porch. Rachel opened the door into a long, bright kitchen that smelled of good strong coffee and fresh pastries. Rachel led them across the kitchen into a breakfast room.

Max looked toward an archway into the huge reception area. "We can go through there to the main hall, can't we?"

"Sure." But Rachel had taken only a couple of steps when Chief Garrett strode purposefully through the far end of the reception area.

"He's going to the terrace room," Rachel whispered. "Come this way. We can go through the jungle." Rachel darted up a path between huge banana plants.

Annie followed, squinting in the dimness. A shrill scream sounded near her shoulder. Annie jerked her head and looked into currant-dark eyes. Cobalt blue and crimson feathers bristled as the parrot flapped its wings. The bird made no effort to fly. A tether was hooked on one orange leg.

"Shh, Godfrey." Rachel waved her hand at him. "We're almost there," she whispered to Annie and Max. She moved ahead. Moisture clung to ferns and fronds. The smell of dirt mingled with the heavy scent of sweet blossoms. They reached the north end of the terrace room just as Chief

Garrett came through the archway from the reception room.

Donna whirled from a window to glare at Garrett. Her fox-sharp face looked old and raddled. "Officer, I demand to be released from this absurd detention. I have no idea what happened this morning, but I am definitely not involved. I am willing to give a statement, but I refuse to be treated like a common criminal."

Terry came to his feet. "My sister damn well has a point, man. What's going on here? I haven't even had breakfast."

Alice sped toward Garrett. "Miss Dumaney must be seen to. I must go to her."

Joan brushed a hand through her wispy gray hair. "I have no experience in police matters, but it does appear that this investigation lacks direction."

Only Wayne remained calm, slouched on a wicker divan, arms folded behind his head, feet crossed. He watched with cool detachment.

Garrett ignored them. He walked directly to the bar, where Pudge sat on a red leather-topped stool, his elbow propped on the bar, his chin in his hand. In the mirror, his face looked old, deep lines splaying from sunken eyes and tight lips.

"Mr. Laurance." Garrett was staring into the mirror. "I'm taking you into custody. I'll ask you to come with me." Garrett jerked his head toward the archway.

Pudge blinked in surprise. "Me? Why? I've told you everything I know."

Max squeezed Annie's arm. "I'd better go with them and get in touch with Johnny Joe."

Garrett was brisk. "Interfering with an investigation, tampering with evidence, giving false information. That's enough for a start, Mr. Laurance. When you are represented by counsel, we will have a formal interrogation. Come this way."

Pudge called out, "Rachel —"

"That's enough," Garrett said sharply.

Pudge ignored Garrett. "Annie, take care of Rachel."

"Let's go, Mr. Laurance." Once again Garrett's hand rested on his holster.

Pudge shrugged and turned to leave.

Fear swept Annie, making it hard to breathe. Pudge didn't know about the bloody raincoat found in his suitcase. That was why Garrett was taking him into custody. There was simply too much involving Pudge: the missing weapon, his flight in the rowboat, his quarrels with Happy, his confession. The police would test his clothes and find traces of Happy's blood on his slacks. There was fact after damning fact.

In Pudge's defense, what could be said? He was trying to protect Rachel so he grabbed up a bloody poker and ran with it. As for the quarrels with Happy, would he admit they were on Rachel's behalf? Annie was afraid he wouldn't. If he refused to explain, the police would draw their own conclusions. As for his confession, he'd admitted it was false, and obviously — at least to

Annie — he'd had no idea that Happy's death occurred hours before he entered her room. That, in the eyes of the police, could be seen as a clever bluff.

Garrett paused in the archway. "Ladies and gentlemen, I regret the inconvenience to the household. I will appreciate your further cooperation. Each of you will be interviewed as soon as possible by Officer Cameron. Until then, it will be necessary for everyone to remain here."

Annie carried the tray down the crushed-oyster-shell path. It was such a relief to be out of the house with its strained silences and restless occupants. After Billy Cameron completed the interviews, the members of the Ladson family wandered aimlessly, avoiding solitude. Marguerite, finally attended by Alice, remained sequestered in her quarters.

Rachel waited on the sunny gazebo steps, chin on her knees, arms wrapped around her legs. It was one of the island's sparkling December days, the temperature right at sixty, the chalk-blue sky crisp as freshly starched oxford cloth.

Annie dropped down beside Rachel, put the tray between them. The wooden step held a faint warmth from the thin sunshine. Annie unwrapped ham sandwiches, opened a two-sided plastic container with apple slices and wedges of Gouda.

Rachel didn't look at the food.

Annie understood, but Rachel needed to eat.

Annie unwrapped two big dill pickles and unsnapped a cup filled to the brim with yogurt-covered raisins. Annie rattled the raisins. "The cook said you love these. She said you like mustard, not mayonnaise, on your sandwich, and rye bread. And spicy chips. She fixed a thermos of hot chocolate." Annie held out a blue plastic plate and a napkin. "Here, Rachel, she went to a lot of effort."

Rachel sat up straight and took the plate and napkin. "Sookie's nice." She poured a mound of the white candied fruit beside the sandwich.

"Sookie?" Annie took a big bite of her sandwich. She was ravenous. Breakfast seemed several eons past.

Absently, Rachel popped a half dozen of the raisins in her mouth. "Sue Kay. But Pam calls her Sookie. Pam's her daughter. She's a cheerleader and a merit scholar. On the weekends, she works in the kitchen at Parotti's. She wants to be a chef. A famous chef. She's going to go to a culinary school."

Annie leaned back against the step, enjoying the sun and the warmth, the food and the faint touches of color in Rachel's face. Annie wished they could keep on talking about Sookie and Pam and cooking school. The easy conversation built a cocoon of normalcy and Rachel slowly began to eat.

By the time Annie poured them each a cup of hot chocolate, Rachel had finished her sandwich and was rolling out the last few raisins on her palm.

Rachel broke the spell. She neatly folded her napkin, placed it and the plate on the tray. She pushed against her temple as if her head ached. "Annie, when will Pudge come home?"

The onshore breeze was freshening. The glossy leaves in a nearby magnolia rattled like hurried footsteps. Spanish moss in the live oaks swayed. In the inlet, Terry's big cabin cruiser rose and fell. Far out in the channel, three motorboats spaced about twenty yards apart moved slowly in apparent concert. One paused and a man in back pulled up a net, scanned the contents, tossed it back again.

At the Dumaney dock, the rowboat was gone but Annie and Max's motorboat was still tied to the dock. Annie realized Max must have ridden with Pudge and that she could take the boat home and get a car. She realized, too, that the missing rowboat had likely been taken by the police for examination. Would there be traces of Happy's blood in the boat? Quite possibly, and that would be another fact lined up against Pudge.

"Annie?" Rachel's tone was puzzled. "Pudge'll be home pretty soon, won't he?"

"That depends." Annie tried to sound reassuring. "Captain Garrett will want to know where Pudge threw that stuff away." And more, much more.

"Oh." Rachel looked puzzled. "But that's not the main thing. When will he arrest that man?"

Annie didn't have any trouble following Rachel's thoughts. No wonder Rachel appeared relaxed. She thought the murder was solved when she told Garrett about Swanson, and she obviously had no idea of Pudge's real situation.

"Annie." Rachel leaned forward, frowning. "What's wrong?"

"Rachel, I'm sure Chief Garrett will find out what he can about Dr. Swanson." Annie put her napkin and plate on the tray. "He'll check to see if Swanson has an alibi —"

Rachel burst out, "He won't. He can't. He killed Mom."

"— but the police have to have proof." Yes, there would have to be proof and an explanation for the raincoat and some kind of link established between Happy Laurance and Emory Swanson.

"Wait a minute." Rachel's tone was hot. She jumped to her feet. "Do you mean the police still think it was Pudge? Because he threw that stuff away and that raincoat was in his room?"

Rachel was just a kid, a kid who'd lost her mother in a shocking, brutal way, but she was too smart to lie to. Annie didn't try. "I'm afraid so, honey." She lifted the tray and stood. "Don't worry, Rachel. Max is with Pudge. And I'm going to see what I can find out. Will you be okay if I leave for a while?" Annie looked doubtfully toward the house.

Rachel looked surprised. "Sure." Her voice was patient, as one explaining the obvious. "That man's not here."

Annie hesitated. Although it would be a swell solution for everyone at the Dumaney house,

Annie had no real belief in Emory Swanson as a stealthy, slicker-garbed murderer. Pudge had told Annie to take care of Rachel. Obviously, he thought someone at the Dumaney house had killed Happy. Was it foolish to go away and leave Rachel alone? "I don't know," Annie said doubtfully.

Rachel stared out at the boats. "I guess they have to keep looking. But that's not what matters. We've got to find the papers. I've got to figure out where Mom put them."

"You're sure —" Annie began.

Rachel nodded vehemently. "Mom said she had papers that would keep him from getting Aunt Rita's money." Her forehead crinkled. "Mom must have known something really bad about him."

Annie didn't doubt there might be bad things to know about Emory Swanson, who had prospered by bilking the credulous. But how could Happy Laurance have obtained that kind of information? She didn't seem the kind of person to hire a private detective. A careful study of her checkbook might answer that question. Annie wondered if Chief Garrett had taken any of Happy's personal papers with him.

Annie looked up at the house, the huge house with so many rooms and so many places papers could be kept. Or hidden. "Where did your mom keep her checkbook, things like that?"

Rachel said uncertainly, "I think in the desk in the library. I'll go see." She was poised to rush up the path.

Annie gripped her arm. “Wait, Rachel. You and I can look together when I get back. Why don’t you go up to your room and write down everything you can remember about yesterday and what your mom said and did. That would be the best help.”

Rachel thought it over. “Then we’ll look together for the papers?”

Annie thought the possibility of finding Happy’s “papers” was about as likely as Chief Garrett releasing Pudge.

“That’s what we’ll do.” Annie turned to go.

Rachel called after her, “What are you going to do? Check up on that man?”

“I’ll see what I can find out.” Annie waved and hurried toward the dock. There was no way she would tell Rachel her true plan.

# Seventeen

Max deliberately chose a chair in the corner of the conference room. He sat very quietly, knowing he was there on sufferance. Johnny Joe Jenkins made no objection because Pudge had insisted that Max be permitted to remain while Garrett interrogated him. Garrett didn't care as long as he got answers and as long as those answers were captured on tape. Bright spotlights beamed from either side of the videocam stand.

The bright lights illuminated every line, every crease in Pudge's face, every gray strand in his blond hair and mustache. Whether from the harsh lighting or fatigue, Pudge's skin looked as pasty and shiny as bread dough. Even though the room was cool, tiny beads of sweat clung to his forehead. He sat stiffly on a yellow oak straight chair, his body still, his gray eyes alert and wary. Beside him, Johnny Joe Jenkins folded his arms, his strong face impassive. Across the narrow conference table, a loose-leaf notebook open before him, sat Garrett.

Max listened as Garrett punched on the videocam and repeated the Miranda warning. "Mr. Laurance, I'd like to get a little background here. Give me your name, residence and relationship to the deceased."

"Patrick Laurance, most recently living in Puerto Vallarta, former husband." He seemed to relax a little against the chair back.

"You arrived here when? And for what purpose?"

"Last weekend. On Saturday. Happy invited me to spend Christmas with them. But I actually came because I wanted to find my daughter." He looked toward Max for an instant. "When Happy called, she was upset. She wasn't really specific about the problem, but it was something to do with her sister and this psychic business. I didn't see that I could help, but I was eager to visit the island, so I agreed to come."

"Did Mrs. Laurance tell you she had papers containing information about Dr. Swanson that could discredit him?" Garrett's hand was poised over his notebook.

Pudge looked surprised. "Papers? No, she didn't say anything about papers. I don't remember exactly what she said, but she went on and on about how awful it was, that Swanson was a crook and he was taking advantage of Rita. Happy was really upset after the dinner Wednesday night when Rita said she was going to sign over everything to Swanson for some kind of Golden Path. I didn't quite get it, but Rita thinks she's communicating with her dead husband through this Swanson fellow. She's decided to give him money to create some kind of psychic foundation. As a matter of fact, the whole family was livid."

"Did your former wife tell you what she intended to do about Dr. Swanson?"

"Do?" Pudge tugged at his mustache. "What could she do about it?"

"That's what I'm asking you, Mr. Laurance."

Pudge ran his fingers through his hair. "I don't know."

"What conversation did you have with Mrs. Laurance on Thursday?"

"I — I don't exactly remember."

Garrett flipped through the pages. "I have an eyewitness who said, 'Happy and Pudge were yelling at each other. I didn't hear a lot of it. I walked on, but she was crying and he told her he'd had enough and he was getting out and he stormed up the stairs.' "

Johnny Joe Jenkins leaned close to Pudge, murmured in his ear.

Pudge shook his head.

The only sound in the windowless interior room was the whir of the videocam.

Pudge clamped his hands on the edge of the table.

"What were you quarreling about, Mr. Laurance?"

"It wasn't a quarrel. She was acting like an idiot. That's all. I told her so."

"You went upstairs and packed?"

"Yes."

"But you didn't leave. Why not?"

"I changed my mind." Pudge's lips closed tight.

"Why?"

Pudge didn't answer.

"When did you next talk to Mrs. Laurance?"

"I didn't."

"That was the last time you spoke with her?" Garrett's voice was heavy with disbelief.

"That's right. I didn't see her again until I found her body this morning." Pudge's blank look splintered for an instant, his face creasing with pain and remembered horror.

"Tell me about this morning, Mr. Laurance."

Pudge moved restively. "I've told you."

"I'd like to hear it again, Mr. Laurance. Start from the first. What time did you get up?"

"Around seven-thirty. I shaved and showered —"

"You showered?"

"Yes." Pudge's eyes darkened with anger.

Garrett made a note. "You dressed? Can you give me a list of the clothing you brought to the island?"

"I can. I sure as hell can. Two pairs of khakis —"

Max liked Pudge's combative tone. He got it, of course. Garrett was trying to make him account for his clothes. But if Pudge had killed his ex-wife, he would simply leave something out. Garrett would talk to others at the house, get a description of what Pudge had worn each day. If any outfit was missing, it would be indirect evidence against Pudge.

"— four sports shirts, two sweaters, a navy suit, black loafers" — Pudge pointed down to his shoes — "a sweatshirt, sweat pants, jogging shoes, two pairs of white socks, two pairs of black socks, four T-shirts, four pairs of boxer shorts, blue cotton pajamas. And that's all. You'll find every piece of it in my room."

"In your suitcase?" Garrett watched him closely.

Pudge was completely relaxed. "Right. Take a look."

"We have, Mr. Laurance. We found the yellow raincoat."

Pudge was still relaxed. "I don't have a yellow raincoat. Or an umbrella." His lips curved in a small smile. "I guess I'm of the old school. Men don't carry umbrellas. I figured out I wouldn't melt a long time ago."

There was no answering smile from Garrett. But his eyes were puzzled.

Max felt like jumping to his feet and shouting hooray.

Garrett pushed back his chair. "I'll be right back."

As the door clicked behind him, Pudge turned toward Max. "What's the big deal about a yellow raincoat?"

The soft hum of the videocam continued.

Johnny Joe looked at Max, too.

Max diverted them. "Johnny Joe, can you see about getting bail set?"

"Sure." His mellifluous courtroom voice filled the small gray-walled room, added life and color. "As soon as we get finished here, I'll pop over to see the judge." He grinned approvingly at Pudge. "You're doing fine."

The door squeaked open. Garrett stepped inside, carrying a blue soft-sided Pullman-size suitcase. His hands were encased in plastic gloves. A white tag dangled from one handle. He set the case on the table.

"Can you identify this suitcase, Mr. Laurance?"

Pudge craned his head. He pointed at a metal nameplate dangling from a leather strap. "Sure. See, there's my name. It's mine."

Garrett stood beside the table. He leaned over and carefully unzipped the case. He lifted the lid.

Pudge jerked back from the table. His eyes widened. He stared at the crumpled yellow slicker with its dark maroon stains. "My God, that's awful." He stared at the bloody plastic in horror. "That's not mine. I didn't put that in my suitcase. Somebody else did."

"Who, Mr. Laurance?"

Pudge glared at Garrett. "How should I know? How the hell should I know? I never saw that in my life."

Garrett folded his arms across his chest. "You don't recognize the raincoat?"

"No."

"Would it surprise you to learn that this raincoat belongs to your stepdaughter?"

Pudge froze. The anger fell away as quickly as the sun sets in a tropical sea, there one instant, gone the next. "Who says so?"

"She does."

Pudge said nothing.

Garrett bent forward. "Isn't it true, Mr. Laurance, that you found this raincoat, recognized it and took it from Mrs. Laurance's room?"

"No." Pudge stared at the open suitcase.

"There was no sweater, was there, Mr. Laurance?"

"I saw a sweater. I thought it was Rachel's. I must have been wrong."

"What did you take from that room, Mr. Laurance?"

Pudge rubbed his eyes. "The sweater." His voice was stubborn. "And the poker. I wrapped them in an afghan."

"You took a poker?"

"Yes."

"What poker, Mr. Laurance?"

Pudge shook his head irritably. "There was a poker lying there. It was" — he swallowed — "covered with blood."

"There is no poker missing from that fireplace."

"Then somebody brought it from somewhere else."

"We've checked all the fireplaces, Mr. Laurance. The fire tools at each fireplace are complete."

Pudge stared straight ahead. "All I know is what I saw. I don't know anything about the poker or where it came from."

"Or anything about this raincoat?" Garrett pointed at the opened suitcase.

"I've never seen that raincoat. Never."

Garrett leaned over the table, closed the case, zipped it. He still wore the plastic gloves. He picked up the suitcase. "I'll be right back."

The door closed behind him.

Pudge turned quickly to Max. "Is he telling the truth? Is that Rachel's raincoat?"

"She said it was. But she was as shocked as you are, Pudge."

"I don't understand. I packed up Wednesday night and I was living out of my suitcase. I didn't unpack."

Max nodded. Johnny Joe listened intently.

"This morning I got out my shaving kit. I left the case open on one of the beds when I went down the hall to Happy's room. I don't see how that raincoat got in my suitcase. Or when. It sure wasn't in Happy's room this morning."

Max punched a fist against his palm. "That means the raincoat was taken from the room after Happy was killed. It must have been hidden somewhere else. Sometime this morning, somebody put it in your suitcase. That gives us a couple of things to look for: the first hiding place for the raincoat and who had access to your room between the time you left in the boat and Garrett brought you upstairs."

But Pudge was staring at the table, his face creased in thought.

That was when the door opened and Garrett walked inside. He wasn't alone. Billy Cameron followed, cradling a spread-out black garbage bag.

"Put it on the table, Billy."

# Eighteen

"Thanks, Ingrid. If you'll take care of everything at the store . . . No. Nobody knows what happened." Annie reached out to stroke Dorothy L. as she rolled on her back on the kitchen counter next to the phone. "Apparently Happy was killed around midnight. No suspects yet." Except her father, but Annie wasn't going to put that into words. Of course, Rachel was convinced that Emory Swanson killed her mother. Annie rubbed behind Dorothy L.'s ears. Emory Swanson . . . "Listen, Ingrid, see what you and Duane can find out about Emory Swanson. There's a suggestion Happy Laurance knew something that would keep him from getting big bucks from Marguerite Dumaney. . . . Right. I'll check with you later."

Annie hung up the phone and scooped up the purring white cat. "Nobody knows more people than Ingrid and Duane." Ingrid not only worked at the bookstore, she and her husband, a retired newspaper editor, managed Nightingale Courts, a complex of rental cabins on the Sound. Annie nuzzled Dorothy L. "From little acorns . . ." she murmured. Who knew what might happen if a rumor swirled around the island that the murdered woman and Swanson were at odds?

Annie glanced around the kitchen, at the breakfast dishes still unwashed. Carrying Dorothy L. over her shoulder, she wandered to the kitchen table and picked up the rest of her sweet roll. Breakfast seemed eons ago. But she knew she was dallying. She didn't really want to do what had to be done. Would Rachel be furious? Oh yes, of course, if she learned of Annie's efforts.

Rachel. Pudge. They both mattered to her. She didn't want to choose between them. But she would not protect one at the expense of the other.

Frowning, Annie picked up the memo pad beside the phone and found a pen. She wrote fast, ripped off the sheet and propped it beside the phone.

It was only two blocks from the Broward's Rock Police Station to Parotti's Bar and Grill. Max walked fast. Pudge in jail. Garrett on his way back to the Dumaney house. At the pay phone in front of Parotti's, Max plunked in the coins. He tried home. No answer. He left a message, then dialed Annie's cell phone. No answer.

"Damn." Max looked across the street. The island's one taxi was parked in front of the ferry boatdock. Its owner, Joe Bob Kelly, sat on the pier, legs dangling, holding a fishing pole. A good day for black drum or flounder. So, one problem solved. He could get a ride home and get his car. But Garrett was on his way to the Dumaney house. Max yanked up the phone, dropped his coins and called information. He was taking a lot on himself, but he felt there was no time to lose. If only Judge (ret.) Halladay was home. And if only Max could persuade him to take on a client, who needed help now. The operator came on the line. Max added fifty cents for the number to be dialed. A gruff voice answered and Max spoke urgently. "Judge Halladay . . ."

Two cars were at the pumps at Parotti's Gas'N'Go. Annie waited until both drivers had paid before stepping inside the convenience store. Sleigh bells jingled as the door closed.

Mike's eyes were startled, then eager. He came around the counter, hurried toward her. "Is Rachel all right? I can't get through to her. I called as soon as I got her message. But I had to come here after school."

Annie studied him, large dark eyes, regular features, dimpled chin. He was boy-next-door handsome. "She called you?"

"This morning. But I'd already left. I didn't pick up the message until I got here." He clenched his hands. "She was crying and she said somebody'd killed her mom and everything was awful, but I should wait to hear from her. I've been trying to get somebody to take over for me, but it's Christmas. Everybody's busy. I get off at five. I'll go over." He rubbed his face. "I guess I can't go to the house. Could you ask her to meet me at the gazebo?"

Annie said offhandedly, "Is that where you met last night? Before you went up to Rachel's room?"

He blinked in surprise. "Did she tell you? I thought —" He broke off.

"That she wanted you not to tell anyone?" Annie was sure that had been part of Rachel's message to Mike. "But" — and she kept her voice matter-of-fact — "we need to figure out if you saw anything last night that could help."

"Last night?" He sounded puzzled. "Why . . . ?" He stared at her. "Was that when it happened?" His voice was hushed.

"Yes. So it's important to know whether you saw anyone around the house. Or if a boat came up to the dock or if there was a strange car parked near the drive." Or if, still angry, you stopped by Happy's room when you left the house last night. But that was a question that belonged to Chief Garrett.

Mike frowned, jammed his hands into his jeans pockets. "I was on my bike. I came on the bike trails and the golf cart path. I was never near the front of the house."

"Why don't you tell me what happened from the time you arrived." Come into my parlor . . . "You might remember something that would help."

The sleigh bells jangled. Mike looked past her. His face lightened. "Hey, Jimmy, listen, man, could you take over here for me for a few minutes? Just long enough so I can" — he looked through the plate glass — "check this lady's car for her?"

Jimmy was stork-tall with arms that dangled to

his knees and a long face that looked patient and equable. "Sure, Mike."

"Thanks, Jimmy. I'll be right back."

Annie followed Mike outside.

"Why don't you pop the hood," he suggested.

Annie slid into the driver's seat, pulled the lever.

Mike lifted the hood and she joined him.

Crows cawed, hopping along the road. Annie spoke over their raucous cries. "What time did you get to the house last night?"

"I didn't get off work until ten. I went home for a sandwich, then I rode my bike over." He unscrewed the oil cap. "It was probably around eleven."

"Was Rachel waiting at the gazebo?"

Mike used the dipstick, replaced the cap. "Yes. We sat there for a few minutes, but it was pretty cold, so we decided to go up to her room." He avoided Annie's eyes.

Annie wasn't interested in romantic interludes. She said briskly, "Before you went in the house, did you see anyone in the garden?"

Mike rubbed his face. "It was real dark last night. No moonlight. We didn't see anyone, but I thought I saw a light near the maze. Maybe it was just headlights in the lane. Rachel said nobody'd be coming out of the house this late. We ducked down on the floor of the gazebo." He frowned. "I was almost sure I saw a light, but I didn't hear a car. Maybe it had stopped. Anyway, we waited a few minutes, then we went up to the house. Rachel said nobody would come to her room. So we snuck up on the grass. We didn't walk on the path because the shells make too much noise. When we got in the house, I thought I heard somebody ahead of us in that big room. We listened, but nothing happened, so we hurried through that room and up the stairs."

"Was everything quiet on the second floor?" The floor where Happy died. The door to her room was not more than twenty feet from the stairs. Annie watched his face and wondered at the odd light in his dark eyes.

"Yeah." He spoke in a whisper. "Rachel pointed at her mom's room and told me to be quiet. There was a light under her door. She said her mom must still be up. We tiptoed up the stairs."

So Mike knew which room belonged to Happy.

"Did you hear any noises when you were in Rachel's room?" The house was huge and well built. But how could a woman be battered to death and no one hear any sound of struggle or call for help? If the first blow was unexpected and brutal enough, Happy might have fallen without a cry. The only sound would have been the weapon striking bone and flesh. Annie did not want to imagine that sound.

Mike's shoulders hunched. "Nothing. We didn't hear a thing. We had on some music."

"Did Rachel come downstairs with you when you left?"

He shook his head. "No. I know my way out."

Annie guessed this wasn't the first evening he'd ridden his bike through the darkness and met Rachel in the gazebo and crept up the stairs to her room. But that could also be a question for Chief Garrett.

"How about Happy's room? Was there still a light under the door?"

Mike jammed his hands into the pockets of his jeans. "I don't know. I didn't look."

A young man stealing down a staircase after an illicit visit to a girl's room would surely check the door to her mother's room. If for no other reason, to be sure the door remained shut. What if that door had opened?

There were other questions that could be asked, but not now and not by Annie. What had he worn last night? Could he produce those clothes? "When you got outside, did you see anyone? Hear anything?"

He shook his head. "I ducked off the path and ran down to the gazebo. I'd left my bike there. I got on it and rode home. I didn't see anybody."

Judge Halladay lifted grizzled silver brows. "Most irregular." He made no move to open the car door. "No mother or father." His big shoulders heaved impatiently and he lifted a massive hand. "All right. I remember. I'm not in my dotage. Stepfather's in jail. The girl's your wife's younger sister. So you're the brother-in-law." His cold brown eyes scanned Max. "I've seen you at the club." The judge was a scratch golfer. "You're pretty good. Well, let's get on with it. No need to sit here all day." He opened the car door, pulled himself out. He'd topped six feet five inches in his youth. Now he bent forward, moved like an old but still powerful bear, wisps of white hair falling over a broad, mottled forehead, small wire glasses perched on a bulbous nose, a wiry beard fluffing from his heavy jaws.

Max hurried to keep up. The judge was irascible and unpredictable, but if he committed to a client, he was unstoppable. The judge ignored the whale fountain and the dragon's head poking out of the fake cave. Max thought that after half a lifetime on the bench, nothing surprised him. Or amused him.

This afternoon the glass bubbles on the front door were dark. Max pulled the silver chain.

The judge looked at the curving drive with brooding eyes. "Police chief's car," he observed.

"Yes. That's why I hurried. He's here to talk to Rachel. I hope we're in time." Max impatiently jerked the chain again.

The Broward's Rock Police Department was in a pastel building with a great view of the small harbor. Annie jolted to a stop and slammed out of her car. She scanned the parking lot. It held one police cruiser and the small Honda that belonged to Mavis Cameron, Billy's wife and the station dispatcher and chief clerk.

Annie pushed in the door and smiled at Mavis. They'd met years ago when Mavis had fled to the island to escape an abusive marriage. She and Billy had since married.

Mavis looked up and her kind brown eyes were worried. She didn't smile.

Annie understood. "My dad's here?"

Mavis nodded. "He's talking to his lawyer."

"How about Max?" Annie peered down the corridor. It was hard to miss Max's voice.

"He just left." Mavis beckoned to Annie.

When she reached the counter, Mavis whispered, "He went to get a lawyer for that girl. Annie, you'd better hurry back there." She paused, bit her lip, then said unhappily, "That's all I can say."

# Nineteen

The Volvo squealed into the Dumaney drive. Annie jolted to a stop behind Max's crimson Ferrari and realized he'd reached home and retrieved his car. She slammed out of her car and ran up the wide, shallow steps. As she pulled the chain, she tried the knob. She was in no mood to wait.

The door was unlocked. As she stepped inside, Max hurried toward her down the hall. "Did you get my message?"

She shook her head. "No, what's happened?"

"Bad stuff." His dark blue eyes were dark with worry. "Garrett's in there" — he jerked his head toward a closed door — "with Rachel. I brought Judge Halladay out to represent her. Thank God the old warhorse was curious. I guess he's bored and this is a little bit of entertainment. He's got about as much warmth as a swarm of piranhas, but he's a canny old devil and he'll protect Rachel."

Annie took a step toward the door, chin high. "Is she in there by herself with the chief and the judge?"

Max grabbed her arm. "Better not. No. Her aunt's with her."

Annie's eyes blazed. "Dammit, she doesn't like Marguerite."

"Garrett insisted. He wouldn't let me stay. But at least Marguerite agreed to have the judge there for Rachel."

The long, dark hallway was cold, but Annie knew the iciness that seeped through her was deeper than the chill of the hallway. Max hadn't rousted the judge out of his home and persuaded him to represent Rachel without good reason.

Or a bad reason.

"Max, why is Garrett questioning Rachel?" Garrett couldn't possibly know of Rachel and Mike's meeting.

"It doesn't look good. You see, they found the afghan that Pudge threw into the Sound —"

Footsteps clipped in the hallway. Alice Schiller, her face drawn and tired, walked swiftly toward them. She looked at each in turn. "What's going on? I saw the police car. Wayne said they asked to see Rachel. And I can't find Marguerite."

Max pointed at the closed door. "The police chief is questioning Rachel. Marguerite's in there with them. Judge Halladay's here for Rachel."

"Garrett's questioning Rachel?" Her voice was sharp.

Annie remembered that it was Alice who had thought of Rachel when no one else had, Alice who sent Annie up to be with the stricken girl.

"That's ridiculous." Alice turned toward the door.

Max said quickly, "He won't let you in."

Alice glared at him. "Why Rachel? That's absurd. I'll tell him so."

He spread his hands. "Alice, you said you saw Pudge this morning carrying an afghan out of Happy's room."

Her dark eyes turned accusingly to Annie. "I didn't tell anyone. I told you I wouldn't."

"Pudge told the police himself. That's all right. But" — Max shook his head — "Pudge told them he found the weapon, a poker, and wrapped it up in the afghan and threw it all in the Sound. They pulled the afghan up and brought it to the station. I was there. Billy Cameron put it on the table, the afghan sopping wet." Max looked at Annie. "Pudge slumped down in his chair because he knew what they would find. When they unwrapped the afghan, it wasn't a poker. It was a field hockey stick. Rachel's field hockey stick."

"Oh my God," Alice moaned. She buried her face in her hands.

Annie stared at the older woman, the woman who cared about Rachel. Tentatively, she reached out to touch Alice's shoulder. Annie's fingers tingled with shock. Alice was not sobbing. Her body was rigid, stiff and hard with anger. She dropped her hands, looked at them with bright, hot eyes. "We've got to do something. Anyone could have gotten that stick. Anyone."

Max stared at the closed door. "I wish we knew what was happening."

"Oh, we can do that. Follow me and keep very

quiet." She took a half dozen steps and yanked open a door. She snapped on a light and stepped into a long, narrow coat closet. "Close the door behind you," she whispered. She stopped at the cedar wall at the end of the closet. Reaching up, she pushed on a portion of the top left wall. Slowly, the wall began to move. She gestured for Annie and Max to step past her. The narrow passageway, just wide enough for one person, smelled musty.

"What is this?" Annie whispered.

Alice reached up, pulled a chain. Every ten feet or so, a single light bulb glowed in a socket on the low ceiling. In the harsh light, a brief smile flickered on her worn face. "You have to remember that this place was Claude's dream house. It's honeycombed with secret passageways. Go straight ahead for about twenty feet. Step quietly." Alice pulled the closet panel shut.

Annie didn't like the low ceiling, the constricting walls. This was not her idea of fun. The passageway was probably considered a top location by neighborhood rats and brown recluse spiders. She eased gingerly forward, sweat oozing on her palms.

"Here." The whisper was as light as a spider touch.

Annie wanted to clutch Max's hand, but, hey, she was a big girl. He eased an arm around her shoulders. She gave him a tight smile.

Alice bent close to them. "Lights off now." She pulled a chain and they stood in utter darkness.

Annie's skin crawled. Black pressed against her eyes.

Slowly, a line of light appeared. Alice's hand preceded the light, opening a thin aperture, perhaps a quarter inch wide and a foot long, that provided a view of a narrow portion of the library. Chief Garrett sat on the near side of a long mahogany table. The back of his neck was red and his shoulders were rigid. Opposite him, facing the passageway, were Rachel and the judge. Rachel looked small in her oversize red-and-green striped T-shirt. She sat with her knees to her chin, her arms tightly clasped around her legs. Sullen anger boiled in her dark eyes. Her pale face was set and hard. Only the quiver of her lips revealed her fear.

Annie held tight to Max's arm to keep from erupting. She wanted to burst into that room, snatch Rachel away from Garrett.

The aperture cut off the judge's head and most of his body. An arm in a dark blue suit coat stretched on the table. The fingers of his ham-size hand splayed open, a ruby glowing in a thick gold ring. The body language proclaimed total confidence.

At the far right edge of the opening, the toe of a black slipper tapped impatiently, the only evidence of Marguerite Dumaney's presence.

The view was constricted, but they could hear every word.

The judge's voice, deep and calm, was as overpowering and relentless as the Mississippi rolling to the delta. "My client has answered fully and with candor. There is no point in repeating questions." Once upon a time, he would have said, "The bench won't tolerate browbeating of the witness." The effect was the same.

Garrett bit off his words. "Yes, sir. I do have questions on a different topic."

"Proceed." A deep throat-clearing. The huge arm and hand remained relaxed.

Rachel's eyes flared. Her fingers laced together.

The black slipper stretched forward. Marguerite's silksheathed ankle was trim and attractive.

Garrett tapped his pen on the table. "Miss Van Meer, tell me a little about your school activities."

"School?" Rachel stared at him.

"Yes. What games do you play?" He opened his briefcase, pulled out a sheaf of photographs.

"I don't know what you mean." Rachel's fingers relaxed a little. "Video games?"

Garrett wasn't old, but he wasn't a kid. "No. Outside. Athletic games."

"Oh, sports." Her tone was easy. "Tennis. Soccer. Field hockey."

"Do you have your own field hockey stick?"

The judge's arm moved as he leaned forward.

"Yes, I —"

"Just a moment, little lady. Chief, I'll ask you to lay some groundwork for your question." The deep voice brooked no disagreement.

"All right, Judge. I have photographs here of a field hockey stick and I would like for Miss Van Meer to tell me if it belongs to her."

"Surely you aren't asking this young lady to

admit ownership of any item merely through study of a photograph!" The full tone was shocked, indicating a regrettable lapse in judgment on Garrett's part.

Garrett thrust the photographs toward Rachel.

Rachel reached out, picked up the pictures. She stared at the first, her brows drawn in a tight frown. "That could be my stick, but it's all dirty. Where did you get it?"

"Please look at the third photograph, the close-up of the handle, and the inked initials." Now it was Garrett who sounded confident.

Rachel spread the pictures out, leaned over the third. "Why, that's —"

"A matter to be studied." The deep voice rolled over hers. "My client will decline to —"

Rachel exploded, "Where did you get my stick? Why is it all messed up?"

"Your stepfather didn't find a poker in your mother's room. This is what he threw into the Sound. Now you tell me" — and Garrett's voice was as hard as a steel-toed boot — "where you last had this hockey stick."

Rachel pushed back from the table, came to her feet. She looked down at the pictures and shuddered.

Judge Halladay caught her arm. "It's all right, little lady, you don't have to answer any more questions at this time."

Rachel ignored him. "My hockey stick." Tears trickled down her face. She whirled and ran to the door, opened it and plunged into the hall.

There was silence in the library. The judge heaved to his feet. His blue suit coat gaped, exposing the Phi Beta Kappa key dangling from his watch pocket. "I'll be conferring with my client." For a big man, he moved swiftly.

Marguerite Dumaney's rich voice rose over his. "Judge, I am shocked at what has occurred here. I have no doubt of my niece's innocence. All girls and mothers have moments of stress. That is simply natural." A red-brocaded arm came into view, hand outstretched, ruby-tipped nails glistening. "Chief Garrett, we are all suffering. I will ask you not to add to our troubles. Surely you can see that your suspicion of Rachel is absurd."

Garrett was on his feet, too. Even from the back, he looked satisfied. "I haven't suggested that Rachel is a suspect in her mother's murder. I simply asked where she left her field hockey stick. But perhaps you can explain to me about Rachel's disagreement with her mother."

Alice Schiller's hand moved and the pencil-thin view of the library disappeared. The lights in the narrow passageway blazed. She jerked her head. "Come on."

Annie wanted to protest. What was Marguerite going to say? Didn't Alice understand how damaging this might be to Rachel? But the slender woman was already moving up the passageway and a call to stop her might be heard in the library.

When they reached the main hallway, Annie saw the judge lumbering up the main steps. He would find Rachel. But for now, something needed to be done about Marguerite. Annie said hotly, "We should have stayed. We don't know what Marguerite's told him."

"I know." Alice's tone was impatient. "Come on, let's go out to the garden." She walked swiftly through the huge, untenanted reception room and out the door of the terrace room. "This way." She led them down a path that veered away from the main ellipse and ended at the maze. "There are benches in the center."

As they plunged between the tall walls of shrubbery, Annie wondered if Alice Schiller shared her mistress's talent for the dramatic. But at least the pungent scent of the evergreens was an improvement over the dead air of the secret passageway.

Alice stood by a marble bench. "We can't be seen from the house."

Annie moved restively. "I wish we knew what Marguerite said about Rachel and Happy."

Alice pivoted toward Annie, a hand outstretched. Her narrow, elegant face lifted, her dark eyes glowed. She was transformed from a prim-faced, negligible woman to an overpowering presence. "Poor, dear Rachel. A child struggling with the beginnings of passion. My sister was doing her best" — a freighted pause — "but youth can be so troubled. I know Rachel wishes she could call back, bury deep, those dreadful words of anger hurled at her mother. Yet you and I know" — a strand of auburn hair drooped over that compelling, still-lovely face as she bent close, her husky voice throbbing with sorrow — "that their quarrel can now never be ended." She held the pose for an instant, then straightened up, her face once again prim. "That's what she said." Alice's voice was once again thin and uninflected. "Or something on that order. Marguerite can't help herself."

Max frowned. "Doesn't she know what kind of damage she's doing to Rachel?"

Alice's lips quirked in a bitter smile. "Marguerite neither knows nor cares. But you both seem to care." Her level gaze was intense.

Annie didn't know how to answer. How could she explain the connection she felt to a girl she didn't know existed a week ago? How could she describe the emotions they'd experienced together since Rachel came storming into Death on Demand seeking the big sister she'd never had? "Rachel and I . . ." Annie turned her hands palms up. "I remember how hard it is," she said simply. "I remember. And she loves Pudge." Annie didn't add, *So do I,* but the words lodged in her heart.

"Your father," Alice said wearily, "is a damn fool. If he hadn't tried to get rid of the hockey stick, Rachel wouldn't be in this mess."

Max was abrupt. "How do you think the cops would have responded if they'd found the stick in Happy's room?"

Alice stuck her hands deep in the pockets of her pleated navy skirt. She stared at the dusty ground.

"Who," Max persisted, "would the police see as suspects? Especially as soon as they found out about Rachel's fight with her mother over Mike. As for Pudge, they may not know yet that he and Happy were wrangling over Rachel, but somebody will tell them —"

"Joan already has." Alice's tone was dry. "Joan looks innocuous, but she always manages to be on the periphery if anything unpleasant is happening. I think it's because she leads such a dreadfully boring life. Especially since she and Wayne divorced." She waved a hand impatiently. "None of that matters. What matters is that Rachel mustn't be accused of killing her mother. I know it didn't happen" — she spoke with utter assurance — "so we have to do something to protect her." Her tone was fierce.

Annie's heart ached for Rachel, but she didn't have Alice's apparently gut-level conviction of Rachel's innocence. And not simply because of the hockey stick. Because of Pudge. Had he run with the weapon because he foresaw the police response to a bloodied field hockey stick? Or did he run because he believed Rachel killed her mother in a moment of irrational anger and he wanted to protect her? If Annie knew the answer to those questions, she could be certain. Those answers would never come. Whatever Pudge believed, he would insist Rachel was innocent.

"Someone killed Happy." Max's voice was combative.

Nearby a barred owl hooted eight times, beginning his winter afternoon courtship song. The hoots were uncannily precise. In the shadows of the maze, the air was almost cold. Annie shivered and pushed away a memory of Rachel, her face puffed with anger. No, not Rachel. Not Rachel. But not Pudge, either. Right now, it looked odds on that one of them — if not both — soon would be charged with Happy's murder. There were no other suspects. Marguerite? She was the rich one, not Happy. Wayne Ladson? Donna Farrell? Terry Ladson? They had no connection to Happy. Her death couldn't benefit them in any way. Joan Ladson? She was a vacationing librarian who hadn't seen Happy in several years. Now, if Wayne's head had been bashed in . . . But it was Happy who died and only Rachel and Pudge appeared to have motives. And, of course, Mike, who claimed he'd not even glanced toward Happy's door last night. Annie almost spoke and didn't. What good would it do to throw Mike into the mix? The police might well charge both him and Rachel. Both might be innocent. Or guilty.

Annie clasped her hands tightly together. "The trouble is that there are no other suspects. None."

Max's eyes were bright and sharp. "What about Swanson? Rachel thinks he did it. What about him?"

"Dr. Swanson?" There was an odd tone in Alice's voice. "Rachel thinks he killed Happy?"

Annie quickly explained. ". . . and Happy told Rachel she had papers that could keep Swanson from getting Marguerite's money for his foundation."

"What kind of papers would endanger Dr.

Swanson's cause?" Alice looked puzzled.

"I have no idea," Annie admitted. "It seems impossible. I didn't get the impression Happy had any contact with the man other than here at the house. Maybe Happy learned something from someone in town."

"Gossip doesn't translate to papers," Max pointed out.

Alice paced in front of the marble bench. "Swanson. I don't like him. He's a bad man." The simple words evoked a dark and dangerous image. "I've warned and warned Marguerite against him, but she won't listen. She thinks he's wonderful. In fact" — and her finely boned face was tight with disgust — "she wants to have a séance tonight to see what we can find out about Happy's murder. I've been trying to talk her out of it. But maybe it's not such a bad idea."

"What good would that do?" Annie didn't try to keep the dismay from her voice. A séance! That would be terrible for Rachel.

"It would bring Swanson here." Alice was excited, determined. "If he killed Happy, it's the last place he'll want to come." She clapped her hands together. "I'll talk to Marguerite and let her think she's persuaded me."

"Swanson." Max didn't sound convinced. "How would Happy know anything that could block his plans with Marguerite?"

Annie understood his skepticism. Swanson was a slick customer, that was certain. There seemed little likelihood that Happy could have found concrete evidence of misdoing serious enough to thwart his plans to milk funds from Marguerite. But if she had . . . money is always a lovely motive for murder.

"Money." Annie's tone was thoughtful. "Maybe Rachel's instinct is right. Maybe that's what we're dealing with." She looked at Alice. "How rich is Marguerite?"

Alice smoothed back the fiery auburn hair. "Very. At least ten million. And since the Dow has gone so high, oh, she's very rich. Claude left everything to her, which certainly wasn't fair to his children. But it's always been understood that the greater portion of the estate would go to Claude's children. I don't blame them for being upset. Swanson has no right to that money. And they all need it. It will be dreadful if Swanson isn't stopped."

A murder charge would stop him. But Annie saw all kinds of difficulties. How did Swanson get into the house? Mike thought there had been light near the maze. Could it have been Swanson with a flashlight? But how did Swanson have access to Rachel's raincoat and hockey stick? That might depend upon how well Swanson knew the house and when the crime was planned.

"If Swanson killed Happy, we should be able to prove it." Annie wished she felt as confident as she sounded. "We have to catch Happy's killer. Whoever it is." Annie was clear about that. She wasn't going to see Pudge sacrifice himself.

Almost as if he'd read her thoughts, Max

grabbed her hand. "Listen, Annie, Pudge wants you to stay here tonight with Rachel. He's worried about her. I promised him you would."

Annie gave him a startled glance. "How can I manage that?"

Alice waved her hand. "I'll tell Marguerite the girl asked for you. It will be fine. There's a guest room on the third floor right across from Rachel. You'll be next to Joan."

Would it be fine to stay in a house where death had walked? But Max had promised for her and it was pitiful to imagine Rachel alone. Only Alice seemed to care about her. "All right, I'll stay. That will give me a chance to look around for Happy's papers. Maybe she hid them somewhere other than her room."

"Papers about Swanson . . ." Alice's lips spread in a pleased smile. "Everyone in the house — except for Marguerite — would be delighted to see Swanson in trouble. Let's organize a general search."

The police would carefully check Happy's room. If Swanson had murdered Happy, the odds were very good that he had found the papers. But it wouldn't hurt to search the house. It was clear from Alice's firm expression that a search was going to happen. Annie looked at her curiously. How had she ever considered this woman to be nothing more than a pale reflection of Marguerite? "How will Marguerite respond to that?"

"I'll see to Marguerite. Her practice before a séance is to withdraw and meditate. She'll never know. It won't be hard. She's hurting, you know." Alice's voice was somber. "Everyone sees her as selfish and cold, but she's always counted on Happy. There will be a huge void in her life. I don't know if the reality has set in yet. When it does . . ." Alice's face was suddenly bleak. And angry. "It shouldn't have happened. God knows it shouldn't have happened. It's all Swanson's fault." Her eyes were hard. "He's going to pay. One way or another."

# Twenty

Annie glanced down the hall when she reached the second floor. The crossed bands of yellow tape were stark against Happy's white door. Annie frowned. Surely Garrett would search the room soon for Happy's papers even though he was deeply suspicious of both Rachel and Pudge. Maybe Judge Halladay could light a fire under Garrett, make sure the papers were sought. If the papers were there, there was a good chance they would be found. If they weren't there . . . A cold wave of fear, insidious as seeping poison, washed through her mind. If there weren't any papers . . .

Annie hurried up the next flight. It was very quiet on the third floor. Her knock on Rachel's door seemed almost thunderous.

There was a muffled call. "Who's there?"

"Annie. Will you let me in, please?"

There was a rattle and the door swung in. Rachel gestured conspiratorially. Annie was glad to see that her color was better. In fact, her eyes glittered with energy and her jaw had a pugnacious set. "Annie, the judge told me not to let anybody in. He didn't mean you." Rachel slammed the door, tugged at Annie. "I've been waiting for you. I knew you'd come —"

The total confidence in her voice made Annie's heart ache.

"— and we'd get to work. The judge said I wasn't to worry, that obviously somebody wanted to make it look like me. I told him about Dr. Swanson. The judge said the police would figure it all out." Obviously, Rachel perceived the judge's arrogant confidence in his own ability to protect a client as a statement of exoneration. That was all right. It was far better that she not be aware of her peril. And maybe, before Garrett made a move — and he would be very cautious about charging a minor — Happy's murder would be solved.

"I wrote down everything about yesterday." Rachel grabbed up a spiral notebook and thrust it at Annie. "I don't think there's anything useful about Mom and him except what she told me when we talked in the gazebo."

Annie looked at the notebook. . . . *everything about yesterday.* Annie's hand tightened on the notebook. "Did you write about your mom slapping you?" Garrett must not learn about that ugly incident on the day that Happy died.

Rachel's eyes filled with tears. "Mom didn't mean it. She hugged me in the gazebo. It was only 'cause I hurt her feelings."

Annie flipped open the notebook. She found the paragraph:

*I didn't mean to make Mom mad but she was all wrong about me and Mike and Aunt Rita lied! She acted like she'd paid Mike not to see me but she'd told him I was going to get a fancy car not to see him and it was all just a lie. She's the meanest old woman in the world and poor Mom always made excuses for her and said it was because Marguerite was beautiful and she'd never learned that sometimes you can't have your way. But Mom got all upset because she thought Pudge and Annie were going behind her back and then I said she didn't love me and she slapped me and I ran away. But she didn't mean it. Last night she told me she was sorry and everything would be all . . .*

Annie tore out the page. She ripped the sheet into tiny pieces, walked to the bathroom and flushed the paper away.

Rachel stood in the doorway. "But Mom said she was sorry."

Annie folded the other sheets, tucked them in the pocket of her skirt. "Rachel, if anybody ever asks — like the police — you and your mom and I were talking and" — *quick, quick,* she tried to think, *what could they say because it was always so hard to avoid truth* — "and I tried to explain what had happened about Mike, but she got mad and told me to leave and that made you mad and you turned and ran away."

"Shouldn't I tell the truth?" Rachel's tone was puzzled.

"Not this time, honey. And it's mostly true. We just don't have to tell everything. Besides, your mom was sorry and she wouldn't want anyone to know she'd slapped you."

"You mean it would make Mom look bad? Oh, I don't want that. The police might not understand. Mom just couldn't handle trouble. She never could. And then" — Rachel's voice was suddenly hard — "she decided she had to stop that man no matter how awful it was — and he killed her. Annie, we've got to find those papers."

"I want to talk to you about that. Max and I told Alice about the papers and she thinks we should ask everybody to help search. Everybody except your aunt. Do you feel up to telling the others?"

"Like a big treasure hunt," Rachel breathed. Her eyes glistened.

Annie realized the search for the papers gave Rachel a focus, helped her to vent her misery and fear. Moreover, a search would give Annie a chance to talk to the others. Maybe someone else had spoken with Happy about the papers. Maybe there was a connection between Happy and Swanson, if only they could find it.

That morning when they'd gathered in the terrace room, fear and uneasiness had made faces careful and eyes wary. Now everyone seemed relaxed and comfortable. Rachel perched on the edge of the barstool. ". . . Mom said there was no way she was going to let Dr. Swanson get Aunt Rita's money. Mom said she had papers that would stop it and she was going to put them in a safe place."

Her audience listened intently. Wayne Ladson stroked his Vandyke as he lounged in a green wicker chair. Terry Ladson clapped his hands together, his sunburned face pleased. Donna Farrell, sitting beside him on a chintz sofa, toyed with a dangling silver earring and looked speculatively toward the mass of ferns. "You could hide an army in here. As for the reception room . . ." Her narrow shoulders rose and fell in a shrug.

Joan Ladson stood by herself near the garden door. "Well" — her tone was earnest, her face faintly pink — "this makes more sense than anything else we've heard. Nobody would kill Happy because she was Happy," she said obscurely. "I mean, not for herself. There had to be another reason, and now we know what it is."

Alice Schiller cleared her throat. When she spoke, her voice was as colorless as usual, but her words were decisive. "I think you all agree that Rachel's talk with Happy may lead to solving this terrible crime. I propose that we conduct a thorough search —"

"Of this huge house?" Donna's voice was shrill. "Alice, that's absurd."

Wayne pushed up from his chair and stood, hands in his pockets. "One of your problems in life" — he eyed his sister with disdain — "is the inability to think critically." He held up his fist, popped up a finger with each pronouncement. "To begin, we can cut the search to a manageable proposition. A: Happy obviously would not hide anything in a room occupied by someone else. That excludes most of the second and third floors. B: She would not have hidden papers in her own room, reasoning that would be the first place anyone would look. C: —"

"Oh, now wait a minute, Wayne. Why would Happy think anybody would look through her things?" Terry raised an eyebrow. "She wasn't a CIA agent."

"You flunk, too, Terry." Wayne's tone was biting. "Obviously, if Happy had papers dangerous to Swanson, they accomplished nothing unless she threatened to use them. Ergo, dear brother, if that was Happy's plan, she would put the papers, as she told Rachel, in a 'safe place,' and, equally obvious to the meanest intellect, her room would be a poor place to hide anything. Especially" — and now his drawl was coldly analytical — "if she had invited Swason to come to her room last night to talk. Now, Terry, if you intended to force someone to forgo a fortune and you had papers that made your threat possible and you were going to meet with that person, would you have those papers close at hand where they could be found or taken from you?"

The red in Terry's face did not come solely from his sunburn. He shrugged. "Hell, who knows what a woman will do? Especially one as dippy as Happy."

Wayne ignored him and continued, his tone pedantic but excited. "C: The hiding place cannot be where the papers might be discovered inadvertently. That excludes the kitchen, washroom, garages, housekeeping closets. D: We know that we are seeking a paper or packet of papers that concern Dr. Swanson. This is perhaps the most important qualification, as it will make it easy to scan materials."

Joan glared at her ex-husband. "You are so infuriating, Wayne. You're so supercilious. Didn't you hear what Rachel said? Happy was 'going to put the papers in a safe place.' She *intended* to do so. She hadn't done it yet. So whatever papers she had were probably in her room and they've now been destroyed."

Alice briefly pressed thin hands against her temples. "Happy's words can as easily be interpreted that she had already set up a meeting with her murderer, but that she fully intended to put the papers in a safe place before that meeting took place."

Terry wrinkled his nose. "This is all so much bullshit. How could Happy have obtained any kind of papers that would compromise Swanson? I don't buy it."

Rachel jounced on the barstool. "Mom said so. She meant it."

Donna smoothed her skirt. "It can't do any harm to look. If we can find something about that man . . ." Her tone was venomous.

"We'll give it a hell of a try." Wayne's gaze was steely.

If Emory Swanson was as psychic as he claimed, he should at this moment have been reeling from a bombardment of inimical thought waves. Every face in the room radiated hostility. Rachel's dark eyes burned with hatred. Alice Schiller looked cruelly triumphant. Terry grinned, an ugly, savoring grin. Joan nodded vehemently, her wispy hair wobbling. "We have to stop him."

Wayne looked at each in turn. "We're agreed,

then. Donna, you take the reception area. Joan, you check out the jungle room. Terry, look in the empty guest bedrooms. Alice —"

The triumphant glitter in Alice's eyes faded. She looked uncertain. "Wayne, I will help, but it will have to be later. Marguerite needs me. She still isn't feeling well. I was up with her most of the night —"

Annie looked at Alice sharply. So far as Annie knew, Garrett had yet to reveal the likely time of the murder. The only people who knew were, of course, the police and Annie, who had overheard Burford's comments, and Rachel and Pudge and Max. That piece of information could be important. If Alice had been awake at midnight last night, perhaps she may have seen or heard something that would help. But this wasn't the moment to ask.

"— and now she's distraught over Happy's death. I must go up to her. And" — she took a deep breath — "I must warn you that Marguerite has summoned Dr. Swanson. There will be a séance tonight in the theater at eight o'clock." Alice ignored the shocked cries. "There's no point in objecting. Marguerite's made up her mind. I would advise all of you to attend. It will give us an opportunity to observe Swanson's demeanor. And now" — her voice shook a little — "Rachel and I must go upstairs." She reached out, took Rachel's hand. "Father Cooley is on his way to discuss plans for Happy's service."

Annie lingered uncertainly near the coffee bar

in the terrace room. She'd hated seeing the wash of pain over Rachel's face, but there was nothing Annie could do to help, and certainly she couldn't intrude in this somber family conclave. There was a moment of silence after Rachel's and Alice's departure, then the others scattered to their search sites, a tribute both to Wayne's generalship and to the relief of engaging in activity that could possibly foil Dr. Emory Swanson.

Until Rachel came downstairs, Annie was on her own. She debated going home long enough to pack an overnight bag, but that could wait until later. Instead, she looked vaguely around, realized her purse with a pen and small pad was in the trunk of her car. She stepped behind the bar, rummaged through some drawers and found a white notepad and a pencil.

Settling at the card table, she tapped the pencil on the table and then began to write:

*Possible suspects in the murder of Happy Laurance:*

1. *Dr. Emory Swanson. Motive: To prevent Happy from providing Marguerite Dumaney with evidence of wrongdoing by Swanson.*
2. *Rachel Van Meer. Motive: Anger over her mother's efforts to bar her from seeing Mike Hernandez.*
3. *Mike Hernandez. Motive: Revenge and/or anger over Happy's opposition to his relationship with Rachel.*

4. *Pudge Laurance. Motive: Quarrel with Happy over treatment of Rachel.*

Murder would presuppose escalation of Pudge and Happy's argument beyond any reasonable bounds. Or deep-seated anger festering since their divorce. Annie thought anyone should be able to tell that Pudge did not have a vindictive nature, but Garrett would be prejudiced by the reports of Pudge and Happy's quarrels.

*Other suspects by reason of being in proximity to the crime scene:*

1. *Marguerite Dumaney. Motive: Quarrel over disposition of her estate.*
2. *Wayne Ladson. Motive: None apparent.*
3. *Terry Ladson. Motive: None apparent.*
4. *Donna Ladson Farrell. Motive: None apparent.*
5. *Joan Ladson. Motive: None apparent.*

The summing up left Annie depressed. Once again it seemed clear that the only real motives for the murder were confined to that first short list. The others in the house seemed not to have any reason to be angry with Happy. Annie was sure that was how the case would appear to Chief Garrett. That didn't mean there might not be reasons none of them knew about.

What did she need to find out?

1. *More about Happy. What did Happy do on*

*her last day? Where did she go? Who did she talk to?*

2. *Where was everyone at midnight? Ask Alice what time she was with Marguerite. This could be important. After all, Happy and Marguerite disagreed bitterly about Marguerite's plans to give her estate to Swanson.*

   Annie put a little asterisk and added: *But it was Happy who died, not Marguerite. The plans for the money remain unchanged.*

3. *Did anyone else see a light near the maze last night? It would be nice to confirm Mike's statement. His report could be nothing more than an effort to make it appear someone else was in the garden.*
4. *Has Happy's car been checked?*

Annie had a penchant for tossing odd objects in her trunk. Residing therein at the moment were a carefully boxed porcelain cake server, a catnip-scented Christmas stocking, a pair of airline tickets to Bermuda (Wouldn't Max be surprised!), a manuscript (*The Katydid Killer*) thrust on her by a hopeful writer despite Annie's protestations that she merely sold books, she didn't publish them —

A shriek erupted in the jungle.

Annie stuffed the notepad in her sweater pocket and bolted toward the rock path between the big rubber trees.

As Max chopped up a slice of cooked tenderloin steak and dropped the bits into Dorothy L.'s plastic bowl, he studied Annie's note. Of course, he'd seen her since she'd written it, but they'd had little chance to talk. Her directions were clear: *Check with Ingrid. She's going to round up all the gossip about Swanson. If the papers exist, there has to be a basis for them. Oh Max, I'm so worried.*

Dorothy L. ate and purred appreciatively.

He reached down and stroked her lustrous fur. If Annie was worried then, she must surely be discouraged now. The discovery of Rachel's field hockey stick made it very likely that the teenager's arrest was imminent.

Max glanced at the clock. It was almost four in the afternoon and he hadn't had lunch, which accounted for the slight throbbing in his head. He swiftly fixed a thick sandwich of tenderloin with horseradish and mustard. He poured a glass of milk and ate standing at the counter, his face furrowed.

Four o'clock on Friday afternoon. Pudge was in jail. Although Max didn't think the police chief worried overly about community pressure, certainly the quick arrest would defuse fear on the island. It would also give Garrett time to put together his case and decide when to arrest Rachel. Max felt certain it was a matter of when, not whether.

Max gobbled the last bite, took his glass to the sink to rinse. Garrett might not feel pressure. Max did. Annie was counting on him to figure out what Happy Laurance could possibly have known that led to murder.

Unfortunately, Max wasn't sure he believed Rachel. Or, if Rachel was telling the truth about the conversation with her mother, Max wasn't at all sure whether the papers had any connection to Happy's murder. Dammit, they needed to know a lot more about Happy's frame of mind the last few days. Something more than the fact that she'd quarreled with both Pudge and Rachel. There had to be something more than that! Well, as Rachel had pointed out and as Annie and Max knew from the dinner at the Dumaney house, Happy certainly was upset about Marguerite's plan to funnel a vast amount of money to Emory Swanson and his Golden Path.

Max strode swiftly toward the door. At the moment, he had no idea how Happy might have discovered information detrimental to Swanson.

As the Ferrari zoomed up the dusty road, Max thought about motives and fervently hoped that Marguerite's money truly was the reason for Happy's murder. If it wasn't, the list of suspects narrowed to Rachel, Pudge and Mike.

The parrot cackled, "Gotcha. Gotcha." His dark eyes glittered. Annie wondered if it was anthropomorphic to attribute malice to a bird.

Joan lifted a shaking hand. "That odious creature. He pecked me!" She gingerly felt her scalp. "I don't think it broke the skin."

"I'll look," Annie offered. She skirted far enough from the parrot's perch to escape attack and stood on tiptoe, parting Joan's wispy graying hair. "No. It's okay."

Joan glared at the bird. "I've always loathed him. Wayne thinks he's funny. Sometimes he says the most disgusting things."

As if on cue, the bird rattled words like pellets: "Fatoldbitch, fatoldbitch."

Joan's face flamed.

Annie said hurriedly, "They say parrots are simply programmed, that phrases recur on a pattern." She'd made it up on the spot, but she was pleased to see that some of the anger eased out of Joan's plump face.

"Well, I suppose they can't help what people have taught them. Anyway" — she looked critically at her hands and frowned — "I need to wash up. Everything's really in an advanced state of rot. There's entirely too much water standing in all the pots. I can't imagine who's in charge. I'll speak to Alice. But I don't think Happy would put papers in here. Let's try the terrace room."

Annie followed Joan to the bar.

As Joan washed her hands, she looked critically around. "Not too many possibilities in here. After all, anyone could look through the magazines or open the drawers. Although . . ." She moved along the back wall, easing framed pictures far enough out to peer behind them. "Something thin could be taped . . . But there's nothing here." She worked from one side of the room to the other, checking under chairs, beneath plant stands.

Annie perched on a barstool. "Did you talk to Happy yesterday?"

Joan crouched in front of a sofa, ran her hand underneath. "No. But she's been" — she paused, frowned — "it's so hard to believe she's dead! I got here on Tuesday night and she wasn't herself. Now, you know Happy —"

But Annie didn't, hadn't and now never would. She'd met Happy that one night, been greeted with kindness, then the next day been caught up in Happy's anger with Rachel.

"— always determined to look on the bright side. So damn chirpy. A June Cleaver clone. And she'd had enough happen in her life to know better! Divorced three times. But she wasn't loose." Joan pulled herself stiffly to her feet and scrutinized the hangings at the French door. "Not like that sister of hers."

"Marguerite?" Annie was surprised at the animosity in Joan's voice. "I thought Marguerite was just married once, to Claude Ladson."

Joan's face swung toward her, her eyes hot, her mouth twisted. "She took another woman's husband! Claude was a married man with three children, but Marguerite had to have him, no matter what. Wayne told me it broke his mother's heart to lose Claude. He always felt it killed her. Of course, now no one believes that people die of broken hearts. But I think they can. I've never understood why Wayne was always nice to Marguerite. Of course, they've all been nice to Marguerite since Claude left everything to her." Her round face reddened in anger. "That was a crime. He should have left his money to his children. Look what's happening now! All the money going to that horrible man! My children have a right to their share of their grandfather's estate. Oh, I wish we knew what Happy had found out. Where can those papers be?" Her eyes swept hungrily over the room.

Annie studied the driven, angry woman, fascinated and a little appalled to find so much passion beneath such an ordinary exterior, a mop of wispy graying hair, slightly bulging eyes, plump cheeks, lips with only a faint dash of pink. "Did you talk to Happy about Swanson?"

Joan peered behind a bookcase. "No. Though I suppose that's what she was nattering on about, complaining that she didn't know what to do, that everything was so difficult, that she wished people would just do what they were supposed to do." Joan pursed her lips. "I saw her slap Rachel, you know. I haven't told the police."

Annie didn't ask Joan's intentions. Instead, she said briskly, "Did anything disturb your sleep last night? Around midnight?"

Joan Ladson's face was still, her stare measuring and thoughtful. "Midnight?" She turned away, peered inside a thin-necked vase. "No. Nothing at all. I slept very well."

"Max, will you take these special orders back to the office?" Ingrid pushed her glasses high on her nose. Her usually well-coiffed hair straggled beneath the Santa hat and her eyes were distracted. "Duane's there. Tell him to get on the computer and try to get the books, though you'd think people would know better than to wait until a week before Christmas to order! But they don't. He can bring you up to date on everything we've found out. I can't leave the desk." She turned to face a customer holding up a book. "Oh yes, ma'am, that's Parnell Hall's new series about the crossword puzzle lady. Yes, it's very clever. . . ."

Max slipped away. This time last week Annie would have been ecstatic at the holiday bustle in Death on Demand. She would still be pleased, but at this moment the success of the store had to be far from her mind. The center aisle was crowded and chatter rose from the coffee bar. Max pushed the door to the storeroom.

An irascible voice ordered, "Keep out. Don't you see the damn — Oh hi, Max. You'd think people who purport to read could see the goddam sign on the door. 'Keep Out.' That's what the goddam sign says, and I've been shooing them out of here like chickens running amuck." Duane Webb heaved his stocky body up from his chair and pumped Max's hand. Duane's moon-shaped face, topped by a skimpy wreath of graying hair, had the stolidity of a grizzled goat, but his bright, light eyes shone with a hard, inquisitive, combative intelligence. He gestured at the stool next to the computer table. "Max, I've turned over every rock on the island. Your man's too damn clever."

Max's heart sank. He shut the door and realized he'd been counting on Ingrid and Duane. Especially Duane. Twenty years as a city editor had robbed him of all illusions, but created a mind that could sift cesspools and come up with facts nobody could contest. Duane was a much smarter investigator than Happy Laurance, and that made Rachel's story of hidden papers suspect. How could Happy have discovered material dangerous to Swanson if Duane Webb was stumped?

"Except" — Duane's thin lips spread in a sharklike smile — "not quite clever enough." He swung toward the computer, clicked a half dozen times on the mouse. "Take a look at this. . . ."

# Twenty-one

The half dozen silver bracelets on each arm jangled as Donna Farrell pulled out the desk drawer and placed it on the floor. "Sometimes" — a lock of silver-blond hair fell forward as she bent to peer in the opening — "there's a secret opening behind the drawer. Hmm. Yes, oh, it's opening." Her usually tart tone rose in excitement.

Annie listened to the sound of scrabbling nails.

"Oh damn. A splinter." Donna yanked out her hand. Irritation emphasized the thin lines that bracketed her eyes and mouth. "Empty. Oh well, this whole thing's a fool's errand." She whirled away from the desk. "There's nothing of interest in here." She waved her hand at the huge reception area. "When you look closely, there aren't many places anyone could hope to hide papers. Have you had any luck?"

Annie didn't explain that she wasn't part of the search party. She said vaguely, "Not yet."

Donna brushed dust from her silk skirt. "Well, there are no hidden memoirs, no steamy love letters, not a frigging thing of interest in this dusty room that should have been condemned before it was built." She looked toward a wet bar. "I need a drink. How about you?"

Donna's heels clicked on the stone floor. She stepped behind the wet bar, clicked on a light. "Scotch? Gin? Rum?" She picked up a fifth of scotch and splashed a generous amount in a cut-glass tumbler. She poured in a token amount of water and took a deep drink. "Take your pick." Donna wandered out from behind the wet bar.

Annie found club soda, put ice in a glass and poured. No one had to go far to find a libation in this house, a wet bar here, a full bar in the terrace room.

Donna sank gracefully into a high-backed rose-wood chair with spiral turnings on each side of the densely flowered upholstery. The Elizabethan chair made her look petite, and its heavy darkness emphasized her fair hair and pale skin. She gazed disconsolately around the huge garish room. "How long do you suppose we have to hang around here? I didn't count on murder for Christmas. I wish I'd stayed home." Another deep drink. "Too bad it was Happy."

It would have been a nice enough sentiment if the unspoken words — *not Marguerite* — hadn't hung in the air.

"Did you like Happy?" Annie edged past a suit of armor. She looked doubtfully at the nearest seat, a concave wooden stool, and perched on its edge.

Donna drank deeply. "I've been in flea markets that had better stuff. Don't think I didn't tell Dad, but he just laughed and said Marguerite liked crap. That thing you're sitting on — it's English, supposed to look Egyptian. That was all the rage after the exhibition of tomb stuff in London in 1862. There was a time you couldn't turn around in a Victorian drawing room without looking at a sphinx head or a winged orb or a lotus capital. And this chair" — she leaned her head back against the upholstery — "was hot stuff, too. They called it the Elizabethan style, but actually this kind of chair was built during the Restoration. Marguerite wouldn't know a good piece if she fell over it. If I had the money she's spent on this house . . ." Her words were softly slurred. Apparently this wasn't Donna's first drink of the day.

Annie decided circumspection was unnecessary. "Did you talk to Happy about Marguerite's plans to give the money to Dr. Swanson?"

Donna sipped her drink, held the whiskey in her mouth for a long moment, gently swallowed. "I talked to Wayne. God, he's mad. If they'd found Marguerite with a stake through her heart, I could point to the man. That's what's so dammed odd. Happy! Nobody would kill Happy."

It was like trying to make molasses take shape. Annie said urgently, "What did Happy say?"

Donna tossed down the rest of her drink. "Say? She didn't say anything. She went around bleating." Donna squeezed her face in concentration, then said, her voice high and breathless, " 'Donna, I don't know what to do. I just don't know what to do!' " The sharp-featured blonde's nose wrinkled in disdain, and she spoke in her own acid tone. "That's what she said Wednesday night after Marguerite made her marvelous announcement about her thrilling commitment to the world beyond, which translated to, *screw the Ladsons.* A grown woman with about as much backbone as a stuffed doll. I told Happy that if she could do anything, for God's sake, do it or we were all going to be broke on our ass. Including her, I might add. Happy was a sweetie, but she wasn't above cadging from big sis. She was quiet for a minute, then she said she'd do what she had to do. I wasn't holding my breath. You have to remember that Happy was the world's biggest ostrich. But" — there was an odd look in her eyes — "she's dead, isn't she?"

"Did you see Happy Thursday night?"

Donna flowed up from the chair and back to the bar. She mixed another drink, shook her head. "Not after dinner. But" — she sniffed her drink — "she and Wayne had a big confab in the garden Thursday. I was taking a walk around the grounds before lunch" — her voice was grand, then slid back to its derisive tone — "since there's not a bloody thing else to do around here. God, what a boring place. When Dad was alive, trust me, it was never boring. Have you ever seen any of his movies? We've got them all up in the shrine on the fourth floor. Movies, posters, newsreels — if it had to do with Dad, it's there." She lifted the glass, downed a third of her drink. "I have to hand it to the old bitch, she was nuts about him. And she still puts on quite a show. I didn't like the message, but the birthday bash was star quality. And that was a pretty nifty performance this morning. But back to Happy. She and Wayne never even noticed me walk past." She sounded faintly aggrieved. "I guess the last time I actually said anything to her was at dinner last night. She was awfully quiet. I asked her if she felt okay. She patted my arm and said that everything was going to be all right, that I shouldn't worry. She had a kind of Joan of Arc look. You know, brave and noble. I told her I never worry." Donna stared down into the amber liquid, the bleakness of her face belying her words. "She disappeared right after dinner. I don't know where she went. I got a book out of the library. God, some bestseller circa 1954. I took it up to my room and stayed there. I'd had enough of the family to last me until next Christmas. In fact, if I didn't have to kiss ass for some money, I'd get out of here right now." She blinked. "If the cops would let me."

Annie looked at her petulant, unhappy face. "Did you hear anything around midnight?"

"Midnight?" Nothing flickered in her eyes. "Last night? No, it was as quiet as a tomb. I was slumbering in my bed. Alone. Another drawback to this boring house." She finished off her drink. "God, another whole week until Christmas."

Max studied the computer sheets with a long list of real estate transactions.

Duane looked as satisfied as Agatha with a mouthful of shrimp. "You'll note the dates?"

Max did. The first sheet listed houses sold the second week of January three years ago. The second sheet listed houses sold six months later.

Duane leaned back in his swivel chair. "In January three years ago, one Kate Rutledge —"

Max felt a quickening of interest. Kate Rutledge, the woman at Laurel's, the smiling, slim woman to whom he had taken such an immediate dislike.

"— came to the island, bought a house. The real estate agent was Heather Crane. Six months later, Emory Swanson came to the island, bought a house. The real estate agent was Heather Crane."

"I see that." Max's tone was unimpressed.

Duane's eyes glittered. "Do you know Heather?"

Max did. Heather Crane sold houses the way some people climb the Himalaya: carefully, with enormous effort, perseverance, and total dedication. She was on the far side of fifty, but slim as a thirty-year-old. She lunched on diet drinks, played championship tennis and knew everybody in town.

"Heather takes one holiday a year. She goes to Bermuda and stays at a different luxury hotel each time. She was at the Southampton Princess this past September. She saw Emory Swanson and Kate Rutledge dining together, obviously a couple. The next day Heather ran into Swanson on Front Street and asked about Kate. Swanson looked blank, said he didn't know a Kate

Rutledge. Heather looked equally blank and said she saw them at dinner the night before. Swanson said that he had dined with a woman who lived on the island, that he was in Bermuda by himself on business. Crane said that it was certainly a remarkable resemblance. Swanson smiled and said he would look forward to meeting Miss — uh — Rutledge when he returned to the island." Duane gave a satisfied chortle. "Heather got home and pulled up her records. Kate Rutledge paid for the house with a check drawn on a bank in Seattle. Swanson also moved to the island from Seattle. He bought a house. His check was from the same bank. Heather mentioned it to her secretary, who told her hairdresser, who . . . but you get the picture. Ingrid picked it up from a friend at church."

Max hadn't expected to be presented with a smoking gun. This tenuous connection between Swanson and another recent arrival on the island seemed innocuous in the extreme. So perhaps Swanson and Rutledge knew each other. So they kept it a secret. So maybe they had a tryst in Bermuda. So?

Annie poked her head in the library.

Terry sprawled on a sofa, arms folded. He gave Annie a sly look and struggled upright. "Come on in. You joining the paper chase?"

"I'm looking for Wayne." The library was a long and lovely room with pale orange and deep rust silk draperies at the twelve-foot windows. Mission oak walls gleamed with the richness of sunlit honey. Father Christmas, a pack over his shoulder, stood in the center of the long table.

"I can suggest a better alternative." He grinned and patted the cushion beside him, then gestured at the life-size painting of a tiger above the limestone mantel. "Come enjoy looking at Rajah. That's what Dad called him. I think he believed the big cat was his soul mate."

Annie knew that Terry's objective wasn't to share an intimate moment admiring the oil painting. His objective was to share an intimate moment. She grinned and stayed in the archway. "Your dad must have been quite a guy." It was interesting how all of his children found Claude Ladson's imprint wherever they looked.

Terry flipped a salute at the tiger. "That he was. Now" — he patted the cushion again — "if you want to know more about Claude, I'm the man to tell you. Wayne's a boring dude, you know."

Annie laughed aloud. Terry definitely was of the always-give-it-a-try school of male hopefulness. "Another time. I understand Happy and Wayne had a talk before lunch yesterday."

Terry yawned. "Yeah, I saw Happy hurry after him. I went the hell in the other direction. I wasn't in the mood to listen to her moan about whatever it was that was bugging her." He glanced around the library. "Hidden papers." He heaved a disgusted sigh. "If you believe that, I've got a nifty beachfront house in Utah that I'll sell cheap . . . oh, only a million or so."

Annie said softly, "But Happy's dead."

The derisive look faded. He blinked. "Yeah. There's that. But I have to tell you" — his voice was suddenly serious — "nobody was crossways with Happy except Rachel."

Annie's retort was sharp. "Happy was very upset over Marguerite's plans to give money to Swanson."

"Sure she was." Terry's glance was shrewd. "But all of us were mad and none of us could do a damn thing about it. I don't believe in some magic bundle of papers that was going to save the day." His red face softened. "I'm sorry."

There was kindness in his voice and in his eyes. He didn't believe in the papers. He believed Rachel was guilty. He rubbed his nose, glanced away. "Anyway, for what it's worth, Wayne's nosing around upstairs."

As Annie hurried up the stairs, she tried to dismiss the look in Terry's eyes. She wouldn't give up on Rachel. Not yet. Not as long as there was any hope of her innocence. So far, they had only Rachel's word for the papers, and those papers were the only link to Emory Swanson. They had no proof, no proof at all. But Happy had talked to Wayne. What did she tell him?

# Twenty-two

Max was almost to the door when the telephone rang. He turned, hurried to the kitchen and scooped up the cordless. Maybe it was Annie . . . "Oh hi, Ma. Thanks for calling me back. Listen." He pulled out a kitchen chair. "Tell me about this Kate Rutledge. What do you know about her? How did you meet her? Is she thick with Emory Swanson?"

There was a considering pause. "She's been active with the Friends —"

Sometimes Max wondered if every woman on the island belonged to the Friends of the Library.

"— and we worked together on the garden committee. She's quite knowledgeable about azaleas. She's not one of those women who say much about themselves. I know very little about her even though she is extremely active in island organizations. It was only after Miss Dora asked for my help that I became aware of a curious fact."

Max picked up on the nuance in his mother's voice. Maybe, just maybe . . . "What, Ma?"

"Kate Rutledge cultivates women who have suffered a death in the family in recent years."

"But —" Max broke off. Sure, he knew how that could be done. Back issues of the local news carried obituaries. Deaths of the prominent (which could also translate to the well-heeled) would also be reported in the news columns.

"I didn't make that connection until I decided to lay a little groundwork for my effort to contact the Swanson group. At various gatherings, I told people that I was simply beside myself with the need to communicate with Buddy. It won't surprise you that the word was soon out all over town. It was then" — Laurel's voice was triumphant — "that dear Kate in a most cautious manner began to sound me out. After I'd confessed to a desperate need to contact Buddy, Kate told me a very touching story" — Laurel's husky voice was dry — "of how she had been able to contact her late husband. Of course, I pounced on that and begged her to tell me who could help me. She told me it had been her great good fortune to learn from others here on the island about Dr. Emory Swanson, who had permitted her to attend some of his seminars on the Golden Path."

"She learned from others?" Max was puzzled.

Laurel's throaty chuckle rolled over the line. "Dear Max. Of course that's what she said. But as soon as I was able to attend some of the gatherings, I made it a point to visit later with others I saw there. In every case — and I was so tactful, Max, you would have been proud —"

Max did not question his mother's ability to disguise the point of any conversation in which she engaged. It was, to be truthful, very difficult ever to ascertain Laurel's objective, either in speech or action. Annie had gone so far as to insist that Laurel's thought patterns resembled the records of an earthquake on a seismograph.

"— of my obfuscation. I did so well!"

Max thought Laurel's simple pride was charming. He smiled.

"In any event, I discovered that all the other women had been led to Swanson by Kate Rutledge. I think that's significant, don't you?"

"I see." Max understood. Kate Rutledge was the shill. If true, it could be considered reprehensible. But was a relationship between Kate Rutledge and Emory Swanson reason enough for murder? "Okay, Ma. Thanks."

She heard the disappointment in his voice. "Max, I'm sure Swanson and Kate are working together."

"I agree. But I don't see Swanson murdering Happy Laurance to keep that relationship secret. He and Rutledge could brazen it out, insist she was simply so convinced of Swanson's great gifts she was eager to help others. Who could prove otherwise? Most of the women who go to the foundation are probably so impressed by him, they'd jump to his defense. Including Marguerite Dumaney."

Laurel always knew how to have the last word. She trilled, "You of little faith. Dear Maxwell. Evil will out. Well, if not evil, then surely chicanery. Tell Annie I'm counting on her. I'll meet her at the gate to the Evermore Foundation tomorrow at two o'clock."

"But Ma —" Max listened to the buzz of the empty line.

Annie stood at the landing on the second floor. The hallways were empty. She hadn't expected to find Wayne Ladson here. He had made the point that Happy's papers were surely not hidden in someone else's room, so it was unlikely that he would be in any of the bedrooms. Terry thought his brother was upstairs. That left the third and fourth floors. She looked toward Marguerite's suite and wondered if Rachel was still there with her aunt and Father Cooley and Alice. There was an easy way to find out. Rachel hadn't come downstairs. Annie wouldn't have missed her. Annie hurried to the third floor, tried Rachel's door. It opened to quiet. "Rachel?" No answer.

It took only a moment more to check the unoccupied guest rooms. Annie had the third floor to herself. She looked speculatively at the stairs. The small theater and the rooms devoted to Claude Ladson's memorabilia — or the shrine, as his daughter described it — were on the fourth floor. Annie couldn't imagine why Happy would choose either as a hiding place. It wouldn't hurt to take a look. Wayne Ladson must be up there somewhere.

She made no effort to step softly, but her climb up the carpeted treads was noiseless. She stood undecided on the landing. The doors to both the theater and the room next to it were closed. She took a step toward the theater, not really wanting to enter the stale-aired room with its oppressive ornate decoration and heavy velvet curtains and faint scent of candles.

The museum door opened. Wayne stepped out. He wasn't looking toward her. His gaze was fastened on the door to the theater. His eyes glistened and his lips were drawn back in a wolfish grin. Annie thought he would have made a perfect illustration for Mr. Hyde stealing out of Dr. Jekyll's house for a night of evil.

She drew her breath in sharply.

His head jerked toward her. His eyes flared. With an effort, he managed a normal smile and looked once again like a slightly untidy professor. "Hello there. You startled me."

"Sorry." She took a step back.

He closed the door to the museum. "I have to hand it to Donna. Maybe there isn't a way to search this house. If Happy stuck her papers in there" — he pointed toward the door — "we'll never find them."

His tone was so normal and reasonable, Annie managed to speak in a reasonably easy tone herself. "You haven't found anything?"

"No luck." He tugged at his beard, frowned. "I'm afraid there may not be anything to find. Happy . . . well, there's no telling what she was talking about. Or what she might have thought important. But I guess we should check out the theater."

He opened the door to the theater, turned on the lights.

Annie stood in the doorway, picked up the scent of candles — gardenia — and felt a wash of revulsion. The dark red velvet curtains reminded her forcibly of the dried blood in Happy's room.

Wayne took two strides, stood on the steps to the small stage. He reached behind the curtains, pulled. Slowly they parted. "Don't see how anything could be attached to the curtains." Nonetheless, he shook the heavy material, peered up at the exposed steel girders. "I don't picture Happy lugging a ladder up here. She'd have to bring it all the way from the garages. And it would take a ladder to hide anything up there." He gazed at the small auditorium. Moving swiftly, he flipped up the seats, checking to see if anything had been taped beneath. He finished, turned to her, lifted his hands. "Nothing here."

Annie was glad to get out into the hall. As Wayne closed the door, she said, "Did Happy tell you about the papers?" He shook his head as they started downstairs.

"I thought Happy talked with you before lunch." The conversation between Wayne and Happy had apparently been intense enough to capture Donna's attention.

"Lunch . . ." he said vaguely. "Oh, that. She just wanted to know how to do some research and do it fast. I told her about the Internet. I wasn't about ready to take her over to school and show her. I told her to try the library."

They were almost to the ground floor. "What kind of research?"

"She didn't exactly say. Murmured something about public records. I told her most of the states don't have all their records on-line, but if it was a birth, death, divorce, marriage, the local newspaper probably carried it. If she knew the approximate date, she could check the newspapers for that week and print it out."

Public records. "Did she mention a state?"

They stopped at the base of the stairs. Terry spotted them from the library and pushed up from the sofa. "Rachel's hunting for you, Annie."

Wayne looked at his brother. "I see you were getting a little rest. How hard did you search?"

"Bro, I am not in your classroom." Terry yawned.

"That's your loss," Wayne snapped.

Annie persisted. "Wayne, please, exactly what did Happy say?"

Terry folded his arms and stared at Wayne. "If Happy told you about the papers, why in the hell didn't you say so earlier?"

Wayne rolled his eyes. "Happy did not tell me about any papers." His tone was studiously patient. "Yesterday she came up to me in the garden and, you know Happy, she was breathless and a little confused and very excited and she said . . ." He squeezed his eyes. "As closely as I can remember, she said, 'Wayne, I need your help. You know how to look things up, don't you?' which was Happy's dim understanding of what historians do. I replied, 'What do you want to look up, Happy?' She looked all around, like a silent film heroine searching for the evil Count Casimir, and whispered, 'Records.' She paused and with great effort she added, 'Vital Statistics.' See, that proves even Happy must have read a newspaper once."

Annie continued to look at him pleasantly, but she didn't like his mocking tone. Happy had struggled with knowledge that ended with her death. She might have been foolish, but she had also been brave.

Annie said thoughtfully, "So you explained how to use the computers at the library to look up newspaper archives?" Newspaper archives. "She didn't say what newspaper?"

Wayne gave a long-suffering sigh. "She didn't say. I didn't ask. It was not a fascinating conversational exchange."

Terry punched his brother on the shoulder. "And you were busy brushing her off as fast as you could. Who knows? If you weren't such an intellectual snob, we might have a lead to her murderer."

Wayne glowered. "That's a stretch."

Terry dropped his bantering tone. "No, look at it straight, bro. The woman claims to have the goods on the man who's going to rip off Marguerite and, need I add, thereby impoverish me, thee and the rest of the clan. If you'd only asked her what the hell she was looking for" — Terry held up a thumb and forefinger an inch apart — "we might be that close to foiling the bastard. But we are" — he raked Wayne with a measuring gaze — "who we are. Now, if she'd asked me" — he threw back his head and laughed — "hell, I'd have given her the bum's rush, too. So I can't fault you. But it's tough to know we could have had the answer — and now we never will."

Annie spoke without thinking. "We will."

The brothers looked at her in surprise.

"We'll figure it out. There has to be something about Swanson that Happy discovered. If she discovered it, so can we." If only they knew what newspaper and where . . .

Terry drawled, "You and Rachel are soul mates whether you're sisters or not."

Annie looked around. "Where's Rachel?"

"Oh, she blew through here a few minutes ago, looking for you. Asked me why I wasn't searching. I told her I'd searched. She gave me a look that would have melted a glacier and stalked off." Terry waved his hand toward the cavernous reception hall.

Wayne looked in the library. "Happy kept stuff in that desk, but I don't think it would qualify as a safe place. Not even in Happy's uncritical mind."

Annie clenched her hands. One more crack about Happy and she was going to ask this arrogant know-it-all a few sharp questions, starting with: *If you're so damn smart, who murdered Happy? And why?* Instead, Annie kept her voice even. "Maybe it would make sense to start at the other end. Do you know if she went to the library?"

"She may have." Wayne tugged at his beard. "I'd guess she did. She was pretty intense. I had the feeling she was determined to get some information and get it quickly. But even if we track her to a particular computer at the library, it probably won't be any help. All browsers contain a history file that keeps track of Web sites visited by a user, but libraries install software to automatically clear the history files every time a user quits the program, or at the least, clears it at the end of the day, to control the amount of hard disk space used. Maybe a librarian helped her and might remember."

"I'll check it out." But that wasn't first on Annie's list.

Max unlocked the door to Confidential Commissions and flipped on the light, but he didn't remove the CLOSED sign in the front window. His secretary, who had unfailing good humor and a soft touch with pastry, had left this morning on a Christmas cruise to the Caribbean. Truth to tell — and not a fact Max brought to Annie's attention — the work level at Confidential Commissions dipped to zero when Barb was gone. But he couldn't be expected to seek work during the Christmas season. After all, there were gifts to pursue. He was especially pleased with the authentic treasure map (tooled on worn leather) that purported to pinpoint the exact — oh, say within a meter or so — location of treasure discarded by conquistadores fleeing Tenochtitlan in 1520. Annie was going to love it. And he'd tracked down a rare signed photograph of Mary Roberts Rinehart atop a camel on a trip to Egypt. As Max closed the door, his pleasant thoughts slid away. He had a better gift in mind now: Pudge's freedom. He would do what he had to do to make this present possible and to give Annie a Christmas she would never forget.

In his office, Max glanced at Annie's picture on the corner of his Italian Renaissance desk, steady gray eyes and kissable lips, short blond hair and guileless smile. He looked into the eyes of the photograph, but in his heart he saw Annie and remembered how she'd fought for him when he was a suspect in the disappearance of a beautiful young client. No matter how damaging the circumstances, her faith in him had never faltered. His Annie, stalwart, vulnerable and loyal. And he remembered another face sagging in fatigue as Garrett pounded with question after question. Yes, it was clear that Pudge hadn't told all he knew about Happy Laurance's death, but Max was willing to wager his world that Pudge was innocent.

Max slipped into his chair, punched on his computer.

The kitchen smelled good, the rich odor of roasting beef, the scent of cheese and greens and cinnamon. And it was spotless. Max would approve.

The dark-haired woman at the sink whirled at the sound of the door. Dishwater dripped from her hands. She gave a tiny sigh of relief when she recognized Annie. "Rachel's hunting for you, miss." She pointed to a door next to the pantry. "She just went upstairs."

"Thank you. I'll catch her in a minute. Sookie . . ." She smiled into startled eyes. "Do you mind? That's what Rachel calls you and I can tell she likes you a lot. I'm Annie."

Sookie's plump face eased into a smile. "Miss Rachel is a good girl." Her voice was as thick and soft as honey, but her gaze was combative.

Annie understood. She answered with a firm, "Yes, Rachel is a good girl."

They looked at each other with understanding.

"Sookie, did you see Mrs. Laurance yesterday? Did you talk to her?"

The cook reached for a dish towel, dried her hands. Her face furrowed in thought. "She was at lunch. I didn't pay much mind, but nobody was talking. Except Miss Marguerite. She was telling a story about Mr. Claude. Miss Happy left right at the end of lunch and she came through the kitchen. She didn't stop and tell me how much she liked her food like she usually did. She looked" — a considering pause — "determined, like a woman who's made up her mind and set on her course. She had her purse with her and in a minute I heard her car."

Annie glanced toward the windows that overlooked a drive. "How did you know it was her car?"

"Miss Happy always raced the motor, then took off with a squeal. Oh yes" — her head nodded — "I always knew when Miss Happy was on her way.

That must have been close to one-thirty. She came back about three. I heard a car door slam, then she burst into the kitchen. She darted over there" — a worn hand pointed — "to the scissor drawer. She yanked it open, poked around. She picked up a roll of duct tape and dropped it into her purse."

Duct tape. Annie walked across the kitchen, opened the drawer. Two pairs of scissors, tacks, assorted kinds of tape, everyday tools including a clawhammer. But no duct tape. She looked toward Sookie. "Was she carrying anything else? A sack? Any papers?"

"I didn't see any. But her purse was big." Those broad hands spread more than a foot apart. "One of those big floppy leather bags."

Annie would ask Garrett if they'd found Happy's purse and whether it contained the duct tape. She walked over, looked out the window. The doors to a four-bay garage were closed. Four cars were parked in a graveled area midway between the garage and a toolshed. Annie pointed at a bright yellow sedan. "Is that her car?" Yellow was a color Happy would pick.

Sookie nodded. She hesitated, then pointed at a row of hooks by the back door. "The third hook," was all she said.

"Thanks." Annie took a step toward the back door, then changed her mind. "I'll be down in a minute. I'm going to look for Rachel. If she comes here, ask her to wait for me." She opened the door to the back interior stairs.

---

The printer whooshed out sheets. Max waited, leaning back in his chair. Private eyes used to skulk down back alleys. Now they sat in front of computer monitors and clicked their mouses. It was hard to achieve that old-time swagger when most information came from the tap of a finger instead of the point of a gun. That hoary standby — the stranger in town — was as passé as 1920s slang. Everybody had an electronic trail now. He had taken less than an hour to put together a pretty complete dossier. He picked up the sheets:

> Emory James Swanson, 42. Born in Kansas City, Missouri. Father Herman, an insurance salesman. Mother Louise, a homemaker. Only child. Four-point-plus grade average in high school. President of senior class. Active in drama. Voted Most Likely to Knock 'Em Dead in Hollywood. BA in sociology with honor University of Missouri, 1979. MA, University of Texas, 1981; Ph.D. in sociology, University of Southern California, 1984. Associated with the Friends of Being, a New Age compound, in San Francisco after completion of doctorate. Published three books with Shining Light, a New Age press: *How to Hear with Your Heart, When Those Beyond Speak Your Name* and *The World Beyond Can Be Yours.* Established the New Vision in Nashville in 1985, Points of Light in New Orleans in 1988, the Shim-

mering Spirit in Laguna in 1991, the Golden Road in Seattle in 1994, Evermore Foundation on Broward's Rock in 1997. Swanson's income before taxes for the past ten years averaged between five hundred thousand to seven hundred thousand dollars a year. Swanson operates the centers by himself, hiring new employees in each city. Swanson regularly speaks at library and book functions. He is single. No record of ever having married. He has no close friends and apparently devotes himself entirely to his work. He spends one week of every month in Bermuda.

Kate Eleanor Rutledge, 38. Born in Pasadena, California, second of three children. Father Jeffrey, a film editor. Mother Cara, a scriptwriter. Active in drama in high school. BFA, University of Southern California, 1983. Freelance scriptwriter, San Francisco, 1984; Nashville, 1985–87; New Orleans, 1988–90; Laguna, 1991–93; Seattle, 1994–96; Broward's Rock, 1997 to present. Yearly income has averaged three hundred thousand dollars. In each city immediately joined women's outreach groups and charities. Single. Travels to Bermuda every month.

Max dropped the sheets on his desk. The correlation between the lives of Swanson and Rutledge was clear. A clever accountant could very likely expose her earnings as money siphoned from

Swanson's foundations through dummy companies. Clearly they knew one another. They ran a nice little operation, where she nosed around a city's affluent and grieving women, whom she skillfully directed to Swanson for succor at, of course, a hefty price. Was this information worth murder?

It might well be. Swanson was close to gaining control of Marguerite Dumaney's fortune. The revelation that he and Kate Rutledge had moved from city to city fleecing the vulnerable might be enough to disillusion Marguerite. Maybe Swanson wasn't willing to take that chance.

Right now Swanson and Rutledge must feel very secure. The word would be all over the island about Pudge's arrest and Rachel's hockey stick. Maybe it would be interesting if the covert partners heard the snuffle of a hound at their heels. Max reached for the telephone.

# Twenty-three

Annie heard a thump above her head as she walked in the second-floor hallway past Marguerite's closed doors. She stopped, looked up. Another thump. She tried to picture the area and realized she had no idea what existed on the third floor on this side of the house.

She was halfway up the main stairs to the third floor when she hesitated. She was simply assuming the noise had been made by Rachel continuing her search. But making assumptions in a house where murder had occurred might be hazardous to her health. Turning, Annie ran lightly down the steps to Rachel's door. She knocked and, when there was no answer, opened the door. "Rachel?" The room was empty. Annie looked around, took two steps and picked up a metal softball bat.

She clutched the bat and moved cautiously up the stairs. On the third floor, she looked down a hall that ended at a closed door. She stepped quietly to the door, turned the knob with her left hand, holding the bat in her right.

A line of unshaded bulbs dangled from the ceiling. The huge area was unfinished and crammed with furniture, stacks of boxes, luggage and trunks. Somewhere to Annie's right there was a thud and scraping sound.

Annie stood in the doorway. "Rachel?"

Rachel's dark head popped out into the central aisle. She gestured vigorously. "Annie, come look."

The storage area was huge, encompassing almost half of the third floor. Annie passed a stuffed elk head, a wooden cigar-store Indian, a church pew and a breakfront.

Rachel, her face smudged with dust, a cobweb dangling from one shoulder, crouched in front of a big leather trunk. A mass of papers and books were spread haphazardly around her. She looked up, started to speak, stopped and stared at the bat in Annie's hand.

"Oh." Annie propped it against a stack of boxes. "I heard noise up here. You shouldn't be here by yourself."

Rachel's glance was just this side of patronizing. "Annie, Dr. Swanson couldn't be here in the daytime."

Annie wished she was as certain as Rachel that Emory Swanson was the murderer. Instead, she had a sudden clear memory of the kindness in Terry Ladson's voice when he observed that no one was crossways with Happy except her daughter. Annie steeled herself against that disquieting memory.

Rachel sneezed. "It's so dusty. That's how I found the trunk."

Annie knelt beside her. "What is all this?"

"Mom's stuff from when she was a kid." Rachel's voice wobbled. She took a deep breath. "I didn't know this was up here. I thought maybe Mom might have decided to put the papers somewhere in the attic. I came in and I almost gave up, just looking at all the stuff everywhere. Then I saw the footprints in the dust. I followed them here. It was scuffed in front of this trunk. I opened it and I saw pretty soon it all belonged to Mom, her scrapbooks and diaries and letters and school programs. I took everything out and looked to see if there were any papers about Dr. Swanson." She heaved a tired sigh. "I didn't find anything. Will you help me, Annie? We can look again."

They sorted through the pile of keepsakes, but there was no vagrant sheet of paper, no fresh envelope, no unmarked file among the yellowed papers. Rachel looked forlorn. "When I saw the footprints in the dust, I thought for sure the papers would be in here."

Annie stared at the scrapbooks and diaries and papers on the floor. She felt vaguely unsatisfied. Maybe Happy had indeed hidden something in the trunk and maybe she or someone else had removed it. It was unlikely they would ever know. "We'd better put everything back."

They worked in silence. Rachel shoved papers in haphazardly. Annie picked up a diary, one of about a dozen. The covers told the story of a girl changing and growing. Annie sorted through, found the first diary — 1959 — and smiled at the raised pink umbrella on the red plastic cover. The later diaries had smooth floral cloth covers. Without conscious thought, Annie, as befitted a bookseller, arranged them in order. She put the books in the trunk one at a time, 1959, 1960, 1962 . . . Annie stopped, checked the remainder of the stack: 1963, 1964, 1965, 1966, 1967, 1968, 1969, 1970. She glanced at the floor, then into the trunk. "Rachel, have you seen the diary for 1961?"

Rachel rubbed her nose. "I don't think so." She bent over the trunk.

Annie rechecked the stack. Finally, after sifting through every item in the trunk, she was certain. Happy's diary for 1961 was not there.

Rachel came to the trunk hoping to find the papers her mother had planned to put in the safe place. She and Annie found nothing regarding Dr. Swanson. They could be sure of only one fact. A diary was missing. Had that diary been gone for years? Or had Happy — or someone else — slipped into the storage area, gone to the trunk and lifted out a young girl's scribbles?

Frustrated, Annie riffled through the 1962 diary. The writing was overlarge, somewhat unformed. "How old was your mom, Rachel?"

Rachel's hands tightened on a scrapbook. "Her birthday was July 9. She would have been 50."

Happy began keeping a diary when she was ten. Perhaps a little precocious but . . . Annie opened the 1962 diary to July 3:

I came in second in the butterfly. Julie beat

me. She has a crush on Paul. I wish Paul would talk to me. Uncle Charles was on the phone talking to that lady who lives next door. Mama almost heard him, but he changed what he was saying and pretended it was a business call. I saw him sneak out of the house last night. Daddy's going to take me sailing tomorrow. Marguerite's mad because Daddy won't let her go to that premiere. Daddy said she's too young. I'll bet she goes anyway. Mama said it will be all right. I wish I could go to camp like Julie. She leaves tomorrow. I won't have anyone to hang around with until . . .

Annie shut the diary. The missing volume would have been when Happy was a year younger. Clearly no one would have any interest in the musings of a twelve-year-old. That volume had probably been missing for years. She and Rachel were wasting their time. Maybe Happy intended to hide her papers in the trunk and changed her mind.

"Come on." Annie was brisk. "Let's put this stuff back. Then we'll take a look at your mom's car."

Max dialed. Unlike their home phone, the Confidential Commissions phone number showed up as Unavailable on caller IDs. It would be interesting to see if Kate Rutledge answered. He and Annie always ignored Unavailable calls, Annie singing as she waltzed past the phone, "I'm Unavailable, that's what I am . . ."

"Hello." Kate Rutledge's voice was smooth and self-possessed.

"Miss Rutledge." Max had spent a year abroad at Oxford during his college days and he was enough of a natural mimic that he had no trouble with a British accent. He also raised the pitch of his voice just slightly. "I'm calling from the Tourist Board. We make an effort to follow up on visitors to the island. You visited Bermuda during September and stayed at the Southampton Princess. Were your accommodations satisfactory?"

"Very satisfactory."

"Did you choose the American Plan or the European Plan?"

"The American Plan."

"And your traveling companion, Dr. Swanson —"

She interrupted immediately. "I had no traveling companion."

"No? That isn't the information I have here."

"Who is this?" Her tone was sharp.

Max kept his voice high and accented, but the tone changed. "An interested party, Miss Rutledge. I'll be back in touch."

He hung up. Too bad he wasn't standing beside Kate Rutledge. He was willing to bet she was dialing the Evermore Foundation right this minute.

Happy's car was unlocked. Rachel stood stiffly by the driver's door, staring at the front seat. Rolls of Christmas paper poked out of a plastic grocery sack. Annie peeked into a Belk's sack: two sweaters and a pair of Guess jeans. She shielded the contents from Rachel's eyes, but Rachel was gazing forlornly at the Christmas paper. Annie made herself a promise. She'd wrap these gifts for Rachel and put her mom's name on the cards. She made sure there was nothing more in the sack, folded it shut. She began to scoot out of the seat. "I don't think —" Then she saw a scrap of paper on the floor.

Annie bent over, picked up the scrap, which turned out to be a cash receipt for fifty cents. The date was yesterday. The time, two-twenty-four P.M. The place, the Lucy Kinkaid Memorial Library.

Annie felt a surge of triumph. Here was the first confirmation of the elaborate theory built on Happy's conversation with Wayne. She backed out of the car and turned to Rachel, ready to share the discovery.

But Rachel was looking toward the back door. Alice Schiller hurried down the steps. "Rachel, Annie."

Rachel backed up against the car. "I don't want to talk to Aunt Rita again. I don't want to. I don't want to talk about it."

Annie wasn't sure whether Rachel meant her mother's murder or the plan for the funeral. But clearly, the girl was upset. Annie took a step forward, tucking the receipt in her skirt pocket.

In the late afternoon sun, Alice's face looked weary. One eyelid flickered in a tic. "I'm glad I found you. I suppose you know there's been no luck in the search for the papers. Wayne says maybe there weren't any papers."

"Mom said there were." Rachel's voice rose.

"It's all right." Alice reached out, patted Rachel's thin shoulder. "Perhaps your mother meant she had information that only she understood. I know we were all hoping to find something. Now, we're going to have an early light dinner." She looked at Annie. "Of course, we hope you will eat with us."

Annie had already made up her mind. "Thanks, no. I need to run home and get some things for tonight and see my husband." And make one other stop on the way. Her fingers touched the receipt in her pocket.

Alice smoothed back a strand of dark red hair. "Will you be back in time for the séance?"

Rachel raised her hands as if to ward off a blow. "I can't do that."

Alice slipped an arm around her thin shoulders. "Of course not. I've already told Marguerite that Annie will represent you. It's quite all right, Rachel."

Rachel grabbed Annie's arm. "You'll watch him, won't you? Annie, make him give himself away."

As she drove, Annie called home. No answer. She checked her watch and left a message. "I'm stopping by the library, but I'll be home in a few minutes to pick up some clothes. Let's have dinner at Parotti's. I'll meet you there at six. I've got lots to tell you."

---

Max dug a pair of golf gloves out of his bag. He picked up the sheet of paper from the printer, reread the message:

HAPPY LAURANCE KNEW. SO DO I.

He folded the sheet (one carefully eased out from the middle of a new package of paper) and placed it in a file folder. He picked up the telephone directory, found Kate Rutledge's address. Hmm. She lived not far from Laurel in a house on Marsh Hawk Lagoon. A bike trail ran conveniently near that lagoon.

Edith Cummings yanked at her curly black hair. Her bright dark eyes were pools of concentration. "I know. Oh God, I can almost see it." She whirled away from the bank of computers (all three of them) and paced across the hardwood floor to the Information Desk. Her face sagged like a lugubrious bloodhound. "Yesterday. We had a rush of users. Old Man Fulton was here and he's a case. Wants to stay on the damn machine all day. I keep telling him it's a max of thirty minutes per customer as long as anybody's waiting. It's after school, there are always about six high school boys lurking near him and I know what the hell they're all looking at, but life's short and I am not their mother. Or Old Man Fulton's, either. Anyway, where was I? Oh yes, Happy Laurance. She came in about two and had to wait, but she asked me to show her how to call up newspaper archives. I went through it a couple of times and I got her started." Edith's face scrunched. "What was it? What the hell was it?" Suddenly her eyes flew open, her hands splatted together. "I got it, I got it! The *Reno Gazette-Journal*."

Annie stared at her blankly.

The supreme satisfaction eased out of Edith's gamine face. "So what's the problem?"

"The *Reno Gazette-Journal*," Annie repeated slowly. "As in Nevada?"

"You got it."

"I don't suppose you know what year . . ."

"Annie" — Edith's tone was dangerously pleasant — "I deal with hundreds of questions every day. Be grateful for what you got."

On Friday nights at Parotti's every seat was taken. The jukebox (a real one, circa 1950) flashed red and green. Old songs ("Night and Day," "The Chattanooga Choo Choo," "Sentimental Journey") could scarcely be heard above the blare of conversation, the chink of dishes, and the scrape of chairs on the hardwood floor. Since Ben's marriage, the sweet-scented wood shavings were used only near the bait coolers. Fortunately, the smell of the latter was almost overborne by barbecue smoke and beer on tap. Their booth was the last in the line before the swinging doors to the kitchen, adding the clang of pans and shouted orders to the general noise.

"Nevada?" Max speared a clam fritter, dipped it

in the red sauce. "I don't get it."

Annie took a spoonful of the succulent baked oyster casserole. Honestly, what did Ben's wife put in this dish? Was that a hint of Parmesan cheese? "I don't, either. I mean, what's Reno? Gambling. Golf. Shows."

Max chewed. "A long time ago that's where people went to get divorced. Before divorce got easy everywhere."

Annie wondered if Laurel had dissolved some unions there, decided it might not be politic to ask. "So who's divorced? Besides Happy." Certainly Happy should know where her own marriages had ended, and what would her marital history have to do with Emory Swanson? Annie put down her fork with a bang. "Marriage! Maybe Emory and Kate got married in Reno!" It was also an easy place to get married, everywhere from a casino to a roadside chapel.

Max took a bite of the garlic mashed potatoes. "That makes some sense. We know — or think we know — that Happy wanted a listing from the vital statistics section in a newspaper. That limits it to a birth, a death, a marriage license, a divorce filed, a divorce granted."

Annie finished, regretfully, her portion of oyster casserole. She drank her iced tea (apricot-flavored). "Does Ben have those funny beers? You know, orange and petunia and whatnot?"

Max looked horrified and clutched his bottle of Beck's. "Surely not."

Annie grinned. "I wasn't suggesting he add

them to the menu. It's just that everything's changed so much since he got married."

Max gazed across the packed room. "Not down deep. He always had great food. Nothing ever really changes, Annie. Ben was a spiffy guy waiting to happen."

Annie felt a sudden chill. Max's lighthearted comment could be viewed as either wonderful or awful. "Nothing ever really changes . . ." She repeated the words slowly. If you stripped a heart to its core, discarded the externals, the bedrock would be bared. That's what they needed to do, look past the externals, discover the heart willing to do evil.

If only the choices weren't so limited: Swanson, Rachel, Mike, Pudge . . .

Max reached across the table, grabbed her hand. "Hey, we'll get there, Annie." He frowned. "I wish there was a reason for me to go to that séance tonight. But we're lucky you can go."

Annie didn't feel lucky. She hated the thought. Trafficking with the supernatural was wrong. She knew that, knew it with her heart and her mind and deep in her bones. At least Rachel would not be there. She took comfort in that and in her certainty that Swanson was a fake, that whatever happened would be created. But still . . .

Max gave her hand a squeeze, picked up his beer bottle. "Here's to the vanquishment of our foes." He downed the rest of his beer, planted his elbows on the table. "Pay particular attention to Swanson. See if he's rattled." His grin was part mischievous kid, part combative antagonist. "It's too bad we can't see Kate Rutledge right now. I'll bet she damn sure is rattled. First the phone call, then the letter tucked in her front screen."

Annie looked at him sharply. "Her front screen! What if she saw you?"

His blue eyes gleamed. "She saw an elderly man with a beard wearing a cap and a cape."

"No. Not a beard." Annie looked at him skeptically.

He reached in his pocket, pulled out a shaggy white beard. "Confidential Commissions is prepared for every eventuality."

Her eyes widened.

He laughed. "Not really. I went by the five-and-dime and bought a Santa Claus costume." He looked abruptly serious. "I had no intention of being recognized. Now she'll be on a lookout for a hunched-over old man with a white beard and a British accent. I hope she's worried as hell."

Annie glimpsed a Max she didn't know — a tough, unrelenting, determined foe. "Why do you dislike her so much?"

He looked at Annie gravely. "She's slick, attractive, like glossy china. Sure of herself. Arrogant. But underneath the attractive sheen, she was disdainful of Laurel yesterday, amused that she was distressed. That tells me she despises people who are vulnerable. Maybe it's time she got a little of her own back."

But when Ben brought their check and they

rose to go, Max bent down. "Annie, you don't have to go."

She waited until they were outside, then she stepped into his arms. He held her tight. She took a deep breath, then stepped away. The Christmas lights wrapped around the lamp poles sparkled, spangling the parked cars with red and green.

Max grabbed her hand. "I didn't realize you were so upset about going to the séance. You don't have —"

"Yes. I do." She squeezed his hand. She said lightly, "A woman has to do what a woman has to do." She stood on tiptoe, kissed him, turned away. He didn't call her back though she knew he was watching as she walked to her car. Max understood. Yes, she hated what lay ahead. She was scared and upset and unsure, but Pudge and Rachel needed her help and that was all that mattered.

She slipped into her car. The séance would start in twenty minutes.

# Twenty-four

The candlelight wavered as Emory Swanson closed the door. Shadows rippled across the stage, disappeared in the heavy folds of the curtain. A candle the color of rich cream sat on a gold-leafed pottery tray in the center of the small stage. It was a huge candle, a foot tall, perhaps eight inches in circumference. A faint coil of white smoke rose, swirled to nothing. The heavy scent of gardenia overlay the stale stuffiness of the small theater. In the fitful light of the candle, every face was shadowed, dimly seen. The scrape of Swanson's chair as he took his place between Marguerite and Wayne was startling in the thick quiet. Clasping hands, eight of them sat in a circle around the burning candle. Eight of them, waiting.

Marguerite hunched forward, eyes protruding above jutting cheekbones. Her breath rasped in her throat. With sickening regularity, a tremor swept her.

So close their shoulders touched, Alice's brooding face watched Marguerite. She seemed to absorb some of that recurring tremor, using her own thin body to bolster the woman beside her. The two women were so similar yet so different:

Marguerite's richly red hair long and swaying, Alice's pulled back in a sleek bun; Marguerite scarcely in control, Alice coldly calm; Marguerite's eyes alive with pain, Alice's gaze intent and measuring.

Swanson darted a swift glance at Marguerite, his hooded eyes grim.

Annie watched him intently. Tonight there was no trace of the smiling dinner guest. His heavy face was somber, wary. He didn't look like a man eager to trod the Golden Path.

Wayne cleared his throat, but didn't speak. He was accustomed to talking, being in charge, telling other people what to think. He gave a little shrug and crossed his feet, ostensibly relaxed. A shadow fell across one temple, giving his bearded face a leering countenance like a one-eyed pirate.

Terry pursed his mouth, puffing his red cheeks in disdain, but his eyes probed the dark shadows at the back of the stage. He moved restlessly in his seat.

Beside him, Joan gave a little squeal. "Oh, you scared me."

Donna's thin, petulant face looked uneasy.

Annie felt a sheen of sweat on her face, a faint nausea gathering in her throat. Alice's hand was cool and limp. Donna's touch was hot and dry, like a desert insect in the summer. Annie wanted to jerk her hands away, pull free of this dark circle, dash through the door to air and freedom.

Donna murmured, "Take a deep breath."

Annie nodded gratefully and shot Donna a look

of surprise. She wouldn't have expected empathy from this tart-tongued, bitter woman. Annie had an overpowering awareness of the figures in that tight circle. Marguerite made an odd sound, midway between a moan and a sigh. Alice's shoulders tightened. Donna's hand trembled in Annie's grasp. Joan's short navy jacket trimmed with gold braid and long navy skirt were perfect for an afternoon tea, but her distended eyes and quivering mouth destroyed the illusion of normality. Terry's glare was both defiant and frightened. Wayne poked his head forward, like a man unsure of the path on a dark night.

"Peace." Swanson's voice was deep. "We are ready."

Annie would have liked to hoot and jeer, but there was a terrible gravity to Swanson's voice as if he saw more than they, as if they were ringed by presences. She stared at him, wondered that he didn't feel the force of her gaze. His head was bent, his eyes closed. He held up the hands clasping his. "Peace. We are ready. Peace . . ."

The words rolled over them, the cadence majestic. Annie felt buffeted by emotion, waves of pain and fear, anguish and hope, anger and satisfaction, swirling around her, intangible emanations from the tight, constrained circle. She sat still as stone. If only she could identify the source. Who was so terribly frightened? Someone in this room reeked of terror. Someone had killed and fear reverberated within that mind.

". . . ready. Peace. We are —"

"You should be ashamed of yourself." The voice was faint and muffled but distinctive, the tone sharp but lightly ironic. It was like hearing an echo, near yet far, of a commanding, quick, ebullient voice. There was a sudden, overpowering waft of gardenia, sweet and cloying. "There are definite limits to —"

Marguerite screamed. Her head jerked back, she stared wildly around the dim stage. "Claude, Claude, where are you? Claude —"

"Oh my God." It was a keening wail. "That's Claude. Oh my God . . ." Joan pulled free, came to her feet. Her chair crashed to the stage. "I want out —"

"Hush." Marguerite's cry was terrible. She rose, one hand tight against her chest, wavered unsteadily. "Claude is here. Claude —"

Annie watched Emory Swanson. She couldn't be certain, but there was an instant when his eyes flared in surprise before his face was wiped clean of all expression. Annie was willing to bet Claude was a hell of a shock to Dr. Crystal.

Wayne said sharply, "I don't like this."

Terry's voice was high. "That sounded like Dad. My God, that was Dad!"

"Wait. Quiet, please!" Swanson's deep voice cut across the exclamations.

Wayne moved across the stage, down the steps and flipped on the chandelier. The bright white light was harsh on their eyes. "Let's check this out." He glared at Swanson, stalked up the steps to the stage-left curtain and pulled it open, his eyes raking up and down.

Marguerite swung toward Swanson. She wore a dark purple dress, long and free-flowing. "Where is Claude?" Her voice was piteous. Tears furrowed her cheeks. She looked as gaunt and desperate as a mourning figure pacing a widow's walk.

Swanson was slow in answering. His hooded eyes went swiftly from face to face.

Annie felt a curious pleasure. Swanson didn't know who had rigged this performance. He was afraid to make any claim. And afraid not to. He couldn't be sure what might happen next. If he shouted fraud, even Marguerite might wonder why. She might also wonder how he could be so certain. Swanson's eyes were hard, but he bent toward Marguerite solicitously. "We can only walk the Golden Path in calmness and quiet. Any outburst drives —"

"Claude shamed us." Marguerite spoke with a childlike wonder. "He said there were limits." She pressed her hands against her cheeks, swayed. "I don't know what to do, where to turn. Alice, Alice!"

Alice took her arm, guided her toward the steps. "You must rest now, Marguerite." In a flurry, the two women were gone.

Swanson's eyes glittered. The man was furious. Without a word, he strode off the stage and slammed through the door.

"That was Dad's voice." Terry's red cheeks looked pasty.

"Don't be a fool," Wayne growled.

Donna tossed her head. "I don't pretend to know what the hell this was all about, but it didn't look to me like swami was a happy man when he departed." She stepped to the center of the circle of chairs, bent down, blew out the candle.

Joan smoothed her wispy hair. "A swami is a learned man, not a spiritualist." But her eyes were still rounded. "I don't care what anyone says, that was Claude."

"It might have been Dad's voice," Donna said sharply, "but that doesn't mean he is lurking in this damned room like a ghost."

Annie slipped past them and out the door, glad to escape the bickering voices. The Ladson family seemed in agreement that they had heard their father's voice. Certainly Marguerite was convinced. And distraught. Annie didn't envy Alice the task of calming Marguerite.

The minute Annie reached the third floor, Rachel's door opened. "Annie, I saw Marguerite and Alice go down. And that man. What happened?"

Rachel closed the door behind Annie and popped onto the red-and-black sofa with its geometric designs. She tucked her candy-striped nightdress beneath her knees and looked at Annie, eyes huge in a pallid face. Annie sank down beside her, grateful for the cheerful room and the scent of hot chocolate. No sweet smell of gardenia.

Annie took a deep breath. "It was silly. And awful. All at the same time. A big candle. Everybody sat in a circle and held hands. Nothing happened until a voice spoke, and everyone said it sounded like Claude." She spread her hands. "That's all. Marguerite got upset and left. Swanson was mad. I don't think he had anything to do with the voice."

A small hand clutched Annie's arm. "No one talked about Mom?"

Annie shook her head. "No."

Rachel's taut body relaxed. She held tight to Annie's hand. "I'm glad." Her voice reminded Annie of a distant wind, high and thin. "Mom's safe with God now. I want them to leave her alone."

She leaned forward and Annie held her tight.

The twin bed felt strange, cold and unfriendly. Annie reached out, but Max wasn't there. She turned restlessly and came fully awake. She listened to the strange creaks of the unfamiliar house, watched the pale swath of moonlight spearing through the window. She was tempted to use her cell phone, call and hear Max's dear, familiar, sustaining voice. But what could she tell him? The séance was weird. So what else was new? Claude Ladson's voice had — somehow — been heard. Somebody made it happen — ventriloquism? — and Annie didn't believe Swanson was responsible. As for Swanson, he'd obviously not been happy to be at the Dumaney house, but, equally obviously, when Marguerite called he came. When he left, he'd looked grim. He had to be concerned whether Marguerite would take Claude's pronouncement as instructions to desist in her efforts to contact him. If Marguerite reached that conclusion, Swanson would look even grimmer. That, of course, had to be the hope of the person who staged Claude's vocal performance. But Swanson would surely be in touch with Marguerite tomorrow. Annie was sure Swanson would convince Marguerite that Claude indeed was there and concerned with her welfare, that Claude opposed the violence that had occurred, that he was seeking vengeance for Happy. Or something on that order. Swanson wanted Marguerite's fortune and he was a clever man.

Was he also frightened?

Annie threw back her covers, paced to the window. Swanson was stymied, worried, irritated and uneasy. But not frightened. Yet, if their instinct was right, if Swanson and Kate Rutledge were married, if that's what Happy Laurance knew, then Max's approaches to Kate should have scared the hell out of both of them.

Footsteps sounded overhead.

Annie looked up at the ceiling and listened.

A light step, another.

Annie pulled on her robe, slipped into her slippers. She opened the door to the hall and listened. Had the person upstairs gone into the theater? Or into the memorabilia room? Annie darted to the dresser, opened her purse, pulled out her cell phone. It wasn't a weapon, but it was the next best thing. Moreover, she had no intention of being observed. She simply wanted to see who was on the fourth floor. Perhaps someone had an idea, a middle-of-the-night inspiration, about where Happy might have hidden her papers. Or how Claude Ladson's voice had sounded in the stuffy theater.

Wall sconces provided dim lighting in the hall and on the stairs. Clicking on the cell phone, Annie stepped into the hall, moved swiftly and lightly toward the stairs. She eased slowly up the steps, phone in hand. The fourth-floor landing was quiet. The doors to both the theater and the museum were closed. Annie tiptoed to the theater, turned the knob. She inched open the door to darkness, smelled gardenia. She closed the door quietly, moved across the floor, turned the next handle.

She squinted against the thin line of light, her nose wrinkling at the musky smell of cigarette smoke. She stood frozen, clinging to the hard, solid doorknob, evidence of a real world, despite the sound of the voice, that light, ironic, ebullient voice:

". . . want you to do your best, Donna. Remember that you have to give love to get —"

The voice cut off in midsentence.

Annie edged open the door.

Donna Farrell rested in an oversize green chair behind a massive desk. Her head drooped. She stared at the silent tape recorder. Tears brimmed in her eyes, spilled down surgically sleek cheeks. Sans makeup, her pointed features were fox-sharp and pitifully sad. She looked small in the padded leather chair, a chair meant for a big man. She pulled at the ribbons on the front of her rose negligee.

Annie pushed the door wide. "I heard noise up here."

Donna's somber gaze touched Annie, moved back to the recorder. "I woke up and thought about it. That was Dad's voice in the theater." She lifted a ringless hand, wiped away tears. "He was always too busy to write." Aching blue eyes swung to another portrait of Claude Ladson. "But you know what, he cared about us. He really did. He sent cassettes when we were at camp or in school, even after we got married." She pointed at the recorder. "After Dad died, Wayne and Marguerite put together the museum. Wayne asked Terry and me to send the cassettes from Dad. So" — she spread her hand — "I came up and looked. Here's the ghost." She punched the button.

". . . love. Marriage can be the —"

Her hand darted again to the recorder.

"Did Swanson know about the tapes?" Annie looked at the walnut cabinet behind the desk. The second drawer was pulled out, revealing rows of small tapes.

Donna smoothed her face with both hands. Her sharp features were composed. There was no trace of the tears except for the redness of her eyes. "Oh sure. I suspect he's been through everything in here." Her hand waved around the huge room. "The better to provide Marguerite with tidbits from the Beyond." Her face twisted. "How can Marguerite be such a fool?" Then, surprisingly, her face softened. "Poor Marguerite. It would have been so easy to hate her. She broke Mother's heart, killed her. But Mother should have been tougher. Can you imagine letting the loss of a man ruin your life?" Donna's tone was utterly puzzled. "I always had to admire Marguerite. By God, she was willing to do whatever in the world she had to do to get what she wanted. And what she wanted was Dad." Donna sighed, pushed back the huge chair, rose. "I envy Marguerite. I can't imagine caring that much about anyone."

Annie recalled the words that had hung in the big room: *you have to give love to get . . .* Claude Ladson saw the lack in his daughter, but his words so many years ago could not open a closed heart. No, Donna didn't understand passion or love or heartbreak or despair. But her tears mourned her lack.

Donna bent across the desk, popped open the recorder, picked up the tape. She replaced it in the cabinet, closed the drawer.

Annie gestured toward the theater next door. "Who did it, do you think?"

"Oh hell, that's pretty obvious. I wouldn't put anything past Swanson, but he wouldn't choose that tape. No, my clever big brother probably found that little phrase in a tape to Terry. Terry was always in hot water with Dad: girls, drugs, money, you name it." Her thin lips curved in a cold smile. "Of course, Wayne may clever himself into deep shit with Marguerite. But I don't intend to tell her. And why should you? You're not in Swanson's camp, are you?"

Back in the guest bedroom, Annie turned off the cell phone, dropped it in her purse. She yawned and started toward the twin bed. She didn't know what to do, if anything. No, she wasn't in Swanson's camp. She wasn't in anybody's camp except Pudge and Rachel's. Did Annie owe any responsibility to Marguerite Dumaney? Marguerite was a driven, lonely, vulnerable woman whose foolish quest to communicate with the dead had resulted in death. That was a fair enough judgment, wasn't it? Wasn't Happy's murder a direct result of Marguerite's threat to divert her fortune from its rightful heirs? Happy was determined to prevent Swanson from getting the money and so she died. That couldn't be clearer. She had papers she'd intended to show to Swanson.

If Rachel was telling the truth . . .

Annie shivered. They had only Rachel's word for the papers. Was Rachel clever enough to have created a motive for her mother's murder?

The papers. If only they could find the papers. Annie reached the bed, sank thankfully onto it. She was tired, so tired. Tomorrow she'd talk to Max. The thought curved her lips in a smile. She sank onto the bed, turned off the bedside lamp. What an awful, long, frightening day. She stared into the darkness and saw the odd glow at the windows overlooking the garden. She lay stiffly for just an instant, her eyes wide. She was throwing back the comforter when a siren wailed.

# Twenty-five

Flames spiked against the velvet black of the sky, shooting up in yellow and red bursts. A muffled boom signaled the explosion of a gasoline tin. Helmeted men in heavy yellow fire gear maneuvered thick hoses. One hose wetted down the garage roof, another sprayed the side of the house, a third arched into the fire. Water hissed, turned to steam. The smell of dank smoke mixed with the stench of gasoline. Despite the swirling sparks, Wayne and Terry each ducked into a parked car, drove them into the garden, since the drive was blocked by fire trucks, then ran back to move the other cars. Annie was glad she'd left her Volvo in front of the house.

The firemen had no need to order the occupants of the house to stay back. They'd arrived on the terrace in ones and twos, everyone there by the time the fire trucks arrived, summoned by a next-door neighbor. No one showed any interest in getting nearer to the blaze engulfing the toolshed. Wayne and Terry, both breathing hard, crunched up the oyster-shell path to the terrace to join the silent band. Another muffled boom and one wall of the toolshed sagged in, disappearing in a flare of flame.

The terrace lights shone down upon the watchers. Everyone was in a state of disarray. For once, Marguerite Dumaney was not the star. She was simply one more bedraggled figure in the crowd on the upper terrace, her hair hidden beneath a green silk cap and her jade dressing gown misbuttoned. Alice wore an orange cardigan over her navy wool gown. Wayne crossed his arms over his bare chest and shivered. Faded jeans hung low on his hips. A wisp of Spanish moss clung to Terry's tartan plaid pajama top. Donna's rose negligee peeped from beneath a cream silk raincoat. Joan might have been poised for a swift walk in her green sweatshirt and sweatpants, the athletic picture marred only by pink hair rollers. An oversize white turtleneck hung almost as long as Rachel's nightshirt.

Marguerite clung to Alice. "I don't understand." Her voice was low and thin without its customary husky richness. "Who did this?" In the sharp glare from the spotlights on the terrace, her haggard face was bereft of beauty, her eyes bright with fear. "Tonight Claude said no. And now this. . . ."

Alice snapped, "Don't be a fool, Rita. Can't you smell the gasoline? Someone set the shed on fire."

"Why?" Marguerite's voice rose.

Donna stalked to the end of the terrace, her silk raincoat swishing, and stopped beside Wayne. "No point in looking for the papers out here, was there?"

"Papers in a toolshed?" Wayne's growl was a

combination of defensiveness and derision. "Where any gardener could find them? That would be stupid."

Joan joined them. "Happy *was* stupid. And she was not only stupid, she must have given the murderer an idea where she put the papers."

Rachel bolted across the terrace. "Don't you say that! Mom wasn't stupid. Who are you to talk about my mom?"

"Papers?" Marguerite flung up her head. Her voice was once again piercing. "What papers?"

There was an uncomfortable silence.

"Mom said —"

Alice broke in, loud and definite. "Happy told Rachel she had some important papers hidden. We wondered if that might have something to do with her murder. We've been looking for the papers."

Marguerite tossed her head. "That's silly. Happy was just dramatizing herself. What kind of important papers could she have?"

"If there were any papers in that shed, we'll never know about them," Terry drawled.

The fire was damping down now, just a glow of embers marking the location of the shed. The firemen began reeling in their hoses.

Wayne shivered. "Standing out here isn't going to help us find out who or what started that fire. I, for one, am going back to bed." He turned and strode toward the back door. The others, after a moment's pause, followed. Terry watched them go, then turned to the path leading down to the dock.

Rachel clung to Annie's arm. "The fire proves that Mom had some papers, doesn't it?"

Annie's eyes smarted from smoke and fatigue. "I guess so." She wasn't certain of anything, though there had to be a reason that the shed was set on fire. An accidental blaze seemed unlikely and Annie, too, had smelled gasoline. But, if the murderer knew the papers were in the shed, why set it on fire? Why not simply search it?

Annie and Rachel were the last ones in the terrace room. Alice waited. "I'll lock up," she said wearily. The whirling lights from the fire truck cast alternating bands of black and red in the room. "Perhaps I'd better stay until the firemen are finished. They may wish to speak —"

A muffled scream rose, then broke off.

Alice's head jerked up. "My God, that's Marguerite!" She bolted toward the reception area.

Annie and Rachel were close behind Alice when she reached the bottom of the stairs to the second floor. From above came the sound of voices. Joan was clattering down the steps, her eyes wild, her mouth working. "I've got to call the police."

Wayne shouted down the stairs after her. "Wait, Joan. Let's stick together." He thudded down after her. Over his shoulder, he called, "Terry, you and Donna stay with Marguerite. Don't touch anything."

Alice grabbed Wayne's arm. "What's happened? Where's Marguerite?"

"She's all right. Scared as hell. Somebody's been in the house. The door to Happy's room is open and everything's thrown around. We need to call the cops. You better come with us. We'll have to search the house." He caught up with his ex-wife, took her arm.

Joan shot him a look of surprise. For an unguarded moment, her heart was in her eyes. Wayne stopped short, slid his arm around her shoulders. "It's okay." His voice was gentle, without its usual veneer of disdain.

Alice hurried up the stairs.

Annie squeezed Rachel's hand. "Go on down with Wayne and Joan. I'll see what's happened." Rachel should not look again into that blood-spattered room.

Rachel clung to Annie. "Mom's door open — Annie, what if Swanson set the shed on fire and waited until we all came out? Then he could get into the house and look for those papers, couldn't he?"

Oh yes, certainly Dr. Emory Swanson could have done that.

Yes, if the fire was set to make it possible to search Happy's room for her papers, obviously the only person who would benefit by finding those papers was Emory Swanson.

"Oh, Annie." Rachel's voice trembled. "This will prove he's guilty."

Annie wished that were so. She wished she didn't have a cold and harrowing sense that the fire and search were part of a malignant design that began with Happy's death and was far from complete.

Even though her night's sleep had been broken and disjointed, Annie woke early. She heard the faraway slam of a car door. The windows were gray with the first light of day. She threw back the covers and walked on bare feet across the cold floor to the near window. She looked across the garden to the burned-out shed and the stocky figure standing there with folded arms. Annie dressed quickly, grateful for her lamb's-wool sweater and wool slacks. She checked on Rachel and was glad to see her deep in sleep, only a few dark curls peeking out from beneath a comforter.

Downstairs, Annie found breakfast set out buffet-style on the bar in the terrace room. No one else was in the room. Annie poured two steaming mugs of coffee and carried them with her. She unlocked the back door and stepped out into a chilly morning. The sun was just up and the thin rays sliced like layers of gold through the mist rising from the water and the garden, gilded the tops of the live oaks and magnolias, glistened on the moist roof of the summerhouse, threw a deep shadow from the maze.

The sour smell of charred wood overlay the pungency of the salt marsh. Annie hurried toward the blackened remnants of the shed. Slowly circling the ruin, Chief Garrett studied the ground.

Annie wasn't surprised to see him. The young chief took his duties seriously. He would want to search for clues in daylight.

He looked up as she neared. His round face was

heavy with fatigue, his blue eyes somber. "Morning, Annie." His voice was hoarse.

"Did you get any sleep?" Flashlights had winked in the shrubbery long after the police search of the house had ended.

Garrett rubbed his temple. "Some." He swung toward the ruin. "Set with gasoline." He looked up at the house. "Anybody could have done it."

Annie understood and wished she hadn't. Garrett didn't think an intruder had crept through the night, committed arson, then waited to get into the house as its occupants straggled out to watch the fire.

"Here, Pete." She handed him a mug of coffee.

He hesitated for an instant, then nodded his thanks.

Annie lifted her mug, welcomed the dark, rich taste. "Happy's papers —"

He interrupted, not rudely but with weary finality. "What papers? Do you think if Happy Laurance — a nonstop talker, from what I've heard — had information damaging to Swanson, she would have kept it to herself? Why should she? To protect his reputation?"

It was the only time she'd ever heard Garrett be sarcastic.

He didn't wait for a response. "As for the search in her room" — his shrug was dismissive — "that was no search. Somebody dashed in there, tossed stuff on the floor, pulled out drawers, dumped cushions." He nodded toward the house and the third floor. "Was the kid in her room when you came out to see about the fire?"

Annie didn't want to answer. How had Pete guessed? That had been her first move, to check for Rachel, but Rachel wasn't in her room. Annie drank her coffee. "No."

"Where do you suppose she was?" Blond eyebrows quirked over skeptical eyes.

Annie had no answer. Her hope was that once again Rachel was meeting Mike at the gazebo because it wasn't until later, when the second fire engine pulled up, that Rachel had pelted across the terrace to join the others.

Garrett rubbed the back of his neck. "The circuit solicitor's looked over what I've got."

Annie gripped her coffee cup, wished its warmth could melt the ice sheathing her heart. Garrett was getting ready to make a move, and that was going to be bad for Rachel. The next step would be up to Brice Willard Posey, the circuit solicitor. Annie knew Posey. Once he made up his mind, he was as immovable as a monolith. And, in Annie's opinion, about as bright. If Posey decided to charge Rachel . . .

Annie blurted, "Pete, she's only fifteen. She couldn't have made up those papers. That's crazy."

Garrett gingerly rotated his head. "Damn neck," he muttered. "You don't think she's smart enough? Crafty enough? Cruel enough? You read the newspapers these days? Tell me about teenage killers and how they plan."

Rachel was a good kid. But that's what they said

in so many of the stories, shocked neighbors describing a killer as the boy next door and the accompanying yearbook photo giving no hint of evil.

"Not Rachel." Annie's voice was harsh.

Garrett simply looked at her, a flash of pity in his cool blue eyes.

Annie drank down the rest of her coffee, but even the best coffee can't dispel fear. "Posey wants to charge her?"

Garrett massaged his neck. "If we don't have an open-and-shut case against somebody else, she'll be arrested Monday. And certified as an adult."

Annie refilled her coffee mug. She ignored the buffet. Her stomach was a hard, cold knot. She paced back to the windows, peered down toward the burned-out shed. Garrett was gone. She pictured him driving back to the jail. He would settle in his office and read his notes, study the diagrams of the crime scene, riffle through the pictures, perhaps even run the videocam tape.

But she knew as much as Garrett. There was only one pointer to anyone other than Rachel and Pudge. That was Rachel's report of her mother's intent to hide papers that she was going to show to Swanson to keep him from taking Marguerite's money. Happy knew something she thought was important. She'd gone to the library and checked back issues of the *Reno Gazette-Journal* for vital statistics. That's as far as they were going to get until they knew what Happy was looking for or had a date. Annie felt a sudden surge of hope. Garrett kept emphasizing that they had only Rachel's word for the existence of the papers, but they had more than that — they had Happy's conversation with Wayne before lunch on Thursday and they had her trip to the library.

Annie finished the coffee. Okay, a conversation and the library. Neither was definitive, but both provided support for the existence of the papers and at the very least could provide Judge Halladay with arguments for the defense . . . Arguments for the defense. Rachel in custody. Rachel in an orange jail jumpsuit. Rachel terrified. Rachel convicted. Annie's stomach churned.

"What's wrong?" The voice was matter-of-fact but concerned.

Annie whirled to face Alice Schiller. It didn't seem to matter whether it was day or night, pajamas or slacks, Alice always appeared calm and self-possessed. Last night, she'd worn a navy wool gown. This morning, she wore a purple turtleneck and gray slacks. She moved with the same grace as Marguerite, but her face was bare of makeup, her auburn hair drawn into a tight bun. As she walked nearer, Annie saw the deeply indented lines splaying from her eyes and mouth and the dark shadows beneath her eyes.

"I saw you talking to the policeman." Alice's gaze was direct and demanding.

Annie hesitated, then she remembered the older woman's concern for Rachel, her efforts to protect her. "They're going to arrest Rachel Monday."

Just for an instant, sheer fury moved in Alice's dark eyes.

"No."

Annie turned her hands palms up. "The only evidence they have implicates Rachel. They don't believe the papers exist. They think Rachel made that up." And, though Pudge meant well, his efforts to protect Rachel might well convince a jury of her guilt.

Alice paced to the French door, looked toward the charred rubble. "Swanson's a clever devil. Damn him." Her voice was coldly angry.

Annie had a swift memory of Emory Swanson's uneasy face at the séance in the theater. Was he clever? Oh yes, she'd certainly agree to that. Was he audacious enough to take the enormous risk of setting the shed on fire and entering the main house? If he had murdered Happy, perhaps he'd had no choice.

Annie joined Alice at the window. "Garrett thinks the search of Happy's room was nothing more than an effort by Rachel to throw suspicion on Swanson."

Alice's head jerked toward Annie. "That's dreadful. Why doesn't he see what happened? It seems so clear. Swanson set the fire. He must have. Perhaps he had an idea where the papers might be in Happy's room. If he found them, there was no need for an extensive search. That's the answer: he found the papers." She lifted thin, elegant hands, pressed them hard against her cheeks. "What can we do? We have to do something!" As her hands fell, her dark eyes implored Annie.

Annie couldn't meet her gaze. What was there to do? She had a gut-deep sense that forces far beyond their control had been unleashed with the inevitability of an avalanche or cresting floodwaters. "I don't know what we can do. If the papers are gone, I'm afraid we'll never find out what Happy knew. Now" — and her tone was disdainful — "if that had really been Claude last night, he could have announced the name of the murderer. I don't suppose that's occurred to Marguerite?"

"Marguerite is a fool." Alice's voice was cool, her face remote. "No, I don't think that's occurred to her. But I don't know what's she's thinking." Alice's face creased in a puzzled frown. "She's behaving very unlike herself. She's lying there in bed, staring at the wall, and she won't answer me when I speak to her. I don't know if she's beginning to have some misgivings about Swanson. I've told her and told her he's a fake. If only I had proof. But" — Alice touched her lips with her fingers, stared out into the garden — "perhaps there might be a way. . . ." Her eyes suddenly lit.

"What?" Annie asked eagerly.

Alice shook her head. "I'm not sure. I'll have to think about it." She turned away and walked swiftly out of the room.

Annie stared after her. Something had occurred to Alice, Annie was sure of that. Well, time would tell.

But they didn't have much time.

# Twenty-six

Annie banged through the kitchen door, her face eager.

Max grinned and pushed back from the breakfast room table.

Annie loved the loving light in his eyes, the curve of his mouth. She came into his arms.

"Hey, I missed you last night." He held her tight against him. "Everything go okay?"

"As well as it could." She gave him a hug, stepped away. "Rachel's okay. I left her eating breakfast. She's going to ride her bike to the beach." Annie thought the odds were good that Mike would be waiting for her. Mmm. Max had fixed blackberry spice muffins. (The secret, he always insisted, was to use blackberry jam, *not preserves.*) She put two on a plate and poured a full mug of coffee. When she was seated, she spread whipped sweet cream butter on a muffin and took a bite and a little indistinctly told him of the night before at Dumaney house. ". . . but the séance fell apart when Claude Ladson spoke." Max gave an appreciative nod at the likely use of a long-ago tape. "Swanson was uneasy even before the séance started. He couldn't wait to leave after we heard Claude's voice. I stayed with Rachel for a while afterward, then I went to my room. I don't know when I've ever been that tired. But I didn't get much sleep because of the fire and the break-in."

"Fire!" He looked at her sharply.

She grinned. "Not to worry. Somebody set the toolshed on fire and Happy's room was searched. Sort of." She explained.

Max listened, shaking his head when she concluded with Garrett's warning. "Monday." He shoved a hand through his tousled hair. "I'd better talk to Judge Halladay."

Annie pushed away the plate, leaving a half-eaten muffin, the savor gone. She'd tried not to think about the future, but they had to think and plan and hope and struggle. If they didn't . . . "Max, I'm scared for Rachel."

"Hang on." He tried to sound reassuring. "If it comes to a trial, Judge Halladay can get a lot of mileage out of Happy's talk with Wayne and her trip to the library. If we can't find the papers, we've got to increase the pressure on Swanson. Now, you're meeting Laurel at his place at two . . ."

Max spent a restless hour in his car, fitfully reading, until a sleek black Mercedes turned into Kate Rutledge's drive. The garage door slid up, the car drove in, the door came down. Max swung out of his car, strode to the front porch, pushed the bell. He wondered if she would answer the door. She couldn't have missed seeing his red Ferrari parked in front of her house. He glanced through the open blinds into an austere room with two blue sofas and gray walls.

The door swung open. Kate stood in the entrance hall, red-and-gray-striped walls, a gray stone floor. Brown hair curved back in waves from her forehead, emphasizing the strength of her face, wide-spaced eyes, long nose, square chin. She stared at him unsmilingly and said nothing. A heavy gold link necklace glistened against the moss green of her sweater. The green was repeated in the minute check of her wool skirt.

"Did you know," he asked conversationally, "that a coconspirator in a murder case can also receive the death penalty?"

She drew her breath in sharply. Her hazel eyes flared. "Are you mad?"

"You've worked with Swanson for years. I can prove it. If you cooperate with the police now —"

"Mr. Darling, I have no need of cooperating with the police. Not now. Not ever. The fact that I may have known Dr. Swanson before he moved here is none of your business. In fact, Mr. Darling, if you don't stop harassing me, I will get in touch with the police myself." The door slammed in his face.

Annie checked her watch. Almost two. She should have called, checked with Laurel. However, Max certainly could be counted on to relay messages accurately. Laurel had specifically asked that Annie be at the gate to the Evermore Foundation at two o'clock.

Annie opened the car door, slipped out. She'd parked deep in the shade of a live oak. She shivered in the dim coolness beneath the glossy-leaved low branches and wished she'd worn a jacket, not just her rust-colored cardigan. Annie walked out to the dusty gray road, acorns crunching underfoot. She paced as she waited, impatient to be accomplishing something to protect Rachel and free Pudge.

A rustle sounded behind her.

Annie whirled, remembering the dogs who'd leapt at the fence. She could see the fence just beyond the tree.

A raccoon swiped up a handful of acorns, then stopped, his dark eyes peering at her. Suddenly he lowered his head, flattened his ears, bared his teeth and growled, the fur rising on his neck and shoulders. Annie's heart thudded. The raccoon stood between her and the car. But — her breath eased out — those dark eyes stared away from Annie. In the cool gloom, she saw another raccoon, almost a mirror image, head lowered, ears flattened, teeth bared, fur rising and heard the guttural growl. "Oh fellows," Annie murmured, "she's probably already made a date with someone else." The growls, deep and malignant, continued for a moment more, then the first raccoon sidled away, disappearing behind a clump of yaupon holly. By the time Annie looked back, the second suitor had also disappeared.

Laurel's Morris Minor eased to a stop in front of the gate. The window slid down and pink-tipped fingers gestured energetically.

Annie hurried across the road.

"Hop right in, dear child." The throaty voice brimmed with good cheer and utter confidence. Laurel looked as jaunty as one of Santa's elves in a bright red wool suit with a Christmas tree brooch, tiny emeralds and rubies glittering against silver branches.

Annie gritted her teeth, but did as directed. Dear child. How would Laurel like to be called dear aged one? The thought was so appealing, Annie smiled as she slipped into the sumptuous comfort of the soft cream leather seat.

Laurel smiled in return. "I knew I could count on you, Annie." Laurel tapped her horn. The huge gates began to open.

Annie said hurriedly, "Better roll up the window. Or we'll have a Doberman riding with us."

"Oh," Laurel said carelessly, "Emory always puts the dogs up when there is company. I told him" — Laurel's tone was waggish — "even the hardiest of spirits might find Brutus and Cassius dispiriting."

Annie tried not to grin, did and was rewarded by an approving glance from blue eyes which, at the moment, did not look the least bit spacey. But Annie surreptitiously pushed her own button to make sure the window was up.

The dusty gray road looped around a stand of pines. The Chandler house nestled in a clearing surrounded by pines and live oaks. There were no cars parked in the front turnaround. This same view would have greeted long-ago travelers in a wagon, jolted by the long journey from Charleston, the red bricks heavily mortared, the columns of the piazza shining white.

Annie craned to see if a car might be parked on one side. "Do you suppose he's there?"

"Of course. He's expecting us." There was a slight pause. "That is, he's expecting me. But that will be all right." Laurel parked near the twin stairways to the front piazza. She reached over and patted Annie's hand reassuringly.

Annie's skin prickled. Why should she need reassurance? She stared at Laurel. "Wait a minute, Laurel. What's going on?"

Laurel beamed. "Annie, it will be so easy." She reached into the backseat, pulled over a red velvet sack. "Here's what I want you to do . . ."

Max dropped the ball on the indoor putting green and picked up his putter. He bent his knees, kept his eyes down, his head still. He made a short, compact swing. The ball curved on the undulating surface, made a slow arc and rolled into the cup.

Max stared. "I'll be damned." He walked slowly across the green, bent down and retrieved the ball. He'd not really been thinking about the putt. He was still puzzling over his dismissal by Kate Rutledge. She had threatened to go to the police. That was not the response of a guilty woman.

Max rose and walked to his desk, bouncing the

ball in his hand. He flung himself into his red leather chair, leaned back and stared at the ceiling. Okay, Kate Rutledge wasn't scared. Either she had nothing to be scared about or she didn't know she should be scared. Or, to look at it another way, if Swanson had killed Happy to keep a marriage quiet (or for any other reason), Kate Rutledge didn't know about it.

Max pushed the button, and the chair came upright. He flipped the ball over the desk and heard it thunk on the green. He pulled out a legal pad, grabbed a pen and stared at the paper. Maybe it was time to look hard at what they knew. He scrawled:

1. *Happy Laurance was murdered around midnight Thursday.*
2. *Present in the house at that time:*
   *Marguerite Dumaney, Happy's sister*
   *Rachel Van Meer, Happy's daughter*
   *Pudge Laurance, Happy's former husband*
   *Wayne Ladson, Terry Ladson, and Donna Ladson Farrell, children of Claude Ladson*
   *Joan Ladson, ex-wife of Wayne*
3. *Familiar with the house and easily able to gain access:*
   *Mike Hernandez, part-time gardener and Rachel's boyfriend*
   *Dr. Emory Swanson, Marguerite's psychic adviser*
   *Sookie, the cook*

4. *Happy had been upset since Marguerite announced she planned to give the bulk of her fortune to Dr. Emory Swanson's Evermore Foundation.*
5. *According to Rachel, Happy said she had papers which would prevent Swanson from getting the money and that she intended to put the papers in a safe place. She further stated, according to Rachel, that she would show the papers to Swanson.*
6. *Happy asked Wayne how to access newspaper files.*
7. *Happy went to the library the afternoon she died and printed out some material, possibly from the* Reno Gazette-Journal.

Max tapped his pen on the desk. Dammit, everything came back to Swanson. No one else appeared to have a reason to want Happy Laurance dead. Sweet, indecisive, worried, loving Happy. If she had been at odds with anyone else, someone would have spoken of it. Happy's only disagreement in her last days had been with Swanson. And, of course, with Rachel and Mike and Pudge.

Max looked at the clock. Two o'clock. They had less than forty-eight hours to save Rachel.

Laurel bustled inside as the door opened. Annie followed, wishing she were on a pirate ship on the Yangtze or a stagecoach rattling into Dodge City, anyplace where she might feel more comfortable than standing on the lovely heart-pine floor of the entrance hall to the Chandler house, her hands sweaty at the thought of Laurel's plan.

Emory Swanson's welcoming smile slid away when he spotted Annie. Hostility glittered in his heavy-lidded dark eyes. He suddenly didn't look quite so handsome, his blunt features tight and strained. Although his salt-and-pepper tweed jacket, bright red tie and gray wool slacks were perfect for a country gentleman greeting guests, there was no amiability in the elegant Georgian hall and Scrooge would have felt right at home despite the Scotch pine with its red and green tartan bows.

Laurel beamed at their unresponsive host. "Emory, you are so sweet to have me this afternoon. And you promised a Chandler house tea, a gastronomic delight to be treasured forever. Which" — her voice was suddenly soft — "surely reminds us all that earthly joys must be appreciated at the moment because" — a light laugh — "even though we may transcend the here and now and reach into the Great Beyond, we know there won't be any coconut cream pie there." Her regret was evident. *"Carpe diem."* Laurel slipped an arm through Swanson's and gently nudged him toward the drawing room.

His choice was to be churlish or to yield.

He yielded. Annie, clutching a bulging red velvet sack, followed them into the elegant drawing room with rose silk hangings at the enormous windows, an Aubusson rug with a rose and green pattern, and rose-and-white-satin Louis XV chairs and divan. Tea was set on the low rosewood table in front of the divan.

Laurel sank gracefully onto the divan. "Emory, do please sit beside me." She waved a hand toward a Hepplewhite chair. "And dear Annie. Oh Emory, I knew you would be so pleased that my sweet daughter-in-law was able to come with me. Without her, my visit could not succeed!"

Annie sat stiffly on the edge of the chair.

As Swanson's head swiveled toward Annie, his expression indicating the kind of delight he might take in the arrival of a black mamba, out of his view Laurel made a circle with her index finger, then a U within the imaginary circle.

Annie forced a smile.

Laurel gave a tiny head shake, but her face was glowing when Swanson looked toward her. "I am simply having a glorious Christmas season and feeling quite elfin. Annie is my cheerful assistant, helping me deliver Christmas presents and in a minute" — Laurel clapped her hands in anticipation — "while you and I enjoy our repast and I know that you and I are here and you cannot therefore be there —"

Swanson looked bewildered.

Annie didn't blame him. She might not be bewildered, but she was damn bothered. If only she had Laurel's élan, her ability to dare an outrageous performance while looking bewitchingly lovely, golden hair perfectly coiffed, ocean-blue eyes sparkling, patrician features regally confident. Instead, Annie's stomach ached, her hands sweated and her face felt as stiff as the meringue on one of the lemon tea tarts on the silver tray. She was sitting only a few feet from a man who may have killed Rachel's mother. Annie stared at his bold forehead, jutting nose and blunt chin, at the lines indented by his thin mouth, a cruel mouth, a merciless mouth. If he killed Happy and if he decided Annie and Laurel were a threat . . .

"— then dear Annie shall take the utmost pleasure in secreting" — Laurel's smile was beatific — "oh, you may think this is a most childlike enthusiasm on my part, but I know you will indulge me, dear Emory. I feel so confident of your kindness toward me since you have made it possible for Buddy —" She gave a little gasp and pressed fingers lightly against her shell-pink lips. "Now I mustn't say more, that is our secret. But I am compelled to demonstrate my gratitude and I could think of no better way." She inclined her head toward Annie. "Do take wing, my dear, trip on elfin feet. . . ."

Annie struggled to her feet, clutching the red velvet bag. "Fresh from Santa's workshop." She wished her voice sounded less like a croak.

Swanson started to rise.

Laurel's hand shot out, gripped his arm. "No, dear Emory, Annie won't join us. She" — and her wink was roguish — "is my very own Christmas elf. Here, let me pour you a cup of tea. No, you first." With incredible speed, Laurel poured the steaming tea and thrust the cup and saucer at him. "No better way of showing my heartfelt gratitude than to afford you a Christmas surprise. Dear Annie will hide a small memento, and who knows when you shall find it. I hope this will be a thrill. Ah, the days of youth and the incredible expectancy. . . ."

Annie hurried across the wooden floor of the entry hall and into the library. She darted the length of the room to the oversize Louis XV oak desk. Several folders were stacked on one corner, an in box, a speaker phone, a tall crystal vase with fresh daffodils. But she didn't see . . .

Was that a footstep? Oh God, had Swanson pulled away from Laurel? Surely Laurel would hold him somehow. Sit on his lap, nibble on his ear . . . Annie plumped the red velvet bag on the corner of the desk and pulled out the top box with its gay red-and-white-striped paper and red bow sparkling with gold flecks. She burrowed beneath other boxes, grabbed the hard plastic of a picture frame, tugged it to the top, all the while searching. Not on the desk. He must have moved it. Relief swept her when she spotted the ornate plastic frame holding Laurel's photograph on a wooden console behind the desk. Swiftly Annie moved around the desk, picked up that frame, replaced it with the identical frame and picture from the velvet bag. She stuffed the retrieved frame to the bottom of the velvet bag. Holding the candy-striped box, she moved quickly away from the desk, seeking a hiding place. She tucked it beneath the fronds of a Whitmani fern in a green pottery jardiniere next to a long Empire sofa.

Footsteps sounded in the hallway.

Annie composed herself, hoping she looked like a successful Christmas elf. She was halfway across the room when Swanson and Laurel appeared. Annie tried to swing the gift bag casually even though she was so aware of the purloined frame it might as well have emitted beeps.

Laurel clapped her hands. "Annie, you won't believe this!"

Annie thought she would.

"Dear Emory is simply as determined as a six-year-old boy." Admiration overcame a hint of petulance. "He insists he gets to open his present now. This minute! But I insist" — her tone was arch — "that he must find it. Now, you can tell him whether he's warm or cold." With a trill of cheery laughter, Laurel settled on the edge of the desk, crossed her legs, showing a length of silk hose.

Swanson paced down the room, his eyes sweeping every surface. He went first to his desk, yanked open drawers.

"Cold." Annie's tone was far from arch. Dear God, if they could just get out of here. What if Swanson grabbed the velvet bag? She resisted the impulse to clasp it to her chest.

Swanson paced behind his desk, slid open the doors to the console.

Annie edged toward the front hallway. "Cold."

Some of the tension eased out of Swanson's face. He looked around the room, took a step toward the windows and the Empire sofa.

"Warmer." Annie backed closer to the hall.

Another step.

"Warmer, warmer . . . oh" — he was nearing the sofa — "you're getting hot." She willed: *Look in the damn fern, buddy, look now.*

Swanson glanced at the sofa and at the fern. He took two steps, pulled apart the fronds, lifted up the box. "Well . . ." He turned, managed a tight smile. "Very nice of you, Laurel."

Laurel leaned forward in anticipation.

Swanson jerked at the box, ripped off the paper and lifted the lid. He stared into the box.

Laurel slipped from the desk and hurried to him. She lifted out the big gray shell with rugged peaks. "I thought this was simply perfect for you, Emory. A knobbed whelk. Of course, it is empty." She sighed. "Poor dear snail. But" — a bright smile — "he leaves behind such a lovely reminder. And now I know you will often think of me." She whirled and carried the whelk to the console and placed it lovingly next to her photograph. She picked up the frame. "So dear of you, Emory —"

Annie could have strangled her. Without a qualm. Why did she have to focus his attention on that damn frame?

"— to keep my picture so near." Laurel placed it by the whelk, turned and sped toward Annie. "Ah, but now we must be off. There are many presents yet to deliver."

All the way to the front door, Annie found it hard to breathe. Laurel chattered. It seemed to Annie that Laurel's farewell to Swanson was interminable. Finally they walked down the steps and to the car. Annie slipped into the passenger seat and shut the door, locking it.

As the car started and Laurel gave one final farewell wave toward the unsmiling Swanson, Annie almost spoke, then subsided. She didn't say a word when Laurel idled her car next to Annie's. She got out, swung the door, but at the last minute poked her head inside. "Laurel, why a whelk?"

Laurel's deep blue eyes, dark as ink, were thoughtful. "The perfect gift is often so hard to find." Her voice was cool. "An empty shell . . ."

Max pulled four chicken breasts from the refrigerator. "Wish I could have seen you skulking around the man's library." He grinned.

"Oh yeah, laugh. How funny would it have been if Swanson had found the twin to Laurel's picture? I would damn sure have been holding the bag, right?" Annie glared.

Max reached over, ruffled her hair. "Aw, come on, Annie. You have to hand it to Ma. She's in a class by herself."

Annie thought that wasn't quite accurate. She was in a class with Raffles, Miss Melville, Bulldog Drummond and Pam North. Especially Pam North.

Max picked up the broiler pan. "After all, she's got the goods."

"We hope." Laurel was even now listening to tapes of Swanson's phone conversations which had occurred since Laurel presented him with the framed picture Wednesday evening.

Annie leaned against the kitchen counter, hands deep in her skirt pockets. "Max, what if there's nothing incriminating on those tapes?"

"We keep digging." He studied the spice cabinet.

"Not too much rosemary," Annie warned. "Max, what should we say tonight?"

He looked at her soberly. "Nothing."

"Rachel has no idea —"

"That's good. There's no point in scaring her. We're doing everything we can, Annie. I spent the afternoon digging up information about the Ladson family. And on Happy. I even ran a check on the cook. Ma's listening to Swanson's tape. So tonight we'll have a good dinner and we'll talk about Christmas. Why don't you get out the stuff to make divinity?"

So they were going to have a happy Christmas evening. Annie loved making divinity for her friends. Tonight Rachel and Mike could help. It would be fun. King's X on murder. A fine plan — if she didn't picture Pudge sitting in a narrow cell or think about Monday.

# Twenty-seven

Annie shivered, watched the patterns of moonlight and cloud against the dark screen. She'd pushed the guest-room windows up, welcoming the familiar scent of the marsh, but sleep didn't come. This second night at the Dumaney house was no more comfortable than the first. Though surely there would not be a fire tonight. Don't borrow trouble, her mother always warned, but trouble was as close as a shadow and could not be forgotten. Was Rachel sleeping? After all, this was her home. But no one at the Dumaney house had seemed to notice or care that Rachel was out until almost nine. Of course, Annie had called and left a message for Alice that they were having dinner and would be in later. Still, when they came up the stairs, no one popped out to greet them. Rachel's aunt was either unthinking or uncaring. Whichever, this was not the place for Rachel to stay. Perhaps, when Annie returned home, she could invite Rachel to come and stay. If Rachel was still free. . . .

Annie folded her arms behind her head. Max wouldn't mind. In fact, tonight he'd enjoyed the kids. Maybe all of them had worked at it, but the evening had been fun. They'd popped popcorn and made popcorn balls as well as the divinity. Mike had eaten five popcorn balls.

She wished Chief Garrett had been at their house tonight. If he'd seen Rachel and Mike . . . Annie moved restlessly. If Garrett ever learned that Rachel and Mike had been in the garden the night Happy was murdered —

The single popping sound was sharp and distinct.

Annie pushed up on her elbow, listening. Fireworks? Car exhaust? Gunshot? Her ears sorted sounds of night, the *qwawk* of night herons, the throaty murmur of mourning doves, the rattle of magnolia leaves, the sough of tall pines. Then came an unmistakable *killdee, killdee,* the shrill scream of the killdeer when alarmed.

Annie flung back the covers and raced to the window. She peered out into the garden. The piercing scream of the birds continued. Was that a shadow darting across the back of the garden? Annie blinked and it was gone. In a moment, the cry of the killdeer subsided.

That popping sound . . . Annie grabbed her robe, slipped into her house shoes. It took only a moment to plunge across the dimly lit hall — Annie was grateful for the yellow gleam from wall sconces — and tap on Rachel's door. "Rachel, it's me, Annie."

The door opened and a sleepy Rachel, eyes blinking, looked at her uncertainly. "What's wrong, Annie?"

"I don't know." But, in her heart, she did. She

knew the crack of a gun. She might be wrong. She hoped she was wrong. But something scared the killdeers and Annie intended to find out what was responsible. Or who. “It’s okay. Go back to sleep. I thought I heard a noise.”

Rachel yawned, nodded and started to close the door.

“Lock it,” Annie ordered.

She didn’t move away until she heard the click of the lock. Just for an instant, she hesitated; then, with a decisive nod, she turned back to her room. Inside, she closed the door and turned on the light. She checked the clock — five minutes after one o’clock in the morning — and reached for her cell phone.

“What the hell . . . ?” Wayne Ladson peered at her groggily, his hair tousled, his beard matted. He held a comforter to his bare chest.

“I’m sorry to bother you.” Annie felt the beginnings of embarrassment. But, dammit, she was sure that had been a gunshot. Almost sure. “I don’t want to disturb Miss Dumaney, but I need for someone in the family to come downstairs with me and wait for the police.”

“Police? My God, what’s happened?” His voice was sharp.

“I heard a gunshot. In the garden.”

His eyes were suspicious. “What were you doing in the garden this time of night?” His eyes noted her orange cardigan and khaki slacks.

“I wasn’t in the garden. I was in my room, and I heard a shot. I called the police and got dressed.”

She didn't mention her quick check of Rachel's room.

He rubbed his beard. "Wait a minute." The door slammed.

Annie buttoned her cardigan. It was going to be chilly outside.

The door swung open. Wayne had pulled on a navy sweatshirt and sweatpants and running shoes. He hadn't taken time to comb his hair or smooth his beard. "Okay. What's going on?" He moved toward the stairs, moved fast.

Annie hurried to keep up. ". . . and I'm sure it was a shot."

"One shot?" He thudded down the stairs.

Annie was right behind him. "Yes."

At the foot of the steps, he turned toward the reception room.

Annie stopped. "I said we'd wait at the front door."

"Please yourself." He sounded irritated. "I'm going to turn on the garden lights. You can send the cops back there."

Annie called after him, "But if someone has a gun —"

He looked over his shoulder. "You heard one shot. If it was a shot. Which I think is damned unlikely. I'm going to check out the garden. If the cop comes while I'm out there, fine. If not, I'm getting the hell back to bed and you can explain it to him."

Annie hesitated, then followed. She'd talked to Billy Cameron and he would likely come to the garden when he saw the lights. If there had been a gunshot, there was no reason to think the person with the gun was still in the garden. Annie began to feel more and more uncomfortable. Maybe she should simply have come downstairs and looked before calling the police and rousing Wayne. The house was silent with the deep quiet of late night — no light, no movement, no sound. There was no hint that any member of the household had been outside. So what difference did that sharp pop make?

Wayne flipped up a bank of switches when they reached the terrace room. He unbolted the door and stepped out onto the brightly lit veranda. The entire garden was thrown into sharp relief by bright spotlights high in the live oaks. A single light near the dock marked the bow of Terry's boat.

Wayne walked to the railing of the veranda, surveyed the garden.

Annie joined him. The only movement was the gentle sway of the pines in the offshore breeze as the cool air from the land rushed seaward to replace the warmer air rising off the water.

"Nobody's out there." Wayne glared at her.

On Terry's boat, light glowed suddenly in the cabin. Had the lights in the garden awakened him?

"Something startled the killdeers." Annie tried not to sound defensive.

"Before the 'shot'?" His tone put quote marks around the word. "Or after?"

She didn't have to think about it. That loud pop, her rush to the window. "After."

A dark figure moved on deck of the cruiser, came over the side, dropped to the dock.

"If there was a shot, you'd think Terry would have heard it." Hands on his hips, he watched his brother stride up the dock.

Annie felt her face flush. Wayne didn't have to be sarcastic. She turned, hurried down the veranda steps and walked swiftly on the curving oyster-shell path. After a moment, she heard a crunch behind her. She was no longer concerned about safety. No intruder would lurk in this lit enclave. In fact, she realized this was probably going to be a pointless exercise, but she wanted to look down near the dock. It seemed to her that the sound of the frightened birds had been deep in the garden. Was there a gate to an adjoining property? Perhaps Terry had heard something. It wouldn't hurt to ask. She walked fast, pausing only to decide which way to veer when she reached the maze. The maze, in fact, formed an impassable barrier between the upper and lower terraces. Paths curved to each side, the south arm leading to the gazebo, the north to the arbor.

A muffled shout sounded past the maze. "Hey," Terry's voice rose in a shout, "Wayne, hurry! Christ, come here!"

Wayne lunged past Annie, his shoes crunching the shells. Annie ran after him, but he was already beside his brother at the foot of the gazebo steps when she came around the maze.

Terry grabbed his brother's arm. "She's dead, isn't she?" Terry's voice shook. In the stark light beneath the live oak, his face was gray beneath the sunburn. He wore an undershirt and faded dungarees.

Annie heard their voices, but they seemed far away. She stared at the crumpled figure lying at the foot of the gazebo steps. Yes, Marguerite Dumaney was dead. The bullet had apparently struck her midchest, knocking her onto her back. She lay with her arms flung wide. The front of her green silk robe was terrible with the bright stain of blood. The crimson of her lips made a vivid splotch against the stark white of her face. In death there was no hint of the power she had exuded in life. Despite the deep sockets of her eyes and the jut of her cheekbones, her features lacked sharpness and her face was no longer beautiful. The once-lovely red hair made a ghastly frame for the dead face.

Wayne took a deep breath and turned toward the house.

"Yo?" came a call.

"Billy," Annie shouted. "Oh, Billy, we're down here. At the gazebo. Hurry."

Billy was big, but he could move. He careened around the maze, stumbled to a stop. "Don't move. Anyone."

"It's too late for that." Wayne hunched his shoulders. "For God's sake, we just found her."

"I have to secure the crime scene." Billy pulled his cell phone from his pocket. "Have any of you touched anything?"

"Billy, it's all right." Annie pointed at Wayne. "He and I came out to see if we could find anything. Wayne turned on the lights —"

"— and I saw them." Terry swallowed. "Wish to hell I'd turned over and gone back to sleep. But hell, it looked like Broadway, it was so bright. And that was strange as hell. And those damned birds had waked me up."

Wayne glanced toward Annie.

Billy clicked on his phone, punched the number.

Annie took a step toward Terry. "Did you hear the shot?"

Terry's head swung toward the gazebo. "No. I didn't hear that."

But the shot startled the birds and their cries awakened Terry.

"I have the scene under control, sir. . . . Yes, sir." Billy clicked off the cell phone. "The chief requests that you remain here until he and the crime unit arrive. Please refrain from talking."

Wayne smoothed his beard, almost spoke, shrugged. He wandered toward the maze, plopped onto a wooden bench. Terry hesitated, then joined his brother. The brothers avoided looking toward Marguerite's body. Annie stared speculatively at the gazebo. It was shocking to find Marguerite Dumaney dead, but astounding to find her dead by the gazebo. Annie didn't profess to be an expert on Marguerite Dumaney's habits, but the only time she'd ever seen the woman outdoors was when Marguerite arrived — dramatically — to publicly accuse Pudge of murder. Once they knew why Marguerite was at the gazebo, they'd be well on the track of discovering who killed her. But the reason seemed obvious. She must have come there to meet someone. That surely wouldn't include anyone in the house. Why come outside when there were many private nooks in which she could easily speak privately to anyone in the house? So not someone in the house. With a surge of relief, Annie realized that included Rachel. Moreover, after Annie had heard the shot, she'd knocked on Rachel's door and roused her. Rachel could not be accused of this murder. Since Marguerite's death must hinge directly upon Happy's murder, Rachel was exonerated. And Pudge was in jail, so he was exonerated, too.

Although it wasn't long — perhaps fifteen minutes — it seemed forever before car doors slammed and Chief Garrett and Lou Pirelli, both dressed but unshaven, strode around the maze. Garrett ignored them all, walking straight to the steps of the gazebo. More doors slammed; the whirl of a police light flickered from the drive.

Perhaps it was the noise, perhaps the continuing blaze of lights in the garden at this too-late hour. The terrace room door was flung wide and a figure strode to the railing of the veranda.

"What is this?" The piercing voice cut through the night, the sharp yet husky, unforgettable voice.

Every face swung toward the starkly lit veranda.

She stood, dark red hair streaming to the shoulders of her scarlet kimono, haggard face imperious. "Who's there? What's going on? Answer me." There was no mistaking the deep-set eyes, high cheekbones and scarlet lips, the features cold and haughty and demanding. Oyster shells rattled. Marguerite came down the path so quickly, the swish of her silk kimono sounded like the flutter of shuffled cards, shockingly loud in the silence that awaited her. She lifted an arm, pointed at Garrett. "My good man, I demand —" Then she saw that still figure. For an instant, she was frozen in motion. Slowly, her eyes widened, her cheeks went flaccid, her arm fell. "What . . ." She took a deep, sobbing breath and walked forward, one leaden step after another, her shaking hand outstretched.

Garrett stepped in front of her. "Ma'am, I'll have to ask you to stop here. No one can —"

Marguerite's head jerked up. Eyes glazed, mouth trembling, she swayed on her feet. Garrett turned toward Wayne. "She needs —"

Marguerite flung herself past Garrett before he could reach out. She flew to the gazebo, fell to her knees beside that still body. She pulled up a limp hand, clutched it to her face and began to moan, "Alice, Alice, Alice . . ."

Garrett was there in two big strides, pulling a sobbing Marguerite to her feet. He gripped her arms, snapping at Wayne. "Come here. Take her in the house."

Marguerite resisted, her eyes wild, her body trembling. "Look at Alice! She's wearing one of my gowns. She has on makeup. She never wore makeup. Never." Marguerite shuddered. "I see myself lying there. Someone tried to kill me! Oh my God."

Garrett gave Marguerite a hard stare. "Why should" — he paused, dredging for the name — "Miss Schiller dress like you? Why should she come out here in the middle of the night?"

Marguerite pressed her hands against her cheeks. Her eyes widened. But she made no answer.

Annie stepped forward. "Ask Marguerite what Alice told her."

Marguerite's eyes blazed. "She's wrong, she's . . ." A deep breath. "Oh God, Alice was wrong. Not Emory. I can't bear it if it's Emory."

Annie felt sympathy war with disgust as she stared at the elegant, still haggardly beautiful woman, beautiful despite the ravage of tears. Perhaps her beauty was indestructible because every thought was directed within. Everyone and everything served as an extension of herself. Marguerite obviously had not realized that if murder did not come from without, it must have come from within the Dumaney house. Would she rather see Emory Swanson as the murderer of Happy and the woman he believed to be Marguerite or would she rather look for the eyes of a killer in the faces of her family?

Marguerite's face suddenly crumpled. Her eyes shut tight. She cried like a child, tears flooding, breath catching. "Happy . . . Alice . . . I need them. Oh God, I need them." She sagged against Wayne.

Marguerite's anguish seared through Annie. Everyone who mattered the most to Marguerite was now dead: her sister, Alice, her husband. Was it any wonder that she clung to her faith in Emory Swanson? If she lost that faith, she would lose everything.

Wayne jerked his head at Terry. "Come on. Let's get her inside."

The two men, supporting Marguerite between them, moved slowly up the oyster-shell path. The only sound was the crunch of footsteps and the harsh gasp of Marguerite's sobs.

# Twenty-eight

An uneasy quiet lay over the Dumaney house. Joan and Donna were upstairs with Marguerite. Wayne and Terry stood at the french door of the terrace room, staring grimly out into the floodlit garden. Annie held her cell phone, but decided against calling Max. Let him rest. There was nothing he could do to help right now. Dr. Burford came and went, taking time to see Marguerite. Rachel snuggled beneath an afghan on a sofa near the indoor garden and fell asleep.

"What the *hell* did Alice think she was doing?" Wayne spoke softly as they watched the crime unit continue its slow and painstaking exploration.

"She told me she had a plan." Annie rubbed eyes grainy with fatigue. "But I don't understand why she tried to trap Swanson by herself."

Wayne moved his shoulders, trying to loosen tight muscles. "What kind of plan?"

Terry held up a pot of freshly brewed coffee. "Anybody join me?"

Annie hurried to the bar, took a mug for herself, carried one to Wayne. She smelled the steaming, strong coffee, waited for it to cool a bit. "We can figure out part of it." Although Annie still had trouble believing that Alice — careful, calm, intelligent Alice — had faced Swanson by herself, her death made that conclusion inevitable. "We know that she was pretending to be Marguerite. That's obvious from the kimono and the makeup. There could only be one reason. Swanson wouldn't come if Alice called him, but he would come for Marguerite. Alice must have called Swanson, pretended to be Marguerite and asked him — told him — to meet her in the gazebo. We don't know what she said. Did she accuse him of murdering Happy? Or did she profess to be puzzled and uneasy because her sister had told her about some papers concerning him? Whatever she said, Swanson came, and, believing Alice to be Marguerite, he shot her."

Terry dumped three teaspoons of sugar in his coffee. "Wasn't that killing the golden goose?"

Wayne gave a short laugh. "If he'd killed Happy and thought Marguerite knew it and could tell the cops, he'd sure as hell chop the little goose's neck. First things first. Rita's money wouldn't help him if he was convicted of murder."

Terry stirred his coffee. "Alice was nobody's fool. If she thought the man killed Happy, why did she try to handle him by herself?"

There was no answer to that. The body lying near the gazebo was proof of a plan gone awry.

The door to the terrace room opened. Chief Garrett stepped inside.

Annie took a deep gulp of coffee.

He started with her, of course. "You called 911 at" — he checked his notes — "one-oh-six, reported hearing a gunshot. What time did you hear the shot?"

Annie figured out loud. "I heard the shot, then the birds cried. I got up and went to the window — I think I saw someone —"

"Who, for God's sake?" Wayne demanded. "You didn't say anything about seeing anybody."

Annie held up her hand. "It was dark. I looked down in the garden and I thought there was movement."

"Where?" Garrett snapped.

Annie pointed to her left. "That way. Away from the gazebo."

Wayne swung back to the window, peered out. "There's a path there. It leads to a dirt lane that runs between this house and the next one."

Garrett made quick notes. "Okay. You saw somebody. You think. But I still want to know when you heard the shot."

"Maybe three minutes before I called, maybe four." She nodded. "So it must have been just about one o'clock."

"What took so long?" Garrett's eyes were suspicious.

She remembered how grateful she'd been for the soft yellow lights in the wall sconces. "I went across the hall and knocked on Rachel's door."

Wayne frowned.

She said quickly, "I didn't mention it when I came for you. I didn't think it mattered. But I thought it was a shot and I wanted to be sure Rachel was all right."

Rachel shivered. "You didn't tell me about a shot. I would have come with you." Her eyes were huge. "I'm glad I didn't. Poor Alice."

Garrett glanced toward the garden, still starkly lit. "You and Mr. Ladson got down there when? Five minutes later?"

Annie shook her head. "More like ten. After I made the call, I went and woke up Wayne. He dressed. We came downstairs. It was probably —"

Terry interrupted. "It was twelve after one when the garden lights came on. I came out to see what was going on."

Garrett looked at Annie and Wayne. "You didn't see anyone when the lights came on?"

Wayne stared out into the garden. "No. There was nobody in the garden. No one at all."

"There was plenty of time for the murderer to get away." Annie locked eyes with Garrett. "My father's in jail." She didn't go on to say he couldn't have been shooting Marguerite in the garden. She didn't need to say it. "When are you going to let him out?"

Garrett wasn't going to be stampeded. "The investigation isn't complete." But he had to know that Alice died because she confronted Happy's murderer. "As soon as —"

The terrace door was flung open. Lou Pirelli, out of breath and excited, yelled, "Chief, we found the gun!"

Annie snapped shut her overnight bag. She glanced around the room. She'd not forgotten anything. How wonderful to know that in only a few minutes she would be home. And not alone.

The door opened and Rachel stepped inside, a stuffed backpack dangling from one thin shoulder. Her eyes uncertain, she said diffidently, "Annie, are you sure it will be okay with Max?"

"I talked to him a little while ago." Annie's ear still tingled. Max was not happy that she'd found a body and not called him. But, as she'd pointed out, what good would it have done for neither of them to get any sleep? Her ear tingled, but her heart glowed. His tone was sharp because he pictured her walking out into a garden when death waited, and he hated that. He'd been forced to admit that she'd not been foolish, first calling the police and seeking out Wayne. And he'd agreed at once that she should bring Rachel with her. "He said to tell you Dorothy L. is thrilled. She thinks we're pretty boring. He'll have hot chocolate ready for us."

Tears glistened in Rachel's dark eyes. "I went down the hall. I thought maybe I had to tell Aunt Rita, but she's still asleep. Joan said she was sure it was all right."

Nobody cared where Rachel went. Both of them knew it.

Annie grabbed her suitcase. "Let's go."

"It's tilting to the left. No," Annie urged, "a little more this way."

On his hands and knees, Max steadied the trunk of the pine in the metal base, screwed a support prong tighter. "How's that?"

Dorothy L. crouched and arched through the air to land on his back.

"Ouch." Max bent forward, but the cat merely dug her claws deeper.

"Annie, do something!" Max reached back.

Delighted, Dorothy L. used one paw to swipe at his groping hand.

Rachel teetered forward on her toes and laughed. "Annie, she thinks Max is a bridge. I'll bet she climbs to the top of the tree. Look!" She giggled.

Annie laughed, too. She hoped trimming the Christmas tree might be the first glimmer of happiness in Rachel's dark and difficult days. Tomorrow would be very hard. Happy's funeral was set at ten. But for now . . . Annie hurried to Max and loosened Dorothy L.'s claws, scooping up the fluffy white cat.

Max dramatically rolled onto his back, hands and feet in the air, growling, "Does Dorothy L. want to spend Christmas at the store? Agatha will turn her into a rag doll cat."

Rachel's eyes were round. "Doesn't Agatha like Dorothy L.?"

Max sat up and waved a hand toward Rachel. "Come close and you shall hear the piteous tale of —"

The phone rang.

Annie was laughing as she hurried to the kitchen. Max loved to tell the story of Dorothy L.'s arrival at Death on Demand, a helpless foundling in need of a home, and her reception by pampered, mistress-of-the-manor Agatha. Agatha's heartbreak had reminded Annie that even a cat can be jealous. The story had ended happily, with Agatha living at the store and Dorothy L. at home.

". . . Agatha wouldn't eat. She bit Annie. She hissed. She . . ."

"Hello." As Annie picked up the phone, she checked caller ID. *The Island Gazette*. For a moment, her chest tightened. On Sunday afternoon? Oh, of course. Vince was at the office, covering the murder of Alice Schiller, which would surely dominate page one tomorrow. But she gripped the receiver tightly.

"Annie." This time Vince's voice was robust. He wasn't calling to tell her the police had an APB out for her father. "Hey, I've got news."

Annie started breathing again.

"Things are breaking fast on the Schiller murder. Here's what we know: Death was instantaneous, single gunshot wound to the chest, burst the aorta, .22-caliber pistol, clear fingerprints on the grip belonging to . . ." A dramatic pause.

"Come on, Vince." She was stern.

"Sorry. Couldn't resist. But you're not going to believe it. The fingerprints belong to Dr. Emory Swanson, the island's chief spirit seeker. Everybody's stunned because gossip had it that Marguerite Dumaney was eating out of his hand. Talk about a shock."

Annie leaned against the kitchen counter. Yes,

she was astounded. Not, as Vince expected, at the identity of the murderer, but shocked that Swanson's fingerprints were on the murder weapon. He was not a stupid man. How in the world had he made such an egregious mistake? She felt a flood of relief. With that kind of evidence, it might not be necessary for Laurel to give her tape to the police. That tape would require some difficult explanations. As for the tape, Laurel had reported to Annie and Max that it contained several cynical comments about "idiot women who believe they have a pipeline to the afterlife" and clearly reflected an intimate connection to Kate Rutledge. But, as Laurel put it, "Unfortunately, we simply picked the recorder up too soon. If we'd left it in place, we might have a record of his conversation with Alice." A regretful sigh.

"Once they ID'd his prints, they traced the gun. Slick work," Vince said admiringly. "Swanson bought the gun last year, presumably to pot at rabbits eating his spinach. His gun, his prints. Of course, by the time they picked him up, there was no trace of nitrate. He'd had plenty of time to wash his hands and, for that matter, his clothes. There's icing on the cake: The neighbor to the south was up with a toothache and saw lights turn into that road between his house and the Dumaney place. It was about a quarter to one and he told Garrett there was no reason for any car to be going down that stretch of lane. It's private property. He went outside to look and saw a

Mercedes with a vanity plate, 'EVERMORE.' To clinch it, Garrett matched tire prints — that's a dirt road — and it was definitely Swanson's car."

Annie covered the mouthpiece and called out. "Max, Rachel, come here. They've traced the gun to Swanson." She dropped her hand. "Have they arrested him, Vince?" She reached down and punched on the speaker phone.

Max and Rachel skidded to a stop on either side of her.

Vince's voice boomed in the kitchen. "You bet. Took him into custody about an hour ago. At the Savannah airport. With a ticket to Atlanta, then on to Dallas and Mexico City. It's a hell of a story."

Rachel pulled out a kitchen chair, sank into it as if her legs wouldn't hold her.

Annie reached out, gripped her hand.

"So you can take a little drive in a few minutes."

Annie stared blankly at the speaker phone. "Drive?"

"I hear there's a guy who needs a lift home. Name of Pudge Laurance. Down at the —"

"Oh, Vince." Sheer happiness lifted her voice. "Thank you. Thank you." Annie punched off the phone and headed for the door, Max and Rachel right behind her.

Rachel stood next to Pudge in a corner of the terrace room. She looked small and forlorn in a navy dress with a white piqué collar. Pudge pulled at his tie and Annie guessed he rarely wore one.

She reached them, carrying two filled plates. Max was behind her with their plates.

Marguerite had decided upon a graveside service for Happy. Although the day was sunny, the shadows of the pines had been dark and somber. Mercifully, the service was swift, and the funeral cars brought them quickly back to the house. Annie would have been happy never to walk into the huge, strange house again, but Rachel had to be there.

"Fried chicken," Annie announced cheerfully. "I'll bet Sookie makes wonderful fried chicken. And mashed potatoes and gravy."

Rachel managed a smile, though her face still looked pinched and her eyes were red with crying.

Marguerite, all in black, swept to the center of the room. "My cherished ones." Her deep, husky voice reached every corner.

The jerky beginnings of conversations stopped. Everyone looked toward Marguerite. Every face appeared strained and tired. Who could wonder at that? They had been close to two violent deaths and this morning attended the funeral of a sweet woman they'd known well for many years.

Wayne slouched against the bar, his dark brows raised. His silvery hair and trim beard were neatly brushed, his narrow face sharply attentive. He looked at Marguerite with marked skepticism, as he might observe a politician or a cabaret singer or an economist.

Joan fluffed her wispy hair. Her dark green dress was too tight to be flattering.

Terry had pulled off his navy blazer, loosened his rep tie. He held a plate heaped with food.

High heels clicking, Donna swished toward a small sofa, her discontented face alert and wary.

Marguerite waited until there was no sound. She lifted her head and she was the Marguerite Dumaney they knew well, blazing eyes, hollowed cheeks, bloodred lips — haggard, yes, but still beautiful, beautiful and mesmerizing. Her perfectly cut black suit was as glossy as a raven's wing, the single strand of pearls at her throat emphasizing the midnight hue of the silk.

"I must confess." Her voice fell, deep and sad as the cry of a loon.

Annie felt suddenly disoriented. The early morning news shows in Savannah had been dominated by the news of Swanson's arrest. There were a half dozen film clips, including a pale and grim Swanson flanked by Chief Garrett and Officer Cameron, a suave Swanson speaking at the November meeting of the Men's Dinner Club, the Chandler house several years earlier during a garden tour and a shot of a Doberman lunging toward the gates. A voice-over had announced: "Residents of Broward's Rock Island were shocked this morning to learn of the arrest of Dr. Emory Swanson for a murder early Sunday morning at the home of reclusive actress Marguerite Dumaney. Shot to death in a gazebo behind the house was Miss Dumaney's longtime companion, Alice Schiller. Swanson settled on the island two years ago, buying the Chandler house, a famous

Low Country plantation long famed for its azaleas and dogwood. Swanson established a foundation which champions crystals as a link with the afterworld. Miss Dumaney is reported to have sought contact with her late husband, Claude Ladson, the movie producer. After taking up residence at Chandler house, Swanson installed gates and the grounds are patrolled by two Doberman pinschers. Swanson is to be arraigned this afternoon in Beaufort. Police have given no motive for the slaying of Miss Schiller. Her death follows the bludgeoning death Thursday night of Miss Dumaney's sister, Happy Laurance. Police will not comment upon whether the two crimes are linked. In national news, the White House . . ."

Annie had noted at the time that Marguerite, as always, got top billing.

Marguerite lifted a hand now to touch the pearl necklace. Her eyes downcast, her head bent like a bereft swan, she spoke so softly they strained to hear. "I am responsible for Happy's death, for Alice's death. I must wake and sleep with that knowledge. I must forever realize in my heart" — her hand spread across her chest, her voice deepened with sadness — "that my innocence" — she slowly lifted her face, stared from one to another, her eyes soft with unshed tears — "blinded me to the snake in our midst. I trusted Emory Swanson. That foolish misstep on my part" — her hand swept out, palm upward, beseeching — "has led us to this sad day when we put to rest my beloved sister —"

Pudge slipped his arm around Rachel's shoulders.

"— Dear Happy. She always sought the good of the family. She and Alice warned me. I don't know" — a deep sigh — "how Happy threatened that evil man. We do know that she faced him and that she died for all of us, seeking to keep our family intact. Alice, too. I can only ask forgiveness. I shall never forget their sacrifice." Her chin rose. Her soulful gaze moved from face to face.

Annie glanced toward Rachel and was glad to see that Rachel recognized this moment as a performance crafted for its audience, vintage Marguerite, and therefore somehow reassuring, a return to normalcy that both Happy and Alice would have welcomed.

"We shall from this moment forward" — Marguerite's voice was vibrant — "remain forever united. Despite our grief, we shall share the good cheer of this Christmas season."

Instead of a vision of sugarplums dancing, Annie suspected the Ladson siblings, their eyes bright and faces wreathed with smiles, suddenly pictured a parade of dollar signs. The threat to their great expectations was ended.

Annie looked from face to face. Swanson had almost gotten away with the Ladson fortune. The resolution of the crimes could not have turned out better for Wayne, who liked to putter among his books, and Terry, who could now afford to cruise wherever he liked, and Donna, who could search for ever finer antiques, and Joan, who would not have to worry about her children's expenses. They could not help but think that all's well that ends well.

Annie pointed at the box of books. "Pudge, if you'll open the carton, Rachel can shelve the books." It worried Annie that Rachel was still so pale. The morning had been long and difficult, Happy's coffin left beneath its mound of flowers, Marguerite's emotionally draining oration. Annie knew shelving books didn't follow the pattern for a funeral day, but Rachel needed distraction, and working at the store during Christmas rush would surely provide that. The store was jammed. Max and Ingrid had lines five deep at the cash desk. A book club from Savannah, mystery readers all, chattered and milled, their high soft voices flowing into the storeroom.

". . . been looking for a first of *The Transcendental Murder* . . ."

". . . absolutely adore Katherine Hall Page's books . . ."

". . . *Who Rides the Tiger* is chilling, simply . . ."

". . . still think Leo Bruce's *Case for Three Detectives* is the best locked-room mystery ever . . ."

". . . hope there's a new book by Sister Carol Anne O'Marie. I have all . . ."

Rachel stacked the books, recent titles by Barr, Crais, Scottoline and Trocheck, on a dolly and pushed the door wide. She edged around a group of women staring up at the watercolors. There might be a winner today. Annie reached out to pull the door shut. She needed to check the order list, see if she could fill some late customer requests for Christmas. Pudge lifted another box of books to the table. She slipped into the chair in front of the computer.

The door opened. Max poked his head inside. "Annie, Pudge, we have a visitor." There was an odd note in his voice. He held the door. "Kate Rutledge wants to talk to us."

# Twenty-nine

Kate Rutledge walked into the small storeroom. Max closed the door behind her. Suddenly it was quiet. Annie and Pudge stared at the slim woman with the squarish face, perfectly waved shining brown hair, soft yellow cashmere sweater and brown wool slacks. She might have been any attractive late-thirties Christmas shopper except for the blazing anger in her eyes and the sharp lines in a face gray with shock and fatigue.

She leaned back against the door, stared at them. "I hope you're all satisfied now. You've accomplished your goal, haven't you, getting an innocent man arrested."

Max gave her glare for glare. "Miss Rutledge, the evidence —"

"Listen to me." She pushed away from the door. "You think Emory killed Happy Laurance and Alice Schiller? That's right, isn't it? The two of them? That Alice Schiller pretended to be Marguerite and he killed her because she accused him of killing Happy?"

"That's right." Max folded his arms.

She whirled toward Pudge. "You were there in the house. When was your wife killed?"

Pudge looked toward Annie.

"Around midnight." Annie remembered so clearly Dr. Burford's crisp declaration.

"Then listen to me." Kate's voice shook. "Emory was with me. He came to my house about ten. He didn't leave until the next morning, just before seven. He was with me all night. All night!" Tears burned in those hot eyes. "I told the police. They won't listen. They think I'm lying. But I'm not. Damn you to hell, he was with me."

Max's dark blue eyes were skeptical. "He wasn't with you Saturday night. He was in the gazebo. He brought a gun. The bullet from that gun killed Alice Schiller. His fingerprints are on the gun. Tracks from his car are in the lane next to the Dumaney house."

Kate shuddered. "He was there. But he didn't kill her. He had no reason to kill her because he didn't kill Happy Laurance. He told me what happened at the gazebo and he told the police. They don't believe him. Yes, he ran away. You would have run, too. He knew they would come after him." She swung toward Pudge. "They arrested you first. I don't know why. You claimed you didn't kill your wife. How would you feel if nobody believed you? How would you feel if you were still in jail, waiting to be charged with murder?"

Annie reached out, held tight to Max's arm. Of course, Kate Rutledge would lie for Emory Swanson. But what if she was telling the truth?

Pudge's genial face creased. "I'd be scared. I was scared." His voice was low.

Kate held out trembling hands. "The police aren't going to help Emory. But you can help him. If you will."

"Why should we help him?" Max bit off the words, his disdain clear. "A man who takes advantage of those in grief. A man who stays in a town just long enough to milk money out of vulnerable women."

"Because someone else killed those women." For an instant, Kate pressed her hands hard against her face. Then she looked at them, despair warring with anger. "You don't care. You'll let the real murderer go free."

Pudge stepped forward. "No. We won't do that." He looked at Annie, appeal in his eyes.

Annie tangled her fingers in her hair. Didn't Pudge see what he was doing? What if they convinced Garrett that Swanson had not killed Happy? Even if Garrett charged Swanson with Alice's death, it would reopen the investigation into Happy's murder and put Pudge and Rachel right back in the center of the bull's-eye. Dammit, didn't Pudge see that? Two murders and two murderers?

But surely Garrett would dismiss that possibility. All along it had seemed obvious that Alice, masquerading as Marguerite, was killed because she threatened Happy's murderer. In fact, they knew without any doubt that Alice believed Swanson guilty of Happy's murder. Alice had told

Annie there might be a way to trap Swanson. Alice engaged in a complex subterfuge that resulted in her death. How could the killer be anyone other than Swanson?

Yet Annie felt cold inside. If Swanson didn't kill Happy, he didn't kill Alice. She stared at the angry, frightened woman demanding justice for Swanson. Why should they believe her? Because of her unconcealed rage? She didn't approach them with a smooth, calculated alibi. Kate Rutledge attacked them.

Perhaps Kate saw the uncertainty in Annie's eyes. "I don't know what you can do." Her face was suddenly empty and bleak. "Maybe no one can do anything. But will you talk to Emory? Will you listen to him?"

Chief Garrett pointed down the hall to the third door. Billy Cameron, big and imposing, dwarfed the little metal folding chair. He scrambled to his feet, nodded hello, his face impassive, his eyes warm.

Max lifted his hand. Annie smiled. "Hi, Billy."

Garrett was as crisp as a new twenty, his round face smooth-shaven, his eyes bright, his khaki uniform board-starched. He looked at them curiously. "Prisoners have a right to visitors upon proper application." Proper application had consisted of Max signing an identity sheet and stating that he and Annie were there at Swanson's request. "You can have half an hour. Knock twice when you want out."

Billy unlocked the door and they walked into a small, square room with no windows, lime-green walls, a plain wooden table, green cement floor. As the door clicked shut behind them, Emory Swanson looked up. He was no longer handsome, his heavy, sharp features sullen and frightened. His manacled hands lay on the table. The too-small orange jail jump-suit pulled across his chest.

Max's shoes grated on the cement. He pulled out a chair for Annie, another for himself. They faced Swanson. "Kate Rutledge asked us to come."

Swanson lifted his hands, used his knuckles to rub against his chin and, Annie realized, to hide lips that trembled. "Yeah. Kate knows I didn't do it. I was with her the night Marguerite's sister was killed." He didn't bluster. He spoke in a weary, hopeless voice.

Annie wished she were not in this room. Despite the newness of the jail, this room had already held within its walls emotions and secrets Annie had no desire ever to know. This afternoon a man who had exuded confidence stared at them like a fox in a trap, a grievously wounded animal.

Swanson shifted in his chair, as if he could find ease from the chains. The clank beneath the table indicated his ankles were chained, too. "Somebody set me up for this."

"You were with Kate Thursday night?" Max spoke quietly.

"We're married." Swanson's voice was dull. "She helps me. She goes to a new town first, gets established. When I get there, she's gotten to know the women —" He broke off.

"Credulous women?" Max's voice was hard.

Swanson's head lifted. "Hell, man, they're rich. And lonely. I make them feel better. I give them their money's worth. They want to talk to somebody who's died. I hold their hands and we look into a crystal and pretty soon they're happy as can be, talking their hearts out. What harm does it do?"

"You scam away their money." Annie's tone was derisive.

Swanson shrugged. "I just take some of it . . ."

Annie thought about Miss Dora's friend who had given away everything she had.

". . . and it's their money. Sure, some of their greedy relatives don't like it, but a lot of them are sitting around waiting for the moneybags to die. Why should I care what happens to them?" He looked at them defiantly, a riverboat gambler caught with extra cards and contemptuous of the marks. "I'll tell you for sure, I never hurt anybody. Never. You can check every place I've ever lived. I never hurt anybody. And I'm in some wills. You know that? This whole thing" — he looked down at the manacles — "is crazy. They say I killed Marguerite's sister and somehow Alice knew it and dressed up like Marguerite and accused me and I shot her. That's crazy."

Wondering if she was succumbing to Swanson's most clever scam yet, Annie asked warily, "What happened at the gazebo?"

Swanson flung his arms onto the table and the chains clattered. "I should have known better than to go there. The setup was nuts, even for Marguerite. But she was always difficult and I knew I had to keep on top of things with her or the whole thing would be ruined. Somebody was trying to screw things up for me. It started at the dinner when she told the parasites they weren't going to cash in when she died. They looked like scalded cats, mad as hell, ready to bite and scratch, but not sure which way to jump. Somebody pulled that stunt with the gardenia. Marguerite was thrilled, sure the gardenia came from Claude. I had to be very careful what I said. Anyway, I thought everything was fine, but then her sister got killed. Marguerite was really upset. She was scared. She called me a half dozen times that day and insisted we try to get in touch with Happy that night. And that voice . . ." Swanson's eyebrows rose. "That was strange. It must have sounded like her husband —"

"From some old tapes," Annie explained.

Interest flickered in his eyes, then faded. "Whatever. I knew somebody was really gunning for me. She called Saturday afternoon. She was talking really soft and hurried and she told me she was terrified, that someone was trying to kill her and she needed a gun. She wanted me to bring a gun to her Saturday night."

"How did she know you had a gun?" Max had pulled a small notebook from his pocket.

"I don't think she did." He lifted his shoulders

in disgust. "She was always unreasonable. I suppose she thought I'd go out and buy one. As it happens, I had a gun. At this point I was just trying to settle her down. She was hysterical. Anyway" — he heaved a tired sigh — "I agreed to bring the gun at twelve-forty-five and meet her in the gazebo."

"Why was the gun loaded?" Max demanded.

Swanson hunched over the table. "Jesus, I thought about it. I almost unloaded it. But she knew how to shoot a gun. Some of those damn movies she made. I was afraid she'd check and then she'd be furious. God, I wish I'd taken those bullets out."

Annie and Max simply looked at him.

He jerked his head. "Look, I know it sounds crazy. And I guess I was crazy. But, God, it was so much money. . . ."

So much money. Enough to kill twice? What price an alibi from Kate Rutledge?

"No." The word came from deep in his throat with an explosive force. "No, dammit. I did not shoot her." He leaned forward, glaring at them. "She said to come to the gazebo at twelve-forty-five. I did and she wasn't there. Of course she wasn't. She was never on time in her life."

Annie felt a chill. No, but she — actually Alice Schiller — had been on time for her death.

"I paced around in front of the gazebo. I guess I'd been there about five minutes or so, and here she came, running down the path. She stopped, looked back, then rushed up to me. She said,

'Emory, thank God you've come. I was right. I'm in danger. Do you have the gun?' She held out a soft bag. I pulled the gun out of my pocket and dropped it in the bag. She said, 'I'm going to have to —' Then she stopped and looked out into the garden. 'Was that a noise? I'd better see. Wait for me. I'll be right back,' and she dashed off before I could say a word. I almost left, but I thought what the hell, I'd gone to this much trouble. In a couple of minutes, I saw a flashlight bobbing. She was almost to me. Only a few feet away. She called out, 'Emory —' A shot rang out. I threw myself on the ground. I heard some noise in the shrubbery and then it was absolutely quiet. I got up and looked toward the flashlight and I could just see a dark shape there. I ran over and dropped down beside her. I picked up her wrist. There wasn't any pulse. I grabbed the flashlight and looked for the bag she'd carried, but there was no bag — no bag and no gun. I used the flashlight to check out the ground around her, but I knew I had to get out of there."

"There wasn't any flashlight there when we found her," Annie said.

"I took it with me. I ran like hell to get to my car." He rubbed his cheek and metal jangled. "I threw the damn thing in the lagoon when I got home. What difference does it make?"

Swanson was right. Producing the flashlight did nothing to prove or disprove his story.

Annie's eyes were sharp. "They arrested you at the airport in Savannah."

Swanson slumped in his chair. "I knew they'd be after me. I've got some money —" He broke off. Yes, no doubt he did have money available in another country, perhaps under another name.

They sat in silence. What an absurd story. No wonder Garrett didn't believe Swanson. Annie studied the big man slumped in the chair, deflated and defeated.

Max looked down at his notebook, pushed it close enough for Annie to read:

*SWANSON CLAIMS*

1. *Alice, pretending to be Marguerite, calls, demands gun, sets up meeting at the gazebo.*
2. *Swanson arrives at the gazebo at twelve-forty-five, bringing gun.*
3. *Alice (pretending to be Marguerite) arrives at twelve-fifty-five.*
4. *Swanson drops gun in her bag.*
5. *She asks him to wait, runs into garden.*
6. *She returns with a flashlight, calls Swanson's name.*
7. *Unknown shoots Alice, believing the victim to be Marguerite.*

Annie could imagine the circuit solicitor's attitude if Chief Garrett presented this summary to him. *Hogwash* was a sanitized version of the likely response. Because it was much more likely that Alice called Swanson, pretending to be Marguerite, and that she threatened him, something on the order of, *I need help to escape these terrible vi-*

*sions. I keep seeing you attacking my sister.* Swanson would talk fast, as fast as he'd ever talked in his life, to convince her that she was simply overwrought but that he would come very late and they would have a private session in the gazebo and he would be able to banish these phantasms from her mind. He came with a gun, not because Alice asked him to bring one, but because he intended to commit murder.

A reasonable scenario, except for the gun. If Swanson committed the murder, he certainly would not have left the gun unless he lost his nerve, dropped it in the dark, didn't have a flashlight, panicked and ran.

The gun. Wouldn't it be odd if the gun that cinched his arrest turned out to be the one reason to believe every word he said?

Max tapped his pen on the table. "The phone call — you thought it was Marguerite?"

Swanson shifted in his chair. "Of course I did. She *said* she was Marguerite. She . . ." His face hardened. "Damn the bitch, I should have known. It didn't sound quite like Marguerite. But close. Alice never did like me."

Alice didn't like Swanson, but more than that, Alice had been convinced that Happy had possessed papers which discredited Swanson.

"Okay" — Max looked quizzically at Swanson — "let's say it happened just the way you've told us. Who shot Alice? And why? How could that person have been Johnny-on-the-spot? And how the hell did this unseen murderer get the gun?"

"Wait!" Annie shoved her hands through her hair. "Wait a minute." She squeezed her eyes shut, thoughts caroming like maddened billiards: Alice set this up . . . Alice looked like Marguerite . . . Alice planned to trap Swanson . . . the gun . . . why the gun?

"Alice planned it!" Annie's eyes gleamed. "That's what never made sense. Why would she set up a meeting all by herself with a man she believed to be a murderer? Maybe she didn't!"

Max squinted at her. "But she did," he said patiently. "We know she called Swanson. That we know for sure."

"But we don't know what else Alice planned." Annie hitched her chair closer to the table, looked eagerly at Swanson. "Alice believed you killed Happy. Obviously she hoped to trick you into a confession. But Alice was certainly not stupid enough to make a date with a killer and be defenseless. She asked you to bring the gun because her reason for calling as Marguerite was to pretend fear and demand a means of protection. It was dramatic enough that she was sure you'd respond to the call. But even with a gun, she had no intention of facing you down by herself." Annie briefly pressed her fingers against her temple. "Not alone. Don't you see? After she got the gun, that's why she pretended to hear a noise and said she'd better go see. She ran out into the garden and gave the gun to the person waiting there, the person she'd asked to help her set a trap —"

Swanson watched Annie in dumb fascination.

"— the person she was depending upon to burst on the scene with the gun after she accused you and provoked you into attacking her. But Alice made a mistake. She chose the wrong confederate. Moreover, she was masquerading as Marguerite when she chose that person. Alice knew that the family members would never turn down a request from Marguerite. What a perfect setup. Here was a chance to kill Marguerite with a ready-made scapegoat at hand. Marguerite had announced her plans to give the money to the foundation, but she hadn't signed away the money yet. With Marguerite dead, the money would never again be in jeopardy."

Max leaned back in his chair, shaking his head. "It won't work, Annie. Either Alice was damned unlucky and just happened to confide in Happy's murderer or we are talking an opportunist second murderer and we still don't know who killed Happy. And we are almost certainly talking a second murderer because the motive to kill Happy was to stop Happy" — he glanced toward Swanson — "from using those papers that she claimed would prevent Marguerite's money going to the Evermore Foundation."

"I don't know who killed anybody. But I didn't kill Happy. I was with Kate." Swanson banged his hands on the table, the chains rattling. "For God's sake, you've got to believe me."

# Thirty

Annie smiled as she walked up the stairs. From the game room came the cheerful click of billiards as Pudge and Max played a rousing game with cries of anguish and whoops of triumph.

On the second floor, Annie stopped at the door to the first guest bedroom. She tapped lightly.

"Come in." Rachel's voice was sleepy and contented.

Annie poked her head in the door. "Just wanted to say goodnight."

The room had been a favorite of Laurel's when she first visited the island, rose walls, white wicker furniture, a rose comforter. In the soft glow from the night-light, the room had a sweet warmth. Rachel's dark hair was loose on the pillow. One small hand was tucked beneath her chin. "Good night." Her eyes wavered, closed.

Annie gently shut the door. She walked slowly down the hall to their room. She heard Max and Pudge climbing the stairs. Pudge's room was across the hall from Rachel.

Annie was slipping into pink shorty pajamas — rather lacy for winter, but Max liked them — when Max opened the door to their room and stepped inside. He looked at her appreciatively. He closed the door firmly. "Everyone is snug in their place."

"I wish that were so." Annie walked slowly to the sofa, dropped onto it. "Max, what if Rachel has to go back to that house? What if Swanson didn't kill Happy and Alice?"

Max looked at her soberly. "I know. I've been thinking about it. The more I consider Swanson's story, the more I'm torn. It's so damn nutty, it may be true."

"Which means" — Annie's eyes were wide — "that Marguerite Dumaney is in danger."

Max shook his head. "Nope. Swanson's arrest took care of that. As long as she doesn't make any move to siphon away the money, she's okay."

Annie shoved a hand through her thick blond hair. "Is she? Maybe somebody who's already committed murder won't hesitate to kill again. After all, waiting for an inheritance isn't quite as satisfying as claiming one."

"No." Max tossed his shirt in the laundry hamper, hung up his slacks. "No more murders. That would prove Swanson's innocence, reopen the investigations. The murderer has a goat. He'll sit tight."

"He?" Annie admired his smoothly muscled shoulders and legs.

"He or she." Max turned toward her. His eyes brightened.

Annie sat cross-legged on the sofa, her pink pajamas a bright contrast to the green-and-blue-plaid fabric of the cushions. She looked across the room at the table in an alcove of the sitting room. A notebook rested there beside a pile of file folders. Maybe they should start over, go through that record, sift every word. If Swanson was innocent, they had to find the murderer. Rachel must not return to live in a house with a killer. That must not happen and, yes, if Swanson was innocent, he must go free. He might well be an unprincipled con man, but that crime was far short of murder.

Max dropped onto the sofa beside her, but his gaze was focused on a portion of a slender length of leg, specifically a creamy thigh. His hand reached out.

Annie absently picked up his hand, moved it aside, dropped it.

He reached out again.

Annie shifted position, but with unexpected results. "Max!" He grinned happily. "You know" — his tone was conversational, but he slipped his other arm firmly around her, pulled her close — "often ideas come to you when you are asleep, and I know just the thing to help you relax. . . ." The last few words were indistinct as his lips found hers.

The cheerful whistle brought her awake. Max pushed open the bedroom door, carrying a tray. "They're still asleep. I made apple muffins and left a note about the coffee for Pudge."

Annie slipped out of bed and padded toward

the white oak table that sat in a bay window overlooking the backyard and the lagoon. "Max, look! Hurry!" She stretched out her hand.

He joined her in the alcove. A winter visitor, a sharp-billed woodcock, rose against the pale blue sky, spiraling higher and higher, fifty feet, seventy-five, a hundred, a hundred fifty. After a final spiral, the game bird's body went limp. Max opened the window, stepped out on a balcony. Making a three-note whistle, the bird drifted down like a falling leaf until almost to the ground, when he zoomed into a grove of pines. "What a guy will do . . ." Max mused. He was smiling as he unloaded the tray, a bowl of papaya for him, orange juice for Annie, muffins and butter. He put the notebook and file folders on the windowsill.

Annie poured their coffee. "I'm sure she is very appreciative." Max always took a deep interest in courtship rites. In the summer, he had been known to urge bullfrogs to bellow a little louder, just in case she wasn't listening or had moss draped over her ears.

"I've been thinking." Annie picked up the still-warm muffin. Mmm. Whipped sweet cream butter. "I don't buy two murderers."

Max dropped into his chair. He speared a piece of papaya. "Does anything else make sense? Why would any of the Ladsons want to murder Happy?"

Annie said tentatively, "Maybe Happy knew that someone planned to kill Marguerite."

Max slapped his hand against his temple. "I

know. They saw it in a crystal."

She gave him a cold look. "Look, two murderers is nuttier than Swanson's story." She reached over to the windowsill, retrieved Max's notebook and tore out a couple of sheets. "We can figure this out." She wrote industriously for a moment, then pushed the sheet to him.

Max ate and read.

*<u>HAPPY'S MURDER</u>*

*Possible suspects, alibis, motives:*

1. *Emory Swanson. Alibied by Kate Rutledge. Motive: To prevent Happy from making public information which might discredit him with Marguerite Dumaney.*
2. *Rachel Van Meer. Alibied by Mike Hernandez. (Although there was still time for Rachel to attack her mother either before or after Mike's visit.) Motive: Anger over her mother's efforts to keep her from seeing Mike.*
3. *Mike Hernandez. Alibied by Rachel. Ditto in re timing and motive.*
4. *Marguerite Dumaney. Alibied by Alice Schiller. (Cannot now be confirmed. However, Schiller's comment to Annie made casually.) No known motive. The sisters were quarreling about Marguerite's plan to give the bulk of her money to Emory Swanson.*
5. *Alice Schiller. Alibied by Marguerite Dumaney. (Can be checked but no need as Alice subsequently killed.) No known mo-*

*tive. On good terms with Happy Laurance.*

6. *Wayne Ladson. No alibi. No known motive.*
7. *Terry Ladson. No alibi. No known motive.*
8. *Donna Ladson Farrell. No alibi. No known motive.*
9. *Joan Ladson. No alibi. No known motive.*

## *ALICE'S MURDER*

*Possible suspects, alibis, motives. Note* bene: *Killer thought the victim was Marguerite so motives evaluated in terms of Marguerite.*

1. *Emory Swanson. Admits being present at the time of the murder. Motive: To escape arrest as Happy's murderer.*
2. *Rachel Van Meer. Alibied by Annie Darling. No known motive.*
3. *Mike Hernandez. Alibi? No known motive.*
4. *Marguerite Dumaney. No known motive.*
5. *Wayne Ladson. No alibi although apparently awakened from a deep sleep not long after the shot. There would have been time for Wayne to return to his room between the shot and Annie's knock on his door. Motive: To secure the family fortune.*
6. *Terry Ladson. No alibi. Ditto.*
7. *Donna Ladson Farrell. No alibi. Ditto.*
8. *Joan Ladson. No alibi. Ditto.*

Max sipped his coffee. "If both murders were committed by the same person, and assuming the alibis stand up, the suspects are limited to that cheery group of inheritance-assured Ladsons:

Wayne, Terry, Donna, and Joan."

Annie tapped Wayne's name. "After I heard the shot, I checked on Rachel and called the police before I went to his room. You're right, there could have been time for him to come inside and get to his room. Let's think about Alice for a minute. Remember, she's convinced Swanson is guilty. She's looking for a backup. She certainly couldn't go to Marguerite. Who would she pick?"

Wayne, Terry, Donna or Joan.

Max's tone was thoughtful. "But not a motive among them to kill Happy."

"There has to be a reason we don't know about." Annie reached over to the sill, scooped up the folders. "Are these the dossiers on the Ladsons?"

"Be my guest. If there's a pointer to Happy's murder in those files, I missed it." He flipped to a fresh page in the notebook and began to write.

Annie skimmed the dossiers. She knew that the Ladson siblings were born in Beverly Hills. After Claude's divorce, their mother moved with them to Laguna and they grew up there. It was no surprise to learn that Wayne excelled in school all the way through postgraduate studies, Terry barely made it through high school and Donna went to an elite, expensive junior college for rich girls with no career aspirations. Joan Ladson née Lewis was a superior student whom Wayne met at Stanford while working on his doctorate after his return from Vietnam in 1974.

Annie wasn't interested in the bones of their

lives. She wanted the flesh. One fact was common to all four: They needed money. Wayne wanted the Dumaney house. Donna's antique store was strapped for cash and so was she. Terry was in arrears in paying the note on his boat. Joan lived modestly, but she had high ambitions for her children.

The need for money may have led one of them to commit two murders. Annie pushed away the niggling inconsistency that Happy's murder was of no financial benefit to this group. It was time to narrow the focus, grab what was possible, and it was abundantly clear that someone had seized an opportunity to shoot Marguerite and that someone had to be Wayne or Donna or Terry or Joan.

Annie stacked the folders. Max was right. There was no hint of disagreement between any of the Ladson family and Happy. Maybe that didn't matter right now. She saw other pointers. Maybe figuring out who might kill would get her and Max started in unraveling the crimes. After all, the cast of possibilities was limited in the gazebo murder. If she focused on that crime, she had a good idea of the killer. "We need someone who's smart, impulsive and tough. Terry's impulsive, Donna's tough, Joan is smart. But only Wayne is impulsive, tough and smart. Max, he's the one." She put the folders back on the windowsill.

Max pushed his notebook toward her. "You keep focusing on the murder at the gazebo. It didn't start there."

Annie picked up the notebook.

*MAX'S TIMETABLE*

*Thursday:*

- *Happy talks to Wayne about researching vital statistics.*
- *Happy goes to the library, calls up the archives of the* Reno Gazette-Journal.
- *Happy returns to Dumaney house, gets duct tape from the kitchen.*
- *After dinner, Happy talks to Rachel in the gazebo, tells her she intends to stop Swanson from taking Marguerite's money, that she has papers and she's going to put them in a safe place.*
- *Midnight, Rachel meets Mike in the gazebo. Mike sees a light near the maze.*
- *Midnight, Happy is beaten to death with Rachel's field hockey stick.*

*Friday:*

- *Pudge discovers Happy's body, sees the hockey stick, grabs it and runs.*
- *Alice finds body, Wayne calls the police, Pudge is taken into custody, hockey stick found.*
- *Swanson holds a séance and Claude Ladson speaks, thanks to a tape from the museum, probably courtesy of Wayne.*
- *That night someone sets the tool shed ablaze, apparently as a decoy. Happy's room is searched.*

*Saturday:*

- *Alice tells Annie she has an idea of how to trap Swanson. At some time during the day, pretending to be Marguerite, Alice calls Swanson and demands that he bring a gun late that night to the gazebo. If this is true, Swanson is innocent. If Swanson invented this reason for the gun, he is guilty and, his alibi from Kate Rutledge for Happy's murder is fake.*
- *Max tries to rattle Kate Rutledge.*
- *Annie and Laurel visit Swanson, retrieve the tape. Laurel listens to the tape.*
- *Near one A.M., Annie hears a shot. Alice, dressed as Marguerite, is found dead near the gazebo.*

*Sunday:*

- *Gun found, traced, search set in motion for Swanson. Swanson arrested in Savannah.*

*Monday:*

- *Kate Rutledge seeks our help.*
  *Swanson describes shooting.*

Annie went back to the top of the timetable. Max was right. It all began with Happy's murder. If the murders were linked (and this wasn't Shakespeare with Enter First Murderer, et al.) and the alibis were real, Emory, Rachel, Mike, Marguerite and Alice were innocent of both crimes.

So? Annie felt a tingle of excitement. Yes, that moved them forward because finally they could believe what these people said. Most especially and most importantly, this validated Rachel's claim about papers that could keep the Ladson fortune from going to Swanson and it validated Rachel and Mike's report of their meeting in the gazebo on Thursday night.

"Max" — she tapped the first page of the timetable — "Mike thought he saw a light near the maze Thursday night."

Max looked at her inquiringly.

"Don't you see? If Swanson's innocent, there's no reason for a light in the garden. Anyway, the maze isn't on the way to the house, either from the boat dock or the lane. So why the light? And why there?"

Max shrugged. "How could Mike be sure where the light was?"

"He works there part time as a gardener. He said the light was near the maze. He was definite about that." Annie's eyes glowed. "So who was in the maze? Not the murderer, whoever the murderer is. There would be no reason. But if you wanted to hide something and you didn't want to put it in the house where it might be found . . ."

They parked in the side lane and slipped quietly into the garden.

Annie glanced toward the house, an interesting mélange of colors in the early morning sunlight, the metal tower shiny as a space saucer, the art-glass windows glittering like rubies and emeralds, the yellow stucco soothing as fresh cream. They would easily be visible from the terrace room or from the windows overlooking the garden. But why should anyone care if they entered the maze? Annie had her story ready: Rachel had asked them to drop by and look for a book she'd left in the maze.

At the opening of the maze, Max squinted at the six-foot-tall glossy-leaved walls of boxwood. "Happy could have pushed something in the center of a hedge wall anywhere and there's no way we'll ever find it."

Annie moved eagerly ahead. "Duct tape, Max. Happy got duct tape from the kitchen. Come on." She wrinkled her nose. She didn't like the rank, sour smell of boxwood. They walked forward, hesitated at an opening, took a left turn, ran into a dead end. They came back, took a different turn, found another dead end.

"Let's go back," Max suggested. "Somebody once told me that if you followed the hedge without a break, you'd get to the center."

After two false starts, they found their way back to the beginning. Max put his hand on the hedge and followed the wall of greenery that had no breaks. Leaves rustled beneath their feet. A crow cawed. A red-tailed hawk, its wings outstretched and still, circled above the maze, which was likely a nice hiding place for mice and rabbits. Annie shivered and walked faster. The hawk was looking down with eyesight eight times better than theirs. Suddenly the hawk zoomed down out of sight. They came around a corner into the center of the maze just as the hawk rose, a rabbit gripped in its talons. If only they could see as well to capture their quarry.

Max looked toward the house, but it wasn't visible from the center of the maze, the view blocked by the spreading limbs of a huge live oak. "Happy picked a good place. She could use a flashlight here and no one would see." The hedge walls would block light from the ground, the live oak from the house.

The open space was about twelve feet square, the gray dirt hard-packed. Two marble benches flanked a sundial.

Max walked to the far bench, Annie to the near. Annie reached beneath her bench, gingerly ran her fingers against the smooth, cold stone. "Max!" She pulled, tugged, wrenched the taped packet loose and held it up for Max to see.

# Thirty-one

Annie stared at a dark oblong on the wall of Pete Garrett's office. That's where Chief Saulter had hung his poster of the Ian Fleming portrait by Amherst Villiers that appeared as a frontispiece in the first 250 numbered and signed copies of *On Her Majesty's Secret Service*. One of Frank Saulter's continuing ambitions was to own one of those copies. Since Pete Garrett had taken over as police chief, more than the decorations in the small office had changed. Frank's office had been untidy, with books piled in the windows and files stacked against the old-fashioned wooden cabinets. A rack of pipes, still fusty even after years of disuse, had sat next to a chipped pottery tray filled with jelly beans in the summer and foil-covered chocolate kisses in the winter. Garrett's office was as austere as a monk's cell. An aerial map of the island filled one wall. A framed certificate behind his desk attested that Garrett had earned a degree with highest honors in criminal jurisprudence. The walls were pale gray, the filing cabinets and desk gray metal. There were no photographs on the desktop, which was bare except for an in box, an out box, and a lined yellow legal pad. If an office reflects personality, this one shouted that its occupant desired order, eschewed flamboyance and prized privacy.

Annie popped to her feet and paced toward Max, who sat in casual ease despite the hard wood of the blond oak chair. Annie stopped in front of him, riffed her hand through her hair. "What if he doesn't tell us what was in the packet?"

Max didn't answer directly. His blue eyes were troubled. "We had no choice, Annie. This is a murder investigation."

"He's stopped investigating." They'd wrangled all the way to the police station. "What if he says he can't release information about evidence?" Annie clenched her hands. She was positive that they had held in their hands, even if only fleetingly, the solution to Happy's murder. Held, because of Max, very fleetingly. He'd whipped off his sweater to carefully wrap the duct-taped, quart-size plastic bag. Annie had glimpsed several sheets of paper. Would that be all she ever saw?

The door opened. She scarcely glanced at Garrett's sober face. Her eyes were on the slim manila folder in his hand.

She surged toward him. "Chief, you've got to tell us what the papers said. Is it information about Swanson? Don't you see?" Max was tugging at her hand. "These are the papers Rachel told us about and Happy hid them just before she met someone in her room. The papers have to be important." Annie could see it all in her mind, Happy clutching papers that someone would kill for, trying to safeguard the papers, settling finally for a hiding place beneath a stone bench in the maze.

Garrett pointed toward the other straight chair that faced his desk.

Max tugged again and Annie sat, but she leaned forward like a greyhound poised to race.

Garrett sat behind his desk. He placed the folder — the closed folder — precisely in the center. His round young face creased in indecision. "I appreciate your cooperation as citizens. As a matter of policy and law, an investigating officer never releases information about evidence from —"

Annie lifted her hand. Max grabbed it and pulled it down.

"— an ongoing investigation. However, in the process of investigating, an officer often must share information in order to gain information." He looked at Annie. "I have here copies of the papers which you discovered this afternoon. The papers and the duct tape contain the fingerprints of the first victim. Since that victim is your stepmother, I would like to ask you to tell me the significance of this material." He stood and held out the folder to Annie.

Late afternoon shadows threw dark streaks across the gazebo. The onshore breeze rattled the palm fronds, kicked up little spits of gray dust. Rachel's overlong sweater dangled to her knees. Pudge stood protectively at her side. Donna pulled up the hood of her blue silk coat, muttered,

"What a nasty day." Wayne stroked his beard and looked speculatively toward the gazebo steps, where a haggard Emory Swanson waited. Billy Cameron, one massive hand resting on his holster, stood a few feet away from Swanson. Terry rubbed his red face. His worn blue blazer was shiny in the sunlight. Joan's eyes were watchful. As always, Marguerite was striking, her fine bones set in sorrow, her deep-set eyes dark with horror as she looked down at the ground where her longtime companion's body had lain.

"Officer." Marguerite placed her red-nailed hand at her throat, the color bright against a jade green silk blouse. "Although I wish more than anyone in the world to see justice done, I find it terribly difficult to be so near the man who killed my sister and my dear Alice, the man whom I trusted with my deepest family feelings. But if this reenactment you desire can be of use against him" — she swung, one hand flung in accusation toward Swanson — "let us proceed."

"We believe the reenactment will make clear what occurred." Garrett's tone was stolid.

Annie felt cold despite her thick wool sweater. Now it was up to her, and she wished she felt the confidence she'd shown to Garrett. Could she pierce the shell of this clever, audacious, calculating killer? They had not a single particle of physical evidence. All they had was surprise.

Annie shook open a paper sack. "I will play the role" — and wasn't that a perfect description — "of Alice Schiller on Saturday night. Emory, please show us what happened."

Swanson lifted his heavy face, gave Marguerite a defiant, angry stare. "I didn't kill anybody. I came here because you — I thought it was you — called and said you were frightened and asked me to bring a gun. I parked over there" — he gestured toward the gate — "and I came here. . . ." He walked up to the gazebo. "You weren't here. I waited, and in a few minutes I heard running steps."

Garrett nodded sharply at Annie.

Annie walked swiftly down the path, holding a paper sack. She hurried up to Swanson. "Oh, thank God you came. Did you bring the gun?" She held out the sack.

Swanson reached in his pocket. He pulled out a small silver gun.

"Ooh." Donna took a step backward.

Wayne's eyes narrowed. "Just a toy."

Swanson dropped the gun in the sack.

"Oh, I hear . . . Wait, I'll be right back." Annie hurried down the steps, ran up the path. She stopped near the terrace door, where Max waited. She knew it was Max, knew his oatmeal cashmere sweater, his navy slacks. But this figure wore a sack with eyeholes and slick vinyl gloves.

He reached in the sack, took the gun and strode swiftly down the path and circled behind the gazebo.

Annie came down the path, stopping a few feet from the steps, just where the body had lain. "Emory, I'm so glad —"

The masked figure drew out the gun, lifted it.

Click.

It would have been a bust in an old-time western, the small snap from a play gun. But the sound seemed inordinately loud in the strained, frightened silence.

Annie looked at each face in turn. "Who shot Alice?"

Terry's hand shook, but he pointed at Swanson. "He brought the gun."

"I brought the gun. She took it." Swanson took a step forward. Billy moved, too. Swanson ignored him, staring at the members of the Ladson family. "One of you got the gun. That's what happened. She gave it to one of you and —"

"Wait, wait, wait." Marguerite's voice rose imperiously. "I don't understand this. You are saying that Alice took the gun from Emory and gave it to one of the family? Why would she do that?"

"For protection. She wasn't a fool. She thought Swanson was a murderer." Annie ignored Swanson's angry growl. "Alice's plan was to accuse him of Happy's murder. Her confederate would be waiting in the darkness with the gun. Alice made two mistakes. She was afraid to ask for help on her own, so she pretended to be Marguerite. No one in the family was in any position to refuse Marguerite. That was her first mistake. Her second was in the confederate she chose. She forgot that everyone in the house wanted Marguerite's money."

"Oh, that's not fair," Terry blustered.

"How dare you?" Donna's voice was shrill, but her eyes slid away from Annie's.

Joan's plump face congealed like stale pudding. "You're saying that one of us killed Alice. That's dreadful."

Wayne ignored them all. "Wait a minute." His face hard and intent, he stalked up to Garrett. "The autopsy should answer some of this. Where was Alice shot?"

Garrett was an instant long in answering. Cops like to get information, not give it. But the autopsy report would soon be released to the media. His voice was clipped. "In the chest."

"The distance?" Wayne's eyes flickered from the place where she fell to the hooded figure near a thick stand of hibiscus.

A reluctant admiration shone in Garrett's eyes. "Approximately sixteen feet."

Everyone looked at Swanson. He stood only three or four feet from where Alice had fallen.

Wayne looked past Swanson to the hooded figure. "You're saying one of us took the gun from Alice, thinking she was Marguerite, and ran around the gazebo. When she spoke to Swanson, she was shot."

Garrett looked sharply at Wayne.

"It was almost a perfect crime." Annie spoke soberly. "Marguerite shot with Swanson's gun with Swanson's fingerprints on it and with Swanson present. There was no risk, no danger for the murderer. So if this is what happened, who is the murderer?" She pointed at each in turn as she spoke. "Terry, Donna, Joan, Wayne?"

Donna yanked tight the belt of her silk coat. "I don't have to listen to another word of this. I'm going back to the house." She swung around.

"Donna." The husky, volatile voice was compelling.

Slowly Donna turned and looked at Marguerite. "You can't believe this?" Donna reached out her hands.

Marguerite backed away.

Donna's hands slowly fell.

Tears trickled from Marguerite's eyes. "Who?" The single word was heavy with heartbreak.

"Whom would Alice turn to?" Annie's words dropped slowly into a pool of silence. "Not Marguerite. Marguerite believed in Swanson. Who's left?" She looked at a circle of faces: Joan's resentful, Terry's defensive, Donna's strained, Wayne's skeptical. "Who did Alice know best? Who lived in the Dumaney house? Who served in Viet—"

Joan bolted across the dusty ground to stand in front of Wayne like a lioness defending a cub. "No. Not Wayne. Never Wayne. And" — she spit out the words, her voice shrill — "he couldn't have done it. I spent that night with him."

"Sheesh." Terry's eyebrows quirked. "I thought you hated his guts."

"Actually," Donna drawled, "if anyone did it —"

Joan whirled. Her hand whipped through the air. The sound of the slap was sharp and distinct.

Donna stumbled back, her cheek flaming.

Wayne was between them in an instant, his arm around Joan, pulling her along with him. "Hey, it's all right. I didn't shoot anybody." He looked down at his former wife, his face puzzled. "Hell, you never lie about anything."

She looked up, her face turning a bright red, her lips trembling. "I know you, Wayne. You don't care about money. You love the house, but you'd never hurt anyone, not really hurt them. You wouldn't shoot Marguerite."

"How can you know that?" His eyes sought hers.

She looked at him without pretense, the love and sadness and heartbreak there for him, for everyone, to see. "I know you."

He put his hands on her shoulders. He looked straight at her. "If you know me, why did you believe I'd drop you for a girl? Why didn't you ask me about her?"

"Wayne?" It was scarcely more than a whisper.

"I didn't care about her. She chased me. She was a tramp and she thought I was rich. I never gave a damn about her. But you heard the gossip and you left." He bit his lip, struggled, then said, his voice shaking, "You left."

And, with a sigh, she was in his arms.

"I suppose he does want the house." Marguerite's voice was cold, remorseless. "Is that why he killed Alice?"

Wayne gently disengaged from Joan, though he held tight to her hand. "Let's get this straight, Marguerite. It's a damn clever scenario, but there's one piece missing." His bright eyes bored into Annie's. "You're missing a little step in your equation. Sure, you can spout why one of us might shoot Marguerite, but none of us, not a single one, had any reason to kill Happy. I sure as hell didn't."

Annie hoped for the right words because this was the moment. "Wayne is asking the right question. Who killed Happy? Anyone could have killed Marguerite at any time. That didn't happen. Instead, Happy died — good-natured, kind, silly Happy. Everything else that happened flowed from Happy's murder. That's what we realized this afternoon when we found Happy's papers."

Annie saw an instant of utter stillness on the murderer's part, the physical reaction to an utterly unexpected and shocking revelation.

Annie watched that still face. "Chief, please read what we found."

Chief Garrett, his round face intent, pulled two sheets of paper from his pocket. He cleared his throat. The only sounds were the rustle of palm fronds in the breeze and the faraway whistle of the ferryboat. "These papers" — his voice was uninflected — "were discovered this afternoon by Mr. and Mrs. Maxwell Darling. They had been fastened with duct tape to the bottom of a marble bench in the center of the maze . . ."

Rachel pressed her hand against her mouth.

". . . and contain the fingerprints of Mrs. Happy Laurance. There are three items, all Xerox copies: two sheets from a girl's diary, a printout of the vital statistics column from the May 24, 1961 issue of the *Reno Gazette-Journal* and the envelope in which the three sheets were contained." He unfolded the sheets. "The diary excerpt reads: 'Daddy is so mad at Rita. She was gone a whole week with that man from the ski place. Daddy got a private detective to find her and bring her home. Daddy told her he's paid the man off. Rita is mad as she can be. She told me she'd have her way because Daddy didn't know they'd got married. Daddy said we can't go back to the lake and I hope it doesn't ruin our summer. I'm going to get to go to camp pretty soon anyway and that will be fun.' " Garrett cleared his throat. "The copy of the vital statistics lists twenty-six marriage licenses issued." He lifted his eyes and looked across the dusty ground at Marguerite Dumaney. "Including a license to Wendell George Harrison, thirty-four, and Marguerite Dumaney, eighteen, both of Los Angeles."

Marguerite waved her hand in dismissal. "A youthful foolishness, Captain. Certainly nothing that matters now. It was annulled, of course. I was just a girl."

Garrett held up an envelope. "On the outside, your sister had written in capital letters: 'NO DIVORCE.' "

The silence was broken by a whoop. "No divorce!" Terry's eyes glittered. "You were never legally married to Dad. No divorce! The money" — and his voice was rich with satisfaction — "belongs to us."

Marguerite fingered the golden necklace at her throat. The only hint of strain in her beautiful haggard face was the guarded watchfulness in deep-set dark eyes. However, she managed a derisive smile. "I see this as simply an effort to protect Rachel. After all, it was her hockey stick that was used to kill Happy. No one could ever say that I had any reason to kill my dear Alice."

Annie began to feel a sweep of panic. Marguerite seemed impervious. And yes, even if it could be proven that the long-ago marriage occurred and that there was no divorce and that the Ladson fortune was not hers, that was no proof of murder — and still there was the hockey stick with Rachel's fingerprints and the gun with Swanson's fingerprints.

Marguerite continued to smile.

Annie stared into those dark eyes and knew that she was looking into the soul of a murderer.

Wayne stared at the gazebo. "Marguerite's got a point there. Why the hell would she go through that charade that Alice cooked up? Or are you saying it was Marguerite who called Swanson?"

Annie pressed her fingers against her temples. No. Alice had told Annie that she had a plan. Annie remembered that moment — her head jerked up. She looked at the old actress with her perfect features and eyes filled with darkness.

"Alice." Annie spoke the name with force and a curl of horror. "Alice called Swanson. She met him. She took the gun. Then she ran up the path and here came Marguerite. Alice had told Marguerite that Swanson would meet her that night. Alice told Marguerite that Swanson was waiting." Annie pointed toward the hooded figure. "It was Alice who came around the gazebo, Alice who used the gun to shoot Marguerite. It was Alice who would do anything to keep Marguerite from losing the money, the money that made Alice's life in comfort possible. Then, with murder done, Alice saw how she could enjoy that money even more. She became Marguerite."

Alice Schiller, her face sharpening into ugliness, turned to run.

# Thirty-two

Rachel looked back one more time at the two new graves, sisters buried side by side. Mounds of flowers still covered the humped gray dirt on each. But Rachel had found a place for the red-and-white-striped cane made of carnations. "Mom loved candy canes."

Annie slipped her arm around Rachel's shoulders. They followed the dusty gray path to the road where the car was parked. The cemetery was quiet, late on this afternoon before Christmas Eve. As they got into the car, Rachel said softly, "I'm glad it wasn't Aunt Rita. She and Mom loved each other even if they fussed a lot."

Dust rose behind the Volvo. Annie drove slowly through the thick shadows. "I'm glad, too."

Rachel's hands locked tightly together. "How did you know it was Alice?"

Annie slowed for a big-antlered deer. He certainly had the right of way as far as she was concerned. On the main road, she picked up speed. "I almost didn't," she said ruefully. "If I hadn't figured that out, Alice would have gotten away with two murders. Even with your mom's papers, there was no proof. But once anyone questioned 'Marguerite's' identity, Alice was done."

Rachel was impatient. "How did you know?"

"I looked into her eyes." Annie would never forget that moment. "She was so sure of herself, so confident, so utterly composed. Yet, only a few days before, Marguerite had been so distraught by her sister's death that she insisted Swanson come and hold a séance that very night. Would a murderer who believed in contacting the dead arrange to contact her victim? I don't think so. The next day Marguerite remained in her room. Why? Because she was grieving. Yet at that moment near the gazebo, she looked at me, unmoved by the accusation that she'd murdered her sister. And Marguerite never lost faith in Swanson. The only suggestion that Marguerite was suspicious of him came from Alice. Alice told me she had a plan. I'll say she did. She knew about Marguerite's first marriage and she knew it had never been dissolved. She knew the money belonged to the Ladsons. Alice didn't want that money to be taken away, so she killed your mom, trying to make it look as though you were guilty. Then she had a brilliant idea. Entice Swanson to the garden, have him bring a gun, get that gun, excuse herself with a promise to return. In the meantime, she'd arranged for Marguerite to come down to meet Swanson. The minute Marguerite arrived, Alice shot her, tossed the gun into the shrubs and hurried back to the house. She was already dressed as Marguerite. She simply waited for the body to be discovered. Now she was sure of the money and finally she was the star, the star she'd always wanted to be."

Rachel shivered. "She was evil."

Who was Alice? Annie knew they would never be certain. She was a beautiful woman, an accomplished actress. She'd been tempted and had succumbed. Was she prompted by fear of losing the only home she'd known for much of her life? Had jealousy festered within her since she was young and Marguerite was the star and she only the pale imitation? Was she frightened, angry, jealous or simply an opportunist? "She was formidable." Annie shot a quick glance at Rachel. "But that doesn't matter now. What matters now is the future. Hey, did we remember the popcorn balls?"

Rachel craned to look in the backseat. "There they are. Annie, can I hand out the popcorn balls?" Her eyes brightened; the tension eased in her hands.

"Sure. But don't let Agatha get one. The last time we had an open house, somebody dropped one and it stuck to her tail. I've never seen a madder cat."

Rachel giggled.

Annie drove a little faster. They were almost to the harbor. "And one time, we had a whole tray of shrimp and . . ."

"Santa Claus Is Coming to Town" boomed from the CD player. The tip of Ingrid's Santa Claus hat hung dangerously near the punch bowl as she added another half gallon of lime sherbet. The second bowl glistened with the rich yellow of egg nog. Trifle filled the third bowl.

Max carried a tray of raspberry brownies. "So who says raspberry brownies aren't Christmas cookies?" Annie had demanded pugnaciously. She reached for a brownie and was rewarded with both her favorite sweet and a rollicking smile from the world's most handsome husband. Rachel darted in and out of clumps of revelers, holding up a plastic bowl filled with popcorn balls. Pudge was working the cash desk. Laurel spooned dollops of whipped cream onto steaming mugs of cocoa and dealt graciously with a coterie of male admirers, her faithful beau Howard, new stalwart Fred Jeffries, pink-faced Pete Garrett, the club golf pro, penguin-shaped Mayor Cosgrove, and a jaunty Terry Ladson.

Familiar faces were everywhere. The doyenne of Chastain, Miss Dora Brevard, was deep in conversation with Emma Clyde, creator of world-famous sleuth Marigold Rembrandt. Annie wondered what they were discussing. She slipped around a group debating — and the level of discourse might be described as heated — the primacy of Agatha Christie or Raymond Chandler.

Miss Dora, dark eyes glittering in her parchment face, exuded satisfaction. "Dear Laurel got the goods" — her word choice reflected a fondness for Erle Stanley Gardner novels — "on Dr. Swanson. There's no doubt about it. The Evermore Foundation is closed, monies have been returned to those fleeced and Swanson and his lady have departed from the island."

"Good show." Emma shrugged her large shoulders, and her red-and-green-striped caftan rippled like Christmas candy. Her piercing blue eyes swung toward Annie. "Oh, there you are. I know you don't think it's fair —"

Footsteps marched smartly down the central aisle toward the coffee bar. Henny Brawley called out, "Hello, hello, hello, I didn't know whether I'd ever get out of Pittsburgh except by dog sled, but here I am. I couldn't miss the Christmas party."

Annie hurried up to give her a hug. Certainly no Christmas party would be the same without Henny. Before she could say a word, Henny glanced up at the watercolors over the fireplace.

Emma, her square face utterly determined, snapped, "*Without Lawful* —"

Henny was not to be bested. She rattled off the titles, "*Without Lawful Authority* by Manning Coles, *Green for Danger* —"

A male voice overrode both Emma's deep growl and Henny's light tone.

"— by Christianna Brand, *The Clock Strikes Twelve* by Patricia Wentworth, *Man Running* by Selwyn Jepson, and *The Franchise Affair* by Josephine Tey."

Pete Garrett's face turned from pink to red when he realized he was the focus of bemused fascination by Miss Dora, Emma, Henny, and Annie.

Emma, known for her forthrightness, made it clear. "How could you possibly know those books? They are all by British authors and were published in the 1940s."

"Before you were born!" Henny added darkly.

"We used to spend Christmas with my grandmother." He grinned. "My granddad brought home a war bride from England. But" — he was magnanimous in victory — "I'd say we had a three-way tie."

Three faces turned expectantly toward Annie.

Three free books?

Oh hey, it was Christmas!

The employees of G.K. Hall hope you have enjoyed this Large Print book. All our Large Print titles are designed for easy reading, and all our books are made to last. Other G.K. Hall books are available at your library, through selected bookstores, or directly from us.

For information about titles, please call:

(800) 223-1244
(800) 223-6121
To share your comments, please write:

Publisher
G.K. Hall & Co.
P.O. Box 159
Thorndike, ME  04986